What Readers Are Saying About *Perfecting Kate*:

"If Bridget Jones could get her act together, lose her Diary, and pick up a Bible, she still wouldn't be half as charming as Kate Meadows in Tamara Leigh's *Perfecting Kate*. Leigh has crafted a heroine who is both winsome and wistful, engaging the reader from the first line and inviting us to tag along on her transformational journey. Every woman will hear a bit of herself in Kate's voice—sometimes I wondered just how much time Leigh spent eavesdropping in my bathroom."

Allison Pittman, author of *Ten Thousand Charms*

"Journey with quirky, sweet Kate Meadows as she confronts issues all women face: balancing her career, love life, and the pressure to be perfect—inside and out. Tamara Leigh's *Perfecting Kate* will have you turning the pages."

Rachel Hauck, author of *Lost in NashVegas*

"Women worldwide can easily empathize with the realistic, heartfelt characters in Tamara Leigh's *Perfecting Kate*. Her story is sassy, classy, and fun—in a word, perfect!"

Betsy-a

Perfecting

Kate

[A Novel]

Tamara Leigh

Multnomah Publishers

PERFECTING KATE
Published by Multnomah Publishers
A division of Random House Inc.
Published in association with the literary agency of Alive Communications, Inc.,
7680 Goddard St., Suite 200, Colorado Springs, CO 80920,
www.alivecommunications.com.
Original photo in cover image by Getty Images

© 2007 by Tammy Schmanski
International Standard Book Number: 1-59052-927-8

Unless otherwise indicated, Scripture quotations are from:
The Holy Bible, New International Version
© 1973, 1984 by International Bible Society,
used by permission of Zondervan Publishing House

Multnomah is a trademark of Multnomah Publishers,
and is registered in the U.S. Patent and Trademark Office.
The colophon is a trademark of Multnomah Publishers.

Printed in the United States of America

For information:
MULTNOMAH PUBLISHERS
12265 ORACLE BOULEVARD, SUITE 200
COLORADO SPRINGS, COLORADO 80921

Library of Congress Cataloging-in-Publication Data
Leigh, Tamara.
Perfecting Kate : a novel / Tamara Leigh.
p. cm.
ISBN 1-59052-927-8
1. Chick lit. I. Title.
PS3612.E3575P47 2007
813'.6—dc22

                                     2006031278

07 08 09 10 11 12—10 9 8 7 6 5 4 3 2 1 0

To my husband, David, who loves me regardless
(and I you, babe) and whose antics and sense of
humor are a ready source of material with which to
frustrate—er…amuse—my heroines (just ask Kate).

ACKNOWLEDGMENTS

As always, there are so many who stand behind a book and without whom it would not be possible to capture the dream: my irreplaceable agent, Beth Jusino, who goes above and beyond and is a blessing to work with; the gracious Kevin Marks, who brought me into the Multnomah family; my exceptional editor, Julee Schwarzburg, whose insight and direction made the dreaded editing process fun (really!); Multnomah's fiction marketing guru, Sharon Znachko, who listens, responds, and is patient, with a halo on top; the wonderful readers who embraced my journey from medieval romances to Christian "chick lit"; my Bible study buddies, who came alongside me when I needed the support—Susan, Susan (that's not a stutter), and Lucinda; and my Lord and Savior, whose timing never ceases to amaze me.

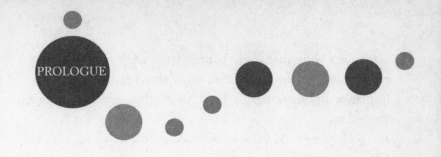

I never asked to be made over. In fact, I was perfectly content with Katherine Mae Meadows just the way she was—twenty-nine years young (and holding), five foot seven (on tiptoe), 110 pounds (wrung out), and completely "au naturel" (in my line of work, who has time to fuss with hair and makeup?).

Yep, content. And the more I told myself that, the more I was convinced. Then one so-called friend commented on my shortcomings to one Dr. Clive Alexander. And the louse concurred! But I'll explain about the good doctor later, as he definitely bears mention.

Okay, so I wasn't content. But I'm not alone. After all, whose legs (other than those of digitally enhanced models) can't stand to lose a tangled web of spider veins and a tub of cottage cheese? Then there are wrinkles—as in wrinkle here, wrinkle there, wrinkle, wrinkle everywhere. Oh! And not-so-strategically-placed moles.

The point is: There's something somewhere on every

someone's body that could benefit from some type of beauty enhancement (e.g., sclerotherapy, dermabrasion, lift, tuck, implants, liposuction). At least, that's the thinking I came around to.

So I guess I did want to be made over. Sort of. And it's all Clive Alexander's fault—

Oops. Like I said, I'll explain about him later.

As for the beginning of the end of Kate as I knew her, it started when a makeup artist and his crew stopped me and my housemate on a San Francisco street and asked if we'd like to be made over for an upcoming issue of *Changes* magazine.

Tempting, especially as I'd recently cornered my reflection and decided that something had to be done to stop the downward slide of the woman in the mirror. Which brings me back to Clive Alexander. Again!

Anyway, call it fate or just plain chance, standing before me was the fashionably bald Michael Palmier. And he wanted to transform me, among other things. Turns out he's also a pretty good kisser, though not as good as Clive—

I digress. Or should I say obsess? Of course, I suppose that's my cue to rewind and begin with the night Clive entered my relatively uncomplicated sphere of existence. The night those unblinking eyes swept through me as if I were invisible. The night I took up residence in front of my bathroom mirror instead of cracking open my Bible. The night I excused myself from Bible study by calling the exercise before the mirror "soul-searching."

Soul-searching—ha! Couldn't have been further from the truth.

h, my. Is it my imagination, or did a tuxedoed Brad Pitt just walk through the doors of one of San Francisco's most exclusive children's clothing stores?

I blink behind my rectangular specs to bring his profile into sharper focus. But as it's been ages since I've seen a pic of Brad sporting anything other than bed-tousled hair, I can't be certain if this clean-cut male specimen is him. Definitely calls for a closer look.

As I step forward, a voice at my back murmurs, "*GQ*. Very *GQ*."

I look around and up into the boyishly handsome face of Beau, co-owner of Belle and Beau's Boutique. From his hiked eyebrow, the peak of which disappears into the dark brown hair playing across his brow, it's obvious he's also taking in the Bradish guy.

Giving my best don't-even-think-about-it glower, I cuff his shoulder. "I'll tell Belle."

He grins. "You know I'm kidding."

Of course I do, as he's never given me cause to think he

might revert to the days before he wandered into our church. However, just as he never misses an opportunity to rib me, I never miss the opportunity to return the favor—even though we sometimes push it too far.

He lifts the hand that bears a gold band and wiggles his fingers. "I'm a reformed man. Belle's the only one for me."

Ah... Momentarily forgetting my on-again, off-again "thou shalt embrace singledom and be unbelievably, inconceivably happy" creed, I wish someone felt about Katherine Mae Meadows the way Beau feels about Belle.

"I know," I say on a breathy note, which snaps me out of "here comes the bride/happily ever after" mode. Thankfully. Despite marriage's supporters, it's not for everyone. Not that I rule it out completely. Rather, singledom is simply the conclusion I reach each time something promising dissolves into something...not so promising. As an added benefit, the dry spells inherent in selective dating are a little easier to bear.

Selective? As in must have credentials, and topping that list is that "The One" be a Christian. Not that I haven't fudged a time or two...make that three ("I *know* I can change him"), but without fail I've regretted lifting the ban on what others call a "discriminatory" practice. Of course, some of my Christian dates haven't gone much better, but at least those losses don't seem to cut as deep.

"Earth to Kate." Beau waves a hand inches from my nose. "Hellooo."

I blink and push my specs farther up my nose. "Do you think that's Brad—?"

"No, but he does bear a certain resemblance." Beau smoothes his linen jacket, presses his shoulders back to attain his full five feet ten inches, and winks. "Meet and greet time."

He walks toward Brad-ish, who's standing with arms

crossed over his chest and head back to scan the three-story three-dimensional wall that's my crowning achievement—and for which many of the Bay Area's mommies and daddies have turned out this evening.

As I sidle nearer, Beau halts to the left of his target and thrusts a hand forward. When Brad-ish turns to him, I'm treated to a head-on view.

"Shucks," I mutter as he accepts Beau's handshake with a stiff á la carte smile that bares no teeth, grooves no cheeks, and lights no eyes. Definitely not Brad. Smile aside, his eyes are less-than-unearthly blue, jaw relatively narrow, and skin on the weathered side. As for his size, though his shoulders are broad, his height falls short. Not that *ex*-Brad-ish isn't attractive. He's simply not flawless. In his midforties perhaps?

"Kate Meadows?" A hand grips my arm. "Are you Kate Mae Meadows?"

I look beside me. "Uh, yes."

The young woman, casually elegant in a soft black skirt and cream-colored blouse, sighs. "Love your work! How *do* you do it?"

My gaze follows hers as we look from Kapok tree to toucan to waterfall to jaguar, several of which project off the wall. Nice. Although I sometimes forget to step back and marvel at the talent God has given me, once a project comes together, I'm amazed—and humbled—as there's no denying that it wasn't a solo undertaking.

I sigh. "Just the right mix of imagination and inspiration, I guess."

She presses something into my hand—my dozenth business card this evening. "The name's Olivia. My little girl would love a Kate Mae Meadows room."

Guessing her daughter to be quite young, as mommy

appears to be all of twenty, I nod. "I'm booked for the next three months, but—"

"August then!"

I smile. "I'll call you."

With a wave, Olivia glides off among the racks of trendy children's clothes. Shortly, she loops an arm through that of an older man, who regards her with an I-am-so-bored expression that brightens only when a server appears bearing a tray of desserts. He helps himself to one but shakes his head when Olivia reaches for the tray.

Mustn't ruin that pretty figure, I surmise as I watch her sparkle sputter. Why, oh why, do so many sacrifice so much for the sake of outward appearances?

I yank my thoughts back. Who knows? Maybe Olivia is cavity prone…or diabetic…or allergic…

Belle, the first half of Belle and Beau's Boutique, appears before me. "So?"

I meet her hazel gaze and smile. "Great turnout. I really appreciate your putting on this 'do.'"

"Good for business, too." She smoothes the golden wisps escaping her French roll and glances around. "Who's the overdressed guy with Beau?"

I look to Brad-ish, who, despite the upscale attire of the others in attendance, definitely stands out—and not just because of the tux. "I don't know."

"By himself?"

"So far, no S.O. in tow."

Ugh. Did I really say that? I've heard S.O. so often that it has crept into my vocabulary. S.O., as in significant other, which is what the uncommitted committed are fashionably called. Why, even some husbands and wives refer to the other as an S.O. It's so…impersonal. As if a loved one warrants little more than the status of something approaching a scouring pad.

Belle's lids narrow. "From the interest he's showing in your wall, might be another client."

Focusing on Brad-ish, I sigh. "I certainly hope so."

She chuckles. "Now that's a rather enthusiastic response. Mind if I read something into it?"

"Oh, stop! You know I've given up on men."

Her eyebrows rise. "Second time this year, right?"

Twice. So what's the big deal? Makes it sound as if—

"And of course, it is only March. Who knows, but at this rate, you might just top last year's New Year's—er, New *Month's*—resolutions."

She has a point, but this time I mean it. In the unlikelihood that I finally meet "The One," it will be because God dropped him in my lap. Hmm…

I glance at Brad-ish. Sure would be nice if he was searching for a soft landing. Maybe I *am* being a bit hasty with my "thou shalt embrace singledom and be unbelievably, inconceivably happy" creed.

"Could be the one," Belle singsongs.

"Fat chance."

"You never know." She slides a hand across her waist, and as with each time I see her caress her unborn child, I pause. All thoughts of my moratorium on men take a giant step back. *Please, God, let this baby make it. Belle's strong, but another miscarriage—*

"Past the halfway mark," she says.

Peering into her angular face, the edges of which pregnancy has begun to soften, I pop a worry-free smile in place. "Four months to go." Best-case scenario, but if she can just make it two more months…

I click my tongue. "Well, guess I'll make the most of this

last hour and shmooze up some more business."

"You do that, and I'll trawl around for a date for you."

I give Belle the evil eye. "No more blind dates, literally or otherwise."

She snickers at the reference to my most recent date—one of her suppliers who she'd only dealt with over the phone. And the reason I've given up on men. Again. No, Charles wasn't ancient or enormously fat. In fact, he was something of a looker. Literally, though, think dark specs, white cane, and guide dog. Not that I have anything against the visually impaired, but when he used his disability as an excuse to grope me—

Honestly! Right there in the restaurant in front of everyone. I felt like an overripe melon. And I feel melon-y enough with a bosom that defies the most stalwart support bra, threatens to topple me when I lean forward, and makes my back ache to the point of tears. Speaking of which, I probably shouldn't mess with what God gave me, but one of these days I'm going to do something about my chest. First I have to get up the nerve. And an excess amount of cash.

Belle sobers. "Sorry about Charles. I didn't think he was your type, but I figured a night on the town would do you good."

And I'm twinged at wringing yet another apology from her. "I appreciate your efforts, Belle."

Her eyes flash—an indication that she has every intention of continuing those efforts to see me as happily married as she.

Oh, well. As it's better to know up front who she's throwing my way, I hold up a finger. "If you insist, but this time make sure he's a Christian."

Not that she doesn't feel the same way I do about dating. She's just become, for lack of a better word, desperate. After all, the Bay Area isn't exactly teeming with single Christian men. And she has to be thinking that if Beau, with his seemingly insurmountable past, could be converted, I might also be blessed.

"Ch-ching," Belle murmurs her rendition of a cash register as a woman floats past with an armful of hundred-dollar girlie-girl dresses. With a slight roll in her pregnant step, she hurries off in flat-soled shoes, the likes of which I'll never get used to seeing her wear. A lover of heels that elevate her above her slender five and a half feet, Belle is rarely seen in anything under three inches. But now that her pregnancy is well under way—

Deep laughter sidetracks my musing.

Brad-ish? The air in my cheeks developing a leak, I blink him into focus and glimpse grooves on either side of his mouth.

Nice teeth, but it's the laugh—the kind that turns heads without crossing the line to obnoxiousness—that's responsible for the humming at my center. Manly. Very manly.

Though it's unlikely that Brad-ish meets my selective dating criteria, is he even eligible for fantasizing—as in single? Of course, my housemate, Maia, would probably overlook a little thing like a wedding ring. She's already done it—or rather *is* doing it. For the past year, the five-foot-ten-inch, 120-pound stockbroker has been seeing a married man. Or, as she calls him, *unhappily* married. She really needs to find Jesus, and if I can just—

Brad-ish's eyes land on me. It may be a second our gazes hold, it may be a dozen, but when he returns his attention to Beau, I nearly wilt.

With heightened curiosity over his marital status—not that I've abandoned my resolution—I lower my gaze to find his arms crossed over his chest again, left hand gripping right bicep, fingers curled out of sight. Of course, if I work my way around, I should have a clear view.

Smoothing the shirt that tops my jeans, I step past a rack of Easter outfits, weave a little left, then a little right, and station myself between a collection of little boy duds and little girl tutus. However, no sooner do I spy the elusive hand than Beau's voice carries to me.

"Though Kate may not be much to look at, you have to admit her work is beautiful."

I slam my gaze to Beau to determine if he's aware of my eavesdropping and is just making the most of it—in a rather cruel way—but he appears oblivious.

"I agree," Brad-ish says.

The humming caused by his laughter seeps out of me. I attempt to shore up the leak by telling myself he's concurring about my work and not my looks. And it helps for all of two seconds.

"Of course, it's inner beauty that matters." Brad-ish sounds oddly distant.

Beau shrugs. "You're right. I'm just one of the lucky few whose wife possesses inner *and* outer beauty."

Which you don't deserve, Beau-zo! And which you wouldn't have if I hadn't put in a good word for you!

Not that it's news to me that I'm less than "model perfect," but when I put forth the effort, I clean up well. Unfortunately, with all the last minute touch-ups to the Amazon wall, I didn't have time to give it my all. With forty-five minutes to spare, I hurtled home, dragged my curls into a ponytail, and pulled on the first clean top and jeans to come to hand. The *only* clean ones, owing to laundry put on hold to complete the wall. Fortunately, the event is just right of casual and left of elegant. Even more fortunate, allowances are made for artists, especially those of the *San Francisco* variety.

Brad-ish glances at his watch. "How about an introduction?"

Realizing that I'm the introduction he seeks and that I'm

about to be caught eavesdropping, I swing around and suppress a groan as discomfort strikes between my shoulder blades.

Oh, my aching back...

Still, I pick up the pace and am within feet of the restroom when Beau calls.

"Kate, darling!"

Darling! Not his darling—*ever* again!

Knowing that Brad-ish is likely watching, I paste on a smile and turn. "Yes?"

Beau clasps my shoulder. "He'd like an introduction."

"I need to freshen up."

"Freshen up?" He frowns down me and up again. "You look..."

Go on, tell me I look great...pretty...any old lie-through-your-teeth compliment so long as I can bite your head off!

He sighs. "You *have* looked better."

Ah!

"Come on." He tugs my arm. "Dr. Alexander only has a few minutes before he has to leave for some swanky fund-raiser."

Which explains the tux.

I cross my arms over my chest. "And he wants to squander them on Kate Meadows, who according to the latest poll isn't much to look at?"

Though the politically correct thing would be to show surprise, transition to horror, and end with an apology, Beau grins. "Thought I'd give you something worth eavesdropping on."

Then he— "That's low! Even for you."

He shrugs. "I know, but extreme situations call for extreme measures."

"Extreme? Then you meant it?"

He screws up his eyes. "I keep telling you, some rollers, a little makeup, fitted clothes, a few less doughnuts—"

"I don't eat doughnuts!"

He gives me a "yeah, right" look.

Okay, so once in a while I treat myself to a doughnut, but I'm only supporting our church's doughnut ministry. Yeah... *doughnut* ministry.

Beau sighs. "As I was saying, the right clothes and color go a long way. Now back to Dr. Alexander."

I stare at him through narrowed lids.

"Think *client*, Kate."

Client...

"Think *BIG project*."

I grit my teeth.

"Good. Now get to it."

I shift my gaze to Brad-ish, who is once more consulting his watch. "All right, but if you think you're back in my good graces, *Beau-zo*, you're mistaken." I step away.

"Uh...Kate."

I twist around.

"The glasses." He taps the bridge of his nose. "Lose them."

Had I thought of it myself, I would. "No." I shove them up on my nose and, with Beau in tow, cross the store. As we near, the divinely tuxedoed Dr. Alexander looks around, and I'm jolted by the gray-blue eyes that capture my reflection.

Steady, girl.

I halt before him and, for a moment, can't remember what comes next.

"You're Kate Meadows, I presume." The frown on his brow contradicts the á la carte smile on his lips.

"Uh...yes."

Beau steps into my peripheral vision. "Kate, this is Dr. Alexander."

Now I remember. And become aware of the hand the doctor has extended—I have *no* idea for how long.

I thrust my hand into his and wince at the feel-good attraction that zips from fingertips to palm. "Nice to meet you, Dr. Alexander."

When he eases his grip, I almost gasp as his fingers brush my palm in reverse. He lowers his arm.

Rats! I still haven't checked out his hand. Would it be too obvious—?

Stop it! This is the man who concurred that you're not much to look at. And who, at this moment, is looking through you.

"I've been admiring your work, Ms. Meadows. You're very talented."

"Thank you."

He reaches into his jacket and pulls out a business card with his left hand, the ring finger of which bears a gold band. Married then.

Not that there was much chance of us hitting it off, especially considering my disregard for appearance and manners, but it was a nice thought.

"Ms. Meadows?" He extends the card nearer.

Not again! Accepting the card, I drop my chin to hide my toasted cheeks. Printed at the top is a hospital's name, center is *Clive Alexander, MD*, followed by an array of letters that surely denote his specialty, and at the bottom are his work and cell numbers.

"An acquaintance recommended you."

"Oh?" I look up and, more out of habit than a need to see more clearly, push my specs up. Not a bad move, as it brings his features into sharp focus. Definitely attractive. Of course, what man garbed in a tuxedo doesn't exude some level of yum?

In the next instant, his lips form words, and like a movie

where a voice is out of sync, I hear him say, "He passed on an article that featured your work."

I start to ask the identity of the one to whom I should be grateful, but he says, "I believe the publication was *Upscale*."

As in *The Bay Area's Finest Homes*—my first appearance in a magazine. "Oh, yes."

"I was particularly impressed with the playroom and the children's library."

"Thank you. Child-friendly environments are my specialty." Not that I planned it that way.

He inclines his head. "Your work is incredible."

"Really?" Yes, I'm fishing. And smiling straight up to my cheekbones. But as I struggle to subdue my mutinous mouth, Dr. Alexander smiles back, and this time his eyes crinkle at the corners.

"You have a unique style."

I moisten my lips. "So…uh…what are you interested in? Revamping your child's room?"

As if my question committed some heinous act, his smile slips. "I'm overseeing the expansion of our children's burn unit and need to secure an artist to create something that appeals to children." He nods at the wall. "Like this."

Wishing his smile back, I reach into my shirt pocket and remove a brightly colored business card. Though mine isn't as impressive as his, it is kind of cute. I hand it to him. "I'd love the opportunity to work up a proposal."

"How far out are you booked?"

"Right now—"

"Clive!"

As he turns toward the flutey, singsongy voice, I peer past him. The woman, wearing an elegant sheath and with fashionably cropped hair accenting her cheekbones, crosses the boutique on stilettos.

So this is the Mrs.

"We're late, Clive." She lays a hand on his arm—her left hand, which is accessorized by a single diamond ring. And a pinkie ring at that.

Oh. *Not* the Mrs.…

She leans in and kisses his jaw, and I imagine Dr. Alexander's wife and children sitting at home oblivious to his extracurricular activities. How sad.

"Adelphia, this is Ms. Meadows, the artist who created the Amazon wall." He nods at my creation.

She doesn't even feign interest but scans me up and down. Then, as if assured I present no threat, she gives a smile that is all the brighter for her findings.

"Ms. Meadows, this is Adelphia Jamison, a colleague of mine."

Colleague. Right. Feeling like a sack of cocoa beans alongside a box of gourmet chocolates, I reach forward. "Nice to meet you."

She clasps and unclasps my hand. "Mmm. Same. We really must go, Clive."

He meets my gaze. "If I don't phone within the next week, give me a call and we'll discuss the project."

"I'll do that."

Adelphia something-or-other loops her arm through his.

"Great-looking couple," Beau murmurs as the two walk away.

"Hmm…wonder what his wife would say about that."

"It's probably something she accepted long ago."

"I'd *never* accept it."

He puts an arm around my shoulders. "Considering your keen fashion sense, there doesn't seem much likelihood you'll be asked to do so."

I duck from beneath his arm. "You're definitely in the doghouse, *Beau-zo*."

"Not much to look at…"

I stare at my reflection in the bedroom mirror—seeing myself as Dr. Alexander and that Adelphia woman saw me. I have looked better. Though Beau may be in the doghouse, I'm the one going to the dogs. Granted in an artsy, free-spirited, semi-Bohemian way, but…

"Not much to look at."

Though I'm hardly leggy and thin, neither am I as stubby as my top and jeans make me appear. Focusing on the former with its button-down front and fringed hem, I wince. If I didn't know better—*way* better—I'd say I was pregnant.

What am I doing hanging on to clothes like these? Why, I can't even remember when I plunked down good money to look like this. It had to have been years ago—

Ah. Post-Christopher, as in the year following his request that I return his engagement ring. I'd given it back, all right (would have nailed him between the eyes if he hadn't ducked), then spent the rest of the day tearing apart my wardrobe. Everything red—his favorite color—landed in the donation pile. Unfortunately, as the majority of my clothes had been purchased with Christopher in mind, I'd had to go shopping afterward, as evidenced by the clothes to which I fell victim this evening.

I turn from the full-length mirror and eye the mounds of clothes, the laundering of which is seriously overdue. Of course, if I pulled out a trash bag, that would solve the problem. But then I'd be down to a bare-bones wardrobe. And that would mean a shopping spree. Which would mean a drained checking account. Which would mean a dip into savings—

Unless I use my credit card.

I consider the piece of plastic that I suppose I should use from time to time to build credit. And it's not as if I'd carry a balance and be subject to an outrageous interest rate. I'd pay off the bill the moment it arrived.

So how much *would* it cost to update my wardrobe? Unfortunately, I really like the stretchy hip-hugging jeans Belle talked me into months back—pricey at seventy bucks a pop. In fact, had I caught sight of the price tag before trying them on, I *wouldn't* have tried them on. But they fit so well, and it had just been the one pair. Now, though, we'd be talking at least four more, which translates into nearly three hundred dollars, and that's before I even look at tops—

Forget it! I am *not* spending seventy dollars on jeans destined for paint splatters. Call me cheap, but that seductive little piece of plastic isn't getting anywhere near a cash register.

I drag my top off and straighten my skewed specs. The mistake I make is in taking another peek at my reflection. The relaxed-fit jeans—of the high-waisted, full-seated variety—make me wince. And groan when I look over my shoulder at my rear end, which appears to be a mile high.

"That's it!" I step out of my sandals, unzip, tug, wiggle, shake, and kick the jeans aside. So maybe I will be purchasing more seventy-dollars-a-pop—

I hear a gasp, but it's only my grandmother who raised me from the age of three, following my parents' death. Though she passed away years ago, her gasp when I did something she did not approve of is so ingrained that it's as if she's in the room now. She would *not* approve of seventy-dollar jeans. In fact, she'd be scandalized, much to the delight of my grandfather, whose memories of his beloved wife kept him going the two years he outlived her.

Throat tightening at my loss, I swim back to the shallow end of Kate's emotional pool. So maybe I can find a cheaper version of the jeans…

Though tempted to content myself with the quick fix of *frugally* updating my wardrobe, I know that Beau's "not much to look at" comment went beyond clothes. Thus, clad in bra and undies, I return to the mirror and position myself with one foot in front of the other, abs sucked in, shoulders back.

Ladies and gentlemen—Katherine Mae Meadows, thirty-three years old (did I actually admit that?), *five foot three* (must have shrunk), *125 pounds* (water retention is such a drag). Reality is a real drag too, which says that as much as I'd like to be twenty-nine, five foot seven, and 110 pounds again, it's not going to happen.

I lift my chin and…grimace. Hoping it's the angle, I turn to the other side. Not much better. Face forward. Ooh. Over the shoulder. Ugh.

Must be objective. And realistic. After all, outside of a pair of heels, I can't do a thing about my height. Outside of traveling back in time (pure drivel), I can't do a thing about my age. And outside of cruel and unusual punishment (a.k.a. exercise), there's not much I can do about my weight. Except…

I scowl at my breasts, which present a few choice pounds I'd love to shed, as in breast reduction. Not only does the weight wreak havoc on my posture, but it's a source of endless backache. Unfortunately, as I'm self-employed and have yet to obtain affordable insurance, I'll have to finance the reduction myself. But if business keeps going well, it's doable. In the meantime, there *is* cruel and unusual punishment.

I consider my abdomen and thighs, evidence that I've gained a few pounds. Or more. Moments later, I enter the bathroom, domain of the all-knowing scale—giver of truth, enlightenment, and deeply abiding remorse.

How bad can it be? After all, it's only been a month since I weighed myself.

As I step toward the scale, I catch sight of the thick dust covering its top.

Make that two months. Maybe three…

Gripping the towel bar to avoid jolting the ultrasensitive instrument, I plant the first foot, then the other. Hmm. One hundred and five pounds. Now for the last *little* bit. I release the towel bar and…

The dial spins wildly left.

"One hundred and thirty-five pounds?!" I jump off and glare at the dial as it returns to—

"Well, lookie there." At rest it reads one pound. "Ha!" I fiddle with the dial until the needle settles to zero—well slightly under—and repeat the mounting ritual.

One hundred thirty-four. A nine-pound weight gain, as opposed to ten. Not so bad. And, of course, everyone knows one should only weigh oneself first thing in the morning following a trip to the bathroom. So 134 pounds it is. Perfectly acceptable.

Just who am I kidding?

I stomp off the scale. A nine-pound weight gain doesn't have me rolling down any aisles, but at this rate none of my clothes will fit by summer. How could this happen? Surely I should have felt it in my pants—

Ah, relaxed-fit jeans! Stretchable hip-huggers! No accountability *whatsoever*.

Determined to take a closer look at this heavier version of

Katherine Mae Meadows, I step to the bathroom mirror. The first thing I notice (how could I not?) is the mole that practically jumps off my cheek. Wish it would.

I remove my specs, which causes the edges of my face to blur. And for once, I'm grateful. Okay, let's see…

Hair. When was the last time I had it styled, let alone *cut*? I tug the band from the dark mass of curls and peer at a handful of dull strands victimized by split ends. And for one crazy moment, I consider adopting a fashionably cropped do like the one sported by Dr. Alexander's mistress. Moving on…

Eyes. More gray than blue, not unlike Dr. Alexander's—
Best to steer clear of that man.

Nose. A little narrow, but attractive.

Cheekbones. Present, though that unsightly mole—
I grunt.

Mouth. Good teeth, small gap notwithstanding.

Ears. A little large, but flat to the head and nicely appointed with double piercings—

I know. Belly, nose, and tongue piercings are all the rage, but I'm not that progressive (if one can call it that). When I need to "find" myself, I scrape away a layer of paint. When I need to "express" myself, I open my mouth. Of course, sometimes I insert my foot. Much like Beau.

Well, maybe not, as his comments about my looks *were* premeditated. "Not much to look at," I mutter.

However, considering all the evidence, his words don't pack the punch they did earlier, and I grudgingly admit that had I not ignored his advice these past months, my appearance wouldn't have gotten so out of hand.

Unfortunately, as much as I'd like to blame the lapse on my flourishing business, it's more than that. It's called *apathy*. As in "Why bother?" which is highly compatible with "Thou shalt embrace singledom and be unbelievably, inconceivably happy."

I'm tired of the hopelessness of dating. Christian or non-Christian, the result is the same. And, in the rare instance a promising candidate comes along, his expiration date becomes apparent the moment children enter the picture. Or, in my case, don't.

I press a hand to my abdomen and am stung that the bulge beneath my fingers will never be the result of a growing child. Early menopause—Premature Ovarian Failure (POF)— took care of not only that, but also my fiancé. Despite Christopher's profession of undying love, he couldn't accept adoption as an alternative to biological children.

I drop my hand from my abdomen. I've accepted my loss. Accepted it and am grateful, as it led me to Jesus. With that reminder, I touch the blue glass and sterling bracelet that was a gift from Belle. She was the first to approach the abject young woman who slipped into her church eight years ago—a lost soul who had left everything behind in Redding to follow her fiancé to San Francisco. When that same young woman accepted Christ a year later, Belle presented her with the bracelet. And it's been on my wrist ever since.

I touch the silver cross, then the medallion with its inscription *Believe*. Always a comfort, it reminds me that God is in control. Thus, it's possible my life will eventually include a husband. Of course, it sure would save time to know at the outset where a man stands with regard to perpetuating the human race. If I had my way, men who require biological children would wear some identifying mark like married men wear wedding bands.

And no, I haven't limited myself to men without pasts. In fact, for a while I believed that those with children were the solution. Wrong. The first widower I dated was so *not* "The One" that it took just one date to mark him off. The next wanted more *biological* children. The third made it clear up front that he was done with marriage. I even dated a divorced guy with partial custody of his three children. He had issues. Last, there was the singleton with a child out of wedlock. As evidenced by his one-night stand overtures, he hadn't learned the error of his ways.

So maybe I am destined to remain manless, but that's no excuse to allow my downward slide to continue. Thus, tomorrow I'll start toning up, courtesy of the yoga class I committed to last month—and for which I have yet to attend a single session. But I *will* get my money's worth!

I glance at my watch. A quarter till eleven. Too late to look up Scripture and analyze how it relates to my circumstances. As for my prayer journal, surely the soul-searching before the mirror will suffice. Yeah.

I excuse myself—something I do more of lately and seems directly proportional to the number of jobs I accept. Much as I hate to admit it, stuffing God in the backseat is becoming habit.

I sigh. Guess it's time for my nightly cocktail.

From the medicine cabinet, I remove four vials: estrogen, progesterone, vitamin E, and calcium—a hormone "cocktail" better known as HRT, or hormone replacement therapy, which protects against everything from heart and bone problems to uterine and ovarian cancer to sleeplessness and osteoporosis.

It takes a full glass of water to get them all down, and I nearly choke on the last.

Ah, the joys of menopause before one's time. Of having one's reproductive ability ripped out from under her.

"Oh, stop it!"

Retrieving my pajamas, I determinedly recite, "Thank You,

God, for life without menstrual cramps." I drag the top on. "Thank You for the absence of PMS." I thrust into the bottoms. "Thank You that I don't have to worry about embarrassing accidents. Thank You—"

A commotion downstairs announces the return of my housemate. I scowl. She's brought *him* home again—Mr. Unhappily Married!

Feeling an ache behind my eyes, I pray it's not one of my rare migraines, courtesy of Premature Ovarian Failure.

Failure. I *really* hate that word.

Rubbing my forehead, I step from the bathroom. Though I know I should hit my knees for prayer, I curl up beneath my comforter and clasp my hands.

Dear Lord, I know You want to use me, but won't You please have a chat with Maia about Mr. Unhappily Married?

2

Saturday, March 17

Good morning, Lord!

Thank You for a fabulous turnout at Belle and Beau's, a feast of business cards (keep 'em coming!), Brad Pitt look-alikes (or maybe not), and enduring friendships (Beau-zo excluded).

Help me forgive Beau for his comment about my looks (and those who agree with him, e.g., Dr. Clive Alexander), help me guard my tongue and become a witness to Maia, and help me be content with the me You made. (Did You really intend for me to have breasts like these?) Above all, please keep Belle and Beau's growing child safe and healthy.

Yours,

Kate

PS: Sorry about missing my Bible time last night. Sooo tired. But I'll do it tonight! Promise.

*PPS: Please help me not to strain anything in that yoga
class I'm taking. Speaking of which, that new body I get
when I make it to heaven? It won't need to be exercised,
will it?*

"And...downward-facing dog," the instructor intones.

Not again. Not the dog thing. *Puh-lease!*

With a whimper, I look to the woman on the sticky mat
beside me—housemate and yoga enthusiast, Maia Glock.
Without visible effort, she shifts her legs back. As she settles
into the pose that appears to be the precursor to a man's push
up—except for the upward-facing tush—I grunt and step a foot
back.

How much longer? It's been... I check my watch. Twenty
minutes? That's all? Oh no. And this is only the first step in
reclaiming Katherine Mae Meadows. Hmm. Maybe I should
give her up for dead. Or at least curvaceously content.

I glance at the door. Would anyone notice if I slipped out?
After all, they're so *into* it.

"Keep going, Ms. Meadows." The instructor's bare feet appear near my hands. "That's it. Gently walk your feet out behind
you."

Singled out. Nowhere to run.

Gritting my teeth, I step my aching right leg back, then
the left.

"A bit more." She pats my thigh.

If I were a pit bull, she wouldn't dare. Baring my teeth,
which my downward-facing mutt conceals, I step back twice
more.

"Good. Now let's hold it."

How about *she* holds it? Arms trembling, calves burning,

back straining with the effect of gravity on my well-endowed chest, I glare at the sticky mat.

Downward-facing dog! Who comes up with names like that? Next thing I'll be told to hike my leg with some "tree-ward-facing dog" move. Or perhaps "fire hydrant–facing dog."

"Now walk your legs back to standing." The instructor's voice drifts away as she moves down the line of students.

I try. I really do, but there's nothing left. I drop to my knees, sink back on my heels, and press my cheek to the cool mat.

"Kate!" Maia whispers above the *plunk-tinkle-tinkle* music.

I meet her gaze at about the level of her knees. Oh, maan! She's bent double like a hinge.

"Get up!"

I close my eyes. "No." Intrigued by the floaty threads behind my lids—what exactly are those things, anyway?—I follow one, then the other.

"Kate!"

"Can't." I sink deeper into the mat.

"Come on. You're embarrassing me!"

"You?" I follow a floaty thing that looks like a warm and chewy cinnamon roll. What has *she* got to be embarrassed about? *I'm* the one ready to pass out.

"Yes, me, the one who went out on a limb to get you a spot in this class."

Out on a limb? *She* insisted I join. All I did was pay through the nose for the privilege. And pray through the heart that our regular outings would allow me to witness to her.

"Get up, Kate."

I crack open an eye. Even bent upside down with sweat on her brow, she looks great.

"Nuh-uh." I lower my lids, and for all of ten seconds, my world is right. No stretching, no straining, no—

"Up, Ms. Meadows. You won't see results unless you push yourself." The instructor pats my thigh again.

Down, boy, down!

Pressing my lips to keep my fangs in check, I lift my head and the sticky mat follows, only to release from my cheek with a *shloop* heard 'round the room.

I sit back on my heels and look up at the semi-earthy woman whose pink-striped hair is confined to a thick braid draped over one shoulder.

She arches an eyebrow, then turns to the others. "And now we roll up slowly and exalt the sun."

Somehow I don't think she means God's Son, Jesus. The other members of the class straighten and lift their arms.

Pressing my hands to the mat, I nearly stumble as I rise. "You're probably wondering what I'm doing here." I drag my moist palms up my sweatpants.

"We all must start somewhere, child."

Child…With a sneaking suspicion she's quoting Confucius, I say, "And end somewhere." I give her an apologetic smile. "I don't think this yoga thing is working for me."

"If you mean twenty minutes of it, you're right." She turns her head and calls out, "And roll down again."

Before I can escape, she settles a hand on my shoulder and bends so near that her forehead almost touches mine. "Ms. Meadows, it requires commitment to make the changes necessary for one's body to find its balance in nature."

Confucius again? And hasn't the woman heard of personal space? I ease back a step. "What I'm saying is I think I'd be better off sticking with aerobics." Of course, I haven't stuck with it, have I? Though exercise is prescribed alongside hormone replacement therapy, I've been bad. Very bad.

She releases my shoulder. "If this is all aerobics has done for you, you're at the right place."

Now that's just plain nasty. However, a reminder of this morning's devotional about guarding one's tongue holds me in check.

I shrug. "Obviously, I've been away from it for a while, but when I—"

She raises a silencing hand. "And back to downward-facing dog."

What's with this lady and dogs?

"Trust me, Ms. Meadows. Given time and discipline, you'll see results. Now let's give it another try."

I'm not a confrontational person. In fact, I'm a pushover, but this is a bit more than I can handle. "Look—"

"Kate."

I turn to Maia, who's peering at me from her doggy pose. "Just do it, okay?"

Hemmed in on all sides. Not an ally in sight. Only tushes. And more tushes, many of which are remarkably firm and narrow—doubtless just the way Dr. Clive Alexander likes them.

Why does that scallywag keep invading my thoughts?

Making a face at Maia, I mutter, "Okay."

Hours later—honestly, it feels that long!—Maia and I emerge from the vile studio into a bright San Francisco morning. Almost immediately, we become the recipients of appreciative glances. Well, actually it's Maia that a passing group of men admire—she of the long legs, perfect posture, tousled tresses, and glistening glow.

I blow a breath up my face, which causes my specs to fog. Great.

I follow the cloudy figure of Maia, who doesn't notice I've

fallen behind. Have I been too hasty committing to such rigorous self-improvement? Granted, besides the one yoga session, I've only managed to trim my split ends, but that took a good ten minutes and resulted in a shorter-than-intended prayer journal entry.

Is it worth it? After all, what's the likelihood that a trimmer, coiffed, and fashionably attired me will land more jobs? Nor will my attempts at self-improvement guarantee that I finally catch a man. Considering the serious compatibility issue, finding *him*—if he exists—is a job for "Super-God." As for the quality of my life, on the surface, self-improvement *would* make me feel better about myself, but will it outweigh the commitment?

God, send me a sign, 'cause I'm sooo tempted to back out!

"You're really out of shape, aren't you?" Maia calls over her shoulder.

I falter. Was that a sign? Would He actually speak through her? Nah, that was all Maia. Scowling, I pump my legs faster and am panting when I draw alongside her.

"Coffee?" she suggests over the sound of an approaching cable car.

Though I know I'll be hurting if I don't get into a tub of hot water soon, I say, "Sure," and give a little shiver as my overheated skin awakens to the chill morning air.

When we stop at the crosswalk to wait for the light, I loosen my sweatshirt from around my waist and drag on the garment. As my head pops through the neck, the telltale clanging that precedes the appearance of cable cars rises above the street noise like a powerfully beautiful voice among croakers.

Partial to San Francisco's only moving historic landmark, I turn my head to the right just as the rectangular box comes into view. *Love* cable cars, especially those bearing riders gleefully clutching the poles and hanging out the sides.

As it rumbles past, sounding its bell, I follow its progress—and would follow it down the hill and out of sight if not for Maia's hefty sigh and "Hmm, nice," drawl.

Curious, I track her gaze to the sidewalk across the street. Standing outside the corner coffee shop is a middle-aged bearded guy with a camera around his neck, a fashionably bald thirty-ish guy, and a cute twenty-ish woman. And they're staring at us.

Us? Not just Maia? Strange.

Maia presses her shoulders back, putting her chest front and center. "The bald guy seems familiar."

I narrow my sights on him. He doesn't look the least bit familiar; however, he is attractive—in a bald way.

The light changes. As we cross the street, I note that the sway in Maia's step is more pronounced. Expecting her to stop and flirt, I'm surprised when she sweeps past the small group.

Ah, the old coy trick.

As I follow her into the coffee shop, I glance over my shoulder at the bald guy and am given what seems a genuine smile.

The coffee shop is an old place with faded paint, worn chairs, lopsided tables, and bookshelves swollen with dusty books published eons ago, but that's why I like it. Those other ones—the yuppified coffee shops that have invaded so much of the city—are simply too sterile, too consistent, and too expensive.

Jolene waves us in. "Yo, Kate! Maia!"

Breathing in the smell of fresh-ground coffee beans—so rich it leaves a taste on the tongue—I return the wave. "Yo, Jo Jo."

As the tie-dye clad Asian woman sets her magical machine to humming, she gives us the once-over. "Working out?"

I grimace as I settle in a creaky chair at the table Maia

claims in front of the window. "How can you tell?"

She grins, revealing a missing incisor. "You—easy. Ms. Maia—could be a front."

Maia snorts. "Who's the one in shape, hmm?"

Was that a slam?

Jolene laughs. "You born that way." She plunges the steaming wand into a pitcher of milk. "The rest of us gotta work hard to look half so fine. Huh, Ms. Kate?"

Another slam. "Humph," I grunt.

Shortly, Jolene sets our drinks in front of us, mine a decaf. Though following my diagnosis of Premature Ovarian Failure I adjusted to decaffeinated coffee, I can't help but be jealous of all that caffeine doing a backstroke in Maia's cup. Unfortunately, caffeine really sucks down my calcium.

"Oh!" Jolene's eyes widen. "Almost forgot. As you working out now, Ms. Kate, I give you sugar-free vanilla syrup. You like." She bustles away.

Decaf *and* sugar free? That's almost too much to bear.

I grimace. "I don't like sugar free."

Maia flips up a hand. "Obviously." Then, as if having merely commented on the weather, she lifts her cup.

Tongue! Guard your tongue! You'll never reach her otherwise.

But how, exactly, am I to witness to her when my wounded ego is conjuring images of torture—a nice, slow drip or maybe splinters beneath her fingernails?

"So…" Maia returns her cup to its mismatched saucer. "You made it through the entire class. What do you think?"

"That what happened to me ought to be illegal. I'm going to be *so* sore."

"That's the idea."

Great. I lift my cup only to pause and lean in. "At the end when we clasped our hands and bowed, the instructor said, 'No mustache.' What does that mean?"

Maia's eyes widen. "No mustache?"

Okay, so I heard wrong. "No mistake?"

Her eyes widen further, then she squeals.

I roll my eyes. "Whatever it was, I didn't get it."

"*Namasté*, Kate. Nah-mah-STAY."

A foreign word. Surely I can be forgiven. "Okay, Nah-mah-STAY. What's it mean?"

She sinks back in her chair. "Something to do with saluting the god in each of us."

"The god?" As in the Holy Spirit?

"Yeah, we're all gods in our own right, you know."

I'm not Catholic, but the temptation to cross myself is overwhelming; however, I calm myself with the realization that this is an opening to witness. "No, I don't know. In fact, as a Christian, I—"

"Uh-uh." She shakes her head. "Don't go there."

Shot down before liftoff....

I sigh and raise my cup as the group that watched us cross the street enters the shop.

Maia leans near. "It *is* Michael Palmier."

"Who?"

She gives me a do-you-live-under-a-rock? look. "Palmier, Kate. You know, the makeup artist who works on all the big models? The one daytime talk shows call in to transform the impossibly unattractive?"

"Uh…"

She rolls her eyes. "The one who put out last year's bestselling *The Makeup Bible*?"

Bible? I nearly gasp in concert with the memory of my grandmother, while slightly more distant I detect my grandfather's chuckle. Though grandmother was a Bible toter, grandfather was an agnostic who loved to pick at his wife's beliefs—in a strangely loving manner.

I clear my throat. "Did you say *Bible*?"

With a mewl of exasperation, Maia shifts her attention to those at the counter.

Wondering how God feels about someone attaching *Bible* to a work of vanity, I peer at the bald guy.

"Hmm," Maia murmurs.

Coffee cup perched before my mouth, I watch her drag the ponytail band from her hair, give her head a slow-motion shake, and go from beautiful to gorgeous.

So much for coy…

Not that I'm surprised. Maia and I may not spend much time together, but when we do socialize, it's always the same. If her flirtations were done with a view to replacing her current love interest, it wouldn't be so bad, but it's all fluff. Though Mr. Unhappily Married has yet to deliver on the divorce he assures her is in the works, she's holding out for the two-timer.

"Think he'll ask me out?"

Did I hear Maia right? I lean across the table. "I thought you were taken."

Her eyes snap. "No, Kate, my boyfriend is the one who's taken."

Do I detect bitterness? Have they had an argument? Perhaps she's finally realized that *unhappily married* doesn't necessarily translate to *happily divorced*.

"Yes, he is." I take a sip of coffee only to grimace when the artificial sweetener hits my taste buds. "Yuck!" I push my chair back.

The group at the counter steps aside to allow me past, and I catch sight of the bald guy's left hand. Not married. Could be just what Maia needs.

"Sorry, Jo Jo." I set the cup on the counter. "Gotta have the real stuff."

She tsk-tsks, and I snatch a biscotti. As I swing away, *The Makeup Bible* guy's eyes meet mine. And he smiles again.

Nice smile.

I head back to Maia. "He's good-looking."

She shrugs and stares out the window.

"And he's not married."

She jerks her chin around. "Oh? And where did you come by that information?"

It's all I can do not to roll my eyes. "No wedding ring." *Duh!*

Her brow buckles. "Wake up, Kate. Maybe your padded world excludes you from men who pass themselves off as single, but in the real world, they exist."

Oh.

"Unfortunately, by the time a woman pieces the puzzle together, she's hooked."

Guessing she's talking about Mr. Unhappily Married, my heart constricts. "I hadn't considered that."

As she buries her nose in her coffee cup, I look to the opposite side of the shop where Michael Palmier sits. *Is* he married? Surely not.

When I turn back to Maia, she's staring out the window at a curbside municipal bus that shrills as it raises its front end. *Hate* that obnoxious sound. Shortly it pulls away, and I'm relieved that we have ten minutes before a repeat performance.

When my replacement drink arrives, I sigh over genuine, unadulterated sugar—worth every single calorie.

Maia pushes her cup away. "Almost done?"

"Done? I just got my coffee."

She sinks her chin into an upturned palm and looks toward

the makeup artist. For the first minute or so, she drums her fingers on the table, but then she smiles almost shyly, which is so *not* Maia. Sending up a silent prayer that Michael Palmier's ring finger doesn't lie, I sip the hot liquid. However, it's not long before Maia starts frowning and glancing between me and the other table.

I shake my head. "What?"

"Feel as if you're being watched?"

"Uh…no."

She relaxes into a smile. "For a second, I thought it was you he was interested in. Funny, huh?"

I nearly nod. True, it would be surprising if a man preferred me over Maia, but funny? That hurts. Why do I persist in concerning myself over her well-being when I could use a little attention myself? A hot bath, for starters! I lower my cup. "Ready to go?"

Her eyes widen. "Um…" She glances across the room.

I pull a five-spot and a single from my fanny pack and drop them to the table to cover our bill and a tip. "Coming?"

"Oh, all right." Like a nymph rising from the surf, she stands.

I step ahead of her and call, "See you, Jo Jo."

"See you, Kate. And you, Maia."

Outside the shop, I draw up short at the realization Maia is no longer following. I peer over my shoulder at where she stands before the shop door. "What?"

"I…uh…need to run to the market to pick up a few items."

Is this her way of getting rid of me so she can pop back in and introduce herself to Michael Palmier? Fine.

I shrug. "See you later then."

"Kate!"

"Yes?"

She juts her chin in the direction of the studio. "Same time tomorrow?"

I shake my head so hard my neck twinges. "In case you didn't notice, yoga doesn't agree with me."

Her jaw drops. "Surely you're not going to walk away from your membership? That wasn't cheap."

Remembering the one-year contract, membership fee, and monthly draft out of my checking account, my resentment over her "funny" comment deepens. "I know."

"What about Pilates?"

"Pilates?" Not that I haven't heard of it, but I know little more about it than yoga.

She nods. "The studio also offers Pilates. In fact, I sometimes alternate between the two."

Might I possibly salvage my membership? Moreover, do I even want to? After all, my poor fit with yoga could be the perfect excuse to back off this whole self-improvement thing.

"At least give it a try."

I start to shrug off Maia's plea only to realize that it *is* a plea, that she's anxious for me to accompany her. Me—an out-of-shape wuss who usually warrants little more than a passing wave. Am I finally reaching her? Have I become more to her than a tenant whose monthly rent allows her to afford a house in San Francisco?

"What do you say, Kate?"

Stirred by joy, I blink. "What?"

"Pilates. Puh-LAH-teez."

"Oh. Do they use words like *nah-mah-STAY*?"

She rolls her eyes. "No."

"Well, maybe I could—"

"Great! Let's get together again tomorrow."

"But we worked out today."

She gives me the once-over. "And a lot of good that did."

That was below the belt. However, despite the uprooting of my joy, I manage to respond with, "They say it's best to give your body a day to recover from a workout."

She puts her hands on her hips. "Look, Kate, if you're going to shed the weight you've piled on—"

Piled on! It is *not* piled on!

"—you have to commit. So tomorrow it is. Bright and early."

I struggle to hold back words I'll regret. In the end, my best defense is that tomorrow is Sunday. Meaning I have an excuse, a legitimate one. Ha!

"Sorry, Maia, but tomorrow's church."

She groans. "Don't you ever get tired of that Holy Roller garbage?"

Tongue, Kate! Tongue! "We're not Holy Rollers, and there's no garbage about it. You know, if you'd attend a service with me, I think you'd be impressed." Hopefully not by the number of wedding bands in the pews.

Ooh, that was an ugly thought.

Maia makes a gagging sound. "Oh, please. Do you honestly think I have some kind of death wish to be stoned?"

Her choice of words surprises me, as it reveals she's not unaware that what she's doing is wrong. "No one's going to stone you, Maia—literally *or* verbally. We all do things we—"

She throws a hand up, but before she can admonish me, the shop door opens and Bald and Good-Looking and his companions step to the sidewalk. "Ladies, may we have a word with you?"

Maia drops her arm to her side and smiles. "Of course."

However, it's me he's staring at. Funny…

"Michael Palmier." He thrusts a hand forward. "My assistant, Trish Jacobs." He nods at the young woman. "And *Changes* magazine's photographer, Arnie Simpson." The bearded guy.

As I stare at the hand he extends, Maia claims it. "Palmier... uh..." She taps her lips with a manicured nail. "Makeup artist, right?"

Is she good or is she good?

"That's right."

"A pleasure. I'm Maia Glock, stockbroker."

"Nice to meet you." He disengages and returns his attention to me. "And you are?"

I meet his warm, green eyes and slide my hand into his. "Kate Meadows."

He squeezes my fingers. "I thought so."

"Huh?"

"Last month's article in *Upscale: The Bay Area's Finest Homes.*"

He recognized me from the stamp-sized picture at the bottom of the spread of the children's library?

"Fantastic work you do."

My business sense kicks in. "Are you interested in making over a room, Mr. Palmier?" I start to withdraw my hand, but he closes his other hand over ours to hold me there.

"Actually, it's *you* I'm interested in making over."

"What?"

"You're perfect."

The last person who called me perfect was my fiancé, shortly before he asked for his ring back. I tug at my hand, but the man holds firm.

"I'm sorry." I give another tug. "I don't understand."

"We're out today searching for mismatched girlfriends to make over for the anniversary issue of *Changes* magazine."

"Huh?"

"You and Ms. Glock. Mismatched girlfriends."

Guessing this is about to turn into another "funny, hmm?" comment, I try again to release my hand.

"One tall, one short," he continues. "One light, one dark. One thin, one—"

"Thick?" I supply with not just a little animosity. And another tug.

He laughs. "Hardly, Ms. Meadows—er, Kate. I can call you Kate, can't I?"

Forget the tug. I jerk hard, and if not for his quick reflexes, the freeing of my hand would have set me on my tush. He grips my arm and, once I regain my balance, has the good sense to release me.

"No offense, Kate." He flashes a boyish smile. "It's just that you have incredible potential. You know, you're really quite pretty."

"Which is what I'm always telling her." Maia steps alongside and loops an arm through mine. "We'll do it."

We'll do it? "I don't think—"

"Here." He thrusts a business card at me, which Maia swipes. "Call me this week, and we'll set up a time."

I take a step toward him. "But—"

"Will do," Maia purrs.

The bearded one raises his camera. "All we need are a few pictures."

Before I can protest, or at least run a hand over my mussed hair, he snaps a half dozen pictures of beautiful Maia towering over pitiful, shell-shocked me.

"Nice to meet you, ladies." Michael gives me a parting smile. "I look forward to seeing you again."

As I watch him and his companions head away, I grumble, "Well, I don't."

Maia snorts. "Believe me, if anyone needs a makeover, it's you, Kate."

That cuts, especially as she said Palmier is the one talk shows call in to transform the *impossibly unattractive*, which I'm *not*! Beginning to boil, I reflect on Beau's "not much to look at" comment, then Maia's "you're really out of shape" comment, next her "funny" comment, followed by her "piled on" comment, and now this. It's—

Maia sighs. "He was nice."

I follow her gaze, which is following Michael out of sight.

She sighs again. "And quite the flirt. In fact, if I didn't know better, I'd say he was flirting with you."

Wait just a minute! That was another slam! And I'm not taking it anymore. "Are you saying there's no way he would flirt with me?"

"Well…"

I open my mouth. "You know—"

Tongue! Guard your—

"—stoning might just be too good for you."

Though normally I'd immediately wish back such un-Christian words, I'm too riled to force an apology. Which is just as well, as the anger that flashes in Maia's eyes evidences that no amount of groveling will mend what's broken.

"Have a nice day," she growls and turns on her heel.

I watch her go from sight, then glance heavenward. "We'll talk later." Beginning to feel the first pangs of regret, I head home.

Saturday, March 17

Oh Lord,

I botched it, didn't I? But how can she say things like that and expect me to turn the other cheek? Okay, so I should have turned the other cheek, but I'm not perfect, You know. Of course You know.

In the future, please help me guard my tongue better, help me make amends and become an effective witness, and help me discern between right and wrong (sorry about the namasté thing—I didn't mean it). Help me find a way out of this makeover gig without further alienating Maia. As for this achy-breaky back—help! Above all, please continue to keep Belle and Beau's baby safe and healthy.

~~Yours,~~

Almost forgot—thank You for dogs with wagging tails and lolling tongues that no more attempt to imitate humans than we should attempt to imitate them (downward-facing dog!). Thank You for great java, old coffee shops, and nicely shaped bald heads.

Sorry about missing my Bible time again. That yoga really took it out of me. Tomorrow night! Promise.

Yours,

Kate

3

At least Maia's talking to me again. No more of the silent treatment I've been subjected to these past four days, despite my attempts at reconciliation. Not the least of which was accompanying her to that blasted Pilates class. No namasté, but plenty of ungodly torture. Of course, I'd be a fool not to realize that Maia's sudden thaw has everything to do with this makeover fiasco—which I *really* don't want to do. And if not for our run-in outside the coffee shop, I wouldn't. Hence, punishment for not guarding my tongue.

"Ow!"

My squawk causes Michael's assistant to grimace in the mirror I've been seated in front of this past hour while she and Palmier consult over the transformation of Kate.

Trish tries again to draw the comb through my hair. This time when the teeth snag, I come up out of my seat.

"Sorry," she mutters, and I just know she's guarding *her* tongue.

I rub my temple. "Believe it or not, that hair is attached to my head."

Nodding wearily, she urges me back down.

As she aims the comb at my hair once more, I pull my arm from beneath the plastic cape and glance at my watch. "How much longer is this going to take? I have a four-thirty appointment on the other side of town." With Dr. Clive Alexander, no less, whose secretary called this morning before Maia and I blew out the door to catch a city bus.

"Not to worry," Trish says. "It's only noon now."

Maia swivels her chair around. "Honestly, Kate, must you carry on so?"

Easy for her to criticize. When she settled in for Palmier and his assistant to work on her, they pronounced her perfect: hair, makeup, *and* clothes. Then they turned to me…

Trish glances over her shoulder. "Arnie, I'm ready to make the first cut."

Brandishing his camera, the photographer appears.

Snap, snap, snap.

Snip, snip, snip.

Snap.

Snip.

Snap, snap.

Snip.

Having accepted that I'll walk out with a minimum of four inches weed-whacked off my hair, I watch as she lops off my dark curls.

Arnie sticks his lens in my face, only to scoff at my feeble smile. "Come on, Miss Meadows. You can do better than that."

"Of course, she can." Michael reappears after a phone call that pulled him away.

Out of the corner of my eye, I see Maia straighten. She's definitely attracted to him, even though I've yet to see any reciprocity. Despite her assertion outside the coffee shop that

Michael was flirting with *her*, it's me he keeps smiling at, my shoulder he keeps touching. Of course, it's also me who requires all the work. He's probably just trying to put me at ease.

A moment later, Michael bends near. "Give it up, Kate—for me."

I really don't want to, but it's been so long since a man looked at me with a twinkle in his eye that I can't help myself. Thus, the smile I flash is genuine and is captured by Arnie.

"Great!" Michael smiles but then frowns when he zooms in on my mouth. "Have you considered bonding, Kate?"

Bonding? Is he trying out some new line on me? "Uh…"

"That gap between your front teeth." He taps his own perfectly joined teeth.

Think I would have preferred it to be a line.

"Nowadays, with bonding and laminates, dentists can do wonders with such imperfections."

Imperfections! A far cry from our meeting outside the coffee shop when he pronounced me perfect. Behind pressed lips, I slide my tongue over the gap that has never bothered me much. Why do I suddenly feel self-conscious? After all, it's a very small gap.

"Never miss an opportunity to shine." Michael pats my hand, causing Maia to stiffen.

And my self-esteem, which is still walking around in a sling fashioned by my housemate, goes up a notch.

While Trish continues to *snip* and Arnie to *snap*, Michael leans against the counter and surveys me. "Glasses have to go. Have you tried contacts?"

First my teeth, now my eyes. "No." I peer at him through the rectangular specs I insisted remain on despite Trish's protests. "Glasses suit me fine." Especially since a side effect of taking estrogen can be an intolerance to contacts.

Michael shakes his head. "No, they don't."

I grit my teeth. "Easy on, easy off. Works for me."

"They clutter your face, Kate. And you have a pretty face. A pity to hide it behind frames."

"I agree," Maia puts in. "I wear contacts myself."

Michael looks to her. "Yes, I noticed." Back to me. "Think about it."

I push the glasses farther up on my nose. "I like my specs."

A frown nudges his eyebrows. Does he regret choosing me for the makeover? "All right, but take them off for the photo shoot, hmm?"

"I can do that."

"Good." He stares at my forehead. "Trish, think you can manage some wisps?"

"For all of five minutes. Her hair's too thick and curly. Better to work with it than risk it going frizzy and have me running back and forth with a curling iron."

"Maybe a little shorter—"

"No. By the time her hair dries, she'll lose two inches to curls."

He sighs. "Your call."

Silence descends until the mirror reflects a very thin woman behind me.

"Lois!" Michael beckons her forward. "Let's see what you came up with."

Arms loaded, she sweeps forward. "All size ten except for the pantsuit." She lowers the bagged garments to the counter. "It runs small, so I pulled a twelve."

Maia gasps as though a bowl of slugs has been set before her. "Twelve?"

Why did I agree to this?

Michael holds up each of the garments, narrows the field

to three, then looks at me. Despite my annoyance, I'm relieved he's smiling again.

"What do you think?" He peels the plastic from a black knit dress and jacket.

Snap, snap, goes Arnie.

If not for the fuchsia that edges the hems, lapels, and flared cuffs of the narrow-sleeved jacket, I'd pass, but its understated elegance appeals to me. Also, as I'm certain Michael is aware, knits make a better fit for someone whose waist and hips are considerably out of proportion with her chest.

"I like it."

"Thought you might." He picks up a smart-looking ensemble. Though it appears to be this side of purple, when he lifts the clear blue plastic, I nearly recoil.

Red—the very shade Christopher loved; the shade that is long gone from my wardrobe. *Never* to return!

I shake my head. "No."

His eyebrows perk up. "You don't like the cut?"

"Uh, color. I don't care for red."

"It's a beautiful shade."

"Sorry, but it's not me."

He steps to my back and lifts the ensemble alongside my face. "Red is definitely your color."

"I agree." Maia nods. "Not only does it brighten your face, but it makes a great contrast for your hair."

In the mirror, I catch Michael's momentary look of surprise, which turns to admiration as he glances at Maia.

Trish props her hands on her hips. "Red is really you."

Three against one. Do I hear four? I look to Arnie, but he's preoccupied with the stuck zipper on his accessory case. Not that one more vote would have any bearing.

I sit taller in the chair. "It'll have to be one of the others."

For a moment Michael seems about to argue, but then he shrugs. "One of the others it is." He retrieves the pantsuit. "What about this?"

It does have a nice cut.

A strangled sound jerks my attention to Maia, who curls her upper lip and mutters, "Size twelve."

I will not let her get to me. I will unclench my fingers. And my toes. And my teeth. I will give the pantsuit a try even if it *is* a size twelve.

I return my gaze to Michael in the mirror. "I…"

Size twelve…

Michael raises an eyebrow.

Size twelve…

"I…uh…like the first outfit best."

"All right. Provided we're happy with the fit, the black dress and jacket it is."

Maia crosses her arms. "*I* still like the red."

Before I can stop myself, I snip, "Then maybe *you* should wear it."

Her eyes bulge. "I assure you, Kate, I am *not* a size ten." She gives a horror movie shudder. "Let alone a twelve."

No, you aren't, you Twiggy/Kate Moss–wannabe! And I nearly say it, but the look Michael exchanges with Trish makes me bite my tongue.

"Phone call, Mr. Palmier!"

Michael peers over his shoulder. "Be right there." He turns back to me. "I'll return in a half hour to do your face."

"Make it an hour and a half," Trish says. "Her hair needs highlighting."

"Highlighting?" Assailed by imaginings of the obscene odor she thinks she's going to subject me to, I shake my head. "Oh, no."

She nods. "To perk up the color."

True, it is kind of dull, but—

"Definitely highlights." Michael meets my gaze, and there's that twinkle in his eyes again. "Keep smiling, beautiful."

Beautiful. Imaginings of chemical odors dissolving, I'm tempted to whip off my specs and toss them at his feet. Goodness, it really *has* been a long time since a man looked at me like that.

"See you in a bit, Kate."

As Michael leaves, my attention is captured by Maia whose face tells all—as in, "What am I? Lard?"—and jostles me back to reality.

My self-esteem enjoys the massage of Michael's attention and kind words, but this isn't good. After all, I have to live with the woman. What if she raises my rent? Rent that is already exorbitant, as San Francisco is *not* a cheap place to live.

Hives threatening at the thought of beating out another decent place, I pull my arms beneath the plastic cape and rub them.

When Michael returns to "do" my face, his expression of pleasure at my transformation mirrors my own. There's a sheen to my hair I've never seen, light twisting inside and outside the curls that brush my shoulders. And the side part tosses curls across my brow to give me a...sexy look. Well, semisexy.

"Wow." He surveys me from all sides. "You don't disappoint, Kate."

"Thanks." I glance at Maia in the mirror. To my surprise, there's wonder on her face where she stands to my left.

"You look great, Kate." She shakes her head. "Really great."

That's a first. And I'm not even wearing makeup. Yet. Hmm. Maybe this makeover stuff isn't so bad after all.

Maia looks at Michael. "You're incredible."

He sweeps his gaze down her and smiles wider. "Thank you."

This time, there's no doubt as to who he's flirting with. The beauteous Maia has a bite on her hook.

Not that I'm disappointed—well, maybe a little. But it's not as if I had a chance with Michael. And even if I did, we're hardly compatible. No, Maia's more his type—beautiful, self-assured, and doesn't wear anything approaching a size ten (much less a twelve). Best of all, a few seemingly innocent comments made by Maia to Trish yielded confirmation that Michael is, indeed, single.

"Let's get to it." He reaches to me. "May I?"

I nod and he removes my specs. "Very pretty." He turns to Arnie. "Ready to catch some great shots?"

Fifteen minutes late! I am *never* late for my clients!

I eye the building that rises before me, momentarily wonder behind which window Dr. Alexander's office is located, then give the fuchsia-edged jacket a tug. As I near the lobby doors, I catch my reflection in the tinted glass.

Wow, I really do look good—in a slightly distorted way.

Grateful for the gift of the outfit, hairstyle, and makeup (which I insisted Michael tone down at the end of the photo shoot), I pick up my pace as best I can in unfamiliar heels—for which I am *not* grateful. As the click of my heels alerts the man ahead, he glances around. And once again I receive an appreciative gleam, as has happened several times since leaving the studio. I'm liking it.

He pulls open the door and nods for me to go ahead.

Really liking it. "Thank you."

Stepping over the threshold, I'm met by a large sign: *ALL*

PATIENTS AND VISITORS MUST CHECK IN AT THE FRONT DESK. I head for the desk at the center of the lobby. Unfortunately, the line is a dozen deep.

Is it possible to bypass this step? Perhaps a directory that points the way to Dr. Alexander's office? I scan the large room and spot a bank of elevators. Guessing a directory is nearby, I *click-clack-click* across the tile, only to be disappointed. Obviously administration is all too aware of human impatience. Must stick to the protocol. I shift my overstuffed bag and look around. And there's the restroom. So what's another five minutes?

In the restroom, I slide my specs on to perform a check of my hair, which has retained much of its semi–Shirley Temple curl. Hmm, nice highlights. Of course, when Trish applied the goop it had taken my all not to gag.

As for makeup, Michael's application has done a nice job of accentuating what turn out to be my best features—large eyes and a neat nose. And my outfit! I dropped ten pounds the moment it settled on my shoulders.

I smile at my reflection. *Enjoy it as long as you can, girl.*

Though Michael presented me with a gift bag containing the products he used, it's unlikely I'll be able to duplicate the look when I slump out of bed in the morning. Pity. I could get used to this—except for the *click-clack-click*, the chafing that's bound to yield blisters, and the further strain placed on an already burdened back. Unfortunately, the Birkenstocks I wore to the studio would ruin the look. And I'm liking those appreciative gleams too much to alter a thing.

For a long moment, I waver over whether to leave my specs in place, but vanity prevails. When I return to the lobby, it's to discover that the line at the desk has grown by a half dozen people. Resolved to a bad first impression—or second, if I count the introduction at Belle and Beau's—I hurry to the desk.

As the line inches forward, I scan the lobby with its multitude of chairs overflowing with those awaiting some doctor or other. And it's then that I catch sight of Brad-ish—er, Dr. Alexander. Hands in the pockets of his long white jacket, he stands near the elevators, eyes scanning the lobby.

Did I breeze past him when I came out of the restroom? I pick up my leather bag and *click-clack-click* toward him. Halfway there, his eyes meet mine, and I offer an apologetic smile.

A five o'clock shadow roughing up his jaw, he gives one of his tight, á la carte smiles and looks past me.

He doesn't recognize me. Of course, I *have* morphed from the spectacled, ponytailed, jean-clad, San Franciscan artist he first met. Imagining his reaction when I reintroduce myself, I smile.

With less than ten feet separating us, his attention returns to me. "Ms. Meadows."

Oh. Maybe I'm not all that different after all. True, he didn't appear to recognize me at a distance, but he could be nearsighted. Wish I were.

"Dr. Alexander." I halt before his blurred figure and extend a hand. "I apologize for running late. I was…" At a makeover session? Probably not. "…unavoidably detained."

After brushing sandy-colored hair off his brow, he closes his hand around mine.

It's only a handshake. I feel ab-so-lute-ly nothing—no tingle, no frisson, no attraction. I give a good, firm shake.

He smiles, and I'm startled by how much more attractive he is with his harsh-edged features blurred. I squint in an attempt to determine if his eyes sport an appreciative gleam. Hard to say, though there is something—

He breaks eye contact and releases my hand.

Good idea. Regardless of what he thinks of my transformation, the man *is* married. Not that the wedding band stopped him from enjoying a night on the town with Adelphia whatever-her-last-name-is.

He glances at his watch. "I was detained as well. Thought you might have given up on me."

"I wouldn't do that," I say, while inside I'm slinging "whew!" all over the place. Is this my day or what?

He turns. "Let's go."

I follow him to an elevator that delivers us to the fourth floor. He leads me down a corridor, at the end of which hangs a plastic sheet that denotes one is about to enter a construction area—as does the noise coming from beyond a Construction Workers Only sign.

Clive Alexander, whose resemblance to a construction worker is limited to an unshaven jaw, pulls back the plastic sheet and motions for me to precede him.

As I step past, pain shoots through the back of my right heel. Yep, there's going to be a blister.

Dr. Alexander draws alongside me, and together we pass through a wide corridor that winds back and forth like a lazy river toward the increasing sound of pounding, sawing, and drilling.

Running my gaze over bare walls that curve and wave, some with portholes, others with elaborate glass block windows, I feel excitement uncoil within the depths of my creativity.

"Wow, this is…"

"Yes, it is," Dr. Alexander says, as if he understands what I can't quite voice. Does he? I steal a sideways glance, but his expression is unreadable.

After a bit more winding, the corridor fans out into a large domed room, where a half dozen construction workers are engaged in creating an environment for pediatric burn victims.

As I cross the unfinished cement floor, I slow to take it all in. And just like that, I know what I'd do with these barren walls—a representation of the earth that stretches from the uppermost center of the domed ceiling down the walls to the floor. An "outside-in" perspective, with all nations represented by their colorful children—holding hands, dancing, playing, laughing, praying. Some in relief to make the mural come alive, especially lower, where little ones could touch their counterparts and trace their smiles.

"You'll do it?"

Realizing I've halted at the center of the room, I look around to find Dr. Alexander's blurred figure beside me. "What?"

"Accept the job."

"You're offering?"

"That *is* the reason you're here, Ms. Meadows."

I shake my head. "Of course, but isn't this an interview?"

"No, it's an offer. I've seen your work, I like it, and you're perfect."

There's that word again—*perfect*. So what if it's in reference to my work? "Really?"

He raises an eyebrow. "Really."

"You don't want to see my portfolio?" I pat the bag beneath my arm.

"Not necessary."

"Well then, all right." I shift my weight and nearly whimper as pain shoots through my heel. "Provided we come to terms, I'd be a fool not to accept a project this size."

"Good. We can discuss the specifics in my office." He strides away from me.

As I follow I notice one of the construction workers looking my way. And another. The latter smiles, and I catch that gleam in his eyes. Well, at least *he* appreciates my torturous makeover.

Not that I care what Brad-ish—*Dr. Alexander, Kate!*— thinks. Far from it. He'll be the one judged for adultery, not me.

I hasten after him and, halfway down the winding corridor, catch up with him only to grab his sleeve to keep from falling off my heels.

He steadies me. "All right, Ms. Meadows?"

Averting my eyes, I ease out of his grasp. "Seems I'm developing a blister. I'm not used to heels."

"Then take them off."

I jerk my chin up. "Off?"

"Wear a hole in your hose or your heel." His mouth tilts as if to smile. "Your choice."

And a pretty obvious one. Fortunately, my Birkenstocks are in my bag. Unfortunately, they'll look cloddish with my outfit. Fortunately, it appears the job is mine.

"You're right." I step out of the shoes. Within moments my feet are cradled by Birkies and my back is shouting a resounding "Thank you!"

As I grab the handles of my leather bag, I find Dr. Alexander watching me, a question on his fuzzy-edged brow.

Hoping to tease a smile from him, though why I want him to show teeth I have no idea, I grin. "I come prepared."

"So it appears." No teeth.

A few minutes later, he leads me past a receptionist, down a hallway, and into his office. Gesturing toward the chairs before his desk, he steps around the unpretentious piece of furniture and settles in his own chair.

As I lower, I lift a hand to push my specs up and, in their absence, almost poke myself in the eye. Goodness! Have I developed a habit, or what?

Inwardly shaking my head, I take in the room. Bookshelves.

File cabinets. Tasteful prints. Modestly framed degrees.
Computer. Desk. Credenza. But not a single family photo to
complement the wedding band.

"So do I pass?"

I look back at Dr. Alexander. "Hmm?"

"Inspection."

"Oh. I was just…wondering what kind of doctor you are."

With finality that discourages further probing, he says,
"Plastic surgeon specializing in reconstruction."

That makes sense, as it is the burn unit he's overseeing.

He raises his eyebrows. "How long?"

Honestly, these "men of few words" could use some help
from a big fat dictionary. "I'm sorry. How long what?"

"The domed room and hallways. How long will they take
to complete?"

I lean forward. "Dr. Alexander, shouldn't we bat around
some ideas? You know, get a feel for what's involved? What the
hospital envisions?"

"I presume an artist of your skill has already formed an idea
of what will work best."

"I have, but surely someone will want to approve my idea
before I implement it."

"That would be me."

I sit back. "Then there isn't a committee or…something?"

He clasps his hands on the desk. "Ms. Meadows, the committee appointed me to oversee the construction and design of
our new unit, and as I'm financing a portion of it, approval rests
with me."

Okay. Now we're getting somewhere. I think.

"Thus, I choose you to turn the ordinary into the extraordinary, provided you're up to tackling something on a larger scale
than the children's shop."

"I think I'm up to it."

He frowns. "Think? I need something more definite than that."

Patience, Kate. This could be the job that launches you. And brings about that excess amount of cash for your breast reduction.

"I'm definitely up to it."

"And you can begin in six weeks?"

I sit straighter. "Six weeks?" The deal breaker. I will not turn my back on my other commitments. With a sinking heart, I say, "I'm afraid that's impossible. You see, I'm booked solid for the next four months."

"Too long. The facility is scheduled to open in just under four months."

"And you're only now lining up an artist?"

His mouth tightens. "An artist was contracted a year ago. Unfortunately, because of a family crisis, he had to pull out last week."

"I'm sorry to hear that, and I wish I could help, but there's no way I can fit in a job this size."

He leans back and begins tapping a pen on his chair arm. "A pity you didn't mention your previous commitments when we first met."

The hair on the back of my neck stands. *Guard your tongue! Guard your—*

"Excuse me? If you recall, though you did ask about my schedule, your girlfriend interrupted before I could answer."

His pen ceases its tapping. "Girlfriend?"

"Silly me. *Colleague.*" I look pointedly at his wedding band.

He stares at me. "Yes, colleague."

No skin off my nose. Well, actually it is, but who am I to set him straight?

A Christian, my conscience kicks in. *Set an example. Maybe even witness to him.*

Me? Sharing the roof over my head is Maia of Mr. Unhappily Married fame, and I haven't been able to reach *her*. How am I supposed to reach a man I don't even know? "Nuh-uh," I mutter.

"Yes, Ms. Meadows, a colleague."

Though Dr. Alexander has misinterpreted my dissension, I squelch the impulse to correct him. "It's really none of my business." I retrieve my bag and rise. "I want this job, and I believe I could do something extraordinary, but I have to walk away."

Surprise leaps in his gray-blue eyes.

"Not only is the timing wrong, but it's obvious we rub each other wrong." I thrust a hand at him. "So thank you for the opportunity, and I wish you every success in finding the right artist."

He ignores my hand. "I *have* found the right artist."

Okay. I lower my arm, turn, and walk away. Thankfully, he doesn't follow. I step into an elevator alongside a man and woman with a young girl between them in a wheelchair.

One look is all it takes to ache, and as the doors close, I offer up a silent prayer for this child touched by fire in the cruelest way—much of the right side of her face pink and puckered.

"Going down?" she chirps, reaching to the lobby button though it's already lit.

Guessing she's about eight, I say, "Yes, please."

She jabs the button despite the elevator having already begun its descent. "My name's Jessica."

Friendly little thing. Doesn't seem the least bit self-conscious, which casts concerns about my own appearance in an entirely shallow light.

I smile. "Nice to meet you."

"What's your name?"

Before I can answer, the woman says, "Jess, honey, leave the nice lady alone."

"Oh, she's not bothering me." Still, I'm grateful for the intercession. Not that I don't like children. I do. But when I get close to a child, my longing for one of my own increases, which makes it hurt all the more to know that I'm being denied what I've dreamed of since my world consisted of chubby-cheeked baby dolls.

The irony is that despite my initial attempts to promote my talent in areas other than those that cater to children, it's what most people want from me. And so, in the interest of making a living, it's what I do.

I feel a tug on my jacket and look down.

"What's your name?" Jessica whispers.

"Uh…Kate." I glance at Mom, who offers an apologetic smile.

The little girl tugs again. "You're pretty."

I am unaffected. Forget that she's sweet and cute and flattering. I feel nothing. "Thank you."

As the elevator slows, I lift my gaze. Third floor, meaning two more to go.

"I'm having surgery tomorrow," Jessica says as two men and three women enter.

To make room for them, I step nearer Jessica. "Is that right?"

"Uh-huh. I'll be pretty again. Like you."

She's buttering me up, trying to worm her way into my heart. And as much as I long to remain distant, I'm slipping toward her. Great…

The elevator once more sets to motion, and I glance at her parents. Dad is stiff jawed, but Mom's eyes are moist.

I struggle for something to say until I notice the cross the woman wears. Though the necklace in no way guarantees she's a Christian, I hunker down so I'm level with the little girl.

"You are pretty, Jessica, and tomorrow when you have your surgery, Jesus will be standing beside the prettiest little girl in the world."

She beams. "I know that!" She says it with such enthusiasm that it nearly drowns out the snort of derision above our heads.

Hackles rising, I meet the scornful gaze of a man who entered at the third floor. Fortunately, the elevator stops again, and shaking his head, he and one of the women step from the elevator.

"No, John!" Jessica's mother's hand is on her husband's arm. Guessing it's all that's keeping the red-faced man from tackling the heathen—er, naysayer—I attempt to distract his daughter by sweeping the blond hair off her face.

"I'm glad you know Jesus, too," Jessica says. "It's sad, but some people don't."

Grateful the elevator is on its final leg of the journey, I nod. "It is."

She brightens further. "We can change that, you know— one person at a time."

Past emotion I'd do best not to feel for her, I murmur, "One at a time."

Leaning near, she drops an arm around my shoulder. "I like you, Miss Kate."

Though I know I should extricate as quickly as possible, my defenses have sustained a major blow. I'm crumbling. Of course, it's not as if I'll see her again. "I like you, too, Jessica."

As the doors at my back open and the others step out, I give her a squeeze. "I'll be praying for you."

She loosens her arms and leans back. "Promise you'll visit?"

What? But I just met her! In an elevator. For all of three minutes.

In the midst of my struggle to find a way out, Jessica's mother speaks, and I'm relieved—until her words sink in.

"Dr. Alexander, how nice to run into you."

4

freeze. Dr. Alexander? No. Must be more than one Dr. Alexander. I glance over my shoulder.

It's him.

Meeting his gaze, I cast about for an explanation as to how he made it to the lobby ahead of me. Of course, the elevator *did* stop twice on the way down.

He looks up. "Mr. and Mrs. Robbins," he acknowledges, then turns his attention to the little girl and, in a voice so warm one could almost get a tan from it, says, "Ready for tomorrow, Jessica?"

"You bet."

Dr. Alexander is operating?

Jessica settles a hand on my arm. "This is Miss Kate."

What's he doing here? Did he follow me? Or is this just coincidence, as in he's on his way somewhere? But then why did he appear before *my* elevator?

"Miss Kate and I know each other."

No, we don't!

"You do?"

"We do." He shifts back to Jessica. "So you know Miss Kate, too, hmm?"

The little girl bobs her head. "I do now."

No she doesn't. All she knows is that we share a belief in Jesus—

Of course, that is pretty major.

Stop! Get out while you can!

I look past Dr. Alexander to an elderly gentleman who's waiting for us to clear out. "We're holding up the elevator."

Dr. Alexander lays a hand on the door pocket and motions for us to exit.

Though I'm tempted to shoot past him, courtesy forces me to pause outside the elevator as the little girl's father rolls her out. "It was lovely meeting you, Jessica."

She tilts her head back. "You'll visit me after my surgery tomorrow?"

Courtesy will get you nowhere, Katherine Mae Meadows!

"Well, I…"

"Please?"

Groaning inwardly, I nod. "Of course."

"Great!" She bounces in her chair.

I look to Mom and Dad. "Guess I'll see you tomorrow."

Dad rolls his eyes. "Suuure."

His wife snaps her head around. "John!"

"Yeah, yeah. Let's go for that walk."

Tempted as I am to take offense, I can't. After all, he read me right. Visiting a child I hardly know—one capable of plucking heartstrings best left unplucked—is not something for which I would normally volunteer. It's…complicated.

Jessica waves as her father wheels her away. "Bye, Miss Kate."

I wave back, and a moment later I'm alone with Dr.

Alexander, whose presence over my shoulder I feel sharply.

"So are all children as easily drawn to you?"

I turn and give an uneasy chuckle. "Drawn to me?"

Why the nervous laugh? Nothing to be ashamed of.

No, it's not, but it's still a subject I'm hardly comfortable with. I attempt a blasé shrug. "I get along well enough with children."

"Well enough?" His mouth comes dangerously close to a smile. "I'd say you make friends easily, like it or not."

Broadsided by the realization that Jessica's father wasn't the only one who noticed my hesitation over visiting Jessica, I latch on to the best explanation for what Dr. Alexander witnessed. "Where Jesus is present, it's not difficult to make friends."

Like a shot of air on a struggling flame, his amusement expires. "Jesus…"

So, another heath—er, naysayer. "Uh-huh." I slide my bag off one shoulder and onto the other. "Well, I must be going."

As I turn away, his hand closes over my arm. "Ms. Meadows, it's not coincidence that I showed up at your elevator."

I raise an eyebrow. "What did we leave unsaid that transformed you into some sort of Superman capable of speeding down elevator shafts?"

His mouth twitches. "Plenty. As for getting to the lobby ahead of you, I used the elevator reserved for doctors."

"Then you're human like the rest of us."

Another twitch. "Fallibly so." He nods toward the elevator. "Will you come with me? There's something I'd like to show you."

I glance at his hand on me. The contact means nothing. Nada. "I'm sorry, but I start a new project tomorrow and I have to begin preparations."

"It won't take long. And it will clear up a misunderstanding that's obviously rubbing you wrong."

I give my arm a tug, but he retains his hold with as much persistence as Michael Palmier the day he talked me into the makeover.

Lord, deliver me from manhandling men.

"Dr. Alexander—"

"Please."

I falter at having reduced him to groveling. Bet it's a rarity. "All right, but five minutes is all I can spare."

"It shouldn't take any longer." He releases my arm, and I follow him into an elevator.

Shortly, I once more traverse the winding corridor. This time, however, it's quiet, and when we exit the corridor, the lack of din is explained by the absence of construction workers. Doubtless, they've kicked off for the day.

I try to squelch my vision of an outside-in world as I'm led to the center of the domed room, but my longing to be the one to make it happen sharpens.

I really shouldn't have let him talk me into this. After all, what do I care if he rubs me the wrong way? It's not as if I'm going to have further dealings with him.

"This is what I want to show you." He draws back a tarp to reveal a three-by-three-foot bronze plaque set in the concrete floor:

IN LOVING MEMORY OF

Though the raised words are large enough to read, the edges are fuzzy. Thus, I retrieve my specs—no easy feat, as I was in too much of a hurry to keep my appointment to properly store them. Now they're at the bottom of my bag. And bent,

I discover, when I dig them free. Certain they were victimized by those nasty heels, I attempt a quick repair of the frame and briefly consider switching to contacts as Michael suggested.

There. I slide the crooked specs on my nose and peer at the plaque.

IN LOVING MEMORY OF
JILLIAN LOUISE ALEXANDER
AND SAMUEL CLIVE ALEXANDER
BELOVED WIFE AND SON
ABSENT IN ARMS
PRESENT IN SPIRIT

Alexander...wife...son...absent...spirit...

"Oh." I look to where Dr. Alexander stands, also looking down.

"Though I wear my wedding band, Ms. Meadows, I'm a husband and father without a wife and child." He meets my gaze. "Does that fix the rub?"

You just had to jump to conclusions!

Of course, it's not every day one meets a widower who hasn't shed his wedding ring to begin the quest for the next Mrs.

I read the dates beneath the inscription. Mother and child, aged thirty-six and five, died within days of each other over three years ago.

Mind awhirl with wonder at what took their lives—most likely, fire—and why Dr. Alexander's pain remains so great that he can't bear to display pictures of them, I look up. "I'm sorry— and that I misjudged you."

"I assure you I'm aware of the significance of a wedding band, Ms. Meadows. Thus, I accept responsibility for the mis- understanding." He flips the tarp over the plaque. "Now that we've cleared that up, I'd like to discuss what it's going to take for you to commit to the burn unit."

I frown. "As I said, I'm booked for the next four months."

"You did, and I admire your ethics; however, I believe we can work out something." He glances at his watch. "I need another hour here. Then perhaps you can join me for dinner?"

Dinner? With Clive Alexander who is unattached? Available. Single. Well…except for the wedding band. And that Adelphia woman.

"What kind of food do you like?"

My smile is apologetic. "I already have a dinner date."

Which is so surreal. But then, it's not really a date. Michael Palmier can't possibly be interested in me. By the end of the photo shoot, one would have had to be blind not to realize that, despite his initial lack of response to Maia, he'd warmed to her. Thus, I've narrowed his motivation for asking me to dinner to two things: Either this is a Maia fact-finding date, or the invite—made in front of her—was intended to incite jealousy. Regardless, it makes my matchmaking that much easier.

"How about tomorrow morning over coffee?"

"Sorry, but I start work bright and early."

Annoyance flickers in his eyes, but in the two strides it takes to close the gap between us, he gains control of it. "Ms. Meadows, this project is important to me."

"I don't question that, however—"

"You're the one."

The One? For one cockamamie, out-of-my-mind moment, I apply my definition of "The One" to his words and start to blush.

"I knew it the moment I walked into the children's shop."

Oh yeah, it's my artistic ability he's interested in. "I'm flattered, but—"

"At least think about it."

Wishing there were some way I could take on his project, I stare at him as the attraction felt the night we met returns en force. "Okay." I hold up a finger. "Better yet, I'll pray about it."

As when I earlier mentioned Jesus, his lids narrow and I feel him take a giant, emotional step back. "Whatever it takes, Ms. Meadows. Just get back to me by the beginning of next week."

Reality check, Kate. Not only is your attraction not reciprocated, but he's too far from God for you to get involved.

But what if he does know Jesus? What if this is just a case of deep loss causing a believer to turn away? What if—

Stop it!

I give a tight nod. "I'll do that."

I'm halfway across the room when he calls, "Ms. Meadows?"

I peer over my shoulder. "Yes?"

"Don't forget your promise to visit Jessica tomorrow."

"Of course not."

He fits his hands in his pockets. "She should be able to receive visitors by late afternoon."

"Anything else?"

"Actually, there is. I apologize for not recognizing you when I first saw you in the lobby. You look…different." He sweeps his gaze down me, and on the return to my face there's that gleam to which I've become partial. "Very nice."

Down, attraction! Down!

"Thanks, I didn't think you noticed."

His eyebrows rise. "Was I supposed to?"

Ugh. "Of course not. It's just nice that you did. I'm…uh… undertaking a bit of self-improvement."

His mouth curves. "Well, I approve."

"Oh? And am I supposed to want your approval?"

Not that I don't…

His smile surpasses the one he gave me when we first met. Then he laughs—not as deep and full as the laugh he shared with Beau, but warm enough to jump-start the humming at my center. Were I still in heels, I'd fall right off those silly little pegs.

He settles back into his smile. "Enjoy your date, Ms. Meadows."

My…? Oh. Right. My date. Which is really for Maia. Which I'm tempted to cancel. Which would free me to have dinner with Dr. Alexander. Which—

Would lead to nothing. His interest in you is purely business.

But he said I looked nice.

Flattery, aimed at getting what he wants. And didn't you just swear off men?

Too bad.

I force a smile. "I'll call you next week."

"Fine."

I turn and, conscious of him watching me, concentrate on putting one Birkenstock-clad foot in front of the other. When I finally hit the first curve of the winding corridor and go from sight, I breathe a sigh of relief that momentarily fogs my specs. Specs that are still sitting askew on my nose, as they were when Clive Alexander said I looked nice. Right…

Glad I didn't bend to his flattery and cancel my matchmaking dinner date. I pull off my specs and attempt to straighten the bent frames only to yelp when the metal snaps.

Wonderful. Another trip to the optometrist. Of course, I was wanting to give contacts a try. Or was that Michael Palmier? Oh, yeah—Michael.

• • •

"Can you make that out?" I point to the menu under the large, bold type: *SEAFOOD SELECTIONS*.

Michael scoots his chair nearer. "Lemon herb-crusted bay scallops."

"Sounds good. I'll take it."

"You sure? I can read the rest for you."

Though he knows the situation with my specs—and made no pretense of hiding his pleasure!—I can't stand my visual helplessness. "I like lemon. I like herbs. I like scallops. Works for me."

As he returns his attention to his own menu, I take in the restaurant, which occupies a prominent, high-rent corner of Ghirardelli Square. "Nice place."

Very nice with a tiered dining room, surfeit of mahogany and brass, and a panoramic view of San Francisco Bay. I don't even want to guess what this night is going to cost Michael.

He scoots nearer yet. "*The* place to eat and be seen. And as great as you look, Kate, you ought to be seen."

There's that appreciative gleam again. Wonder if I'll ever get tired of it? Not that men haven't "gleamed" at me before. They have, especially when I was fresh out of my teen years and more concerned with makeup, clothes, and body. Before Christopher asked for his ring—

Stuffing the memory back in its hole, I reach to the blue glass and sterling silver bracelet and rub the *Believe* medallion.

I believe. I do.

"Blah, blah, blah," says Michael.

Well, not "Blah, blah, blah," but that's what my wandering mind hears as I stare out the window toward Alcatraz Island, the infamous federal prison that once housed criminals but now caters to tourists.

Releasing the view back into the wild, I look into Michael's eyes. "Hmm?"

"On a slow boat to China?"

I laugh. "Sorry."

"No problem. I was just saying I'm glad you wore the outfit tonight."

Less my foot-friendly Birkies. Grateful for the tablecloth that conceals the heels I slipped off once we were seated, I inwardly grimace at the Band-Aids required to make the shoes tolerable. What was I thinking? Though the Birkies would have been inappropriate for a night out, I could have worn flats. Vanity is definitely the mother of foolishness.

I finger the jacket's fuchsia edging. "I've received several compliments."

"Is that all?"

I make a face. "I don't get around as much as you, Mr. Palmier."

"Michael," he once more corrects. Why am I having difficulty addressing him informally—especially as he's become *Michael* in my thoughts?

"Sorry—Michael."

He props his chin on an upturned hand. And not for the first time, I wonder how a man who shaves his head can be so good-looking. Maia has to be stewing—or drowning her confusion in her married boyfriend.

Hoping it's not the latter, I remind myself of my matchmaking mission for the good of mankind. Or should I say "married kind"?

"Now, Maia—" I squash the impulse to push up my absent specs—"gets around more than I."

A knowing gleam replaces the appreciative one. "I'll bet she does."

Set myself up for that one, didn't I? "What I mean is that she's worldly."

He slips from attentive to bored. "Like every other woman I meet."

This isn't going the way I expected. Deep breath. "She's really an interesting woman."

"I'll take your word for that."

Oookay. "Did I mention we're housemates?"

He perks up. "That explains a lot."

"What?"

"Why you're so mismatched. You're not actually friends, are you?"

Does this mean he might pull the makeover pictures? Hmm. Might be a good thing. Still, I can't abandon Maia, nor my plans to convert her to single men.

"Though we're not best friends, we are friends. In a way. I mean, we've been housemates for going on three years. After all that time, you get to know one another. And, uh, form a bond. A friendship. Yeah."

His snort causes nearby diners to glance our way. "Admit it, Kate. Maia stays on her side of the house, and you stay on yours."

Uh-oh. "Well, most of the time, but we work different hours and—"

"Kate."

"Did you know she's a stockbroker?"

"So she said—several times." He closes a hand over mine in my lap. "Listen, I don't want to talk about Maia. I want to talk about you."

"Why?" I almost bark, surprising us both.

He recovers before me. "I like you. So if you have some plan to hook me up with your *supposed* friend, I'm telling you it's not going to happen."

Not going at *all* the way I expected. "You like *me*? But Maia's beautiful and—"

"I see plenty of beautiful women in my line of work. That's not what I'm looking for."

I really hope that wasn't a slam.

"I don't understand." Ah. Maybe I *do*. "Has some biological clock started ticking that I should know about?"

He shrugs. "I'm thirty-eight, been everywhere I care to go, seen everything I care to see, and experienced everything I care to experience. What's left but to settle down?"

Yup. *Ticktock, ticktock*, but not with this clock who has sworn off men—even if it is for the second time this year.

"If you're trying to sweep me off my feet, Michael, it's not working."

He chuckles. "I'm being honest." He squeezes my hand. "From the moment I saw you outside the coffee shop, I was enchanted."

"Enchanted?" It's my turn to snort, and I use the moment of levity to pull my hand free. Thankfully, he doesn't leave his in my lap. "If you recall, I was not only wearing specs, a sweatshirt, and exercise pants, but I was rewriting the definition of glowing."

"And you weren't the least bit concerned."

As I stare at him, a thought occurs, as in *Where's the camera?* I eye the ceiling, the walls, the floor. "Is this one of those crazy twists on a *Candid Camera* reality show?"

Michael throws back his head and laughs. *Not* a Clive Alexander laugh—loud rather than full, shallow rather than deep. However, it does prove useful, as it causes our waitress to finally notice us.

Wearing a chic black apron, she hastens across the dining room and shakes her head, which causes her blond ponytail to swish. "Ready to order?"

Michael's laughter ends on a sigh. "For some time now."

With a look of annoyance, she pulls out her pad and raises an eyebrow. "Ma'am?"

"I'll take a dinner salad with blue—"

"That would be our house salad." She proceeds to scratch on her pad.

Right. "With blue cheese dressing—"

"Roquefort." She scratches some more. "And for your en-trée?"

"The lemon scallops."

"Herb-crusted?"

How did my order turn into the third degree? "What other kinds of lemon scallops do you have?"

She sighs. "Just the herb-crusted ones, ma'am."

"Then—" I suppress a smile—"that's what I'll have."

Scratch, scratch. "Good choice." She gives her ponytail an-other swish. "And for your side?"

"Rice."

"Wild rice?"

Here we go again. "Is there any other kind?"

"No, ma'am." She taps her pencil on her pad.

I press my shoulders back. "Then wild rice it is."

Scratch, scratch. "And you, sir?"

Light dancing in his eyes, Michael places his order with pretty much the same result.

When the waitress *swish-swishes* away, I slide my gaze to him. "*The* place to eat?"

Smiling, he crosses his arms on the table. "So why is it hard to believe I'm interested in you, Kate?"

"I'm hardly your type."

"How do you know that?"

"To begin with, I'm thirty-three years old." *Hate* to admit
that.

"Believe me, Kate, thirty-three isn't old. You still have plenty
of childbearing years ahead of you."

Pang. Not my type at all. *So* glad I've sworn off men.

I lift my water goblet and take a long sip. "So, your biological clock is telling you it's time to go forth and multiply,
hmm?"

"Go forth and multiply—I like that." His lids narrow.
"You're religious, aren't you?"

I'm always surprised at how personal a question that is, especially coming from someone of the opposite sex. It's almost
like being asked my bra size. Though I know it's wrong to feel
that way and that I should proudly proclaim my beliefs, I don't
deal well with rejection.

I stiffen my upper lip. "I'm a Christian. And you?"

"Buddhist."

I startle.

He laughs. "Just kidding."

Whew! I think. "Then?"

"Christian."

"Really?"

"Sort of. I was saved at sixteen, but that's pretty much the
extent of my religious experience. So I suppose I'm a Christian,
provided there's no expiration date."

At the realization that I'm not treading on completely foreign ground, I brighten. "Of course there's no expiration date.
Once saved—"

"—always saved."

Hey! Maybe I *could* date this guy. Maybe we're not so different. Maybe there *is* a future for us. Maybe I was too hasty in swearing off men.

"What about you, Kate? Is *your* biological clock telling you to 'go forth and multiply'?"

Maybe not.

I moisten my lips. "Not really."

"Neither is mine."

I frown.

"I just want to find a good woman and spend the rest of my life with her."

"And somewhere in there have children."

"Actually, I could take 'em or leave 'em."

Did I hear right? Did this single, attractive, successful something-of-a-Christian really say that? Might God have finally dropped "The One" in my lap?

It's possible…

"Not only am I the eldest of six siblings—" he gives me a meaningful look—"but between them, they've given me tons of nieces and nephews."

Possible…

"I assure you, if I never have a child of my own, I'm more than covered."

Very possible…

"In fact, I dedicated my bestselling book to the lot of them, including two who weren't yet born."

Realizing he's waiting for a reaction to his author status, I say, "*The Makeup Bible*? Maia mentioned it."

His face brightens. "Did she?"

"Yeah."

"Great title, huh?"

"Well, I did wonder about the *Bible* part of it."

Disbelief crosses his face only to be replaced by an air of

patience. "Think about it, Kate. Isn't the *Bible* considered life's greatest instruction book?"

Though he's misunderstood my concern over the use of *Bible*, I'm pleased by his regard for God's Word. "Absolutely."

"Well, just as the original *Bible* covers every aspect of how to live, *The Makeup Bible* covers every aspect of how to display and preserve a woman's beauty. Clever, no?"

He thinks I'm thick.

"Yeah." I have every intention of dropping the subject, but the thought that follows finds its way to my lips. "Of course, my grandmother might take issue with it."

Michael tilts his head to the side. "She'd be offended?"

I nod. "She was very spiritual."

"Was?"

"She passed away years ago."

"Sorry. Were you close?"

"With the exception of my teen years—yes. She and my grandfather raised me."

"Oh?"

"Um-hmm. My parents died when their two-seater plane went down in the Sierra Nevada mountains."

"That must have been hard on you."

I shrug off the twinge of loss. "I was only three."

A semiuncomfortable silence descends until Michael says, "So your grandparents raised you to be a Christian."

"Grandmother tried, but with the support of my agnostic grandfather, I managed to stay a step ahead of her—or should I say *behind* her?"

Michael smiles. "Is your grandfather still agnostic?"

I feel a twist at my center. "He passed away two years after my grandmother—still the doubting Thomas."

"Sorry to hear that." Before the silence creeps in again,

Michael says, "I'm assuming you have no siblings."

"None."

"So you're pretty much alone in the world."

I've concluded the same thing numerous times, especially at night when it's just me, my pillow, and a bad case of self-pity, but it's not true. Though I'm hardly drowning in friends, there are people who care about me—foremost among them Belle and Beau.

I draw a deep breath. "I'm a Christian, Michael. How can I be alone?"

He breaks into a smile. "I like you, Kate."

"And I like you." Though not as much as Clive Alexander— *Who is strictly business!*

Michael gives an abrupt nod. "Then let's take a chance and see if we make a good fit."

Whoa! This is so…whirlwind. And yet the temptation is there despite the little voice that mutters something about matchmaking and swearing off men. Thus, I find myself mentally constructing a list.

Pros	Cons
He's a Christian!	*Not a practicing Christian.*
Christian groundwork laid.	*May not be truly saved.*
Children not essential to existence.	*May change his mind.*
Great looking.	*Is he balding? Or just fashionable?*
Successful.	*Exposure to lots of beautiful women.*

"Kate?"

My columns dissolve. "Don't you think this is moving a bit fast? I mean, we just met a few days ago."

"Four days."

He's keeping count, is he? "My point exactly."

"Come on. It's not like I'm proposing or asking for exclusive rights. As I'll continue to date other women, I have no objections to you dating other men."

That's assuming there *are* other men. And, lo and behold, Clive Alexander rises to mind again.

Michael squeezes my hand. "I want to get to know you, to see if you might be the one."

That's twice in one day. First, Clive said I was "The One"—well, the one to paint the burn unit—and now Michael. Difference is, it appears Michael and I agree on the same definition, whereas Clive—

Why does that man keep intruding on my date? With a spurt of defiance, I meet Michael's gaze. "All right. Let's get to know each other."

He beams and leans forward.

I catch my breath at the feel of his mouth on mine and nearly pull back; however, the kiss is nice—no pawing, no drooling, no scene setting. Just a kiss.

As he draws back, I lift my lids. "Mmm."

He traces a finger beneath my bottom lip and contemplates my mouth as if there's nothing he'd rather do than take an extended tour of it. As if—

"Have you given any more thought to having your teeth bonded?"

He has no idea how fortunate he is that I'm no longer susceptible to PMS. I lower my smile over my imperfect teeth. "Not really."

He removes a business card from his shirt pocket. "Dr. Neimer, the best in the business. Mention my name and he'll give you a discount."

Staring at the little white card, I bite my lip with the gapped offenders. This was premeditated. He made a point of toting it along to give to me—a woman he claims enchanted him. True, with his help I cleaned up nicely, but if he thinks he's going to completely make me over, he can find himself another girlfriend—

Oh dear, what have I done? At what point did I hop the fence between matchmaker and girlfriend? This wasn't for me. It was for Maia. And here I am contemplating a future with this man. Not to mention tooth bonding! And contacts!

Goodness, it really has been a long time since a man paid me any attention.

"Hey." Michael reaches up and smoothes my brow. "If you keep frowning like that, you'll cause those frown lines to deepen."

Lord, what have I gotten myself into?

Wednesday, March 21
Dear Lord,
    Thank You for caterpillars changing to butterflies, great haircuts, flattering outfits, appreciative gleams, and men who open doors for women. Thank You for little-girl smiles, little-girl courage, and little-girl faith. Thank You for children's hospitals and skilled surgeons' hands. Thank You for misunderstandings set right, widowers who continue to wear their wedding rings, and memorials to lost loves. Thank You for men who don't require children to complete them and who kiss without groping. BTW, did You drop Michael in my lap? If so, does that mean he's "The One"?
    Help me to be discerning in future areas of self-improvement and not to allow the new me to go to my head. As always, help me guard my tongue and not be

quick to judge others. Please be with Jessica during her
surgery tomorrow—and Dr. Alexander! And please
continue to watch over Belle, Beau, and baby.

    Yours,

    Kate

PS: Told You I'd catch up on my Bible time.

5

eow! Refusing to rub my eyes, I blink…squeeze and blink…and squeeze a dozen more times until I realize I've become an object of interest. As I focus through tears on the figure emerging from the hospital room, I nearly groan.

"Ms. Meadows." Dr. Alexander steps toward me. "Are you all right?"

"Yes!" I push off the wall I've been leaning against for ten minutes only to duck my head and rub my eyes.

"What is it?" His shoes appear amid my swimming vision. "Something in your eye?"

"Uh-huh." *Two* somethings. *Rub, rub.*

"Let me see." He lifts my chin.

For a moment, I'm too frisson-wracked to do anything but peer at him through narrowed lids.

"Ah, contacts—and colored ones at that."

Yes, I took Michael's advice, though not intentionally. Curiosity made me ask my optometrist whether I was a candidate. He'd pointed out that women on HRT can be intolerant of contacts, but the only way to know for certain is to give them a try. Next thing I knew, I was pointing to the colors I liked—green and blue—remarking on how easily he fit them to my eyes and exclaiming over how comfortable they felt. What went wrong?

"New, I suppose?"

I jerk my chin in his grip. "Uh-huh."

He sighs then releases me.

Whew! I declare, the man has electricity in his veins and not of the static variety that only makes one jerk. Oh no—the killing kind.

"Part of your self-improvement plan?"

Heat flushes my skin. "Uh-huh." Yikes! What's happened to my speech?

"Do you have cleaning solution with you?"

"Uh-huh."

Words, Kate! Put forth a little effort!

Despite the irritation, I open my eyes wide. "I came straight from the optometrist."

"Then I suggest you duck into the restroom and take care of your problem before you visit Jessica."

"Good idea." I start to turn away only to realize I have no idea where I'm going. "Where's the nearest restroom?"

I glimpse a tolerant smile before I blink and squeeze again. Then to my surprise, he takes my elbow and leads me down the hall. "Here." He releases me.

"Thanks." I grope for the handle, step inside, and close the door.

Five minutes later, I glare at the contacts where they float in solution. Having decided a mere cleansing is too good for them—even if I have to make do with fuzzy edges—I twist the caps closed and drop the case in my bag.

Though I know I won't like what I see, I look in the mirror and recoil at my blurred image. My eyes are *so* red. As for makeup—which took too long to apply after a long day on the new project—much of the mascara has gone south.

I grab a paper towel, moisten it, and gently wipe at the rings beneath my eyes. Unfortunately, gentle doesn't cut it. Thus, I rub at the delicate skin, grateful Michael isn't here to scold me.

Once I'm satisfied that I no longer resemble a raccoon, I fluff my hair, which is in pretty good shape despite my reservations about my ability to duplicate the "look" Michael's assistant gave me. Did Dr. Alexander notice?

Not that I care. I don't!

I step back from the mirror, but as I turn, I catch sight of my tie-dyed shirt and relaxed-fit jeans. Not exactly how I would have chosen for Dr. Alexander to see me again. I *really* need to update my ward—

Aargh! I don't care what he thinks.

I wrench open the door and step into the hall, which, thankfully, is empty.

Shortly, the nurse who asked me to wait outside ushers me into Jessica's room, and I'm once more grateful for Dr. Alexander's absence.

I look to the little girl and am surprised not only to find her sitting up in bed, but that her eyes are bright and lips bowed. Other than the bandages covering the right side of her face, she hardly looks different from yesterday.

"Miss Kate, you came!"

I glance at her parents, who are in chairs pulled close to their daughter's bed. Mom smiles, and once the surprise passes from Dad's face, so does he.

"Of course I came." I cross to the bed and lower my bag to the floor.

Jessica captures my fingers in her small hand. "Thank you."

My heart tugs, but rather than fight the emotion, I turn my hand up and give her fingers a squeeze. "How are you feeling?"

"Good. Dr. Alexander says the operation went well. I might even go home Sunday. Did you pray for me, Miss Kate?"

"You bet I did."

She looks to her parents. "Told you she would."

Her mother meets my gaze. "Thank you for coming."

"Oh, Miss Kate! Dr. Alexander told us you're an artist."

"Did he?"

"Yes. He said you're going to paint the new burn unit."

Grateful for the muscles that prevent my eyes from popping from their sockets, I croak, "Dr. Alexander told you that?"

"Uh-huh. He thinks you're great."

Great? I momentarily forget my outrage. "He does?"

"Oh yes! His eyes change when he talks about you."

"Really?"

"Uh-huh. He told us all about your Amazon wall."

Oh. My art. It's my art he thinks is great. My art that makes his eyes change. Not me. Which is exactly as it should be. I am *not* interested in Dr. Alexander. Michael Palmier is plenty man for me. Well…maybe.

Jessica gives a little bounce. "Dr. Alexander said the trees look like you could climb them and the animals like you could pet them."

Whether she realizes it, the little mite is calming my roiling. But that doesn't mean Dr. Alexander isn't going to hear about this. How dare he tell her I accepted the job!

"So how are you going to paint it, Miss Kate?"

"Hmm?" I blink at Jessica, and her enthusiasm once more causes me to forget my outrage. "I was thinking something on the theme of the world, with children of every nation represented."

The unbandaged portion of her forehead furrows, then she claps her hands. "The dome! It's perfect! And since I'll be coming to the hospital a lot, I'll get to see the world grow bigger and bigger!"

She has vision, and I'm pleased—until I realize I've confirmed my acceptance of the job.

Dr. Alexander, you rat!

Jessica and I visit another ten minutes, during which her mother opens up, and her father makes a comment here and there. When the nurse announces it's time for dinner, I take that as my cue to leave.

Jessica's mother rises from her chair. "Thank you for coming, Miss Meadows. It means a lot to Jessica." She glances at her husband. "And us."

After exchanging phone numbers with Jessica, I slip out.

Now a-hunting we will go…

I approach the receptionist who stands guard over the doctors' offices; however, before I can ask the whereabouts of one Dr. Clive Alexander, the woman says, "Ms. Meadows?"

"Uh, yes."

She sweeps a hand toward the hallway on the left. "Go on back."

He knew! But of course he did. "Thank you."

I traverse the hallway with steps so jerky my chest bounces, placing further stress on my back.

Unhh! Maybe Michael knows a good plastic surgeon who specializes in breast reduction.

As I round the corner, I falter at the sight of Dr. Alexander standing in the doorway of his office, a shoulder against the frame. "You're angry."

I halt before him, reach to my specs, and freeze. Grateful I didn't poke myself in the eye, I do the U-turn thing with my finger and jab the air between us. "You misled that little girl."

His eyebrows rise.

"Don't you raise your eyebrows at me! You told Jessica I accepted the job!"

He considers my accusatory finger. "I thought it might help get you off center."

"Off center! We talked *yesterday*. And agreed I would call you by the beginning of next week. *Next* week!"

He opens his mouth, only to close it when the tread of feet warns that we're no longer alone.

"Clive," a gravelly voice says.

I glance over my shoulder into weathered eyes beneath bushy white eyebrows.

"Adam," Dr. Alexander stiffly acknowledges.

The stout man, whose badge on his white coat identifies him as Dr. Adam MacPhail, gives me a nod, then looks at Dr. Alexander. "When you have a few minutes, I'd like to speak with you about the matter we discussed yesterday."

A muscle jerks in Dr. Alexander's jaw. "I didn't realize there was anything left to discuss."

The older man claps the younger on the shoulder. "You know me better than that, Clive. This afternoon, then."

I glance from Dr. MacPhail to Dr. Alexander and wonder what the "matter" is.

Stop it, Kate! As Eve proved to humanity's regret, curiosity leads to downfall.

"This afternoon," Dr. Alexander begrudges.

"Good." Dr. MacPhail gives me another nod, then continues down the hallway.

I raise my eyebrows, to which Dr. Alexander responds by gesturing me to enter his office.

I frown. "You sure? Your boss seemed a bit—"

"He's not my boss."

"Oh?"

"Ms. Meadows, if you'd like to discuss the burn unit, now would be a good time."

And that's when I remember my reason for hunting him down—to confront him over his dirty, rotten, underhanded tactics.

Jerking my bag higher on my shoulder, I step past him. A moment later, he settles into the chair beside the one I take, and it's all I can do not to demand that he take his proper place *behind* the desk.

Leaning forward, he rests his forearms on his thighs. "I owe you an apology."

I peer at him through narrowed lids. He doesn't look apologetic. "Then you wouldn't do it again?"

"I would if that's what it took to get a commitment out of you."

I jump to my feet. "You are so manipulative!"

He sighs and sits back. "Sometimes I push too hard, especially when it's for a good cause. And this *is* a good cause."

I glare at him, the child in me wanting to stomp out of his office, the juvenile wanting to give him a good dressing down, the adult stuck in the midst of sibling rivalry.

"Please, Ms. Meadows, don't make me chase you down any more elevator shafts." He nods at my chair. "Have a seat so we can discuss this civilly."

"At the moment, I don't feel very civil."

He rises. "Then over dinner?"

What is going on? Not a single date in over a month, and now four invites in two days. "I'm already committed for this evening."

"Oh? Another date?"

I will *not* be embarrassed about Michael's back-to-back invite, even if it is the middle of the week. "As a matter of fact, yes."

His brow lowers. "For being as busy as you say you are, you seem to have a good deal of time on your hands."

Ah! "Well maybe you work sixteen-hour days, but I don't!" Which isn't entirely true considering my pre-Michael work schedule, but what I do beyond an eight-hour workday is none of Clive Alexander's business.

"I apologize." And this time he does look apologetic, sort of. "I'm pushing too hard again."

So what clued him in? My hair standing on end? And just where is all this anger coming from? I am *not* an angry person. And yet I could throttle him!

Deep breath. "Have you heard of Dale Carnegie, Dr. Alexander?"

Surprise flickers in his eyes, but then his mouth tilts. "*How to Win Friends and Influence People*? I assure you, you're not the first to recommend the book."

"Then let me be the last. Get the book, read it, and maybe we'll talk about the burn unit."

He thrusts a hand forward. "I'll be waiting for your call."

Why do I have this sneaking suspicion that he has no intention of going anywhere near Dale Carnegie?

Gritting my teeth, I slide my hand into his and, too late, realize what a bad idea it is. As much as I don't want to be attracted to him, the squeeze of his hand causes funny little things to jump on the trampoline that's supposed to be my stomach. Fortunately, he doesn't sustain the shake longer than necessary.

"Good-bye, Dr. Alexander." I lower my arm to my side.

He inclines his head. "Ms. Meadows."

I hightail it out of there and am surprised—and disturbed—

by a pang of disappointment when I exit the elevator and he's not there to intercept me.

> *Thursday, March 22*
>
> *Dear Lord,*
>
> *Thank You for alternatives to contacts (trying to tell me something?). Thank You for the success of Jessica's surgery and the skilled hands You directed (guess that means I have to thank You for Clive Alexander, too).*
>
> *Help me to be patient, guard my tongue, and not allow myself to be pushed into something that will jeopardize my integrity. Or might the burn unit be Your go-ahead to pursue breast reduction? My back really aches. As always, please keep Belle and Beau's baby safe.*
>
> *Yours,*
>
> *Kate*

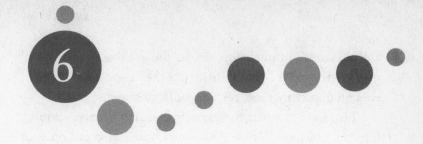

6

And the verdict is…?

Belle's eyes bug.

Beau steps back.

Belle's hand convulses on her expectant belly.

Beau's jaw drops.

"Well?" I stare at them through sapphire blue contacts (yes, I gave them another try).

"You…" Beau shakes his head.

"…look…" Belle sighs.

"…great!" Beau chuckles. "So great I didn't recognize you."

I asked for that. "Gee, thanks, Beau."

"At your service. No doughnut today?"

He just had to remind me! Though the siren song—er, scent—of the doughnut ministry called the moment I walked through the church doors, I'd managed to distract my salivating taste buds. *Thanks a lot, Beau-zo.*

He drapes an arm across my shoulders. "So, tell me more about this Michael Palmier."

I haven't seen Beau or Belle since church services last Sunday, and they aren't in my 8 a.m. singles Sunday school class, so all they know is what I've told them over the phone. Obviously not enough to prepare them for my transformation.

I consult my watch, then look to the churchgoers swarming into the sanctuary. "If we don't hurry, you'll miss out on your pew."

As if someone pulled the fire alarm, Beau drops his arm from me, takes his wife's hand, and hastens her toward the doors.

Beau and his pew—left of center, just the right distance from the speakers, three rows back, end seats.

Me? Though I often join him and Belle, my day goes as swimmingly—or unswimmingly—regardless of where I sit. Thus, when Beau and Belle squeeze out the last two seats of "his" pew and he shrugs apologetically, there are no hard feelings. Determining my chances are better on the balcony, I turn toward the steps.

Thirty minutes later, a half dozen spirit-lifting songs sung out, I watch as our minister takes to the pulpit. Brother Leo's topic is evangelism, and I cringe at not yet having gotten anywhere with Maia. In fact, I'm further out than ever, owing to Michael's attentiveness. Three dates in four days does not sit well with my housemate, as evidenced by her banging around the house last night previous to Michael's arrival to take me out for pizza and a wardrobe-enhancing shopping spree. (My credit card will *never* be the same—and yeah, I did pop for more of those seventy-dollar hip-hugging jeans.)

I consider the new outfit I wore to church, a blue, figure-enhancing pantsuit (size ten!). And that's all it takes to drift from Brother Leo's sermon. As with several of the outfits I ended up purchasing, I initially pooh-poohed Michael's selection, but he really has an eye for cut and color, with the exception of his insistence that *red* is my color.

Smoothing my lapels, I smile. The moment I saw my reflection, I knew this outfit was me. The only outfit with which
I hadn't concurred was an above-the-knee dress that laid bare a
series of spider veins that were a cause of concern for Michael—
so much so that I earned myself another business card. Brother
Leo reduced to white noise, I lift my bag and remove my wallet. Nestled behind the bills are a stack of business cards—Dr.
Neimer, tooth bonding; Judith Westman, electrolysis and laser
hair removal; Dr. Schulze, pest control (mole and spider vein
removal); Dr. Corrigan, breast reduction.

Of course, that last was my doing and grudgingly given, as
Michael tried to convince me that, despite my back problems,
my breasts are fine just the way they are. Hmm.

As for the first three cards, though resentment flared each
time Michael presented one, after some consideration—supple-
mented by time before the mirror—I found myself concurring.
So much so that I almost made appointments with Dr. Neimer
to advise me about my gap and Dr. Schulze to evaluate my
"pest" problem. Almost…

Nibbling my inner lip, I tell myself to toss out the cards
and stop worrying so much about my appearance. And I know
I should; however, the favorable reaction to the "new and improved" Katherine Mae Meadows makes me return them to my
wallet. Mustn't be too hasty. I'll just think about—

"Pray about it!" Brother Leo booms.

I am jolted, causing the elderly woman beside me to gasp
and clutch her chest.

"Sorry, Mrs. Farmer." I glance at Brother Leo to confirm
that he isn't speaking to me. He's not. I think… "Powerful message today, hmm?"

The woman lowers a trembling hand to her lap. "Not really,
dear."

So much for excusing my bodily outburst.

She draws a deep breath and leans near. "I thought perhaps something bit you."

Something *did*, but not anything creepy crawly. With an apologetic smile, I return my attention to the minister.

"The opportunities are boundless! The needs many! There's no excuse to look the other way." He points left. "The lost are waiting for you!" Center. "And you." Right. "And you." He jabs at those seated on the balcony. "And every one of you."

I know... I just don't know how to reach Maia without incurring rejection. And anger, as there's no doubt she's attracted to Michael. Oh, why does he have to like me? Moreover, why do I like him, especially considering his aversion to my imperfect self?

Complicated, but let me count the ways:

1. Though he may not be a practicing Christian, he's the closest I've come in a looong time.
2. Though I'm not nearly as attracted to him as I am to Clive Alexander—nix that!—he's good-looking.
3. Though his kisses don't exactly make me melt, he respects my limitations on physical contact.
4. Above all, each time I "feel him out" about perpetuating the human race, he remains indifferent. Surely I ought to be able to turn the other cheek when he points out a flaw. After all, nobody's perfect.

By the time the sermon ends, the offering plate makes the rounds, and the blessing is spoken, I'm wrung out. So I decline Belle's invitation to lunch and promise that later I'll fill her in about Michael, who as it turns out is waiting for me at the house.

His voice hits me as I step into the foyer, followed by a

chuckle and, not too far behind, Maia's husky laughter.

What is he doing here when I told him I rarely return from church before one? And what are he and Maia laughing at?

Anticipating the worst—after all, if Maia has no inhibitions about a married man, she's not likely to have any over her house-mate's something-of-a-boyfriend—I step into the living room.

And there's Michael on the sofa with Maia sitting in the chair opposite, a good six feet separating them.

Both look around, and in an instant, Michael's on his feet. "You're back early, Kate."

A good hour early. And if I hadn't been? As the possibilities sweep through me, I return my gaze to Maia, who remains seated with her bare legs curled under her. Why have I never before noted her resemblance to a cat?

Oh no! Is that jealousy coursing through my veins? It is. Jealousy when I should be pleased to see these two hitting it off. And I would be if Michael hadn't made it clear he was interested in *me*, not Maia.

Add to that the sorry fact that it's not every day I meet someone with whom I don't have major compatibility issues, and I suppose it's only natural for the green-eyed monster to put in an appearance.

I force a smile as Michael steps alongside me. "I thought we agreed to get together around the middle of the week."

"I know." He slides an arm around my waist. "But when I woke this morning thinking about you—" he squeezes me to his side—"I had to see you."

Even as his choice of words eases my jealousy, in the distance I detect the *ticktock* that, in a staccato tone, warns this is too fast, too strange, and too un–Michael Palmier. As if this is who Michael *wants* to be and not who he really—

"Oh!" He releases me. "I brought you a gift."

I momentarily forget his biological clock. What could it be? Flowers? Candy? Tickets to a—

"Autographed." He thrusts forward something thick and scentless, dry and tasteless, heavy and joyless: *The Makeup Bible*.

I stare at the tome that lands in my hands without so much as a loopy bow or length of ribbon. "Wow." As in who'd believe instruction on a woman's appearance could fill up something the size of…well…a Bible. A *large*-print Bible.

"I brought one for Maia, too. Of course, I didn't know she'd already purchased a copy."

"And read it cover to cover," she chimes in.

He winks at her. "Smart girl."

Mustn't take that wrong. I glance from Michael, who beams admiration at Maia, to Maia, who beams it right back.

She pats her copy, which sits on the end table. "A wealth of knowledge. And as everyone knows, one can never have too much."

"Mmm," I murmur.

Michael nods at my book. "Go on, read the inscription, Kate."

He inscribed it? Wrote a personal message? Ahh. Probably something sure to make me feel bad for suspecting he's transferred his affections to Maia.

Eagerly I flip to the title page where "To Kate" is written with a flourish, followed by "Lots in here that should help."

Lots?

He closes with "Enjoy!" and signs it "Michael." In *red*.

I eye Maia's copy and wonder at *her* inscription and what excuse I can give for whipping back the cover to see for myself. However, it's the vision of doing just that that pulls me back from the brink.

Michael's gift is a nice gesture, and I don't care what he

wrote in Maia's copy. I smile. "Thank you. I can't wait to spend some time in it." Okay, so I'm exaggerating.

He grins. "I've put sticky tabs on the pages I thought would be most helpful."

And so he has… I glance at the multicolored tabs that protrude from the top edge of the book. Must be a couple dozen.

"Have a look, Kate."

Reluctantly, I turn to the first, a chapter titled "Hair of Biblical Proportions." And among the sections listed are "Did the Delilah?" and "Having a Samson Hair Day?"

Oh…my…gosh. Lowering my chin to hide compressed lips, which are all that's holding back laughter, I draw a long breath.

"That's a great one to start with." Michael taps the page. "All kinds of tips on how to deal with uncooperative hair."

Despite the negative connotation, I must admit that *uncooperative* about sums up my hair. "Great." I sneak a peek at Maia's copy, the top edge devoid of sticky tabs.

"So, join me for a cup of coffee?"

I make a face. "Sorry, Michael, but I chugged down two cups in Sunday school. That's pretty much my limit."

Though I try not to see the disappointment that throws a shadow across his brow, guilt floods me. "But I haven't had lunch, so maybe a Polish dog at Fisherman's Wharf?"

His face brightens.

"Polish dog! And undo all your Pilates work?" Maia grabs her thigh and makes a pretense of jiggling fat that doesn't exist. "Trust me, Kate, it'll go straight to your tush and thighs."

Considering her attraction for Michael, I'd think a bit more fat on Kate would make her happy!

I shrug. "One Polish dog won't hurt." Of course, I do have to watch my fat intake because of the HRT. And last night I *did* indulge in pizza.

"Maia's right. How about we grab a salad somewhere?"

And all I wanted was to spend a nice, quiet Sunday afternoon with a turkey sandwich, my Bible, and my daily planner—as in, is it at all feasible to take on Dr. Alexander's project? So much to do…

I nod. "A salad sounds great."

"Good choice," Maia says with an air of approval that makes my emotions stand on end.

Biting my tongue, I slip from beneath Michael's arm. "I'll just change clothes and we can go."

"Fine. I'll visit with Maia—turns out we've got a lot in common."

I'll bet they do.

I swing away.

"Hey, beautiful!"

I pause, afraid to look around in case Michael's speaking to Maia. But then no need to call out when she's so near.

I meet his expectant gaze over my shoulder. He *did* mean me. "Yes?"

"Did I mention how gorgeous you are in that new outfit?"

Gorgeous. I tug the hem of my blue jacket. "Thanks."

"You're welcome." With a jaunty smile, he turns his attention to Maia, who gives a feline stretch…offers a feline smile…

"There."

"Where?"

"There." Michael reaches across the table to point to the left of Maia's luscious lips, nearly touching the glob of yellow. "Right there."

Narrowing my green gaze on the two—yes, I changed eye color—I wonder again how Maia finagled an invite to the wharf. Most unsettling is that she finagled it out of *me*! All I did was ask how she planned on spending the afternoon, and the next thing I knew I was suggesting she join us.

She dabs at the corner of her mouth, narrowly missing the mustard. Intentionally missing it, as how can anyone not feel a glob that size?

"Allow me." Michael rises from the bench beside me, steps around the table, tilts her face up, and sweeps the mustard away with his napkin. "Got it."

Maia smiles. "Thank you, Michael."

"Anytime." The breeze off the bay ruffles his collar in the absence of hair, and he returns her smile.

She bats her lashes. Honestly!

He blinks and faces me. "Uh…ready, Kate?"

Feeling jealousy dig deeper, I pat my stomach. "All full." On greens, reds, whites, and yellows—as in lettuce, tomatoes, Dungeness crab, and fat-free something-or-other dressing. A *far* cry from the Polish dogs on which he and Maia fed.

I know. Dungeness crab isn't exactly chopped liver. In fact, the flaky meat brought in from the wetlands of the upper San Francisco Bay really is divine—at least until one's taste buds go numb from overindulgence. As mine wore out years ago, it takes something slightly more potent to satisfy them. Something like a Polish dog.

I glance at Michael and Maia's plates, streaks of mustard and ketchup the only evidence of their gluttony. Why did I let them guilt me out of a dog? It should have been *my* mouth Michael wiped mustard from.

Maia rises beside Michael. "That was good, wasn't it?"

Go ahead, rub it in a bit more just in case good ol' Kate doesn't realize what she missed.

Michael nods. "Best Polish dogs in the city."

I thrust up so suddenly that were the bench not connected to the table, it would have toppled. "Sure are," I say as their surprised countenances turn to me. "And talk about a great salad. You'll have to try one next time."

Maia glances at my Styrofoam container and wrinkles her nose. "Crab is for tourists."

You are sooo in the litter box!

"Think I'll stick to dogs," Michael concurs. Again.

Well, aren't they compatible?

And that word *compatible* reminds me that I originally hoped to match these two. I should be thanking God for the opportunity to turn Maia from Mr. Unhappily Married, making plans to move her to the next step of attending church (with the aid of "once saved, always saved" Michael). However, while part of me urges me to "hand over the boyfriend" and cut my losses, the other part reminds me that Michael and I are also compatible—at least where biological children are concerned.

"You okay, Kate?"

I focus on Michael. "Yeah. I'm great."

"You sure?" Maia comes around the table. I half expect her to look pleased, but she doesn't. In fact, her concern appears genuine.

I put a hand to my chest. "Just a bit of indigestion."

"Oh?" She loops an arm through mine. "Good thing you didn't go Polish, hmm?"

Why does it always come back to dogs?

Shortly, I find myself strolling the wharf, Michael and Maia on either side of me. Feeling like a shelf-worn book between beautifully matched bookends that are just being kind in propping me up, I consider my go at self-improvement. Maybe I really don't look all that different from a week ago. After all, it was just a change of clothes, a new hairstyle, a bit of makeup, and a switch from glasses to contacts. As for Pilates, thus far all I have to show for that is muscle ache and stiffness. Maybe I need to do more. Maybe I should make that appointment with Dr. Neimer. And Dr. Schulze.

Or maybe I should pull out my Bible....

Beginning to feel tangled and knotted, I attempt to distract my emotions by taking in this small slice of Fisherman's Wharf through the senses of the tourists who throng to San Francisco's most popular destination.

Yes, the endless variety of shops and eateries is stimulating. Yes, the street entertainers who dance, juggle, pantomime, sing, strum, and perform sleight of hand are amazing. Yes, the barking of the sea lions that congregate at Pier 39 is...

Actually, it's pretty obnoxious, but I'm probably among the minority who feel that way.

As for the fishing fleet that brings treasure from the sea into Pier 45, it tempts one to nostalgic musings. Then there's the aroma of fresh seafood and sourdough bread that, mixed with the brisk salt air, piques ones nostrils and palate—

Aargh! For all my straining to tune my senses to the pleasures of Fisherman's Wharf, the majority of my perceptions are straight out of a travel book. So I abandon the exercise and turn my energy to disconnecting from Michael, as I've done with others whose futures held things mine didn't.

Okay, God, if not Michael, who? Or is there anyone for me? Would it be better if I did swear off men? As in ONCE AND FOR ALL?

Divine intervention? Biting my lip, I lower the phone and shift my attention to the planner I laid open on my desk minutes before the call from Mr. Deveraux. According to the burly voiced man, he and his wife are putting their house up for sale. Thus my services are no longer required, which frees up a month of working time five weeks from now—when Dr. Alexander proposed I begin work on the burn unit. Strange.

Attempting to relieve my strained back, I roll my shoulders and once more consider the stack of business cards—in particular, that of the doctor who specializes in breast reduction. The surgery costs a small fortune, but of all things I might do to improve myself, it carries the most weight (no pun intended), as vanity has little to do with it. And if I can fit in Dr. Alexander's project, there should be enough funds to pay for the reduction.

"All righty, then." I draw a line through each *Deveraux* entry. Unfortunately, it will take longer than a month to complete the burn unit. I flip to the following month where *Fischer* is penned in for two successive weeks—another children's library. Then there's the Hilo Youth Foundation, which I quoted out at three weeks. Maybe if I—

I sigh. "And when are you supposed to live? Not to mention *sleep*?"

I tap the planner. Though I try to keep my working hours from eight till four—nine till five when I attend Pilates with Maia—I could cut out Pilates (shucks) and work seven till three, thereby allowing me to put in a half dozen hours at the hospital during the evenings. Of course, there's always Saturdays. I grimace at the realization that that leaves no time for dating—

No, I haven't opted for a split personality, and yes, I was on my way to disconnecting from Michael; however, when we returned to the house and it was just the two of us on the doorstep, his kiss held no hint of good-bye. But the real clincher was when he said, "I'm really starting to love you, Kate."

Thus, against all logic, Michael and I are still on. But do I decline the biggest job of my career on the chance it could mean the difference between making it with him and not? If he truly cares, surely he'll hang on despite the long work hours. That, or have a few more heart-to-hearts with Maia....

I look up and eye *The Makeup Bible* on the corner of my desk. What *did* he write in Maia's copy? Probably the same as mine. Mustn't make mountains out of molehills. Or infatuations out of mere acquaintances.

Unbidden, a mental snapshot of a certain doctor rises to mind. "So what do I do about you, Dr. Alexander? Where do you fit in?" I return my attention to the planner and snort. "Or should I say *squeeze?*"

I flip through the months, hash and rehash the pros and cons, and finally acknowledge that I'm not where I need to be.

Returning to my bedroom, I scoop up my Bible and settle into a worn armchair for an evening of soul feeding.

Forget about Michael. Forget about Maia. Above all, forget about Dr. Clive Alexander and the call he's expecting. And I do— for the fifteen minutes I'm allowed to poke through Proverbs.

The phone beside my bed rings for the third time, and I consider ignoring it. But it could be a client, and as I forgot to turn on the answering machine, I have no choice but to check caller ID.

I cross the room and peer at the small screen, which comes up "private."

On the fifth ring, I lift the receiver. "Katherine Meadows."

"Ms. Meadows, Adelphia Jamison. I'm sure you remember me." The consciously cultured voice brings forth an image of the polished woman I believed to be Dr. Alexander's paramour.

As I struggle with the temptation to disavow all remembrance of her—terribly un-Christian—she prompts, "We met at the children's boutique."

"I remember. What can I do for you, Ms. Jamison?"

"Dr. Alexander asked me to set up a meeting between the three of us."

"He did?" I say with restrained rebuke. "Surely he told you I haven't committed to the job."

"Yes, though he said you agreed to give him an answer by the beginning of the week."

"That's true; however, I'm still attempting to free up the time required to accept such a large project." Too, I really need to pray about it.

"But you will accept the job."

That wasn't exactly a question. "I should know by tomorrow."

"Then let's make the appointment." I hear the rustle of paper. "Tomorrow at two works for me."

"Ms. Jamison, if I don't accept the job, an appointment won't be necessary."

"But if you do, the appointment is in place."

"Ms. Jamison—"

"Ms. Meadows"—*huff!*—"I'm a busy woman. Go with me, will you?"

Silently chanting "guard your tongue," I pull the handset away and glare at it before putting it back to my ear. "Ms. Jamison, what role do you play that requires your presence?"

"I head up the financial end of the hospital's expansion projects. I'm the one who approves payment for your work."

Then this is the "colleague" part of her relationship with Dr. Alexander.

"Two o'clock tomorrow afternoon?" she presses, and I just know she's penciling me in.

"No."

"Excuse me?"

"I'll be up to my elbows in paint at two o'clock. However,

if I accept the job, I can meet with you and Dr. Alexander around—"I make a quick calculation of the time required to get from the project in Sausalito back to the city—"four o'clock."

"I go home at four, Ms. Meadows."

Then I'm the only one required to make sacrifices? "Meaning you work until four?"

Huff. "Exactly."

"So do I, Ms. Jamison—and often later." I really don't mean to be antagonistic, but it's sloughing off me like dead skin. But then, this woman is a bit of a pumice stone. "I'm willing to kick off early, as long as you're also willing to accommodate."

Heavy sigh. "Though it will put me in the thick of rush-hour traffic, four it is."

"Provided I accept the job."

"Of course."

"All right. Unless you hear from me, I'll see you and Dr. Alexander at four o'clock."

"Good-bye, Ms. Meadows."

As I lower the handset, I consider calling it a night; however, I haven't been in my Bible enough. Determined to stick it out, I swing back toward the chair.

"Oh, my back!" Kneading the muscles along my spine, I once more consider calling the surgeon Michael recommended. Which is one of the best reasons for accepting the burn unit job.

As I lower to the chair, I mentally set up a pros/cons list for my reduction.

Pros	Cons
Less weight up front = less back strain.	*Surgery is gonna hurt.*
Better-fitting clothes.	*Recovery is gonna hurt.*
Fastest way to drop a few pounds.	*Possible complications.*
Proportioned figure.	*Downtime following surgery.*

Able to sleep on stomach.   *Uh…no built-in canopy for*
Jogging a possibility?   *my shoes.*
Oh! Bathing suits and nonknit dresses!

Looks like Dr. Alexander just might get his way…

Sunday, March 25
Dear Lord,

Thank You for Brother Leo and sweet little old ladies like Mrs. Farmer. Thank You for shopping sprees and modest credit card limits. Thank You for outfits that flatter and coordinating eye color (maybe I can get used to contacts). Thank You for vicarious feeding on Polish dogs, last-minute cancellations (was that You?), and Belle's growing baby.

Help me overcome my jealousy toward Maia. (Would I be breaking any commandment if I took a peek at what Michael wrote in her copy of The Makeup Bible?) Help me guard my tongue and curb my antagonism toward that Adelphia woman. Help me be discerning about this stack of business cards. (You wouldn't mind a bit of spider vein removal, would You? Oh, and this gap!—my fault, not Yours. Probably all that thumb sucking as a kid.) Help me make the final determination about the reduction (I really want this one). Whew!

XOXO
Kate

PS: Tithe coming soon!

7

"Sign here…" Adelphia Jamison taps the contract. "Here… and here." She looks up. "Provided we're in agreement."

How could I not be? I stare at the big fat numbers that follow the dollar sign. That's a lot of money. Had I quoted the job, I would have bid it at two-thirds. But she said that was the budget, take it or leave it. Decisions, decisions.

"Are we in agreement, Ms. Meadows?"

With a glance around the conference room that has yet to admit Dr. Alexander, I nod. "Everything appears to be in order."

"Good." She thrusts a pen at me.

My own nails sharply contrasting with hers—paint beneath the tips and in the curves of my cuticles—I accept the pen and set my signature to the blanks that commit me to a ten-week time frame and severe penalties for delays. But there won't be delays. I'll make it work, even if it kills me. Which it might…

Adelphia sweeps up the contract. "I'll make a copy, and that will conclude our meeting."

And not a minute too soon if she wants to beat the worst of rush-hour traffic, I mull over as she exits the room. I declare, her whirlwind explanation of the contract made me feel like she was speaking a foreign language. Thus, I insisted on reading every line. Throughout, she sat with pinched lips, folded arms, and foot drumming the floor. None of which deterred me from watching out for my best interests. In fact, it only prolonged her misery, as the distraction forced me to reread several times. But now she can leave, and I can go home and figure out how I'm going to juggle this project without losing my mind. Fortunately, it's five weeks before I begin work on the burn unit. Unfortunately, once it's underway, it's going to be a bumpy ride.

I glance at my robust chest. "I hope you're happy."

"Me?" A masculine voice takes a spin around the confer-ence room.

I jerk my gaze to where Dr. Alexander stands at the thresh-old.

Caught talking to my chest. Lovely. "Uh…um…"

He raises his eyebrows above the glimmer in his eyes. "Or were you talking to someone else?"

Some*thing* else. "You, Dr. Alexander. I was talking to you. I mean—" I shake my head—"who else would I be talking to?"

Surely I'll be forgiven, as God can't possibly expect me to admit to conversing with my bosom. That would be *so* wrong.

"Then in answer to your question—" he steps farther into the room—"I'm happy."

"Good." I stand. "Ms. Jamison is making a copy of the con-tract."

He looks to my JESUS IS KING T-shirt, then my paint-streaked relaxed-fit jeans (can't bring myself to risk the seventy-dollar-a-pop hip-huggers). Unfortunately, though I did allow time to change for the meeting, there was this one wall that stood between me and beginning work with the faux glaze first thing in the morning. Thus, I applied the last of the base coat, and now I'm paying for it. Not that I care if Dr. Alexander finds me presentable. Well, maybe a little…

He returns his gaze to mine. "I apologize for missing the meeting."

"No problem. Ms. Jamison covered the contract." Rather, *I* covered it. Wondering what's taking her so long, I heft my bag onto my shoulder. "So, Dr. Alexander, did you read Dale Carnegie?"

He smiles. "It's on my to-do list."

I wish he wouldn't smile like that. Makes him far too appealing.

"Can you spare an hour or so, Ms. Meadows?"

I frown. "For?"

"To discuss your ideas for the burn unit. Of course, if you have another date…"

"Not tonight."

"Then you'll have dinner with me?"

He didn't say anything about dinner, just a discussion. And why does he keep asking me out? Merely the means by which he conducts business?

"An early dinner," he clarifies.

"How early?"

"We could leave in fifteen minutes."

"Fifteen minutes!" I open my arms wide. "Do you really want to be seen in public with this?"

His mouth tilts. "It's not a date."

"Obviously!" I mentally huff and puff in an attempt to cool the heat rising in my cheeks.

"Well?"

Now that I've accepted the job, I suppose we should discuss it. "All right. Dinner it is."

A moment later, his "colleague" sweeps into the room. "Clive!" She halts alongside him and sinks her red-tipped claws into his sleeve.

Red. Christopher's favorite color. I don't like red. Not candy apple red, not Santa Claus red, not—

Dr. Alexander leans toward her to receive a peck on the cheek.

"Let me guess…" She sparkles beneath his regard. "A difficult surgery?"

"Yes."

"But successful."

"Appears to have been."

She smiles larger, only to drop a size or two when she remembers me. Crossing the room, she extends a sheaf of papers. "Your copy of the contract, Ms. Meadows."

I accept them. "Thank you."

"Well, that wraps it up. Nice meeting with you." She thrusts out a hand that I clasp, only to inwardly grimace at the clammy palm beneath mine.

Thankfully, she quickly disengages and swings back to Dr. Alexander. "Since we've been condemned to rush-hour traffic—"

Thanks to the demanding Ms. Meadows.

"—how about we wait out the exodus over an early dinner?"

First *condemned*, now *exodus*. She really is put out.

Dr. Alexander's face turns apologetic. "Ms. Meadows has agreed to have dinner with me to discuss the project."

"Oh." She blinks. "Good idea." A long pause follows, which I take as an opportunity for Dr. Alexander to invite her along. When he doesn't, she presses her shoulders back. "Well, I'd offer to join you, but my day has been tedious enough as it is."

Was that a slam? Humph! One would think I stole her date out from under her nose. But then I guess I did.

She saunters out of the room but pokes her head back inside. "Forgot to mention that Adam's looking for you."

The name rings a bell, but it's Dr. Alexander's stiffening that returns me to the hallway outside his office the other day when Dr. MacPhail asked to discuss some "matter" with him.

"Thank you, Adelphia."

She frowns. "You're not going to give in, are you?"

He glances at me. "This is not the time to discuss it."

"Oh." Her eyes flit to me. "Of course." Then she disappears.

An awkward silence—weighted by my curiosity—follows. I step forward. "So, fifteen minutes?"

He nods. "Provided you're not opposed to a simple meal, we can walk to the sandwich shop down the street."

Sounds safe enough for someone in my state of dress. "Sure."

"Meet you in the lobby."

Twenty minutes later, we walk side by side through the lowering of day, passing from light into lengthening shadows and exchanging niceties. The nippy air causes me to shiver, and I hug my arms tighter. Why, oh why, didn't I retrieve a sweater from my car? It's not as if I don't know San Francisco's intemperate moods.

The next shiver that runs through me coincides with the ring of Dr. Alexander's cell phone. He pulls it from his belt, peers at the screen, then returns the phone to its holder. Obviously, not someone he wishes to speak with.

I shiver again.

Fortunately, Dr. Alexander slows as we approach one of those chain cafés that dot the city with nearly as much enthusiasm as the trendy coffee shops. As I prefer nonformulaic restaurants, I'm a little disappointed—until he opens the door for me into Home-Baked Breads & Things.

Disappointment taken hostage by the scent of freshly baked warm and crusty loaves of bread and sweetly sticky things like cinnamon rolls and cherry tarts, I drag in noseful after noseful. If not for fear that I might end up in a humiliating heap, I'd close my eyes and transport back to my grandmother's kitchen, which often smelled like this.

Of course, it didn't look like this, I muse as I survey the café with its rustic decor, scuffed cement floors, mismatched tables and chairs, and alcoves that offer privacy to those who don't care to sit in the open. Nice. Now if the food tastes half as good as it smells, this could prove a real find.

"This way." Dr. Alexander leads me past scattered diners to the back of the café, where those waiting to whip up our meal are a surprise themselves. Their aprons are simple white jobs, and all bear evidence of food preparation: mustard stains, oil spots, and various other condiments destined for the plate but sidetracked by a wayward hand.

"What can I get you?" asks a round-faced young man with holes in his earlobes threaded with what seem like small pieces of pipe. I've been seeing more of those lately but still haven't figured out what it's about. Not sure I want to…

I look at Dr. Alexander. "Any recommendations?"

"Carnivore or herbivore?"

I blink. Did he really say that? Hardly original, but definitely cute. "It's Monday, right?"

His left eyebrow goes up. "It is."

"Then carnivore it is."

The right eyebrow joins the left. "Meaning tomorrow is herbivore?"

"Actually, I practice omnivore-ity on Tuesdays."

He gives a short laugh that jump-starts the humming at my center. *Love* his laugh!

"If I'm not careful, I might get to like you, Kate."

Get to like me... *Kate*, rather than Ms. Meadows. I stare at him.

To my relief, he doesn't sink back into his brooding self but turns to the menu on the wall behind the counter. "The turkey club is good, as is the ham and Swiss on Asiago, but if you like—"

"Asi-what?"

"Asiago, a cheese bread. Quite good."

"Say no more." I smile at the holey young man behind the counter. "Ham and Swiss on Asi...uh..."

"Asiago. With everything, ma'am?"

I peer at the small writing on the menu. "Everything but onion."

"And you, sir?"

"The same, less the onion as well." Dr. Alexander looks back at me. "Don't care for onion either?"

I scrunch up my nose. "Wreaks havoc with my breath. And believe me, you won't want to get anywhere near me if—"

I nearly choke. How I hope he doesn't take that any other way than intended.

Something flickers in his eyes. "As I said, it's not a date."

"And thank goodness for that. I mean...not that I...uh, you..."

"I understand, Kate."

Still *Kate*? Why that pleases me, I don't know. Of course, we are going to be working together, so it follows that we should transition to first names.

Soon I carry my sandwich and milk—paid for by *Clive*—

and follow him to an alcove. As always, there's that moment of awkwardness when a Christian knows they should offer up thanks for a meal but hesitates for fear of appearing odd. Even in the presence of fellow Christians, it's not unusual to feel discomfort, but in the presence of nonbelievers it can be excruciating. Of course, Dr.—uh, Clive—could be a believer.

A moment later, he lifts his sandwich to take a bite.

Despite the temptation to follow suit, I lower my head and send up silent thanks for my meal. When I settle back in my chair, I discover that Clive has returned his untouched sandwich to his plate.

"Done?"

I nod. "Brownie points in heaven, you know."

Ooh, I said that aloud, didn't I?

Sorry, Lord. Didn't mean to make light of You. It just…fell off my lips.

I take a bite of my sandwich—not a bad strategy, as the process of digestion curbs a wayward tongue. Not that one should rely on such, as it's the waistline that suffers. And I certainly don't want to work any harder at Pilates.

Still hate the class, but I'm determined to get my money's worth. And I am. Beneath the table, I grip my thigh. Not that it was ever really flabby, but it's begun to solidify.

"How is it?"

I jerk my hand off my thigh, only to realize it's the sandwich he's talking about. "Very good."

"Glad you like it."

Over the next fifteen minutes, we make small talk, during which Clive receives another call and responds to it the same as before.

"So what have you got for me?" he asks once our plates are clean.

I pull my bag onto my lap—a bag that is lighter than it should be. With dread, I open it. "Ohhh. I left my sketchbook at home."

He glances at his watch. "Would you object to me having a look at it there?"

I blink. "I could bring it by the hospital tomorrow."

"I'll be in surgery most of the day."

"The day after?"

"Out of town."

"I…guess you could follow me home."

He pushes his chair back. "Let's go."

Outside, in the dusk of approaching night and a breeze that's gone from nippy to chilly, I shiver again.

Clive halts. "Take my jacket."

I glance behind and discover that he's already shrugged out of it. "Thanks, but it's not much farther."

He holds it open for me. "Your teeth are chattering."

"But you—"

"Don't need it." He smiles crookedly. "Hot-blooded."

I'll bet he is. *Naughty, Kate!*

Clenching my teeth to keep them from clacking, I slide my arms into his warm and toasty sleeves. Mmm…

Over my back, Clive pulls the lapels closed, and I shudder as his hands brush my collarbone.

It's the cold air. Has to be. However, as we resume our pace, I have to admit that I'm still attracted to him. Don't want to be, but it's true. And unwelcome, considering I have Michael who's attracted to *me*, even if his attentiveness toward Maia is greater than it should be.

Twenty minutes later, I find my suspicions all the more founded when I pull into the itsy-bitsy driveway of the Victorian-era house I share with Maia in the Alamo Square

Historic District. Smiling tightly, I wave back at Michael and my housemate where they sit on the top step illuminated by the porch light. So he showed up unannounced. Again.

Stepping out of my car, I glance over my shoulder at where Clive pulls into the single curbside space deeded to our address.

"Kate!" Michael calls as he rises from the step.

"Hey!" I call back.

Maia unfolds alongside him. And, by golly, no amount of jealousy can hide the fact that they're a handsome couple.

"Nice place." Clive steps alongside me.

Grateful for the distraction, I peer at the narrow house sandwiched between two others and silently concur that its whimsical pastel colors and exuberant trim lend just the right amount of charm. Of course, that's what Maia paid me well to pull off three years ago—and how we met.

I look back at Clive. "Thank you."

He smiles.

Like that smile, not to mention the way the breeze fingers his hair and the shadows of night soften his jaw—mere observations, of course.

Clive raises an eyebrow. "Kate?"

"Uh, come on up." As he follows me toward the steps, concern pinches Michael's brow. And he's not the only one to react to Clive's presence. Maia's eyes light up, her tongue sweeps her bottom lip, and she angles her body to best show off her figure (as if she has a bad side!).

The moment I step to the porch, Michael slides an arm around me, pulls me in, and plants a kiss that leaves no doubt that he's marking territory. Might he think Clive and I are returning from a date? Of course, that would mean he's playing dirty by "marking" me in front of another man. Not exactly what one expects from someone who said there was no exclusivity to our dating.

"Missed you." He pulls away just enough to give me air. "So who have you brought home with you?"

I draw back, and after a slight hesitation, Michael eases his hold enough to allow me to turn to Clive, whose smile of moments earlier is gone. Meaning Michael did what he set out to do, which was sabotage my date—

It wasn't a date! It was a business meeting.

"Well?" Michael prompts.

"Uh, Michael Palmier, meet Dr. Alexander. Dr. Alexander—Michael Palmier."

Michael's arm at my waist tightens. "Doctor, hmm?"

Clive inclines his head. "And you, Mr. Palmier?"

"Makeup artist, author of the bestselling *The Makeup Bible*." Michael thrusts a hand forward. "And, of course, Kate's boyfriend."

"Of course." Clive catches my eye as he accepts Michael's handshake.

Warmth flushes me, and my tongue cleaves to the roof of my mouth. When the men unclasp hands, what follows is an awkward silence—until Maia clears her throat.

"And this is my landlady and housemate, Maia Glock."

With a smile that falls just shy of whisker licking, Maia accepts Clive's handshake. "Stockbroker. Lovely to meet you, Dr. Alexander."

"And you." He immediately loosens his hand, causing my housemate to blink. And blink.

Goodness! First Michael, now Clive. This could be bad.

Deciding an explanation is in order, I look at Michael, who continues to hold me to his side. "Clive and I were out this evening to discuss—"

"Clive?" Michael exclaims.

Ugh. Dropped the formality of "Dr. Alexander." If he felt threatened before—

"Dr. Clive Alexander?" He loosens his hold on me. "*The* Dr. Clive Alexander?"

The? Meaning this is no longer about *me?* I narrow my eyes on the object of Michael's interest and discover that the relative ease with which Clive earlier carried himself has gone south. In fact, he's bordering on stiff.

"As in San Francisco's finest cosmetic surgeon?"

Maia gasps. "Really?"

Clive's stiff. Definitely stiff.

"As in best friend to the less-than-perfect rich and famous?"

Stiffer. And yet Michael seems oblivious. Or perhaps he's all too aware.

"As in the toast of plastic town?"

Clive broadens his shoulders with a breath. "I no longer practice cosmetic surgery, Mr. Palmier."

"So I heard. Dropped out, what? Three years ago?"

"Almost four." Clive's gruff voice reminds me of the day he showed me the memorial plaque and told me he was a husband and father without a wife and child. It doesn't take a genius to piece this together. Obviously, the loss of his family is responsible for him giving up his career as a top cosmetic surgeon.

Michael sighs. "Pity—a real loss to the profession."

His regret seems genuine, but then I'm struck by the possibility that his regret is grounded more in the matter of one less business card.

"So how are you keeping yourself busy these days, Dr. Alexander?"

"Reconstructive surgery. Primarily burn victims."

The opportunity is too good to pass up, so I jump in. "Which is the reason we were out this evening, to discuss the job I've accepted for the hospital. Cli—er, Dr. Alexander—is heading up the project."

"Ah, business then." Michael smiles, and I can't help but appreciate how attractive he is in spite of his shaved head. "I suppose I have you to thank for keeping my girl warm." He plucks the collar of Clive's jacket.

Forgot I was wearing it. Of course, its presence probably has a lot to do with Michael's territorial behavior.

Clive nods. "Glad to be of service."

I shrug out of the jacket and hold it out to him. "Thank you for the loan."

His fingers brush mine. "Shall we take a look at those sketches now?"

Trying to convince myself that the shudder that just coursed through my arm and leapt through my heart was caused by a chill, I step from Michael's side and push the door inward. "Come in."

Clive crosses the threshold and is followed by Michael.

Maia halts alongside me. "Nice catch, Kate. Too bad he's married."

Noticed the ring, did she? "He's not my catch," I rasp low. "And he's a widower."

"Reeeally?" And there's more of that whisker licking.

"Trust me, Maia, he's *not* your type."

"Reeeally?"

I open my mouth only to realize that now I'm the one who's getting territorial—and over a man with whom I have no right to be. Besides, maybe Clive Alexander is her type, as in unmarried.

Hmm. Is it possible she could fall for him? Of course, outside of her married boyfriend, has she ever fallen for anyone?

The closest I've seen her come is Michael. But that may be because he's shown little interest in her—at least, in the beginning.

"We'll see." Maia saunters forward and places herself between Michael and Clive—a beautiful stretch of canvas framed by two attractive men.

I close the door and, as I cross toward the stairs, offer Michael an apologetic smile. "I'm afraid tonight's not a good night, so—"

"Don't worry about me. Maia and I'll brew some coffee while you take care of business. Join us when you're finished. And you, too, Dr. Alexander, if you can spare a few minutes."

"I'm afraid I won't be able to." Clive gives me a meaningful look.

Right. I hasten up the stairs, and he follows.

"Oh, Kate!"

I look down at Michael who's moved to the threshold of the living room.

"Did you make an appointment with Dr. Neimer to discuss your gap?"

I frown. "What?"

He rolls his eyes and taps his teeth. "Dr. Neimer."

Embarrassment flushes me. "Yes, I made the appointment today." And have felt guilty ever since.

Michael smiles. "Good girl."

Girl?

"What about Dr. Schulze?" He taps the place on his cheek that corresponds with my mole.

Is he intentionally pointing out my every flaw in front of Clive?

I gnash my teeth. "Also taken care of." Which made me feel guiltier yet.

"Good. I promise you won't regret it."

I already do.

Shortly, Clive and I enter the large bedroom that serves as an office-slash-studio. Spying the sketchbook on my drafting table, I cross to it.

He follows and halts almost shoulder to shoulder as I search out the half dozen sketches. And there's that attraction again.

I tap the first picture. "This is what I envision for the hallways: jungle transitioning to woodland…mountains…hills."

His phone rings, and he makes a sound low in his throat. "Excuse me." Glancing to the small screen, he starts to glower again.

When his eyes dart to mine, I smile sympathetically. "Why don't you just get it over with?"

"All right. I'll only be a minute." Turning aside, he flips open the phone and strides away. "Yes, Adam?"

As in Dr. MacPhail?

Clive halts before my desk. "No, meaning the answer is still no." He looks up then down—at my copy of *The Makeup Bible*.

Uh-oh.

Listening, he lifts up the cover.

Oh, no.

Certain he's reading Michael's inscription, I cringe.

"Listen, Adam—" he snaps the book closed—"I know I owe you, but this is not a good time."

Owes him what?

"Yes. No. Because I can't."

Can't what? Pay Dr. MacPhail what he owes him? As in money? Might Clive be a gambler?

He glances over his shoulder, and I quickly pretend an interest in my sketches.

A minute later, he returns to stand alongside me. "Sorry about that. Where were we?"

I turn to the second sketch. "Here's where we transition to lakes...meadows...farmland—" I turn the page—"rural setting...city." I glance up at him.

Though the tension that first arose during his exchange with Michael has increased, he manages a smile. "Very nice."

"Great." Now for the pièce de résistance. With bated pride (I know, pride goeth before a fall), I turn to a rendering of the domed room. "An outside-in view of the earth with children of all nations represented." I tap a group positioned against the backdrop of Asia. "Holding hands"—tap—"dancing"—tap—"praying—"

"Praying?" Clive leans in to stare at the kneeling figures.

"Yes."

"No."

There's that "fall" I should have been more mindful of. "What do you mean 'no'?"

"No praying."

He's serious. But is this really about my religious renderings, or is it fallout from Dr. MacPhail's call that *I* urged him to take?

I step back. "I suppose you have a good reason for nixing expressions of faith?"

"I do."

"And that would be?"

"It's not what I..." His lips compress. "It's not what the hospital is looking for."

I shake my head. "I don't understand. Nearly all of my work incorporates God on one scale or another. Surely you know that."

"Yes, but it's not necessary for the burn unit."

Indignation sending out roots like nasty weeds, I harden my jaw. "And why is that?"

"I don't need a reason."

I press my shoulders back. "If you intend to deprive children and their families of the comfort of knowing that God is watching over them, you'd better have a reason. A *good* reason."

His lids narrow. "For depriving them of the *false* comfort of God?"

I clench my hands. "False? Ask Jessica how false the comfort of God is."

"She's a child, Kate."

So it's still *Kate*, is it?

"Exactly, *Dr. Alexander*." I poke a finger in his chest. "Even if you want to turn your back on God because of what you believe He took from you, it's not what children and their frightened families want."

Pull back! Pull back!

"They want to know when they're lying in a bed not their own, surrounded by people they don't know, their lives completely turned inside out, that they're not alone. They want to know that God is there. And how better to assure them than to display symbols of His love?"

Clive's gaze drops to my finger at the center of his chest. "I'm not going to argue with you. Like it or not, there will be no religious symbols." He steps back.

"But—"

"In the contract you signed, *I* have final approval, and my approval hinges on a child-friendly environment that doesn't shove religion down anyone's throat. Remember, it's not only Christians who end up in the burn unit; it's children from all religious *and* nonreligious backgrounds."

"But the hospital is called St.—"

"I know what it's called, and no further religious overtones are required."

As evidenced by the wind in my ears, I'm close to hyperventilating. I narrow my eyes on his set face. All right, no overtones. But there will be undertones. Somehow, I'll put God into the burn unit. And if he doesn't like it, he'll just have to take spray paint to it. The heathen!

"Fine," I say, only to realize that I'm close to tears. "Whatever you want."

He stares at me, and something like regret flashes in his eyes. Though I sense he wants to say more, he sets his jaw. "I should be going."

"Um-hmm."

"We'll talk again soon." He crosses to the door and looks around. "Can I offer a piece of advice?"

"And what would that be?"

"Don't try to improve on something that works."

"What?"

"The gap." He taps his front teeth in what's surely a mockery of Michael. "And the mole. In my opinion, neither detracts from your appearance."

His opinion—ha! All the more reason to go through with the procedures. And I will, I decide, ignoring the voice that whispers something about cutting off my nose to spite my face.

I stand straighter. "In *my* opinion, the inclusion of God in the burn unit won't detract from *its* appearance. Rather, it will *enhance* the environment."

His shoulders stiffen. "Which is the reason it's called an opinion."

"All right, then, here's another opinion—the sooner you pay your debts, the sooner you'll get out from under them."

He does a double take. "What?"

"Dr. Adam MacPhail."

Understanding replaces questioning, which gives way to simmering. "Don't assume to advise me on something you know nothing about."

"Don't I? I know that you owe him and are avoiding him. Now the question is: Why haven't you paid him?" I know I've gone too far, but it's too late to place a guard on my tongue.

However, he doesn't unload on me. In fact, his dark expression eases into a bitter smile. "Are you making assumptions about my character again?"

I am, aren't I?

"If you recall, the last time you did so, you got me all wrong."

Which wasn't entirely my fault, as he's the one who continues to wear his wedding ring, thereby presenting a married face to the world.

He inclines his head. "Good evening."

Hands clenched, I watch him go from sight.

"Good riddance," I mutter and swing back to my sketches, only to grimace when a big, fat tear slips down my cheek. Flinging it away, I pull out the stool and plop myself down. Considering how much I have to do to prepare for the burn unit, Maia and Michael will just have to do coffee alone, which shouldn't disappoint. They'll likely be happier without me. *If* they even notice my absence.

I'm slipping into self-pity. I drop my forehead to the drafting table. Why, oh why, did I accept the burn unit job?

I wallow, then reach for the phone. As I'm going to need help, it's time to call in identical twins, Dorian and Gray, whose mother was passionate about the literary works of Oscar Wilde. Though I do most of my own painting, bigger projects call for extra hands. And the best around are those of Dorian and his brother. If they can fit me in, they'll take care of the time-consuming prep work.

A half hour later, Dorian delivers the punch line of a joke that causes my cheeks to burn.

He chuckles. "We'll take care of it, Kate. See ya."

Okay, so how am I going to slip God into the burn unit? I peer at the sketch of the domed room. However, fifteen minutes later, I remain a blank slate while in the kitchen below Michael and Maia remain oblivious to my absence.

I glower. Sure are chummy for two people who aren't inter-ested in each other. And that thought returns me to the secret inscription.

Provided they're still in the kitchen...

I knock my shoes off and pad to the head of the stairs. Determining that the muffled voices are coming from the kitchen, I start down. And all goes well until I place my weight on a step that evidences the house's 120 years. As the creak resounds around me, I freeze. When Maia and Michael's un-interrupted voices assure me my cover isn't blown, I descend the remainder of the stairs and creep into the living room. And there on the sofa table sits Maia's copy of *The Makeup Bible*.

I peer across the room at the doorway that serves as an alternate entrance to the kitchen. It's empty. Guessing the two are at the eat-in counter, I tiptoe around the end of the sofa, retrieve the book, and open to the title page.

To Maia—not that you need any of this. Michael

Not that you need any of this. Unlike Kate...

Monday, March 26

Dear Lord,

Thank You for generous budgets (looks like I'll be able to afford that breast reduction). Thank You for Clive not inviting Adelphia what's-her-name to join us for dinner. Thank You for Home-Baked Breads & Things, Ashigo Asigo Asi—whatever that bread is called—unexpected humor and laughter, first name basis (for as long as it lasted), borrowed jackets with warm, toasty sleeves, and Dorian and Gray.

Forgive me for talking to my chest (I didn't know he was there!), hesitation over public prayer (I'm not ashamed!), and that silly comment about "brownie points in heaven" (didn't mean it). Forgive me for being prideful about my work, poking that insufferable Clive Alexander in the chest, and making assumptions.

Help me with this gnawing jealousy. "To Maia—not that you need any of this"! Meaning Kate does. That HURTS! Not that I'm unaware of my imperfections, but why is Michael pursuing me if he can't be content with me the way I am? And why am I letting him? And why am I making appointments that make me feel guilty? Okay, I know why. But how often does a man who doesn't require biological children come my way? And who's also attractive? And who makes me feel valued (well, when Maia isn't around and my flaws aren't readily apparent). Oh, Lord, am I pathetic or what? I'm shaking my head BTW—see! So help me help me help me. Above all, please continue to watch over the baby.

Yours,

Kate

PS: Be patient with me. I will get back into Your Word soon.

Monday, April 9
Dear Lord,

Well, that wasn't so bad. Thirty minutes and <u>Zip! Zap! Zowie!</u> That pesky little mole is gone. So what do You think? I know You put that "beauty" mark smack-dab on my cheek, but You really don't miss it, do You? I mean, surely its usefulness (whatever that was) had run its course. And it was just the one (of course, still trying to reconcile how half an hour of work translates to almost two hundred dollars—why, that's four hundred dollars an hour!). Though tempted to have the other three moles zapped, I did exercise control. Fortunately, they aren't visible.

So would it be wrong to ask You to speed the healing of my skin? And to ease this incessant itching? I'd really appreciate it.

Thank You for another uneventful week in Belle's pregnancy. Thank You for keeping baby snuggled up where the little one can grow big and strong. Thank You for visible proof that You answer prayers.

I could use some help with the upcoming burn unit—as in staying focused and juggling my schedule. Then there's Michael, who was just a little too thrilled with the removal of my mole, which didn't keep him from adding to my business card collection. As always, help me be patient with Maia and find opportunities to witness. Regarding the bonding on Friday, please let the dentist be worth the eight hundred dollars he's charging to rid me of this gap. (Wonder how much per hour that works out to be!). Hello, savings account...

    Yours,

    Kate

PS: Sorry I missed Sunday school yesterday, but at least I made it to worship. And You do know, don't You, that I'm caught up on tithing? Regarding my time in Your Word, could You help me remember where I left my Bible so I can catch up on it? Sorry...

Friday, April 13

Dear Lord,

    Okay, that was bad. Not horrendous, but bad. Three hours in the dentist's chair, mouth cranked open, cotton stuffed into every saliva-producing crevice, whiny drill "roughening" up my front teeth, nasty gels and bonding materials trickling down my throat, layering, sculpting, curing, and endless polishing. BAD! But what a difference! Surely not even You would deny that my smile has gone from fine to mighty fine. Look at this! Can't believe I never noticed how much that little crack detracted from my appearance. Though I'm still far from model material (ask Michael!), I'm liking me. So I guess he was right...

    Thank You for Dr. Neimer's skill (his chair-side manner could use some work) and for continuing to heal my mole-less cheek. Thank You for Belle's good health, and please let her upcoming ultrasound show that baby's doing well.

    Two weeks until I go in for spider vein removal,

which should pretty much wrap up my major self-improvement issues (excluding the reduction). So one last dip into savings ($350 isn't all that much, is it?).

Yours,

Kate

PS: Can't believe I didn't realize that my Bible was under my pillow (of course, had I time to make my bed, I would have discovered it sooner). Too bad You didn't give us the ability to absorb Your Word simply by pressing it to our heads. Meaning it's time to apply myself. Bible, here I come!

Friday, April 27

Oh. My. Gosh!

Ow! What was I thinking? That so-called doctor turned me into a pin cushion with his lousy saline injections. I sting all over—from my ankles to the tops of my thighs. And the cramping! And for what? True, he said it could take weeks, or even months, to see noticeable results, but surely I ought to see something now. Something besides reddening and bruising. And these support hose! Feels like I'm stuck in a vacuum. No wonder so many little old ladies are grumpy.

The only good is that it's got me sitting—legs elevated. That means maybe I can catch up on my Bible time, which has once more gotten behind.

Ow! Maybe Clive Alexander was right. Why improve on something that works, especially something that 90 percent of the time is covered in jeans! Never again! I don't care if my legs turn into a road map of the United States! I don't care if Michael begs me to do it for him! I am NOT doing it again. No way! There ought to be a

law. Hmm. Wonder what the Geneva convention would
say about this form of torture. Regardless of the fact
it's voluntary, it's inhumane! And Michael's going to
hear about it! (Why do I get this feeling You're less than
sympathetic?)

Thank You for everything, especially Belle and Beau's
baby.

Yours,
Kate

’m obsessed. Or is *vain* the better word?

I sigh, flash another "perfect" smile, and flip up the visor. Though it has been two weeks since the bonding that rid me of my gap and three weeks since the removal of my mole, I still can't get over the new me. And yet sometimes I miss the old me, whose figure was less toned, hair out of control, makeup practically nonexistent, wardrobe comfortably plain, eyes on the dull side, smile a bit quirky, and mole—

No, I don't miss the mole. Nor the spider veins that have started to fade. Pest control is definitely where it's at (within reason—will *not* do sclerotherapy again!).

Fortunately, there's only one thing left to do to perfect Kate, but Michael would disagree considering my collection of business cards and the chapters of *The Makeup Bible* he keeps referring me to. Three months after the burn unit is completed, I'm scheduled for breast reduction. I finally made the consult appointment (in a carefully disguised voice), kept it (slunk into the waiting room wearing dark sunglasses), and endured the humiliation of Dr. Corrigan's exam. An exam that included intense scrutiny from all sides, which made me feel like a very ugly painting.

Then there were the man's murmurings and asides to his nurse, who gave single-syllable responses. Thank goodness the next time I see Dr. Corrigan I'll be heavily sedated and on my way into surgery. It'll be worth it, though. And that brings me back to Clive, who I haven't seen since our disagreement over God.

Hoping—praying—he won't put in an appearance on my first day at the burn unit, I pull into the parking garage, accept the ticket spit out by the machine, and drive up. On the third floor, I groan at the sight of Clive's car in the row reserved for physicians. Great. What are the chances I won't run into him? According to Dorian and Gray, who I've made a point of visiting after hours, Clive has stopped by every other day or so.

Oh, well. If I do run into him, at least I'm looking my best—wearing new hip-hugging jeans rather than the old relaxed-fit (mere coincidence, of course).

Gripped by a need to be certain I'm in top form, I flip the visor down and smile at my reflection. Teeth are perfect.

Returning my attention to the parking garage as a car passes me in the opposite direction, I chance another glance in the mirror.

Hair? Not bad.

Back to the parking garage, where I spot a space ahead. Slowing, I turn into it and, as I ease to a stop, shift my gaze to the mirror for one last look—

Crunch!

I stomp the brake, slam the car into park, and scramble out from behind the steering wheel to confirm what I already know—my left front bumper is crunched.

I glare at the stunted cement pylon that appears none the worse for the hit. The sawed off little—

But not so sawed off that you couldn't have seen it had you been watching where you were going.

I really don't want to hear it.

Ten minutes later, I enter the domed room lugging two bags that contain the various tools of my trade: paints, brushes, thinner, drop cloths, etcetera.

"Thar she blows!" a voice calls, and I spy a man with short spiked hair balanced near the top of a ladder, an arm thrown out in welcome.

Pleased to discover that he and his brother haven't left for the day, I determinedly push the crunched bumper to the back of my mind. "Ahoy, Gray!"

Though he and Dorian finished prepping a week ago, when they said they had nothing in the hopper for the next two weeks, I took it as a godsend. Handing over my drawings and specifications, I put them to work applying textured paint to the designated ocean areas. Time permitting, they'll also lay down the paint for the land forms.

Dorian emerges from the men's room. "Ahoy, new and improved mate!"

Clive Alexander isn't the only one who's given me grief over my attempts at self-improvement, but at least the Oscar Wilde brothers are positive about the changes—changes that have me gawking at my reflection instead of keeping my eyes where they belong!

"Hey, Dorian."

He winks. "What's new?"

Besides a crunched bumper? "Nothing." I lower my bags. "I'm in a holding pattern." No need to let him in on the sclerotherapy.

He halts before me and scans my face and jean-clad figure. "Darn." He shakes his head, causing his long bangs to fall into his eyes. "Gray and I laid bets on your next undertaking."

He makes it sound as if I'm a poster child for plastic surgery—and I haven't even had plastic surgery! Yet.

I shrug a shoulder. "Oh, yeah?"

"He thought *nose*; I thought *lips*."

Trying to ignore the implications, I say, "I see."

He laughs, pats me on the back, then strides toward his brother. "Party time, Gray! Let's wrap it up."

I should let it go. After all, he's only teasing. Or is he? Forgetting the little incident in the parking garage, I mentally shuffle through the business cards and pause on the one belonging to a surgeon who specializes in nose jobs.

Hmm. I run a finger down my nose. It's not that big, is it? At least, it never struck me as being out of proportion. In fact, I consider it one of my better features....

I slide my finger lower and run it across my lips. The last time Michael and I kissed, he did say I should consider "plumping."

I eye the brothers, who are gathering up their tools and, before I can reconsider, cross to them. "Gray?"

The brother with the spiked hair turns to me. "Hmm?"

I touch my nose. "Do you really think it's too big?"

No sooner do I speak than I'm certain he's going to laugh. But instead he straightens and leans near. "Well..." He leans a little left, a little right. "It's..." His lips twitch. "Perfect." With that, he pops a kiss on my nose.

As I lurch back, Dorian chuckles. "Yeah, but you gotta admit, her lips could be fuller."

I return my gaze to Gray, just as he draws near again and focuses on my mouth, with greater intensity than when I landed a kiss on my nose.

I slap a hand to his chest. "Oh, no, you don't."

He groans. "Come on, Kate. When you gonna let me take you out?"

Another admirer. Amazing what a bit of self-improvement can do for one's love life (and self-esteem). Prior to my makeover, Gray wasn't the least bit interested in me. Now every time I see him, he asks me out. But I have Michael, who despite our decreasing time together, recently swore off dating other women.

"It's all you, Kate," he'd said. Of course, the moment Maia walked in, it was all her.

As it seems I've done a hundred times, I push aside my misgivings. "Sorry, Gray, but I'm spoken for."

He sweeps up my hand and cocks his head. "Little lady," he affects a voice that aspires to the timbre of John Wayne, "that's a mighty small ring you got there." He squints. "Can hardly see it. Nope. Can't see it at all."

I tug my hand free. "Not spoken for in that way."

"Ah." He wiggles his eyebrows. "Then say yes."

"No."

He sighs. "All right, I know when I'm not wanted."

"Leave poor Kate alone," Dorian chides.

I look to where he's on his hands and knees folding a drop cloth. He winks.

Gray turns away and glances over his shoulder. "Nice jeans, Kate."

And I blush. "Er…thanks." Now let's just hope I don't regret forgoing my relaxed-fit jeans. As much as I like the fit, feel, and look of my hip-huggers, it's asking a lot to expect them to come away from the job unscathed. Whatever possessed me?

Vanity. You know, that which crunched your bumper. That which has you questioning your nose and lips. The possibility that Clive Alexander might drop by—

With a grunt, I cross to my bags and begin unpacking.

Shortly, the brothers head across the domed room toward the winding hallway.

"Hey!" I call from alongside the scaffold. "Great job, guys."

"Thanks," they say in unison, and I'm relieved when Gray grins. No hard feelings, then.

Dorian waves. "Maybe see you tomorrow."

"Hope so." I start to walk away only to yield to the question pecking at the fore of my mind. "Uh, guys?"

They look around.

"Has he come and gone?"

"You mean him?" Gray nods to where Clive has appeared at the mouth of the winding hallway.

I force a smile. "Yeah." Ha ha. "Him."

Gray faces forward again. "Hiya, Doc."

Clive inclines his head. "Gray…Dorian."

A few moments later, I'm alone with the very person I wished to avoid.

"Avoiding me, huh?" he says as he crosses the domed room.

Why dance around our disagreement? "Can you blame me?"

"No, though I was beginning to wonder if you planned on subcontracting the entire job."

I prop a hand on a hip. "You knew I couldn't begin work immediately."

"I did." His eyes stray to my hip-huggers.

And I'm so glad I'm not wearing relaxed-fit, full-seated—

Not that I care what he thinks. I just…well…

I clear my throat. "Considering the time constraints, I determined the only way to bring the job in on time without stressing myself into an early grave was to hire out the prep work."

A frown speed bumps across his brow as he halts before me. "Understandable."

Then why is he frowning so hard? "G-good." Confusion is

to blame for the speech blip, not his proximity. I avert my gaze. "As for the ocean Dorian and Gray are painting—"

"So you went through with it."

I return my attention to Clive and realize he's staring at my open mouth.

Ah. Noticed my latest adventures in self-improvement, both of which he advised against. I snap my teeth closed. "What?"

"The gap between your teeth—and the mole." He reaches up and lightly touches the flesh where a mole once held court. "Gone."

I pull back from his touch. "I decided I could do without both."

"Hmm. So what does Mr. Palmier have planned for you next? Derriere implants? Rhinoplasty?"

Another reference to the size of my nose!

"Botox? Liposuction?" He shakes his head. "You know what you need, Kate? A man who likes you just the way you are."

"Is that so? And are you applying for the position, Dr. Alexander?"

Oh…my…goodness. Did I say that?

His gaze dampens. "You wouldn't like me."

"I imagine not." However, in the next instant I acknowledge my words for the lie they are. I do like him. Against my will and despite our run-in over God, I like Clive Alexander.

Desperate to change the conversation, I say, "Though it's true that Michael has offered suggestions on improving my appearance, whatever I've done I wanted to do." I have, haven't I? I'm certainly pleased with the results.

Too pleased. Remember the bumper?

I press my shoulders back. "And anything else I have done will be my decision alone."

"Surely you're not planning to—"

"Dr. Alexander, please don't preach at me—you who have nothing that needs improving upon."

He opens his mouth only to close it. Silence stretches until an "almost" smile grooves his mouth. "I'll take that as a compliment."

It *was* a compliment, wasn't it?

A long moment passes. "I'm sorry, Kate. I didn't mean to turn this into another confrontation. In fact, I came to apologize for the last one."

He did?

"I…" He shrugs. "The exchange with your boyfriend…then the call from Dr. MacPhail…"

Clive Alexander at a loss for words?

"Not that it excuses my behavior." He sighs. "I handled our difference of opinion poorly. I apologize."

Then he's changed his mind about allowing me to incorporate God into my work? I start to smile.

"However, I still maintain there are to be no religious symbols."

Heathen. Infidel. Pagan.

In an effort to hold back retaliatory words, I tell myself to accept his olive branch—in all its thorny glory. "Apology accepted." Deep breath. "Now I really must get started."

His hand closes over my arm. "Kate."

No sooner do I settle my gaze on his long fingers than he releases me and both hands take a running leap into the pockets of his physician's coat.

He clears his throat. "I don't expect you to understand. All I ask is that you let the matter lie."

"Excuse me?" I shake my head. "You're the one who broached the subject of our disagreement."

So he might apologize. And it was you, Katherine Mae

Meadows, who assumed his apology meant he'd relented.

As regret washes over me, I once more witness the jaw action that evidences his struggle. In the end, he gives an abrupt nod and turns away. "I'll let you get to work."

I stare after him, struck by a longing to offer an apology but unable to form anything coherent. And pride is the stumbling block. I know it as surely as I know I've messed up Clive's attempt at reconciliation.

Before the entrance to the hallway, he looks over his shoulder. "Though I can't say I approve of the manner of your latest attempts at self-improvement, you do look very nice, Kate."

I do? Then he likes my face better without the mole? My smile better without the gap? My hip-huggers—

Aargh!

I put my chin up. "And just who asked for your approval?" Of course, no sooner are the words out than I'm clenching my hands to keep from clapping them over my mouth. That was another olive branch, wasn't it?

"Touché." With a wry smile, he strides from sight.

A moment later, I'm dealt another dose of French, as in déjà vu, as this is pretty much how our last disagreement ended—censure of my religious convictions and disapproval of my attempts to better myself.

I sigh. Though I like Clive despite our head butting, and for some reason he seems to like me, it's a good thing neither of us is romantically interested in the other. A very good thing—or so I tell myself. Over. And over.

Monday, April 30
Dear Lord,
*　　Thank You for pest control (spider veins continuing to fade). Thank You for an ungapped smile. Thank You*

for Dorian and Gray. Thank You for Clive's compliments, grudging though they were (tells me not to improve on what works, yet sees my improvements as positive!).

Help me be content with me (wish Michael would find another use for all those business cards and stop referring me to <u>The Makeup Bible</u>). Help me not to succumb to vanity and any more crunched bumpers. Help me finish off this run at self-improvement with the reduction. Help me stop obsessing over my nose and lips (that Dorian and Gray!). As always, help me guard my tongue and not fall prey to name-calling, even in my thoughts (sorry about the heathen/infidel/pagan thoughts against Clive). Please continue to nourish and protect Belle and Beau's baby. They are so excited about this incredible blessing!

Yours,
Kate

PS: Sorry I missed church yesterday, but I am catching up on my Bible time! Sort of… And sorry I haven't been a better steward of my money. Still can't think what possessed me to wear my hip-huggers when I KNEW they would end up splattered. Oh well, at least now I have some "look good" painter's pants.

PPS: Having a bit of trouble with migraines again—nothing full-blown, but on the edge. Please help me overcome so my HRT won't have to be tweaked again.

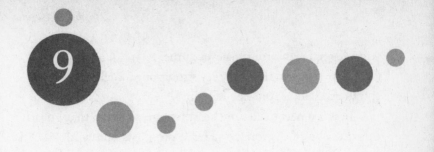

9

"Feel it?"

"Umm?"

"There! Feel it now?"

"I…think…?"

Belle claps a hand over mine. "Come on, Kate. You can press harder."

I feel it then, an undulating movement that makes my heart go bippity-bop. "Ooh," I croon, heedless of the other churchgoers' reactions to the feel-the-baby-move ritual. "I feel it!"

When I look up, Belle's beaming, and the worry that's dimmed her eyes these past months is all but gone. Belle, Beau, and baby are past the critical mark. Not that something couldn't go wrong over the next two months, but they're out of the darkest part of the woods. God willing, Belle will soon be a mommy.

The little one shifts beneath my palm again, then gives a series of kicks that evokes images of a toddler tantrum. "I *really* felt that!"

A passing teenager, badly in need of a belt to hold up his

wide-legged jeans, rolls his eyes at me.

"Yep, our bundle of joy's a strong one." Belle gives a conspiratorial wink. "And he's healthy."

That last part makes my heart twinge, so much that I nearly miss her slip of the tongue. "He?" I prop fists on my hips. "Did you peek?"

She gives an un-Belle-like bob of her head. "I know we said we wanted it to be a surprise, but when we went in for this last ultrasound, the doctor dangled the secret in front of us." She curves an arm over her bulge. "It just didn't seem right that he knew and we didn't. Besides, I was tired of calling our baby 'it.'"

I grin. "Don't think I'd be able to resist either." Of course, the moment the words are out, I feign a sudden interest in the tips of my shoes.

Belle understands, as evidenced by her silence.

Determined not to dampen her joy, I retrieve my grin, lean over her bulge, and kiss her cheek. "I'm happy for you and Beau."

As I draw back, I hear her swallow. "I know you are."

More silence, which could be remedied by joining those entering the sanctuary; however, we're waiting on Beau and Michael, who dropped us at the entrance to save us the walk from the parking lot.

I touch the blue and silver bracelet Belle gave me all those years ago, finger my way to the silver cross, then to the *Believe* medallion.

I do.

Unfortunately, I'll have to believe more deeply if I'm to vanquish all traces of ache.

"How's the burn unit progressing?"

I make a face. "Slow—afraid I miscalculated the enormity

Perfecting Kate 155

of the project. If not for Dorian and Gray, I'd be in deep doo-
doo."

"How much longer before they jump ship?"

"A week, then it's all me."

"And your next project begins…?"

The dreaded overlap. "Three weeks, at which time the burn
unit will be relegated to evening work." Of course, it already
is—day *and* evening, which makes for twelve- and fourteen-
hour workdays. "Can't complain, though, especially as I haven't
had any more run-ins with Clive Alexander." Other than a few
brief sightings, he's remained conspicuously absent.

Belle gives a sympathetic nod, having lent an ear to my rant
over his ban on religious symbols. "Perhaps it's too painful for
him."

Of course, she also lent an ear to the revelation about his
wedding ring.

"Perhaps."

Belle sighs. "You'll be able to bring in the job on time, won't
you?"

"Yeah, though it's likely to mean a bad case of sleep depri-
vation."

Belle's face turns serious. "You have to take care of yourself,
Kate."

"Of course."

"I'm keeping an eye on you."

I shudder. "Scary." And my attempt at lightening the conversation earns me a punch in the arm. "Ow. For a pregnant
lady, you really pack a punch."

"And don't you forget it."

As I rub the sore spot, Belle peers past me. "What's taking
them so long?"

"Probably guy talk."

She smiles. "They seem to have hit it off."

"Yeah." This is only Belle and Beau's second exposure to Michael—the first occurring on a recent double date—but the two men interact as if they've known each other for years.

"Though I don't have much to go on," Belle says, "I like him."

"Hmm?" I bring her back to focus. "Oh, Michael. Yeah. I like him, too."

"But?"

I blink. "Did you hear a *but* in my voice?"

"Big *but*. C'mon, give over."

"Well…" I grope to explain away my big *but*. "I suppose it's—"

"Shoot! They're here—my Beau, your Michael."

My Michael. Wishing "my Michael" sounded right, I look over my shoulder and, from among the churchgoers, pick out Michael and Beau.

"This conversation is on hold, Kate. No hanging up, hmm?"

She knows me well. And I'm grateful, as I could use a sounding board. "No hanging up."

She raises an arm to wave the men toward us only to falter. "Well, howdy-do. It appears that Beau and Michael have hooked themselves a fish called Maia."

"What?" I swing around and, sure enough, alongside Michael saunters my housemate.

What's she doing here? True, I invited her as I do *every* Sunday, but she turned me down as she does *every* Sunday. When last I saw her, she was at the window wearing a robe as Michael and I stepped into Belle and Beau's car. Before heading to church we stopped for coffee, but it couldn't have been more than forty minutes since we left the house. And yet Maia's coiffed, made up, and decked out in a red suit dress.

Red.

Belle nudges me. "Maybe you finally reached her."

I would rejoice were it true. Unfortunately, I suspect Michael is responsible for her setting foot on holy ground. And that makes me stand taller and press my shoulders back despite the shift in weight that causes my back to ache all the more.

A moment later, Beau, Michael, and Maia halt before us.

Michael smiles and nods at Maia, who's standing closer to him than ought to feel comfortable. "Look who we ran into in the parking lot."

"Belle," Maia acknowledges my best friend before swinging her gaze to me. "Kate."

Strangely out of breath, I say, "I didn't expect to see you here. I'm glad you decided to come." That wasn't a lie, was it? I really *am* glad she came.

Maia glances at Michael. "I changed my mind."

Might that have been when Michael appeared on the door-step? As I struggle with resentment, Maia continues, "Though I was resigned to another boring Sunday, when you left I was struck by a need to be among friends."

What? Couldn't call your married *boyfriend?*

No sooner does the vicious thought slip in than I remind myself that it's been weeks since I saw her actively engaged in home wrecking. No late-night comings and goings.

Maia rolls an elegant, red-clad shoulder. "So I thought, what the heck, give Kate's church a try. After all, if Michael thinks it's worth looking into—" she glances at him from beneath her lashes—"maybe I should."

Who do you think you're kidding! Sure, Michael and I aren't married, but we're dating. You—

In an attempt to calm down, I excuse Maia's behavior with the reminder that her interest in Michael is a step in the right direction. A definite improvement over her pursuit of a man who made a lifelong commitment to another woman. But then she winks, and before she speaks, I know my struggle to remain Christlike is doomed.

"And who knows," she drawls, "maybe the experience will make a saint out of a sinner."

Ha! If this were a Catholic church, I'd dump holy water on you. Sssssssss!

Beau steps forward. "Uh, shall we?"

Noting his furrowed brow, I wonder if he picked up on my tension; however, a reality check tells me it's more likely that it's his pew he's worried about. Sure enough, as we move toward the sanctuary, he leans toward Belle. "Why didn't you and Kate secure our seats?"

"The baby moved, honey."

His irritation dissolves. "Oh."

Amid the buzz of churchgoers who greet one another as if it's been longer than a week since they last met, Maia and I sandwich Michael between us as we walk the aisle behind Beau, Belle, and baby. Shortly, we claim a pew two rows back from Beau's regular spot.

Lowering beside Belle, I note that Beau seems only slightly ruffled. Of course, he is preoccupied with his child.

As his fingers span the compact ball, Belle leans near me. "Why do I get the feeling that Maia Glock is one of your big *buts*?"

It's a moment before I tune in, and when I do I'm grateful for the preservice din, which drowns my snort. Big *buts*. Not big *butts*.

Whew! Kind of funny.

Or is it? I glance around and discover that Michael and Maia are chatting.

My hand he's holding. I stare at my lap where our fingers are entwined. *Mine.*

But *his* attention *she's* holding.

Must be the red outfit. Can't *stand* red.

"Yeah." I nod. "She's definitely a *but*."

"Turning over a new leaf, hmm? Stealing them away before the ring's in place." Belle sighs. "Still, I suppose that's progress."

Is she stealing him away? *Is* my jealousy founded? If so, what should I do? Or am I supposed to do anything? Though I've enjoyed the attention Michael lavishes on me—business cards notwithstanding—and his stance on perpetuating the human race makes him a fine catch, perhaps I ought to take the hook out of his mouth and throw him back.

I consider our joined hands and remember all the Sundays when the only hand I've had to hold has been my own. Despite Michael's criticism and pursuit of my perfection, it really has been nice not to be lonely. No, he may not be "The One," but isn't *something* better than all the nothing I've had?

Shortly, we rise to join in hand-raising songs of praise. By the time the worship leader gives us leave to take our seats, my fingers are no longer entwined with Michael's.

As the mustached Brother Leo approaches the pulpit, out of my peripheral vision I see Michael lean near Maia and whisper something. And my jealousy cranks it up a notch. While I struggle with what I try to convince myself is an uncalled-for emotion, our pastor extends a welcome. Then he jumps into today's sermon with, "Fidelity!"

It flashes *huge* on the screens, and I almost choke. Clearing my throat, I glance at Maia, who resembles a taxidermist's prize work, stuffed and mounted.

"Are you struggling to overcome temptation?" Brother Leo sweeps his gaze around. "Contemplating an affair?"

Are you listening, Maia?

"Or have you already lost the battle? Sinned? Betrayed your spouse and children—or perhaps another's spouse and children?"

Dare I gauge Maia's reaction? I go back and forth until Beau overcomes whatever compunction he has and leans forward to see past Michael. And in that moment, my conscience slaps me across the face. I'm gloating. True, Maia needs to know what God says about fidelity, but probably not the first time she sets foot in a church.

Poor timing. And despite my recent bout with jealousy, I feel sorry for her.

"Think!" Brother Leo expounds. "Think of the untold pain you've caused or will cause if you don't turn from this sin."

Looking main floor to balcony, he allows silence to settle, and in the mounting tension, I glance at Maia's pale countenance. She's going to walk out and never return.

"Let's see what God tells us." Brother Leo slides his glasses on. "Open your Bibles to…"

Ears falling deaf, eyes blind to the book and verse that appear on the screens, I grip my Bible. What should I do when Maia walks out? However, she remains until the service ends. Then, like a jack-in-the-box, she's on her feet and heading for the doors. With a word to Belle, I hasten after my housemate as she attempts to make it to the parking lot ahead of the others.

"Maia!"

Though I know she hears me, she uses her long legs to draw farther away. Still, if not for the hand that pulls me back, I could have caught up with her.

I look around into Michael's face.

He shifts his gaze to Maia's receding figure. "Must have hit home pretty hard."

"You know?"

"Yeah."

He says it with such regret that there's no doubt he wishes Maia didn't have the past she does. That she—

I throw my thoughts in reverse. *Past*, I tell myself and am so tempted to reassure Michael that Maia appears to have put her home wrecking behind her—at least temporarily. But that might leave me sans boyfriend...

So I say nothing while inside I war over feelings for him that are more brotherly than loverly, motives that hinge more on his indifference to having children than on a desire to actually spend my life with him, and instincts that warn I'm wasting his time *and* mine.

"Belle and Beau are waiting." He drops an arm across my shoulders. "Let's grab a bite to eat."

"Though Maia is certainly a big *but*, and this mutual attraction you think they share is another big *but*—" Belle folds her hands atop the table and leans as far forward as her tummy allows—"I'd wager the biggest *but* is yours."

I lower my glass of Perrier and turn my attention to the half-eaten Chicken Santa Fe, which appears far less appetizing than it did a half hour ago.

"Talk to me, Kate."

I poke at a glob of congealed cheese with a fork tine and transform it into an un-smiley face. "You're right." I drop back against the padded seat. "The biggest *but* is me." I glance to the strip of floor between restaurant and bar, where Michael and Beau watch the sports coverage of something to do with a ball—one of those small ones that fits into the hand and get the stitches knocked out of it. Just kidding. I know it's a baseball.

"I like Michael." I scan his handsome profile.

"Uh-huh?"

"But something's missing. You know—that feeling."

"Like you had with Christopher."

I could have gone all year without hearing his name. "Yeah."

Belle covers my hand with hers. "You know, not all relationships start with a bang—take me and Beau. We didn't *fall* in love. We *grew* in love."

And I watched the whole thing from the sidelines, impatient for them to progress through the stages that ultimately led them down the aisle. Not surprisingly, Belle refused to be hurried with something as important as with whom she'd spend the rest of her life and have children. Though she had been a good friend to Beau, listening and pointing him to Scripture, that had been the extent of their relationship for two long years. Not until Beau worked through the issues that had led him to an alternate lifestyle and accepted Christ as his Savior did Belle extend the slightest encouragement. Too bad we can't all be as patient and committed as she.

I look at her. "Even at the get-go, didn't you feel something when Beau kissed you? A queasy little flutter?" I press a hand to my stomach. "And when you were apart, didn't you ache? I mean, there you'd be minding your own business and he'd pop into your thoughts and distract you from whatever you were doing?"

Her eyes birth stars and a slow smile curves her mouth.

"That's what I want to feel, Belle. But I don't."

She blinks away the stars and squeezes my hand. "Because you won't let yourself?"

I shrug. "I suppose that's part of it."

"Have you told him?"

"No. Besides the fact that we're only dating, the first time we went out he told me he doesn't require children. Of course, that could change."

"And so you're holding out for fear of rejection, not allowing yourself to feel for him."

As I've done dozens of times, I examine the possibility from all sides, but no matter how honest I am, the answer doesn't change despite the jealous sprite that pops up when Michael and Maia are in close proximity. My feelings for Michael—suppressed or otherwise—are shallow.

I heave a sigh. "Even if I told him and he didn't pull back, I don't believe it would change my feelings for him."

"So you could never love him?"

I consider Michael, admire his strong jaw, broad shoulders, and nicely shaped head. He's attractive, but I'm not attracted to him in the way he and Maia appear to be attracted to one another. "I can see us being friends."

Belle's shoulders slump. "Then why are you dating him?"

"Outside of the fact he's one in a hundred who doesn't require biological children?"

She winces.

"It's nice to be pursued, Belle. Nice to have someone pay attention to me who doesn't slink off the minute he realizes dinner and a movie won't earn him a round-trip ticket to my bedroom. And so I keep asking myself whether it would hurt to settle for friendship in marriage. As I don't want to spend the rest of my life alone, why not spend it with a friend?"

She groans. "As much as I'd like to see you in a good relationship—and Michael seems a peach—I don't think you'd fool him for long."

"Just as he hasn't fooled me regarding Maia."

"You really think there's something between them?"

"I'm afraid his interest in me is all white-picket-fence fantasy."

"So neither of you is being honest." She gives a *tut-tut*. "Well, there you have it. Sounds like it's time to break it off and see if you can salvage a friendship."

Though I know she's right, I recoil. "He's the closest I've come."

Lame. Very lame.

"I've said it before, Kate—a man who does not want-slash-need children should not be your first requirement."

"And as I've said before, better to know up front what a man expects from a potential spouse than waste time and emotion on someone whose heart is set on something I can't give."

Frustration ripples across her brow. "There's always adoption."

Exactly what I presented to Christopher on his way out of my life, but Belle wouldn't know, as I never told her of my last desperate attempt to hold on to him. He'd wanted a little "Jr." who was truly a Jr., not some unknown child with an unknown pedigree. A papered Christopher Stapleton the Third.

Pain darts behind my eyes, and I catch my breath.

"Are you all right, Kate?"

I squeeze my eyes closed.

"Migraine?"

"Trying to be. Might have to adjust my HRT."

She sighs. "You really ought to look into the patch."

She's right. The patch's steady release of hormones is said to be effective against migraines, but its presence would mean advertising my problem to the world.

I creak my lids open. "If it gets bad, maybe I'll give it a try."

"Just don't let it get too bad."

"I won't."

"Back to your future husband. If someone truly loves you with the kind of love capable of weathering the storms inevitable in marriage, your inability to give him biological children won't matter."

Meaning Christopher's love wasn't that kind of love. I know...

When Belle's face wavers, I realize my eyes have misted.

She squeezes my hand. "Trust in the Lord, Kate—in His will for you—and He'll provide." As if to attest to her own answered prayers, she curves her free hand atop her bulge.

I draw a deep breath. "So what should I do about Michael?"

"Let him go so he can pursue Maia, if that's what he wants."

"Just hand him over?"

Belle does a double take. "You don't hand over old boyfriends, Kate. He's not secondhand clothing."

I smile. "I suppose not. Still, they like each other and—"

"No matchmaking. Back out of the relationship, and let happen what may."

"But—"

"If they think you're stepping aside in order to throw them together, they'll feel manipulated."

Like Michael felt when I first attempted to steer him toward Maia.

"But without my blessing—"

"Kate!"

"—they may feel they're betraying me."

She pins me with wide-open eyes. "Just get out of the way, and let nature do its thing."

My shoulders slump. "Okay."

But there's no "okay" about it, I realize as I catch Michael's eye then his smile. Despite those business cards of his, I like him. If only I could love him…

"Can we talk, Maia?"

Silence.

"Helloooo?"

Silence.

"Come on. I know you're in there."

"Yeah." Maia's voice drifts through her bedroom door. "So?"

I press my face nearer the doorjamb. "Can I come in?"

"No."

I know I'm overstepping, but I try the knob—locked. "Okay, we'll talk through the door."

"I'd prefer not."

"Then open the door."

"No."

"Maia, I'm sorry about church. Well…not *sorry* sorry, but sorry. I didn't know Brother Leo was preaching on *that*. Not that I shouldn't have. I mean, he does post upcoming sermons, but I don't pay much attention to them. Anyway, I understand how uncomfortable you must have felt."

"I doubt that, Miss Goody Two-shoes."

I rattle the knob, and to my surprise, the door creaks inward. Aha. I push it wider and meet Maia's gaping gaze, where she sits hugging her knees in a corner of the bay window. Still wearing red…

I smile and give a little shrug. "Guess the latch didn't catch."

She scowls. "I want to be alone."

"I'd really like to talk."

"About?"

I venture a step inside her room. Wow. Though I've always imagined her bedroom resembling a harem, with floaty-floaty things hung from a canopied bed, plump cushions strewn about the floor, and candles set around, I was way off. Soft elegance is more the tone.

"What is so important that you have to invade my privacy, Kate?"

"I feel bad about what happened. I mean—"

"Spit it out."

Why didn't I lie low for a while? "As I was saying before you let me in—"

"I didn't let you in."

"Well, before the door opened."

"With a little help from Kate."

"Anyway—" I say through gritted teeth—"I just want you to know that I feel bad."

"About?"

I don't know what comes over me—actually, I do—but before I can zip my lips, I snap, "Oh, grow up!"

Her jaw drops.

Where is a roll of all-purpose duct tape when you need one?

I cross to the bay window and plop down in the corner opposite Maia.

She draws a shaky breath. "I can't…believe…you said…that."

"I'm sorry. It was very un-Christian of me—"

"Hypocrites, all of you! Judging others, counting yourselves better than those who don't believe that silly little Bible of yours."

Silly? Hardly. Little? Compared to what?

Maia shakes her head. "I'll bet half the married men at your church are unfaithful to their wives. And the other half? Give them time."

Obviously, Brother Leo lit a fuse that could detonate what's beneath if I'm not careful. Ignoring the coward that urges me to tiptoe out of here, I send up a prayer for God to give me the right words.

"You're right, Maia." I slip my feet out of my sandals and cross my legs. "Christians can be hypocrites." Just like everyone else.

Though she glowers at me over the tops of her knees, something flickers in her eyes.

"However, most of us try to be better, more Christlike. Yes, we stumble, but we drag ourselves up, dust off our backsides, and try again. Over and over."

A frown creases her brow, and I pause, hopeful she'll say something to confirm that my words aren't going in one ear and being spit out the other. When she doesn't, I reach across the window seat and lay a hand on her knee. "Christians are still human. Still sinners." Which is what Belle once told this sinner.

"So why bother with all this Christianity junk if it doesn't make a difference?"

"But it does make a difference," I exclaim a bit too passionately. "Er…what I'm saying is that though the acceptance of Christ doesn't make us perfect, being saved changes us."

"Saved from what?"

Hell. No, let's see if I can put it in a more positive light. "Saved *for* eternal life."

"As opposed to eternal hell."

"Uh…yeah."

Maia considers me. "I believe that religion is merely a means of controlling the masses."

Okay, so evangelism is not my strength. I draw my hand back. "Religion, perhaps, but not Christianity."

"Whatever."

I roll my shoulders to ease the tension. "If you're as unaffected by Christianity as you'd like me to believe, why did you attend church today?" Yes, I'm pretty sure Michael was the motive, but what if there was something else? Something she may not be aware of? "I mean, why today and not the other times I've invited you?"

She stares, and I could just shake her.

"Isn't there something in here—" I lay a hand to my heart— "that wants to know a greater purpose in life? To be loved?"

Her bottom lip quivers.

Ooh. Maybe we're getting somewhere. "To be forgiven?"

Her eyes pool.

Yes! "To be free of the burden of guilt?"

She gulps.

On a roll. "To be—"

"Oh, Kate!" She comes across the window seat so fast that the top of her head clips my chin, causing the back of my head to strike the window.

Yeow!

With a shudder, she wraps her arms around me and presses her face to my shoulder. "I felt dirty! And I don't want to feel like that. I mean, if a woman can't hold on to her man, is it my fault? Why do I have to be the bad guy? It's not as if I'm the one who's married." She shakes her head. "Besides, if it wasn't me, it would be someone else."

I raise a hand, awkwardly lay it on her head, and give a little pat.

As if realizing that she's laid herself bare, Maia stiffens;

however, she doesn't retreat. Some moments later, she murmurs, "I thought I was going to die sitting there next to Michael, condemnation oozing out all around him."

"Condemnation? What are you talking about?"

She pulls back and stares at me out of mascara-smudged eyes.

Wow. Who would have thought that Maia Glock was a candidate for tear-proof mascara?

"He knows, doesn't he? You told him!"

Ah. "About your…"

"Affair. Go ahead, say it."

"No, Maia. I didn't tell him."

Though I expect relief, disappointment settles on her face. "Oh." A moment later, her disappointment transforms into such confusion that her brow folds up like an accordion. "But I thought that was why he…"

"Why he doesn't show an interest in you?" I sigh. "Rather, why he *tries* not to show an interest?"

She settles back on her heels. "What are you saying?"

"Michael fights it, but he's as attracted to you, as you are to him."

One moment her mouth is softening; the next, it's tight-lipped. "Who says I'm attracted to him?" She shoves back into her corner. "He's your boyfriend. Though I know I'm not the most moral person, I would never—"

"It's okay, Maia. I—"

"It's not okay! You think I'm after Michael, don't you?"

"No, I don't." Well, maybe I do… "It's just that—"

"You really have a low opinion of me."

"Maia…"

"Thanks a lot! Miss Goody Two-shoes versus the devil with the blue dress."

Red dress. *Red* dress.

"Maia—"

She jabs a finger in the direction of the door. "Out!"

With my teeth, I pin down my tongue. With my throat muscles, close down my vocal cords.

But she just has to jab the air again. "I said out!"

"Look! Do you or don't you want Michael?"

Oh…no.

After a stunned moment, Maia drops her feet to the floor and rises. "Get. Out."

Belle is not going to be happy. But I'm not matchmaking. I'm stating a fact, one Maia would discover eventually. And it would hardly be neighborly not to inform her of my pending boyfriend-less status.

I stand. "I'm breaking it off with Michael."

Her lids narrow. "What's wrong with him?"

"Nothing. It's just that we're not…compatible."

"Out!"

You blew it, Kate. Really blew it…

Sunday, May 6
Dear Lord,

  What was I thinking? What happened to guarding my tongue? WHAT IS MY PROBLEM?!!! Lord, please help me to take my Bible to heart, to apply Psalm 19:14 every time I open my mouth—that my words will be pleasing and acceptable to You. Big order, but I could really use some help down here.

  As for my love life, if You're not going to help out, I really will have to swear off men—ONCE AND FOR ALL. So I'm asking You to somehow…someday…somewhere bring me someone with whom I can spend the rest of my

life. Though You're always with me, I'd really appreciate
a loving earthly relationship. A man who not only
loves me more than the idea of a biological child, but
who loves me just the way I am. Speaking of which, in
looking through past journal entries, I see that I asked
You to keep the business cards coming. You do know that I
meant those related to my business and not my looks? Of
course, You do.

    Apologetically yours,
    Kate

PS: And now for a little time in Your Word! Could You
help me keep my eyes open?

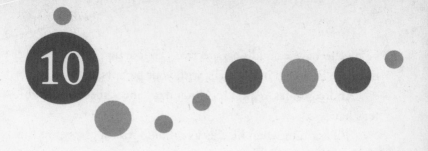

10

’ll tell Michael. Really. Tonight when he takes me out for another late dinner. Or maybe when he picks me up. Wouldn't want him shelling out money under false pretenses. Not that we couldn't go dutch.

Regardless, it's got to be done. Unfortunately, that's what I've told myself every day this week, and now it's Friday, which marks the passing of five days since Maia last spoke to me.

"Miss Kate?"

With a startle, I find myself standing alongside Jessica's hospital bed. "Hmm?" I smile at the little girl who has returned for more surgery—this time on her arm.

"It's great." She pats the portfolio that contains renderings of the burn unit.

As I stare at her, I marvel at Dr. Clive Alexander's God-given skill—deny it though he may—which has gone a long way toward restoring her face.

"I'm glad you like it."

"Oh, yes! Maybe tomorrow I can come see it for myself."

Saturday. Perfect, as I'd planned on working, and it would

be nice to have a child's perspective. "I'd like that." I turn to her mother. "Provided it's all right with your parents."

Andrea smiles. "And Dr. Alexander." She ruffles her daughter's hair.

"I'll ask him when he checks on me." Jessica glances at the clock. "He should be here soon."

And that's my cue to shove off. But first… "Can I pray for you, Jessica?" It's not something I do often due to my own awkwardness—much easier to tell someone I'll pray for them and tag the prayer to the end of my bedtime prayers—but it seems a natural thing to do.

"Oh yes, please." Jessica clasps her hands in readiness.

I bow my head. "Lord, I praise You for all the blessings You've given Jessica. I thank You for Your healing and the skill You've provided Dr. Alexander to do Your will. Lord—"

I lose my place at the sound of the door opening and feel that terrible, unwelcome discomfort at being caught doing something I should not be ashamed of. And I'm not!

In a loud, clear voice, I finish, "Lastly, I ask that You place Your angels around Jessica and guide Dr. Alexander's hands during the surgery." And if he's offended, too bad. "Amen."

"Amen," Andrea and Jessica say with gusto.

Ready or not…

"Dr. Alexander!" Jessica exclaims.

Do I have a sense for this guy or what? Steeling myself for disapproval, I look over my shoulder at where he stands just inside the room. He smiles at Jessica propped against the pillows, but the turn of his mouth doesn't reach his eyes.

He steps forward. "I apologize for the interruption."

"You didn't interrupt. Miss Kate was just praying for me—and you!"

"So I heard." As he nears, I raise my chin to receive his

regard; however, he steps past. No skin off my nose. Of course, according to Gray, I *could* use a little skin off my nose—

I have got to stop worrying about my looks!

"Jessica, I'll stop by tomorrow and, if you're feeling up to it, give you a tour of the domed room."

She turns her smile from Clive to me. "Yes, please."

I swing away.

"Ms. Meadows?"

I halt. "Dr. Alexander?"

His eyes travel down me, making me aware of my state of dress—loose green T-shirt and paint-streaked overalls.

If only my hip-huggers hadn't needed laundering.

"I'd like to speak with you."

Probably wants to ban me from including him in prayer. "I…"

"I won't be but a few minutes."

"All right." I point to the door. "I'll be in the hall."

A few minutes become five…then ten. Not that I begrudge Jessica her doctor's attention, but one really must marvel at doctors' sense of timing, which differs so significantly from those who wait upon them. Every minute that passes, the tighter my nerves draw. And as for the time that could be better spent painting—

Hmm. It's not as if he doesn't know where to find me.

I push aside the plastic sheet and enter the winding hallway. Imagining the transformation to come—mountains, lakes, meadows—I smile. Of course, it's still a ways off.

"Lord"—I blow a breath up my face—"help me make this deadline."

On the threshold of the domed room, I halt. Now this is progress. I look around and imagine the reaction of children to the smiling faces that welcome them. Dare I be so bold as to think *accepted, eager, comforted?*

That last thought draws my eyes to the kneeling boy and girl I completed last night. They face each other, heads bowed—

er, bent…

Hands clasped—

er, reaching…as they pray, er, contemplate.

And what, pray tell, are they contemplating?

Strategically placed wildflowers on which butterflies have lit. Quite clever, if I might again be so bold. So, too, are the crosses I slipped in. Though you have to search for them, they're in the spaces between the children, the folds of their clothing, the rivers that *cross* landforms, the waves upon the ocean…

I sigh, relieved that, thus far, I've received no censure. Of course, Clive can hardly object to what he doesn't know. And the longer he avoids the burn unit, the more I'll be able to work in the symbols of hope so badly needed by the children who will fill this empty space. By the time the good doctor notices—*if* he notices—the work will be too far along.

At the point of becoming dangerously smug, I realize my mistake in allowing impatience to cause him to seek me here. If he looks too close…if he discovers I've gone against his wishes—

I swing around and retrace my steps. Halfway down the hall, I hear the rustle of the plastic sheet that lies beyond the next two curves.

I wring my hands, turn back toward the domed room, wring my hands again, and glance over my shoulder as footsteps echo around the corner ahead.

Don't just stand there! Intercept!

Doing an about-face, I manage two steps before he comes around the corner. "Dr. Alexander!"

He halts. "Are you all right?"

Realizing I'm still wringing my hands, I jerk them to my

sides. And if that isn't suspicious, I throw my palms up. "You startled me."

"You didn't hear me coming?"

"I…" I tap my forehead. "Deep in thought—you know how artists are."

"Not really." He tilts his head to the side. "Sorry to have kept you waiting. Jessica's mother was anxious about tomorrow's surgery."

"I understand."

He takes a step toward me.

Oh no! I hasten forward, halt before him, and hope like the dickens that his offense at being included in my prayer can be handled here. "So, what did you need to see me about?"

The glint in his eyes seems suspiciously like…well…suspicion.

As I silently groan, he glances past my shoulder. "Let's talk in the dome."

"Obviously, I offended you," I spew out.

The triangle between his eyebrows deepens. "How is that?"

"My prayer for Jessica…including you."

"Ah." He widens his stance. "I have to admit it unsettled me, but I'm not offended."

"You aren't?"

"Just because I believe it's a waste of time to expect God to act on prayer doesn't mean you should. Besides, perhaps God is more receptive to your prayers than mine."

I guard my tongue against my next words but, after a moment's reflection, decide they can't hurt. "You sound bitter, Clive."

"That's because I am bitter. You see, God and I are divided."

"How so?"

Without another word, he steps around me and heads toward the domed room.

Shouldn't have asked. Should have guarded my tongue. Should have just listened. But no-oo…

I follow him down the hallway and, when I enter the domed room, find him tossing back the tarp. "This is how we're divided." He looks across his shoulder at me. "These two innocents."

After what seems like minutes, he shoves a hand back through his hair. "I have no idea why I'm telling you this when you can't possibly care."

"But I do care. I can't stand to see someone hurting."

His lids narrow as though to discern my sincerity; however, he shrugs it off. "This isn't why I wanted to talk to you—"

"Was your family Christian?" I blurt out, certain the door he opened is about to close.

"We were."

Were… "Then you should be comforted by knowing that your wife and child aren't forever lost to you."

He's silent for several moments, then flips the tarp over the plaque. "I'd like to discuss the progress you've made and how the timetable is shaping up."

Regret stabs me. My attempt to keep him from scrutinizing my work has failed.

Please, God, let him see something other than the crosses and praying children.

But as I hold my breath, he begins to frown. Shortly, he strides past me and halts before a bowed boy and girl.

I force my feet forward and draw alongside him.

Trust in the Lord. A sidelong glance confirms the tension he exudes.

"I'm not blind, Kate."

And? Dare I hope he'll accept what I've done? That it's subtle enough not to offend? Unfortunately, another glance shows no softening of his profile, and I grasp for something to counter his forthcoming pronouncement.

The deadline! If nothing else, for the sake of the deadline perhaps he'll grant me this one concession. And if he doesn't?

I have only myself to blame. After all, I willfully went against him when he forbade it. I knew what I was doing. I—

Oh, surely there's some way to reach him!

I lay an entreating hand on his arm. "Please don't let the division between you and God deprive frightened and hurting children of His comfort." Nose beginning to tingle, I grip his arm tighter. "Please."

He looks into my face, then lower at my hand on him.

I'm wasting my time, aren't I?

Eyes moistening, I release him and swing away. The sudden movement causes a sharp pain to slice between my shoulder blades. I wince and take the half dozen steps to the cart upon which my tools are laid. From among an assortment of paint-brushes, I choose a two-inch job.

Returning to Clive, I thrust the brush at him. "Have at it, then."

When he doesn't take it, I grab his hand and slap the brush in his palm. "If you want it gone, then *you*—"

His fingers close over mine. "No."

I lift my wet eyes to his and in a creaky little voice say, "No?"

He looks momentarily away, and when his eyes return to me, I detect a softening. "It means a lot to you, doesn't it?"

I swallow. "It does. More, though, it means a lot to children like Jessica."

"Jessica…" He slides his gaze up the wall at my back. "It will set you back if you have to redo it."

Is this going the way I hope—pray? True, I'd prefer him to have a change of heart, but I'll settle for his concern over the timetable. "It will."

The suspense is killing me, and just when I don't think I can stand it any longer, he speaks. "Then it stays."

My heart thumps harder. "Really?"

"Provided you keep it subtle."

I bite my lip to keep from beaming; however, the smile escapes and I feel myself start to glow—from the roots of my hair to the tips of my toes, every pore proclaiming, "Hallelujah!"

"I'm so happy," I gasp.

"Good."

"And excited."

His mouth veers toward a smile. "Great."

"And relieved."

He raises an eyebrow. "I'm sorry."

"And grateful."

He lowers his regard to my mouth. "Don't be."

"And…"

His thumb begins to move on top of my hand, and it's then that I notice him noticing me—*really* noticing me. And he's so close I can feel his breath on my lips. So close that he surely feels mine. And as his head descends, I realize that Clive Alexander is going to kiss me.

Really? This has to be a dream. Any moment now, I'll wake up and have to begin this day all over again with the same worry and stress of being caught doing something I shouldn't. And the reality is that Clive *will* take the paintbrush, *will* X out the crosses and praying children…

"Kate?"

I open my eyes and peer into his face above mine. Nice dream.

"Are you still seeing that makeup guy?"

Not a dream.

I nearly assure Clive of my pending boyfriend-less-ness,

but it strikes me how cheap I'd sound—as if at the mere promise of a kiss, I'd dump one boyfriend for another. So reluctantly I say, "Yes, I'm still seeing Michael."

Clive glances at my mouth once more, then releases my hand and steps back.

So the doctor has morals?

He nods at the wall behind me. "Keep it subtle, hmm?"

Struggling to hide my disappointment, I jerk my head. "Of course. And…thank you."

"You're welcome."

Though I expect that to be the end of our exchange, he lingers. "You recall the debt I owe Dr. MacPhail?"

As if I could forget. Over and again I've told myself it's none of my business, yet it still bothers me. "Yes?"

"It's being repaid."

"Oh. Good." Giving myself a little shake, I smile. "I mean, great!"

"Yeah. I'll be gone—"

"Clive!"

I look past him. And there, at the entrance to the domed room, is none other than that Adelphia woman. Who has a penchant for interruptions.

"There you are," she says as he turns to her. "I've been searching all over for you."

"I dropped by to see the progress Kate's making."

She takes in the room with one quick sweep and nods. "The meeting starts in five minutes."

"I'll be right there."

She crosses her arms over her chest. "I'll wait for you."

After a long, unmoving moment, Clive gives me something of a smile. "Keep up the good work."

That's it? And what was that he said about being gone?

My disappointment over what he leaves unsaid is nearly as sharp as the disappointment when he draws alongside his "colleague" and she loops an arm through his.

I sigh. Why did Clive feel it necessary to inform me of the status of his debt? Because he cares what I think? And why should he? Because he's interested in me? Interested even though, not so long ago, he warned me I wouldn't like him?

Mixed signals, and yet there was nothing mixed about his intent to kiss me and his inquiry into the status of my relationship with Michael—the answer to which denied me a kiss.

Forcing myself back to the present, I consider the walls and nod. "Subtle… I can do subtle." Which is something to smile about.

Thank You, Lord, for hearing my prayers and making Clive receptive. And please help this day go by fast so I can have that talk with Michael.

"Close your eyes."

I frown at Michael where he sits beside me. "Huh?"

"Close them."

"Why?"

"I have a surprise for you."

I start to lower my lids only to be struck by a possibility that packs a punch. What if…? No. He wouldn't. Would he? After all, we've only been dating two months. And that's about to come to an end.

"Kate?"

Panic sets in. "I don't like surprises."

"You'll like this one."

Why didn't I break it off sooner? It's one thing to tell someone the relationship isn't working, another to do so when he's ready to take it to the next level. But surely he isn't proposing. Surely the surprise isn't inside a velvet-covered box.

Fearing I might hyperventilate, I stare at my plate, which I had so wished the waiter would clear away to eliminate the temptation of finishing off the enchilada and taco special. Suddenly grateful my wish wasn't granted, I grab my fork and stab a bite of sauce-drenched tortilla, chicken, and cheese.

"Let me finish this first." Hoping the remains of my meal will buy me five minutes during which I can figure out how to derail Michael, I pop the forkful in my mouth and chew with purpose.

"Oh, come on, Kate!" Michael swipes my plate and sets it out of reach. "Listen to your stomach, not your head."

I feel like a child whose knuckles have been soundly rapped. Though I earlier shrugged off Michael's hint that I order á la carte—as in taco *or* enchilada—there's no hint about this.

He didn't mean to hurt your feelings, rational, turn-the-other-cheek says. *And it's not as if you really wanted to finish your meal.*

True, it was a diversion. But who does he think he is to make that decision for me? And despite my on-again, off-again with Pilates and that I've lost only a few pounds, I'm in decent enough shape. In fact, I feel pretty good about me.

"Ready for your surprise?"

Is he oblivious to my churning, or just trying to lighten the mood? I slide my gaze to him.

He smiles. "Ready?"

Oblivious.

He slaps a magazine down on the table. "Hot off the press."

I stare at *Changes* magazine, the issue that doubtless features my makeover. No ring, then? *This* is my surprise?

Oh, thank You, God. In fact, I'm so relieved it's not a proposal of marriage that I forget Michael's faux pas.

"Wow. This is great. Wonderful. Terrific."

He chuckles. "All that and you haven't even seen the article."

I smooth a hand across the cover, which features a supermodel who's probably gorgeous the moment she crawls out of bed.

"Page 122," Michael prompts.

I continue to stare at the model, who not only plies a perfect smile, but also shows off a perfect mole in the right crease that runs from the outside of her nose to the corner of her mouth. Bet she doesn't have to worry about spider veins, either—all some-teen years of her. Nor her weight, the consideration of which returns my attention to the unfinished enchilada.

"What's with you, Kate?"

"Nothing." I open the magazine and flip past one advertisement after another. And suddenly there's the beauteous Maia Glock towering over pitiful Kate Meadows. Mutt and Jeff...or should I say Jeff and Mutt?

We stand on the street corner outside the coffee shop, Maia glowing in her form-fitting yoga outfit, me...

"Michael, tell me Arnie used a wide-angle lens. Please."

"'Fraid not."

I sigh. Not that I look fat. Just out of proportion. But then, Maia *is* tall. And I'm not.

Why in the world did I allow myself to be talked into the makeover? I read the paragraph that describes Michael's mission and names the two women who submitted to his expertise.

Steeling myself, I turn the page and...am pleasantly surprised by the photographs that capture my transformation. The last page is a spread that compares before and after. On the left, another shot of Maia and me on the street corner; on the right, Maia and me dressed to the nines in Michael's perfectly lit studio.

Michael taps the after version of Katherine Mae Meadows. "That's the best your hair has looked."

Of course it is.

He peers at me. "Speaking of which, you're due for a trip to the salon—you know, to reshape your hair and touch up the color."

I draw a tress through my fingers. The color *is* borderline dull, and the ends are split.

"I guess you haven't had time to read the chapter in my book about the proper care and conditioning of hair."

I cannot tell a lie. "Sorry, I've been busy."

His lips thin. "Well, it's worth the effort—ask Maia. She said my tips made all the difference for her. In the meantime…" He reaches behind him.

Not the wallet! Please, not the—

"…let me give you Amy Om's card." The dreaded wallet appears, and a moment later, so does the business card. "You'll like her. In fact, she's every bit as good as my assistant, Trish."

Though tempted to reject the card, I remind myself that it's just a haircut—and that my hair *is* approaching critical mass. Now, if it were a liposuction referral, that would be different. Unfortunately, that's not paranoia talking, as Michael has started dropping hints about my thighs. It's only a matter of time before some expert in the field of sucking out fat finds his way into my collection of business cards.

"Kate?" He wiggles the card.

"Oh!" I pluck it from him.

He pats the magazine. "So what do you think?"

I consider the picture of the new and improved Kate Meadows, then read the closing paragraph, which surprisingly mentions my work on the burn unit. "What's this?"

"Before the magazine went to press, I asked the editor to drop it in. Not only does it make for a more interesting feature, but considering the importance of the project, it gives you more credibility as an artist. And on the money side, it's bound to drum up more business."

Though I'm grateful, I can't help but wonder what Clive will think. Not that it's a secret I was hired to—

"So what do you think?"

I return my gaze to the magazine. "Once you get past that first picture, it's great."

He nods. "We intentionally chose the worst before picture to give the makeover miracle proportions."

Miracle? Makes me sound as if I was in a world of hurt.

Michael frowns. "Are you okay, Kate? You're kind of…" He peers closer. "…red."

Red.

I mentally bite my tongue. *Lord, help me, because I really don't want to say what I'm thinking.* Well, actually I do, but—

"Speaking of which, have you contacted the aesthetician I recommended?"

I stare at him and wonder how many pounds of pressure my teeth can stand.

"Oh!" Michael reaches again. "Almost forgot."

Not the wallet again. Not the—

"Everyone says Dr. Abrams is *the* best." He extends a silver card and wiggles it as though it's bait and I'm the fish. "Liposuction."

"Ah!" I slap a hand to the table. "This has got to stop. And it's going to. Right. Now."

He pulls back. "Kate?"

Realizing heads are turning, I lean nearer. "Isn't there anything about me you like just the way it is? Just the way *I* am?"

His brow wrinkles. "There's a lot I like about you."

"I'm listening."

He scans my face. "You have…uh…beautiful eyes."

"That would be colored contacts—green tonight."

He swallows. "And your smile—"

"Less the gap."

He shifts uneasily. "Well, yeah."

"Go on."

"You have a pretty face." He smiles faintly. "Real pretty."

"Now that the mole is gone."

He draws a deep breath. "The placement was all wrong. You said so yourself." He closes a hand over my clenched fingers. "Don't you think you're being overly sensitive?"

I pull my hand from beneath his. "I'm tired of all these business cards. Tired of you picking me apart, telling me how deeply you feel for me only to point out my every flaw."

"Kate."

"You might have convinced yourself that I'm ideal marriage material, but what you really want is a perfectly flawless—"

"Kate!"

"Don't deny it. You want perfection, and I am not perfection."

"On the inside you are."

I gape at Michael.

He shrugs. "I like who you are, Kate."

Slowly, I close my mouth. He likes who I am. But if he likes what's inside so much, shouldn't that be enough? Shouldn't—?

I startle when my cell phone gives a shrill *toot-a-ly toot*. I'm tempted to ignore the call, but this is an opportunity to guard my tongue that I'll regret passing. I hold up a staying hand.

The phone *toot-a-ly toots* twice more before I flip it open. "Hello?"

"Oh, thank God."

"Beau?" His voice sounds strained...emotional. "Is every-thing all right with Belle?"

"No. I mean, not exactly. But maybe."

I ignore Michael's questioning frown. "What's happened?"

"She's gone into labor, and the doctors aren't sure they can stop it."

Seven-month mark. She made it to the seventh month.

"I'm on my way."

Beau confirms that they're at the hospital where Clive works, gives me the room number, then hangs up.

The confrontation with Michael forgotten, I meet his concerned gaze as I grab my purse. "Belle's in labor. I've got to go to her."

"Sure." He rises. "Would you like me to drive you?"

I'm tempted to accept; however, as I came directly from the burn unit to dinner, it would mean leaving my car—and having Michael feel obligated to wait around at the hospital.

"Thank you, but I can drive myself."

"All right." He guides me toward the front of the restaurant and halts at the cashier's stand to settle our bill.

Though I have every intention of beelining it to the parking lot, he pulls me back and gives me a quick kiss in spite of…

In spite of whatever set me off before Beau's call. For all its necessary brevity, the kiss is comforting.

"Call me."

I nod, then hurry to my car.

"Please, God." I beseech as I slide into the seat, and my throat tightens.

"Please, God." I implore as I fumble the key into the ignition, and my nose tingles.

"Please, God." I beg as the engine springs to life, and my eyes moisten.

"Oh, please, God." All the way to the hospital.

"Thank You, God," I whisper as dawn creeps through the blinds to touch Belle's restful face. Lifting my head from the arm of the chair I curled into hours ago, I look to where Beau sits op-

posite me. Hard asleep, he rests his head on the mattress near
his wife's shoulder, his right hand entwined with Belle's. The
doctors stopped her labor shortly after midnight, and all is well.
Beau encouraged me to go home, but I wanted to be here for
Belle as she's always been here for me.

I rub the *Believe* medallion on the bracelet she gave me. I
believe. I really do. Though she'll be bedridden until she delivers—for however long baby holds off—her child is safe. And
even if he had been born last night and spent weeks in NICU,
chances are he'd have been fine. Of course, each day he lingers
in the womb increases those chances.

The chair's springs creak as I rise, causing Belle to lift her
lids. "Kate."

I step to her side and claim her left hand. "Sorry I woke
you."

"Glad you did. You okay?"

"Of course. How about you?"

"Tired."

I brush the hair back from her brow. "I'm going to leave you
now so you can get some more sleep, but I'll be back."

She begins to lower her lids, but as I release her hand she
recaptures mine. "My mom?"

I was hoping she wouldn't ask. Her mother doesn't like
Beau. With his homosexual past, she thinks he simply isn't
good enough for Belle. And even now that he's the father of her
grandchild, she's holding out.

"I left her a message. I'm sure as soon as she picks it up
she'll be on her way."

Belle sighs. "Maybe."

And maybe not. I prayed about it in the dark hours of
morning—that her mother would come through for her—but
will God answer another prayer as I hope He will?

As much as I hate to give Belle false hope, I smile. "She'll be here." Even if I'm arrested for making harassing phone calls. And it's a possibility, as she hasn't forgiven me for the role I played in bringing Belle and Beau together.

"'Night, Kate." Belle closes her eyes and her hand relaxes in mine.

I glance at Beau where he continues to breathe deeply, then shrug my shoulders up and down to ease the ache. Worse, however, is the ache in my back.

Rubbing at it, I slip out of the room and head for the hospital garage—first home to change clothes and grab a bite to eat, then back to the burn unit and a day of painting interspersed with visits to Belle. As I enter the elevator, I send thanks heavenward that she was admitted to this hospital. True, her room is in a building separate from the children's hospital and entails a bit of a walk, but it's convenient. And the exercise will do me good.

Shortly, I pull into light traffic and dig my cell phone from my purse. Time to make another call…or two…or three…or however many it takes to reach Belle's mom.

Saturday, May 12
Dear Lord,

Thank You for prayers answered as my heart longed for them to be. Thank You for the extra time You've given Belle and Beau's baby to develop. Thank You for Belle's mom finally answering my call and for having a good reason for not answering the half dozen calls before. Amazing that a woman of sixty-odd years would suddenly take up spelunking. For goodness' sake, she's about to be a grandmother! Anyway, thank You for softening her heart enough to make her crawl out of whatever dark, slimy cave she was in so she could be here for her daughter. And for her not completely ignoring Beau. Of course, I'm grateful she didn't give me the evil eye. (I hate it when she does that!)

Thank You for Jessica's reaction to the domed room. Her squeal, smile, dancing eyes, embrace of the symbols of Your love—all music to my ears and eyes. You really know what You're doing, don't You? Well, duh...

Okay. I hesitate to ask this after all the prayers You've answered—the really important stuff!—but could You help me out with Michael? As much as he likes who I am on the inside, I know it will never be enough for him. Give me the courage and the words to break it off so he can pursue Maia if that's what he wants. Oh, and help me stop worrying about my thighs. They're not that bad. Certainly not bad enough to seriously consider liposuction (still trying to figure out how that business card ended up in my purse). Liposuction—ha! Only when I sit wrong are the dimples in evidence. Obviously, the sooner I break it off with Michael, the better...

Good night!

Kate

PS: Thank You for near kisses. Even though Clive's didn't pan out, it was a boost to know that he was ~~tempted~~ oops...interested.

PPS: Pulling out my Bible. See? And I will be at church tomorrow—even if it kills me!

11

I'm dying. Whatever possessed me to take on the burn unit? Oh yeah, that would be my breasts. Greedy little—

BIG! With a resentful glance at the offenders, I pull into Belle's driveway, switch off the headlights, and drop my head to the steering wheel. Though only three days into juggling two jobs, I feel as if I've been put through the spin cycle. Monday through Saturday, seven until one at the new job, then two until eight-thirty at the burn unit. And forget Pilates! Not that I liked it much anyway, but according to the fit of my clothes and a few less pounds on the scale, it was helping.

I open the car door and, a few moments later, press the doorbell of Belle and Beau's house.

Of course it's Beau who opens the door, as Belle isn't allowed much beyond their bedroom.

"You look awful, Kate."

I shrug. "It's called truth in advertising."

"Ah." He lowers his gaze. "I thought you were going to toss out those baggy old jeans."

I was, especially after all the positive feedback over my hip-huggers; however, after subjecting a second pair to paint splatters, I couldn't bring myself to risk a third.

I step past Beau. "Just trying to get a few more wears out of these old ones."

"Toss them out, Kate." He closes the door. "If not for your sake, then mine."

"I will." Eventually.

He sighs and consults his watch. "Almost nine."

"She isn't asleep, is she?"

"Nah. You know Belle—night owl to the max, especially now that she has nothing to do all day but lie around."

As she's done for the past two weeks, poor thing. "I'll go up, then."

Beau follows me upstairs. As we start down the hall, I falter when I see the nursery door open and the light on.

"Want to take a peek? I hung new blinds today."

I'm sensitive about that room, but not as sensitive as Belle and Beau were following the miscarriages that left it so empty. It's been years since the door stood wide.

"Come on." Beau steers me inside.

I halt at the center of the room and stare at the wall behind the crib, upon which a detailed Noah's ark rocks atop the water. It's some of my best work. Despite the heartache inherent in preparing a room for someone else's newborn, it was my gift to Belle and Beau. I've done a few nurseries since, but I pass when possible. Children's rooms I can handle, but there's something about a nursery...

"Looks as good as the day you finished it."

I survey the other walls, then pause on one of several Scriptures painted in an elegant hand. "It does."

My eyes meet his. "Ready to be a daddy?"

"I've been ready a long time."

Of course he has. "And you're going to be great."

He breaks into a grin. "You're telling me!"

I thump his arm. "Well, aren't you modest?"

"Just stating the obvious." He wiggles his eyebrows. "Let's go. Belle will be wondering what's keeping us."

As I follow him to the door, I glance around at the empty crib that their baby will soon fill. Despite the dull ache at my center, I'm happy for them.

"Hurry!" Belle calls as we start down the hall. "He's on the move!"

We run to the bedroom, where Belle is propped on oodles of pillows in the middle of the bed. She motions me forward. "Come on!"

I drop to the mattress, and she grabs my hand and guides it to her belly. "Feel him?"

She never tires of tracking her baby's movement. Even before she was on bed rest, she would stop midstep...midsentence...midwhatever to savor the miracle.

"I feel him." I return her smile. "Think he'll be a rock climber?"

"Could be."

"I'll leave you to your girl talk," Beau says.

Once the baby stills, I lightly put my arms around Belle and give her a hug. "How are you feeling?"

"Bored, but otherwise great." She nods at a teetering stack of magazines atop the nightstand. "As you can see, Mom has added to my collection."

Mom, who still doesn't like Beau, though she is making an effort to tolerate him.

"Of course, *Changes* magazine is still my favorite." Belle eyes the solitary magazine that features my makeover.

I groan. Since its appearance on the newsstands, the magazine has generated more interest in my work, and I've scheduled two new projects, but it hasn't been without a price. A couple times too often, potential clients have shown up at the burn unit unannounced to consult on projects. The first time was flattering, the second unsettling, the third annoying. And it goes downhill from there, especially as I don't have time for interruptions if I'm to make my deadline. Fortunately, Clive hasn't shown up since he nearly kissed me two weeks ago. Unfortunately, I miss him.

"So, Kate, what do you think of the new blinds?"

I blink at Belle. "Blinds? Oh—the nursery. They look great."

She's watching me. Though previous to her miscarriages she was tuned in to my feelings, experience with her own losses has made her more sensitive.

"Really," I say.

She pats my hand. "How are you doing?"

"I'm tired. Nothing but work, work, work."

"Nothing?" She raises an eyebrow.

I know what she's asking. "As soon as I get the time to sit down with Michael, I'll break it off for good." Not since the night she went into labor have he and I been on a date. But it's not as if I don't have a good excuse for putting off the inevitable. I have several. First, the little spare time I have is devoted to Belle; second, when I make it home at night, I have to deal with a brooding and moody Maia; third, the new project is draining me.

Still, Michael keeps inviting and I keep avoiding. And he's not happy. The message on my answering machine yesterday was that if I didn't fit him into my schedule to discuss our "misunderstanding," he'd camp out on my doorstep. Thankfully, he wasn't there last night. Hopefully, he won't be there tonight.

"Get it over with, Kate." Belle squeezes my hand. "It's not fair to him."

"I know. I'll do it soon."

"How soon?"

I hate it when she holds me accountable. "The next time the opportunity arises."

She screws up her face. "Make the opportunity. In fact, don't visit me again until you've taken care of Michael."

"But—"

"I mean it. Until you stop stringing him along, I'm telling Beau to bar the door."

There's no arguing with her, especially when she's right. "If it's not too late when I get home, I'll call him." As her lids narrow, I cross my heart. "Promise."

"And then?"

I frown. "Then what?"

"You move on."

I snort. "What? Afraid I'll sink into some deep, dark depression?"

"No, but you're going to miss the attention, the companionship."

"Yeah, well, I'll get over it. Always do." Sort of. Of course, this latest letdown could have been avoided had I not reneged on swearing off men. Should have stuck to my resolu—

That's it! I slap a hand to my thigh. "This time I mean it, Belle—*really* mean it."

She groans. "Not again."

"No more dating. No more men."

She sighs back into her pillows. "Okay, but remember, it is only May."

I make a face at her and turn toward the door. "I'll let you get your rest. 'Night."

"Kate."

"Hmm?"

"How are the migraines?"

I shrug. "Still dodging the bullet."

"And still too stubborn to give the patch a try."

"Well, if it ain't broke—"

"If it's cracked, it's broken, Kate."

I smile. "I'm fine. Really."

"All right, your call. Speaking of which…" She raises an imaginary phone to her ear.

Ten-fifteen is too late to call, isn't it? Of course, according to Michael, he's usually up until at least eleven.

I scowl at the phone.

You promised, Kate.

I reach for the handset only to draw back when the doorbell rings. Michael? Surely not this late.

I hear Maia open the door. From the muffled pitch of the voice that slips beneath my door, it's a male visitor. But is it Michael? I hope it is; otherwise it's likely Maia's married man. A few moments later, I have the disheartening answer when the voices drift away into other parts of the house. Not Michael, then.

Once more, I consider the phone but feel my mouth go dry. First hot tea, then the call.

In the event that I happen upon Maia and her night visitor, I pull a robe over my pajamas. It's hardly flattering, thick and worn as it is, but it's modest.

I'm halfway down the stairs when Maia's voice rises from the living room. Tempted as I am to turn back—my mouth *is* really dry—I continue my descent until I hear Maia laugh. And then Michael.

The one stair that creaks loud enough to be heard above laughter protests beneath my foot, causing the two in the living room to fall silent. I'm had, but if I take the stairs two at a time—

"Kate," Maia calls in that indifferent voice she adopts when she deigns to acknowledge my presence, "Michael's here to see you."

Oh yeah? Then why are you only now informing me? The jealous thought springs to mind before I reason that the oversight is cause to rejoice. Despite Maia's anger at me for throwing my "used" boyfriend her way, she has feelings for him.

"Great," I call back. "I'll grab a cup of tea and be right in."

I take another step down only to pause at the sight of my robe. What will Michael think if he sees me, especially after visiting with the beauteous Maia? Doubtless, his mind will race with referrals…wallet hand will tremble…fingers will itch to pinch a business card. That, or he'll break it off with me.

Oh! This could be good. Maybe I won't have to be the bad guy. No explanations. No apologies. No hurt feelings. This *is* good.

I descend the last of the stairs and glance into the living room. "Back in a few minutes."

Maia makes no attempt to hide her dismay at the sight of my robe-clad figure, but Michael does. And fails. As I sweep past, I grin at the startle that preceded his forced smile.

What I don't expect is for them to follow me into the kitchen, thus denying me the time to prepare for the showdown.

I retrieve a tea bag and dangle it before them. "Tea, anyone?"

Michael shakes his head.

Maia tightens the belt of her form-fitting silk kimono. "Uh-uh."

Gosh, they're an attractive couple! What was Michael thinking when he passed over Maia for me?

She smiles at Michael. "I'll leave you two alone. Good night."

Michael smiles. "Good night, Maia."

Then she's gone.

After a long, uncomfortable moment, Michael says, "I apologize for dropping by at this hour, but I knew you'd still be up."

I blow a breath up my face. "Oh, yeah."

He crosses to the eat-in counter and pulls out a stool. "We need to talk."

"I know."

"You've been avoiding me."

"I have."

He clasps his hands on the counter. "I've thought a lot about what happened at the restaurant and what you said about me wanting to perfect you."

Wondering in which cabinet I stowed the teapot, I prompt, "And?"

"And you're right. All I can say is that I never meant to make you feel that all I cared about was your appearance. I'm sorry, Kate."

This isn't going the way I hoped. Fearful that the ball is back in my court, I open a lower cabinet. Where, oh where, is that teapot? And how, oh how, am I to say what needs to be said?

"So, Kate…"

I sink to my haunches before the cabinet, rummage through the pots and pans, then stop. What caused Michael to leave his sentence dangling? I look over my shoulder and find him frowning at my backside. Not a good view, as I'm hunkered down and the thick robe is flared over my hind parts. I nearly jump to my feet, but it occurs to me that perhaps we're back on track.

"Michael?"

He blinks. "Hmm?"

"Everything okay?"

He draws a deep breath. "At the risk of setting you off again, I have to tell you I'm concerned."

"How's that?"

"Maia tells me you're no longer attending Pilates."

Bingo! "No time for it." I continue my search for the teapot. Ah, there it is!

"Well, you need to make time."

Tongue!

I jerk the pot free. "Why?"

"Well, because you're…you're…"

Straightening, I turn to him. "What?"

The dam breaks. "You're potentially fat."

I blink. Potentially. Fat. Did those words really come out of him? Surely I'm hallucinating. Yeah. Too little sleep. Has to be, as no guy would say something like that to someone for whom he claims to have feelings. Would he?

"Look, Kate," he continues with desperation that clues me in to what my face reflects, "if you don't make exercise a priority—"

"Potentially *fat*?"

"Well, it's just the way you were bent down. And the robe isn't exactly flattering, you know."

I gnash my teeth. "I know." Which is the way I wanted it, I remind myself. Must calm down. Must not take it personally. But I do. I slam the teapot on the counter in front of him. "Why are you with me?"

He pulls back. "What?"

"Okay, you said you like who I am, but obviously that's not enough, so why are you with me?"

Maia appears in the doorway. "What's going on?"

I thrust my face near Michael's. "Why are you with me and not—" finger jab—"with her?"

He glances at Maia. "C'mon, Kate. You can't be serious."

"Am I laughing?"

"Uh…no."

"Look, Michael, I'd have to be seriously impaired to not know of your mutual attraction." I glance at Maia, who's assumed a watchful stance. "Sure, you fight it, but it's there. You like Maia. Certainly more than you like me, with all my imperfections."

He waves a hand as though to wipe away my words. "No, Kate."

"Yes, Michael."

"No." His frown lines deepen, and I'm tempted to advise him that he's "potentially wrinkled," but that would be mean. See, I'm not completely hopeless.

"Yes," I say, more forcefully.

"Nooo."

"Yeeesss." I narrow my gaze on Maia.

She's biting her lip. Waiting…

Michael makes a sound of exasperation. "Maia and I are just friends. Yes, we like each other, but not in the way you think." He widens his eyes at Maia in a silent appeal for support.

She folds her arms across her chest.

"Maybe Maia isn't what you're looking for," I say, "but she's what you want—tall, slender, gorgeous, and with a sense of fashion and beauty."

Michael shakes his head. "You're what I want."

"No, I'm not. And—" here comes the really hard part—"you're not what I want."

Hurt darkens his eyes.

"Though I like you a lot," I swallow the lump in my throat, "I don't see our relationship developing into anything beyond friendship. I'm sorry." I push back from the counter. "I know I can't tell you or Maia what to do, but you really ought to examine your feelings for one another."

He stares at me across the silence.

"That's all I have to say." I toss the tea bag to the counter and cross toward the doorway. As I near, Maia sidesteps and averts her gaze, but not before I glimpse moisture in her eyes.

All is hushed as I climb the stairs.

Tuesday, May 29
Dear Lord,

I did it. Boy, did I do it! And I'm sure You're disappointed. I know I am. Not because I did it, but because of how I did it. But, honestly! POTENTIALLY FAT? How was I supposed to react? By turning the other cheek? Oh! That's funny—the other cheek. Get it? Well, almost funny.

What was Michael thinking? And what guy in his right mind says something like that to a woman he cares for? Potentially fat! If he weren't so nice, I'd say he's cruel. But I rant. Potentially fat aside, thank You for Belle holding me accountable, even if the breakup didn't work out the way I'd hoped. And, more important, thank You for keeping Belle and Beau's little bun in the oven. Your blessings abound! Potentially fat!

And now for special requests (I'll bet You get tired of those). Lord, help me keep my nose out of places it doesn't belong, as in the relationship between Maia and Mr. Potentially Fat. You know they're perfect for each other,

don't You? Physically speaking, of course. With regards to
spiritually, that obviously needs some work. If I could just
think of a way to work it so that Michael and Maia—

I know. Keep my nose out of it. Amazing how much
trouble one gets into with that particular member of
the face. And don't even get me started on the tongue!
Speaking of which, please help me use all I've learned
about guarding this nasty little waggler. I'm doing better,
but not good enough. And please help me to stop dwelling
on Clive's near kiss. Must move on. Must not waste time
or thought on something that was never meant to be. It
wasn't, was it? Of course not. Were it, You'd drop him right
in my lap. Yeah.

Always yours,
Kate

PS: As I know You don't want me to worry about my
thighs, I've decided I won't. They're fine just the way they
are. Not perfect, but perfectly acceptable. No liposuction—
gives me the creeps every time I think about a hose
sucking out the fat globules—however, a bit of toning
wouldn't hurt. Maybe a dozen squats or leg lifts before bed.
Pre-bed toning. Sounds good. Starting tomorrow night.

PPS: Regarding my Bible time and Sunday services, it's time
to pick up the slack. Hence "Operation: Perfect Faith." Like
the name? Me, too. Though I know it really isn't possible
to have perfect faith—we are human—one should still
pursue it. And so, instead of expending so much time and
energy on my outward appearance, I'm going to work on
the inner. Stay tuned.

12

Sleep. I had no intention of succumbing, but my head had begun to throb. So I rested my stinging eyes for just a second. However, as evidenced by the cramp in my neck, my aching back, and the hand shaking my shoulder, I did succumb. Without so much as a whimper, I plunged into that black hole that sucks up every minute of a person's productivity. And I have only myself to blame. Well…there is Clive Alexander.

For the hundredth time wishing I hadn't allowed him to coerce me into spreading myself thin, I drop my head back against the wall.

"Hello, Dorian," I murmur from behind closed lids. But then the faint scent of cologne tickles my senses. "Or is it Gray?" Not that there's anything faint about the stuff *he* bathes in—

"It's Clive." The hand on my shoulder falls away. "Sorry to disappoint."

Sucking in a breath, I attempt to focus on the man who's down on his haunches before me. He's back. Not a single sighting for nearly three weeks, and suddenly he's back. Right here. Right now. In the flesh.

Heart lurching, I squelch the impulse to launch myself at him. Where did *that* come from? I mean, it's not as if there's anything between us—

Well, there was the kiss—rather, *near* kiss. And my relationship with Michael is off—at least, where *I'm* concerned. Yesterday, just as I was starting to breathe easier, he left a message suggesting we "talk it over." Probably should call him.

"Kate?"

Realizing how foolish I look with my mouth agape, I close it as I peer into Clive's face—*tanned* face. Not that he's deeply tanned, but he's definitely spent some time in the sun. Has he been vacationing? Laying on a beach soaking up rays?

Feeling a stab of jealousy, I clear my throat. "You're…uh… back."

"And you're sleeping on the job."

Guessing it must be eight in the morning, I grimace. "Unfortunately, not the job I should be at." I turn my watch up and, as I removed my contacts last night to ease my stinging eyes, squint to focus on the digital numbers. Almost nine o'clock. Worse yet.

Straightening, Clive reaches a hand to me. "Juggling two now?"

I know I shouldn't be so eager to accept his assistance, but my hand slides into his as if it's sliding into home plate. And the moment his fingers close over mine, I start to buzz.

Uh, by the way, Clive, I'm no longer dating Michael.

"Yeah," I say as he draws me to my feet. "Mustn't forget my other commitments."

He continues to grip my hand as if I'm still in danger of toppling. "Not getting much shut-eye, then."

I shrug. "Enough."

There's that almost smile again. "Then you meant to fall asleep on the job?"

"Oh no! And I assure you it hasn't happened before. The long days and nights just caught up with me and..." I make a face. "I only meant to rest my eyes."

He peers nearer. "They're bloodshot."

Surprise, surprise. "Nothing a little Visine can't remedy." I pull my hand from his, retrieve my bag, and fish out a miniature bottle. "See? A full month's supply." Actually, more like a week's, but that's between me and Visine.

He frowns. "Are you holding up all right?"

"Sure." Not.

He doesn't seem convinced, and I'm warmed by his concern. And thrilled by the implications.

You do know, Clive, that Michael and I are no longer seeing each other?

Of course, his concern is probably more for whether or not I'll bring in the job on time. "Don't worry, everything's under control."

"Perhaps you ought to call in Dorian and Gray."

"A step ahead of you. As of last week, they're back on the job."

"Good."

"In fact..." I glance at my watch again. "They should be here soon." Frustrated with the fuzzy edges, I shove a hand in my bag, pull out a daisy-bedecked case, and push my specs up on my nose.

Clive's eyebrows take a jaunt up his brow. "It's been a while since I've seen you wear glasses."

It's been a while since you've seen me, period.

Though I'd been tempted to inquire into his absence, I was

afraid my interest would get back to him.

I tap the bridge of my specs. "Good old standbys."

"Then you've adjusted to contacts?"

"I have."

He steps back and runs his gaze down me. "Anything new?"

"What?"

He gives my face the once-and twice-over. "Has your boyfriend determined you're still not perfect?"

Oh. I consider the liposuction card that's still lurking (*must* clean out my purse) and that I did succumb to microdermabrasion's promise to erase some of the lines around my mouth, eyes, and forehead (one last hurrah before launching Operation: Perfect Faith).

"Sorry," Clive misinterprets my musing, "I'm overstepping my bounds."

And I should be offended, shouldn't I? But I'm not. Just embarrassed by my vanity and the chunk of money it's cost me.

As I struggle for a response and a way to work in my breakup with Michael without sounding obvious, silence creeps in…seeps in…begins to flood.

Then my watch beeps the hour, an unwelcome cue to get moving. Though I have every intention of doing so, out of my mouth pops, "I haven't seen you for a few weeks."

"Out of town."

Just "out of town." Nothing about the Mexican Riviera… the Bahamas…the Caribbean…

"Well, welcome back." I adjust my bag on my shoulder. "I'd better get—"

"I'm impressed with what you've done." Clive surveys the walls that have come to life in the intervening weeks.

"Thanks. Subtle enough?"

He looks at me. "If you're asking whether or not I approve, I do."

Whew! "Great. Well, I really need to get—"

"You're incredibly talented, Kate."

Is he stalling? I moisten my lips—a movement he follows. Perhaps I didn't read too much into his near kiss. Maybe he *is* attracted to me.

Hey! You! Didn't you swear off men ONCE AND FOR ALL?

Did I? I meant to, but did I actually say it? Did I—?

Oh, yeah—Belle.

"I'm glad you accepted the job," Clive says.

"Thank you."

And did I mention that I'm no longer dating—?

Pitiful! I do *not* need a man! And the sooner Clive Alexander and I part ways, the sooner I'll believe it. So time to push off. Unfortunately, before I get to my next job, I'll have to stop by the house for the dose of HRT I missed last night.

As I step past, Clive says, "Coffee?"

Absolutely! And…uh… have you heard that I finally broke it off with Michael—

I turn. "Sorry, but I have another commitment. Have a good day."

"You'll be back this afternoon?"

"Considering my late start, it'll be closer to evening." Meaning he'll be long gone.

"I'll see you then."

He will?

He smiles.

Oh no. Must stand firm. Must resolve to be unbelievably, inconceivably happy as a single. I can do it. Sure, I can.

"Bye." I swing away.

But as I cross the room, I'm grateful that today—er, yes-terday—was a hip-hugger day (paint splatters and all). In fact, I ought to toss out every last pair of those horrendously un-flattering relaxed-fit jeans. And I will. Fortunately, I recently stumbled across an alternative to the seventy-dollar-a-pops (half the price and hardly a difference!).

Hmm. Maybe between jobs I can swing by the store and snatch up a few more pairs.

As I step into the winding corridor, I glance behind and find Clive watching me.

Definitely must increase my wardrobe…

I've become a junkie, as in vending machine cuisine. So what's it going to be tonight?

I stare at the machine that boasts rows of snacks. The low-fat baked potato chips are a good choice, as is the low-carb protein bar, neither of which holds the appeal of the cinnamon roll or gourmet chocolate chip cookies. But I'll be good—at least as good as good can be when good is starving. Thus, I pair the "naughty" gourmet cookies with the "nice" baked potato chips. Then, once more erring on the side of "good," I choose bottled water.

Booty in hand, I turn and—

Hellooo Clive.

Having seen nothing of him since resuming work on the burn unit three hours ago, I'd accepted that he wasn't going to show. Now here he is, giving rise to a wave of excitement remi-niscent of a kiddie roller-coaster ride.

"Hello, Kate." He frowns at my dinner.

Squashing the impulse to thrust my guilt-laden hands be-hind my back, I smile. "Well, you certainly have a penchant for appearing out of thin air."

"Hardly thin air, as I've been watching you for several minutes."

"Minutes?" I say, only to back up and latch on to what was surely a slip of the tongue. "Watching me? Why?"

Dismay flickers across his face, but he shrugs. "Curiosity." He lifts a hand, and in it is a magazine. *Changes.*

"Oh." There's nothing to be embarrassed about, but I am.

"Adelphia left it on my desk."

Adelphia what's-her-name, who's popped in several times these past weeks, taken a quick peek at my progress, and withdrawn. Was she reporting back to her absent "colleague"? Checking to make sure I was keeping it subtle?

"Adelphia saw mention of your work on the burn unit and thought I'd be interested."

Groan. Interested in Kate Meadows looking her worst, more like it. Maybe she feels threatened? As if! Of course, Clive did almost kiss me...

I force my feet forward. "Not exactly Kate Meadows at her best."

"I don't know about that."

I halt before Clive. "Then you didn't notice the before picture?"

"Though it's true that the after picture is more flattering and stays true to the formulaic makeover, there's nothing wrong with the before."

"Nothing wrong? Either you need glasses, or you want something from me."

His mouth lifts. "And what might that be?"

The first thing that comes to mind is that he's interested in picking up where he left off with the near kiss, but that's probably wishful thinking, meaning it won't make a hoot's difference when he learns that I broke it off with Michael.

But then why is he here at this time of night? A voice speaks from the recesses of my gray matter—one that refuses to believe in being unbelievably, inconceivably happy as a singleton. Good point.

Of course, considering my day job, afternoons and evenings are really the only time for us to talk about the burn unit. Another good point.

Deciding to make light of the matter, I raise an eyebrow. "What do you want from me? Aha!" I tuck the chips, cookies, and bottled water into the crook of my arm and raise a finger. "If you think you're going to get me to bring this job in ahead of schedule, think again."

He laughs. And what a laugh! Warm and oozing with male hormones that make my spine threaten to take a running leap off my back.

"I assure you, I only meant to compliment you, Kate. Nothing ulterior."

Really? Well then, in case you're wondering, Michael and I are no longer an item.

He glances at the magazine. "So now the question of how you and Michael Palmier got together is answered."

I almost startle at the realization that I've been handed the perfect opportunity to disavow the relationship. However, before I can spit out words so well-rehearsed they're practically tattooed on my tongue, he raises his eyebrows at my armful. "Late-night snack?"

Snooze, you lose…

"Dinner."

The teasing light in his eyes flickers. "*That's* your dinner?"

The rebuke is there, and I feel like a teenager again. Grandmother fixed three squares a day and expected each to be the end-all until the next. Fine with me, at least until my teenage years, when girlfriends and boys came fully into play. Time developed a sort of fast-forward quality, and dinner was more often miss than hit. And so there were the late Friday and Saturday night forays into the refrigerator, where spoonfuls of peanut butter or cookie dough and potato chips tided me over until a hearty breakfast the next morning. Grandmother had not been happy, and she'd looked at me just the way Clive is right now.

I will *not* take offense. "Hardly rooftop dining fare, but it's not as if I'm dressed for a romantic candlelit dinner."

When I look up again, Clive is no longer regarding me with censure but with amusement. "Rooftop dining, hmm?"

And I could just die. Rooftop dining! Romantic candlelit dinner! Might he think I'm an empty-headed romantic?

I cast about for something to turn the conversation, but all I come up with is, "So…care to share my humble fare?"

Did *not* mean for that to rhyme!

Amusement deepening, Clive steps nearer and, with tanned fingers, taps the bag of baked chips. "I suppose this qualifies as a serving of carbohydrates—"

Ugh.

"—and vegetables."

Hmm. Hadn't thought of it like that, but it fits—in a rather processed, less-than-fresh way.

He taps the gourmet cookies. "Another serving of carbohydrates and sugar."

I know. Seriously out of whack with the food pyramid.

"And twenty of the sixty-four ounces of water required daily."

Nothing wrong with that. Quite right, actually. *So* glad I didn't give in to my baser cravings for a soda! *That* would have looked bad.

I meet his gaze, which is not too distant. In fact, the last time we were this close—

"Care to join me?" I blurt out.

As if becoming aware of how near he is, he takes a step back and busies himself with rolling the magazine with those tanned hands of his.

Just where did he get that tan?

When his eyes return to mine, the ease with which he holds himself is only slightly off.

"I don't suppose you'd allow me to take you out for a sandwich?"

Yes! Yes! Yes!

Unfortunately, procrastination has never gotten me anywhere but in trouble. "Sorry, but I'm on a tight schedule. Speaking of which, I really ought to get back to the burn unit."

"I'll walk with you."

I'm thrilled. And dismayed. Wishing I truly believed it possible to be unbelievably, inconceivably happy without a man, I hug my "dinner" to my chest as I walk alongside him. Despite the late hour, there are plenty of hospital personnel around, several of whom acknowledge Clive by name. Thus, our exchanges are kept to a minimum until we enter the construction area.

"So you've found afternoons and evenings are best to work on the burn unit," Clive says.

"Definitely, especially now that the rooms off the corridor are being fit with equipment. Though Dorian and Gray don't mind the commotion, I prefer quiet."

"Understandable."

We enter the domed room.

"Too, my other job can only be completed during the day, so it all works out." And since we're indulging in small talk… "So on which beach did you come by your tan?"

His lips quirk. "I was in Guatemala."

I falter. "Guatemala? Uh, sounds exotic."

"It is, though not in the sense you think. I wasn't vacation-ing."

I halt before the scaffolding. "Then what were you doing—?" I roll my eyes. "Sorry. None of my business."

"But it is your business, as you're the one who sent me there."

"Excuse me?"

"Remember the debt you advised me to pay?"

"Dr. MacPhail's—" I wince as my stomach gives a resound-ing SOS.

Clive's eyebrows rise. "You should probably feed it."

Despite my curiosity over my role in Guatemala, I step to the wall and lower to the floor. And Clive joins me. *Well, isn't this cozy.*

Afraid that my fluster is showing, I dip my head and open the bag of chips, then the gourmet cookies. As my substandard meal hardly qualifies as dinner, I'm tempted to forgo a prayer; however, considering how far I've drifted from God in spite of my good intentions to launch Operation: Perfect Faith, it's the least I can do. So I close my eyes, offer up thanks, and momen-tarily find Clive waiting on me.

"Okay." I pinch a chip from the bag. "Explain Guatemala."

Crunch, crunch, crunch.

He raises a knee and rests a forearm on it. "Contrary to your assumption, the debt I owed Adam had nothing to do with gambling—or even money."

That's a relief. I pinch another chip. "I'm listening."

He settles his gaze on the far wall in the vicinity of South America. "Years ago, Adam did me a favor that I may never be able to fully repay. These past weeks I've attempted to put a dent in my debt." He looks around. "He works with a Christian organization that recruits doctors to perform operations for those who lack access to adequate health care."

I'm all ears. Or should I say eyes? "Then you…"

"Went to Guatemala."

"Wow." And a Christian organization to boot!

"For years, Adam has been after me to get involved, but I've always turned him down. So when a doctor scheduled for the Guatemala clinic pulled out, Adam called in my debt. A debt I declined until you made me relent."

"Me?"

He lowers his eyes to the chip hovering before my mouth and with a wry smile gives my hand a push. "Eat, Kate."

And I do, crunching through the chip without actually tasting it. Of course, it *is* baked.

"I don't understand. Though I encouraged you to pay your debt, I couldn't have been any more convincing than Dr. MacPhail."

His lids narrow. "Couldn't you?"

Mustn't read too much into that. But what exactly does he mean? "Sorry, but I'm still not following."

He shifts, and I feel discomfort rise off him like steam. "Strangely enough, I care what you think of me, Kate."

Gulp. "What?"

"There's something about you, but I didn't see it the night we met—"

That would be pre-Michael, as in premakeover.

"—and tried not to see it the day I showed you the burn unit—"

Oh. Post-Michael. Postmakeover.

"—and told myself I shouldn't see it the day you hunted me

down for telling Jessica that you'd accepted the burn unit job. It was there."

What? What made him care what I thought? Though my go at self-improvement has to be some of it, despite his attempts to discourage me, it's more than that. Could it be my pizzazz?

Hmm…

My calm, soothing disposition?

Uhh…

My sense of humor?

Well…

My faith?

Could be. I *did* stand up for the inclusion of Christianity in the burn unit, and on more than one occasion he has witnessed my prayers, one of which included him. Maybe I've begun to exude that sense of goodwill with which steadfast Christians like Belle perfume the air.

In the next instant, I wince. As evidenced by the decreasing amount of time spent with God, I'm hardly steadfast. I believe, but am not doing much *doing*. Which is all the more reason to put Operation: Perfect Faith into effect tonight. And I will.

"I'm not sure what it is." Clive startles me out of my musings. "But you moved me in the right direction. And I want to thank you."

I blink at him. "I'm glad to have had a positive influence on you."

He turns his gaze toward the tarp-covered memorial plaque, and what rolls off my tongue seems the most natural thing to say. "I'm sure your wife and son would be proud of what you did in Guatemala."

He stiffens, but before I can wish back the words, his

shoulders ease. "I believe they would." Then he draws a deep breath—the kind that signals it's time to shove off.

And I panic. Flounder. Grasp. "So what was it like?"

"What?"

"Guatemala. The clinic."

I watch the struggle on his face, but just when I'm certain he's about to shrug off my question, he says, "Four clinics in ten days, actually. And between the nine members of our medical team, we treated over fifteen hundred people."

That takes my breath away.

"Our first clinic was a refugee camp in the mountains. The pictures you see of places like that, Kate…they're shocking."

"I've seen pictures."

"But that's all they are—pictures that don't come close to revealing the ungodly living conditions." He shifts, so deeply troubled that I feel the weight of his memories. "Incredible need… poverty…and every imaginable disease and ailment. It's not the twenty-first century there, let alone the twentieth."

It takes all my willpower not to give his hand a comforting squeeze.

"That first day we worked eight hours in cramped tents with only a thirty-minute break for lunch. By the time night fell, we hadn't made it through half of those seeking care. The next day, between surgery and dispensing medication, we put in twelve hours—again with only a thirty-minute break, during which I walked around the village." His brow ripples. "I couldn't take more than half a dozen steps without one of the children who danced ahead of me dropping back to touch my doctor's coat as if…"

I catch my breath, but he doesn't finish the sentence. So I do, though not aloud: *As if touching the garment of Jesus Himself. As if they knew who sent Clive to them.*

He draws a breath. "I peered into the cramped huts in which the families lived. They were dark, lit only by fires over which girls labored to turn cornmeal into tortillas." His gaze swings back to me. "Conjunctivitis and lung infections are rampant there. Do you know why?"

"No."

"Their Mayan religion encourages them to build huts without windows in order to keep out evil spirits. Thus, lacking proper ventilation, they live amid the smoke of their fires." He gives a crooked smile. "At one point, I had an urge to grab a translator and make him tell them about Jesus."

I startle, but no sooner does hope bud than he adds, "Fleeting only."

It was something though, Lord.

He begins to massage the back of his neck. "After one more day at the refugee camp, we went on to a beach village on the Pacific Coast. The clinic was a large, open adobe structure with a thatched roof. That first day, we saw over three hundred people, half of them children. It wasn't much different in the next two villages."

He drags his hand from his neck, and the weariness deepening the lines of his face starts to lift. "In spite of it all, Kate, the people persevere. And live. And smile. And laugh. And love. Especially the children. It made me wonder what they have that I don't." His eyes slide to me, and his mouth edges toward a smile. "Maybe I ought to check out the Mayan religion, hmm?"

I can't help my widening eyes, nor dropped jaw. The only thing I do control is my spluttering objection, but only because his smile goes from beginner (a little eye action) to intermediate (lots of eye action) to advanced (loads of eye action complete with a teasing glint).

Despite the fun he's having at my expense, I warm to his gray-blue irises…thrill at their depth…experience rending disappointment when a spasm of unease causes him to break eye contact and his smile to sink below beginner level.

"Probably more than you wanted to know."

"No! It's wonderful to hear how God worked through you to bring healing and hope to those people."

Oh, no. BIG "Oh, no."

Mouth tightening, he rises, meaning soon I'll be as alone as I was before he caught me at the vending machines. Perhaps more so now that I've tasted his company. And enjoyed it. And want more of it. He's leaving. And I have yet to alert him to my boyfriend-less status.

Which is good, especially since I'm determined to remain single.

"It's been a long day." He gazes down at me. "And it's going to be an early morning."

I start to stand, but he waves me back. Urgency pounding at my temples, I crane my neck to peer up at him. "Surgery?"

"Two before noon." He checks his watch. "Perhaps we'll run into each other tomorrow."

"As tomorrow's Saturday, I should be here all day." Hint, hint. "And a good portion of the night."

He nods. "Good night, then—"

"Michael and I are no longer seeing each other," I blurt out. Much to my dismay. Much to my self-loathing.

But much to my relief, his mouth turns up and the resulting smile includes teeth. "Glad to hear it."

He's glad…

"Good night, Kate."

That's it? "Uh, good night, Clive."

Friday, June 1

Dear Lord,

He's back. And there's something about me that makes him care what I think of him. That's good, isn't it? It means... What does it mean? And if it means what I want it to mean, should I want it? I know he has turned away from You, but perhaps he's coming back. After all, surely it was Your will that he travel to Guatemala to aid those in need. Even if I'm the one he credits with pushing him into it, he's heading in the right direction. And that's promising.

If Clive Alexander is the one You've been holding in reserve for me, You wouldn't care to send a sign, would You? Of course, here I go again calling on You when I've been less than faithful of late. Asking for answers when I'm negligent in answering Your call for an ongoing relationship. But that all changes tonight. Tonight I begin Operation: Perfect Faith. (I'm thinking Proverbs and maybe some Luke.)

So thank You for Clive's safe return from Guatemala and that he didn't react negatively when I blurted out the news about Michael (that was obnoxious, wasn't it?). Thank You for Belle's continuing pregnancy. Thank You for spring that unfolds into summer, the absence of another message from Michael on my answering machine, and the absence of notification that my rent is going up (or did that glare Maia gave me this morning mean she's about to sock it to me?). Speaking of which, please help me to resolve the sticky situation between the three of us.

Yours,

Kate

13

KATE MEADOWS is printed in a bold, I-don't-do-flourishes hand that causes the blood pumping through my veins to put the pedal to the metal.

Dragging my bottom lip between my teeth, I pull the taped envelope from the vending machine. It's him. Has to be. After the squandered anticipation of waiting to see him all morning, then afternoon, my hand trembles as I thrust a finger beneath the flap and sweep it along the seal.

"Ow!" I peer at the paper cut, then raise my finger to give it a good suck.

Ooh. Bad idea. Repeat after me: hospital…germs galore….

Lifting the hem of my oversized top, I use the back of it to dab at the cut, then return to the mysterious envelope, gingerly pry at the flap, and pull out a prescription slip headed: RX.

Meet me on the roof (use the maintenance stairs off the domed room). Come hungry. —Clive

Oh, my. Clive…the roof…hungry…

I reread what is the nicest prescription ever written for me. And in a legible hand! Pulse accelerating, I recall my quip that vending machine cuisine is hardly rooftop dining fare. Took it to heart, did he?

With a thrill, I imagine a rooftop dinner like those portrayed by Hollywood—candlelight, white tablecloth, long-stemmed roses, violinist, and tuxedoed gent whose one purpose in life is to sweep me off my feet. And not just any gent, but Clive Alexander, looking like he did the night he entered Belle and Beau's Boutique. This time looking that way for *me* rather than for Adelphia you-know-who. Looking *at* me, rather than *through* me. Admiring *my* figure in an elegant—

I glance down. Guess not.

From my accidentally colorful Keds to my victimized hip-huggers, to my short-sleeved oversized top, I'm far from elegant. Kate Meadows, Hollywood's fleeting sweetheart, better not quit her day job. Not to mention her night job.

Clutching the prescription, I turn from the machines and start back the way I came. As I near the construction area, I turn into the restroom to check my appearance.

Yu-uck! Not only did I become less conscientious of my appearance as the day progressed, but to keep from tumbling off the scaffolding, I'd lurched into a freshly painted wall. Hence the blue blotch on my hair and streak on my sleeve. Though I knew I ought to clean up before the paint dried, I'd given up on Clive. Thus, I'd doggedly set about repairing the smeared wall.

I pick at the blue-coated strands that start at my left temple and sweep backward, but there are too many. Grumbling under my breath, I turn on the tap and stick my cut finger into the stream.

A few minutes later, paper cut soaped, dried, and wrapped

in tissue, I head for the maintenance stairs. Three flights later, I step out on the roof into a relatively warm night. Relatively, as in not certain whether the prickles up and down my bare arms are caused by the breeze coming off the bay or the eerie dim that stretches across the rooftop between isolated pools of light. One thing I do know—no candlelight, white tablecloth, or roses in sight. And no Clive—tuxedoed or otherwise. Of course, maybe once my eyes adjust—

A shift in the darkness ahead, followed by footfalls, causes me to peer deeper. A moment later, Clive strides into the light thrown by the stairway at my back, revealing casual dress of khakis, a button-down shirt, and a light jacket. Not quite the impact of a tuxedo, but certainly an improvement over doctor's attire.

"You came." He halts before me.

How I wish my heart wasn't beating so wildly! "Just what the doctor ordered."

His regard shifts from my blue-streaked temple to my eyes. "Do you always follow doctor's orders?"

As I stare at Clive, who looks exceedingly Brad-ish at the moment, I wonder what it is about the backdrop of night that tempts one to romantic pinings. Were this a movie—

It's not. No candlelight, no white tablecloth, no tuxedo. Too bad.

"Do I always follow doctor's orders? Um…" I smile. "Within reason."

He returns the smile, causing the butterflies to beat more frantically in my stomach.

I pull the prescription from my jeans. "Of course, your invitation was a bit of a surprise."

"But still within reason."

"Well, I am hungry and it did sound like an invitation to a *real* meal."

"It is."

Tucking the prescription back in my pocket, I glance past his shoulder. "Then?"

"This way." He grips my arm and guides me through the darkness. Fortunately, my eyes adjust and pick out the path between metal boxes of varying sizes, all of which undoubtedly keep the hospital running. Many of which are groaning, clicking, and humming.

"Almost there." He turns me toward a large, dimly lit structure before which a brown shopping bag sits. And I can't help but be disappointed. Yes, I accepted that there was no candlelight, etcetera, but in truth I was holding out for something a far cry above a brown-bag meal.

Clive halts before what I guess to be a utility shed and releases my arm. "Sorry I didn't bring a blanket to sit on. We'll have to make do without." He lowers to the rooftop.

I sink down beside him and, with my back to the wall, quip, "Thank goodness for jeans."

"And Home-Baked Breads & Things." He reaches to the bag.

My ears perk at the name of the eatery where he took me the night I signed on for the burn unit. And a memory of the taste of Asi…Ashi—whatever!—makes me salivate.

"Ham and Swiss on Asiago." Clive hands me a paper-wrapped bundle. "No onions."

I blush. "Thank you."

What is it about him that makes funny things happen to my insides? Yes, he's handsome in his own way, but Michael is on the hunk side of manhood. In fact, despite his bald head—or perhaps because of it—he's more handsome than Clive. And younger.

Meaning I'm not shallow? Or could it be I have an "eye"

thing? Though both men's height and breadth and physique are nice, Clive's eyes do something to me that Michael's never did. And his laugh…

He sets another wrapped sandwich between us, and I'm relieved not to be eating alone. Two squat containers appear next. "Soup," he says, "something with lentils. And to wash it down…" Bottled water.

Hollywood would in no way approve of Clive's version of rooftop dining, but I'm touched by his thoughtfulness. And curious about his motive. Much as I'd like to think he has romantic designs on me (so much for being unbelievably, inconceivably happy), I know I shouldn't assign too much to what may simply be a kind gesture. But then, mustn't forget that near kiss. Nor that he was visibly pleased to hear that Michael is out of the picture.

"This is really nice of you."

"Wouldn't do for our resident artist to collapse from a lack of nourishment. After all, you have a deadline to meet."

That's what this is about, my deadline? *Just* my deadline? As I stare at him, his mouth tilts. No, it's more than that. I know it, and he knows it. Unless I'm fantasizing and he's teasing.

I clear my throat. "Thank you, Clive."

My, but I like the sound of his name—the way the *C* and *L* blend so smoothly…the long, drawn-out *I*…the *V* that vibrates across my bottom lip…the strong, silent *E*.

C L I V E. C L I V E. CLIVE.

"You're welcome."

Yanked back to the embodiment of that name, I try to hide my fluster by giving my full attention to the unwrapping of my sandwich.

"Cut your finger?"

I consider my index finger, which has bled through the

makeshift bandage. "Just a paper cut. Not likely to require the expertise of a highly trained plastic surgeon like yourself."

He pulls my hand from the sandwich, and at the rasp of his skin across mine (aren't doctors supposed to have soft hands?), I jerk.

He lifts his chin. "I'm not going to hurt you, Kate."

Are you sure about that?

As past experience whispers across my emotions, I avert my gaze. "I know. You just…surprised me."

How I hope he doesn't look to where my heart is pounding so hard that my top is surely shuddering!

He bends over my hand, unwinds the sorry bandage, and probes the tender flesh. "A bit more than your average paper cut. How did it happen?"

"Used my finger as a letter opener." In the next instant, I roll my eyes at the realization that he might connect my recent injury to his dinner invite.

He looks up. "My prescription?"

Oh well. "That's right. *You* did this to me."

"Then it's a good thing I have malpractice insurance. Of course, if you hadn't torn into the envelope…"

Embarrassment makes the air turn suddenly balmy. "I didn't tear into it!"

He smiles and returns his attention to the cut. "It won't require stitches, but you will want to keep it clean and covered. In the meantime…" He sets my hand on his thigh.

My hand is on Clive Alexander's thigh! Shouldn't be, but is. Shouldn't leave it there, but I do.

"…a proper bandage is in order." He tears a strip from a paper napkin, winds it around my finger, and finishes it off with a sturdy knot. And all the while, attraction skitters up and down my spine like a lab rat on triple-shot espresso.

"All better," he says.

I warm at the warmth in his eyes, almost shudder when those eyes lower to my mouth. Of course, might that be because it's hanging open?

Pulling my hand back, I look away, only to light on the sandwich in my lap. Without thinking, I lift the bundle to my mouth.

"No prayer tonight?"

Oops. I close my eyes and, fifteen seconds later, open them. "Thanks."

"Anytime." He takes a bite of his sandwich.

A moment later, I nearly moan at the pleasure of ham and Swiss on Asiago bread.

"Good?"

"Mmm." Nod. Nod. "Mmm."

After we polish off the sandwiches, we start in on the "something with lentils," the liquid warmth chasing away my chills.

"Better than the vending machine," Clive says as I fit the lid on the remains of my soup and drop the container in the bag.

I lean back against the building. "Thank you."

He also leans back. "Thank you for joining me."

"My pleasure." And it is. Right or wrong, mistake or not, I like his company. More than like it.

As Clive stares out across the roof, I catch movement in his lap, where he's turning his wedding band.

"Do you ever take it off?" I ask in advance of careful consideration. Ugh.

"Hmm?"

For fear that he might think I'm referring to something other than his ring, I nod at his hands. "Your wedding band."

The round and round movement ceases. "It's my constant companion. A reminder."

In deference to his heart's ache, my attraction to him takes a step back. He must have loved her very much.

"Of course, I'm also grateful for the protection it affords," he says in what seems an attempt to lighten the mood.

"From husband-hunting women?"

"Sounds egotistical, but yes."

"Then you're not looking for another wife?" Ugh again.

"Not yet, though three years should be long enough, shouldn't it?"

Yes!

"Uh…I suppose it's however long a person needs."

He gives the ring another turn. "If I marry again, I intend to do it right."

"Then you did it wrong?"

Ah! Who oiled my lips?

"Let's just say I missed out on a lot."

Such as? And if I *am* a candidate, am I qualified to fill his departed wife's shoes?

Candidate! Qualified! How pathetic does that sound?

I softly clear my throat. "Then you're interested in someone like…um…"

He turns his gaze on me. And oh, how I like his eyes. And the line of his nose. And the turn of his mouth. And his firm chin, even if it is stubbled over.

Feeling my cheeks warm, I wish the warmth would spread to my arms. "You're looking for someone like Jillian?"

Surprise crosses his face. "Jillian was a wonderful woman—loving, accomplished, beautiful—but there was only one of her. Just as there's only one of you, Kate."

Nice line. Makes me warm all over (thankfully).

"What I'm trying to say is that should I marry again, I want what I missed with Jillian. And our son."

Eerrrkkkk! Though I already know the answer, I force myself to seek clarification. "Then you want another child."

"Actually—" his mouth lifts in the muted light—"I'd like several."

Whooshhh! Struggling to maintain my bowed mouth, the corners of which feel suddenly weighted, I clench my hands.

It's to be expected. After all, it's not as if I haven't been here, done this. *Many* times. Men may not possess a maternal instinct, but most possess a paternal instinct. Even Michael, who professes a take-'em-or-leave-'em attitude, may find himself on the take-'em end of the spectrum eventually.

Of course, there's adoption. But, as always, I'm panged by the remembrance of Christopher's reaction to the option. Maybe Clive is different.

"But the first requirement," he says, "is to find the right woman, a woman I can love."

Love. Cures all ills, doesn't it? But can the desire for natural children be considered an ill?

"So, until the right one comes along, this stays on." He raises his ringed hand between us.

But all I see is a wall that doesn't look as if it can be scaled.

Clive lowers his hand. "You said you're no longer seeing Michael."

Surprised by the change of subject, I manage, "That's right."

"Then you're done with all this self-improvement nonsense?"

I am, aren't I? Well, almost. Wondering how appropriate it is to mention my breast reduction, I stall. "One should never stop trying to improve oneself."

"Yes, but the self-improvement I'm referring to is of the instant, superficial variety."

"Of which you don't approve."

A shadow crosses his face that has nothing to do with the night. "There was a time when I did. A time when I was as self-absorbed as those who wrap their identity in pretty packages."

"And now?"

He glances at his left hand. "Now I know different. Unfortunately, that knowledge cost me everything."

As his bitterness raises yet another wall, I await enlightenment; however, the silence grows, and I realize he's said as much as he intends.

"So you're done?" he prompts, and it takes some backpedaling to retrieve his question of whether or not I've abandoned my quest for an "instantly" perfect Kate.

I try for a mischievous smile. "Actually, there's still liposuction—"

"Kate."

"—and electrolysis—"

He closes a hand over mine in my lap, causing me to startle.

He thinks I'm serious. But surely my smile didn't escape him. Or did it? After all, I'm more in the shadows than he.

I look up. "You do know I'm teasing, don't you?"

"Are you?"

Though confirmation springs to my tongue, a vision of the business card that yet lurks in my purse rises before me. "Well, sort of. I *was* considering liposuction and electrolysis, but I have decided against both."

"Why?"

It's a trick question. I know it as surely as I feel his warm skin against mine. Unfortunately, it's hard to think straight with him holding my hand.

"Why, Kate?"

"For one, the procedures are too expensive."

"Then you'd go through with them if money was no object?"

Knew it was a trick question! I flex my hand beneath his. "No, I don't think so."

"You don't *think* so?"

I shift around to face him. "If you recall, you approved of my first attempt at self-improvement. And though it's true you advised against the removal of my mole and gap, afterward you said I looked nice."

"I do like the way you look, Kate. Very much."

"Then who's to say you wouldn't like me better if I took self-improvement to the next level?"

In concert with my mental slap upside the head, Clive's left eyebrow soars.

"*Do* you want me to like you better?" His eyes stray to my mouth, and for one lovely moment I'm certain he's ready to deliver on that kiss.

"Kate," he says on a sigh that returns his regard to mine, "of course, I didn't object to seeing you in something other than shapeless clothes and to your hairstyle and use of makeup. In fact, had the mole removal and bonding been your idea, I wouldn't have dissuaded you. However, it was obvious that Michael was pushing, that you, like so many of those I once charged thousands of dollars to 'perfect,' were seeking to please someone other than yourself. And that—" his hand flexes on mine—"is where women fall into the vicious cycle of cosmetic surgery. The never-ending pursuit of something that can never be had, no matter how perfect one's nose, chin, or thighs."

Put that way…

He lowers his gaze, frowns at his hand on mine, then pulls back. "At the moment I may be on the wrong side of God, but I know He wants you to see yourself as He sees you, Kate."

He just said God. All by himself. Without prompting. And last night he mentioned Jesus.

"So, no liposuction, hmm?"

Slightly breathless, I say, "Unless it's something *I* want."

"Do you?"

"Well, I am a bit heavy in the thighs—"

"No, you're not."

He says it with such certainty that I flush at the realization he's noticed that part of me. "You don't think I could stand to lose a few inches?"

Cannot *believe* I'm discussing my thighs with him! And asking for his opinion!

His mouth twitches. "Perhaps a bit of toning."

Making no attempt to fight my own twitching lips, I smile. "All right, no liposuction." Though tempted to change the subject, I know there won't be a better time to come clean. "However, there is a procedure I've scheduled for this fall."

Bye-bye smile. "What's that?"

"Breast reduction." Cheeks warming, I glance down. "In case you haven't noticed—"

"I have."

Of course he has. Doesn't everyone? I give a nervous laugh. "My idea, not Michael's. In fact, it's the one procedure he advised against. Strange, huh?"

His eyebrows lift, but he doesn't voice what I can see he's thinking. A moment later, a sympathetic frown transforms his face. "I imagine you suffer from back problems."

So glad we're on the same page. "Do I ever!"

"Then you ought to have the procedure. However, if you can stand it, I'd advise you to postpone it until after you've had children, as the procedure can affect your ability to breastfeed."

Pang. "I…know."

His lids narrow. "Breastfeeding not in your future?"

He has no idea how near the truth he is. Dare I tell him? And possibly quash any interest he has in me?

Ouch.

I feel like the recipient of a nasty pinch, but it's better to know now where he stands with regard to children. Better to pay now while I'm still dealing in the currency of infatuation rather than in pieces of my heart. I do *not* want to repeat what happened with Christopher.

"Kate?"

I square my shoulders. "Actually, I don't..."

Say it!

"I don't think I'm going to have children."

Think? Did you say think? *There's no "think" about it!*

Clive frowns. "No children?"

"Natural, I mean, er, biological."

"Why?"

"Well, there are so many children in the world who need homes."

Pay me now...pay me later!

"So I'm thinking adoption."

I'm thinking boc-boc-boc!

"And since I...well, I can't..."

"Are you worried about ruining your body?"

I gasp. "Of course not. It's just that..."

Last night's first installment of Operation: Perfect Faith rises before me, specifically Proverbs 11:3, which says that good people are guided by honesty, whereas treacherous people are destroyed by dishonesty. Feeling decidedly treacherous, I long to come clean. But I can't.

"What about you?" I gush. "Would you consider adoption?"

Confusion slides onto Clive's brow. "I suppose, but only after I repeated the experience of having a biological child."

Knew I should have stuck with unbelievably, inconceivably happy as a singleton.

As my heart goes into a nosedive, Clive looks out across the rooftop. "There's something about watching one's child grow, running a hand over the little bump that becomes a bulge…"

Pang.

"…feeling the flutter of tiny hands just out of reach…"

Double pang.

"…the kick of little feet…" He trails off, and in the silence that feels like a weight on my shoulders, I rub my goose bump–riddled arms.

His eyes return to mine. "I want to experience that again. Provided I find the right woman."

Which Kate Meadows is not. And that's okay. Better than stringing myself along and ending up brokenhearted again.

I nod at his ring finger. "Well, until you're ready to begin the hunt for Mrs. Right, I promise not to put out the word that you're eligible. *And* I assure you that you needn't worry about keeping me at bay."

"Then you're not attracted to me?"

I startle.

He grins.

Oh, how I'd like to bite at his hook, but there's Christopher. Christopher who, though I don't doubt he loved me, couldn't face life without a little junior. And Clive has admitted the same, though it seems for reasons other than presenting a Clive-stamped trophy to the world.

I look away. "I admit you're attractive, in a Brad Pitt sort of way."

"Heard that before."

The droll words are too tempting, and I glance sidelong at him. "I'll bet you have."

"Brad Pitt not your type?"

The absurdity of his question causes me to issue a snort so unladylike that I'd be horrified if I were still fantasizing about a future with him. "Honestly, what woman would say Brad Pitt *isn't* her type?"

"Then?"

Why is he pressing me? It's as if it really matters. As if he's decided three years *is* long enough to hide behind his wedding band. Of course, perhaps he's playing with me. Teasing me.

Determined to give as good as I get, I say, "Resemblance does not a Brad Pitt make."

He nods. "So what about me don't you like?"

As I resume my attempt to warm away the goose bumps, I remember my encounter with him the day I started work on the burn unit. "Maybe it has something to do with the warning—"

"Here." He starts to remove his jacket.

Recalling how affected I'd been by his warmth wrapped around me the night we had dinner at Home-Baked Breads & Things, I shake my head. "I'm all right."

"Come on, Kate. You know you want it."

I do. I really do. And the longer I fight it, the more of his warmth steals away into the night. "Okay." I slide my arms into his sleeves.

He sits back. "You said something about a warning?"

As I melt into his heat, attraction resumes its jaunt up and down my spine. I'll get over it. Over *him*. A year from now—maybe two—this moment will be a distant memory.

"So someone warned you off me?"

I lift my chin from his collar. "Um-hmm."

"Adelphia?"

I open my mouth to remind him that it was *he* who issued the warning, but the opportunity to delve into his relationship with that woman is too tempting.

"Why would Adelphia warn me off you?"

Regret etches his mouth. "Because she'd like to take our relationship to the next stage."

So it *has* reached some "stage." "You're no longer just colleagues?"

"Something more than colleagues. Something far less than committed. Was it Adelphia?"

I shake my head. "Someone more convincing, with whom you're intimately familiar."

With a flash of annoyance, he leans nearer. "Who?"

"You." I poke his chest. "Clive Alexander said I wouldn't like you."

His confusion deepens before it clears. "Ah. And you believed me?"

"That *is* what you wanted."

"At the time."

Pleasure runs through me, and for one blissful moment, I let it have its way with me. But the reminder of his desire for biological children resurfaces.

Feeling a tingle in my nose, I latch on to humor, misplaced though it is. "Are you propositioning me, Clive Alexander?"

He looks down at my finger planted at the center of his chest.

Curling the accusatory appendage into my palm, I lower my hand to my lap.

"Propositioning." He draws out the syllables. "A rather strong word for letting a woman know that I'd like to see more of her."

Dear God, why did You allow this? Why tempt me with what can never be?

Of course, maybe Clive would feel different about biological children if he knew I couldn't—

Christopher didn't.

But he's not Christopher.

He feels the same need to perpetuate the human race with a biological junior. Get out before your heart ends up sliced, diced, and pureed!

Clive clears his throat. "Plainly put, Kate, I'd like to know you better."

A combination of longing and fear stirs me. "Why?"

His surprise is palpable; however, it's replaced by a frown that evidences he's giving the question full consideration. "I asked myself that a lot while I was in Guatemala."

Then he thought about me, actually had Kate Meadows on his mind.

Why does that sound like a country song?

"And the more I asked myself 'Why Kate?' the more I noticed that, despite all the hardship those people endure, they still have hope because of those willing to make the lives of those less blessed a little better."

He said "blessed"! Christian-ese at its best. And yet he doesn't seem to notice, as evidenced by the absence of a flinch or stricken look.

He draws a breath. "It opened my eyes to what I have despite all I've lost. And what I could have if I allowed myself to hope like those people. So I did. Do you know what I hoped for?"

I shake my head.

"I hoped that when I returned home, it would be over between you and Michael."

I'm shocked by his honesty. "Oh."

"Now you know," he says almost businesslike. "And your answer is?"

I want it, too, but Christopher looms—as does Clive's desire for biological fatherhood.

"Kate?"

A lump rises in my throat. "I can't."

"Why?"

"For one, my schedule is overflowing."

"I'm aware of your commitments and that I'm largely responsible for your burden, but from time to time you need to come up for air."

Imagine coming up for air with Clive Alexander....

And in a moment of weakness, I do, envisioning the kiss that should have been mine. Hardly coming up for air. More like drowning...

"What other objections do you have?"

"Uh..." I grope until, as if by divine intervention, I'm handed the one thing likely to send him packing. "I'm a Christian, whereas you're...not. Well, at least not a *practicing* Christian, and it's important to me that whomever I marry—"

His face tightens. "This isn't an offer of marriage, Kate."

"Of course it isn't. Still, as marriages typically start with a date, it follows that a person should only pursue another with whom they're...compatible."

"In your case, a *practicing* Christian."

"That's right."

"So Michael is a *practicing* Christian?"

"I...think so."

Clive's eyes bore into mine. "You *think*?"

Feeling like a butterfly—make that a moth—pinned to a board, I say, "He *was* saved as a teenager, and though he hadn't attended church for years—"

"Let me guess, he resumed his pursuit of Christianity once you started dating, even attended church with you. That is, until you broke it off with him."

Though it's too soon to verify, I know it's likely Michael won't be at church tomorrow.

"Is that how you define a *practicing* Christian, Kate? One who attends church in order to impress a woman? If so, I could be persuaded to take a look at the inside of your nice little church."

That last is so punctuated by sarcasm, it stings.

"Any other objections?"

You mean besides the fact you require biological children?

And I nearly say it, but to what end? So that for the remainder of my time at the hospital I suffer his pitying glances every time we run into each other? No. My inability to bear children is nobody's business but my own.

Exactly what about Proverbs 11:3 did you not understand, Kate?

Feeling a sudden need to be alone—to straighten out the kinks in my chest, iron out wrinkled emotions—I spring to my feet. "It's late." I thrust a hand out. "Thank you for dinner. It was delicious."

After a tense hesitation, he rises and clasps my hand.

Resisting Clive's pull, I say, "Now I really must put my nose to the grindstone." I give my hand a tug.

He holds fast. "You like me, Kate. I know you do."

As much as I long to deny it, I'm too transparent. "Yes, but that doesn't change that we're not right for each other. Simple as that."

"No." His breath moves the hair on my brow. "Not simple as that." And to prove it, he looks to my lips…angles his head… bends nearer….

I am *so* sunk.

Though his mouth lightly brushes mine, my senses react with the enthusiasm of flint on steel. Sparks. And more sparks. So bright I gasp and close my eyes to keep from being blinded by the sudden shift from night into day.

Oh, my. Clive Alexander is kissing me, causing a queasy flutter to invade my stomach and pain to prick my heart—not far from what I described to Belle all those weeks ago when I finally acknowledged that Michael wasn't "The One."

Then suddenly it's over, and I blink my way back to the night and the man before me, whose eyes are just this side of triumphant.

Taking a step back, I press fingers to my lips and am surprised when I don't receive a shock of static electricity.

"Complicated is what I'd call it." Clive releases my other hand, which I only then realize he was still holding.

I drop my arms to my sides. "Complicated?"

"Not as simple as you thought."

Oh. "I...didn't want you to do that."

"Yes, you did. You've been wanting it for as long as I have."

"No."

"Careful, Kate." He smiles softly. "Christians aren't supposed to lie."

And I *am* lying.

I take another step back and choke out, "Good night," then hurry across the roof.

Not until I reach the maintenance stairs do I realize that I'm still wearing Clive's jacket. I'd return it to him, but I want another kiss too badly...want more than the secondhand warmth of his jacket...want his arms around me....

"Ah!"

I jerk the jacket off, drape it over the railing, and descend the stairs to the domed room. Ignoring the mess of brushes and open paint cans, I head for the parking garage.

Saturday, June 2

Dear Lord,

I'm a mess. Of course, You already know that. Though Your voice within says, "Tell Clive," fear says, "Why?" After all, what's the likelihood that this man to whom I'm so attracted might come to care enough for me that he would set aside the need to see himself in a child of his own? And even if he did, surely his desire for a biological child would always be there, as would my inability to bear him one. So why complicate matters? Why not just walk away? Yes, honesty would be the "perfect" response, but I'm just not up to perfect. Sorry.

Please help me put this Kate-Michael-Maia triangle to bed, and in such a way that I don't further offend either of them. I know — call him.

Thank You for another good day for Belle and baby. Regarding the baby shower, thank You for Belle's mother stepping up to the plate. I know with You all things are possible, but it would have been hard for me to host the shower.

I will be at church tomorrow.

Kate

PS: Flipped open to 1 Timothy, so I think I'll start there tonight. Mind if I pray myself to sleep afterward?

14

I played hooky again. But it's not as if I didn't try to make it to church. After all, I told God that He could count on me. It's just that *I* didn't count on Michael.

There I was, all spiffed up, when there he was. I caught sight of him a moment before he would have caught sight of me, had I not stumbled back from the doorway of my Sunday school class. Unfortunately, that little move not only cost me my doughnut, which went rolling down the hall with the smug enthusiasm of the gingerbread man before the wolf gobbled him up, but a decaf-splashed blouse. Afraid other stragglers might call attention to my plight, I'd inched along the wall toward my doughnut. Not that I intended to gobble it up—yuck!—but I couldn't just leave it there.

Five minutes later, flapping the front of my blouse in an attempt to cool my flushed chest, I'd jumped in my car and headed out of the parking lot.

So why didn't I stay and talk to Michael? And why am I now hurrying down the winding corridor toward the burn unit on a Sunday? With regard to the former, not only did the surprise of Michael's presence leave my blouse doused in coffee, but considering how we left it the night I blew, church seemed an awkward place for discussion. As for my detour, the mess I left in the domed room called to me on my way home.

I know. Sunday is a day of rest. But it shouldn't take long, and once it's done, I'll be able to enjoy the rest of the day without worrying about what awaits me on Monday. And it's not as if a little paint and turpentine will make any difference to the state of my clothes.

As I step from the winding corridor, I glance at my blouse, visible between the lapels of the buttonless sweater I scrounged out of the backseat of my car. Though the coffee stain isn't as obvious against the taupe-colored material as it was when wet, it's still not a pretty sight.

I tug the sweater closed, only to wince as my fingers graze my skin through the blouse. Dragging at the neckline, I glance at my bright red skin. Still no blistering, but it smarts. Promising myself I'll put something on it as soon as I get home, I cross the domed room.

Something is amiss, I realize as I near the scaffolding. I halt and frown at the tidy collection of paint cans, brushes, and folded tarps. Someone cleaned up after me. It wouldn't be Dorian or Gray, as weekend work is out of the question for those two who have so many parties, so little time. As for the maintenance staff, they stay clear of the construction area. So?

Clive. He would have seen the mess when he came off the roof. But would he have taken the time to put it in order? Especially after the way we parted?

I try to imagine him doing it, and it isn't all that hard. In fact, I'm certain it was Clive, which makes my attraction to him all the harder to fight.

Alternately flapping my blouse and blowing cool air down

my chest, I stare at the work done on my behalf. Why? To impress me? Or was he just being considerate? Or might he be obsessive about cleanliness? Like Christopher...

Of course, Christopher with his big, soft hands—as opposed to Clive's raspy, manly hands—wouldn't have lowered himself to cleaning brushes.

I release my hold on my blouse and glance over my shoulder at the entrance to the winding corridor. Is Clive working today?

It would be best to thank him the next time we run into each other, but I have an overwhelming urge to do it now. Which is likely to send the wrong message. And yet, five minutes later, I'm approaching the burn unit's "command central," a.k.a. the nurses' station.

It appears deserted, but when I peer over the counter, a middle-aged woman looks up from her clipboard. "May I help you?"

"I'm trying to locate Dr. Alexander. Is he in today?"

"No."

As disappointment unfolds, she adds, "Not officially."

"*Un*officially, then?"

She narrows her lids. "You're the artist, right? The one who's doing up the new burn unit?"

"Yes." I reach a hand down to her. "Kate Meadows."

"Alice Apple."

As we shake, I glance at her badge. Alice Apple it is. Cute name.

"I peeked in yesterday when you were working on Australia." She pulls her hand back.

"You did?" Though there were a few comings and goings I'd been aware of, owing to the expectation of seeing Clive, I don't recall her being one of them.

"I didn't want to interrupt you. You looked very into it. Great work you do. I can see why Dr. Alexander chose you for the job."

"Thank you. So is he *un*officially around?"

She raises her pen and points right. "Down that hall, left, and straight through to the noise." At my questioning frown, she adds, "Discharge party for a little boy who's been in recovery for three months. Dr. Alexander likes to send the children home on a positive note, especially as it's usually just the first of many hospital stays."

As it was for Jessica...

She sighs. "Makes it easier for them to return."

Once more plucking at my blouse, I nod. "I imagine so. However, I don't want to interrupt."

"Everyone's welcome." She waves me toward the hall. "Go on."

Should I? After all, this *could* wait until tomorrow.

On top of the foolishness that, against all sense and reason, made me seek out Clive in the first place, my curiosity over the discharge party and the man behind it is roused.

"Maybe I'll stick my head in."

The woman returns her attention to her clipboard. "Have a piece of cake for me."

Shortly, the noise leads me to a set of doors over which brightly colored letters spell out *THE PLAYROOM*—the soon-to-be outdated version of the domed room. Unfortunately, as the narrow window in each door is covered, I *will* have to stick my head in. But if the noise is any indication of the number of people, my entry should go largely unnoticed. I step inside.

The room before me, being less than half the size of the domed room, is crowded. Very few glance my way.

I move to the edge of the fray, and a quick sweep reveals as many as thirty adults, a dozen of whom are garbed in hospital fatigues. A similar number of children are present, among them victims of fire as evidenced by bandages, hospital gowns, and wheelchairs.

My heart constricts at the sight, and it lightens to see their smiles, which in several cases are accessorized by blue and white frosting. And their childish, innocent laughter—

As compared to the deeply warm laughter that turns my head.

I look to Clive, who stands to the far right with his profile to me, and swallow hard as attraction kicks in. Though I tell myself I made the right choice, I find myself entertaining the possibility that it could work out between us. At least until a little boy appears beside Clive and gives his pant leg a tug.

Dropping to his haunches, Clive lays a hand on the child's shoulder, listens to his chirpy little voice, then draws the boy to him for a hug. He wears children well.

Time to go.

I turn away only to hear, "Miss Kate!"

Can I pretend I didn't hear?

"Miss Kate!"

I turn back to Jessica, whose face is bright and smiling despite yet showing evidence of the fire. She waves, says something to her mother, and heads toward me.

She draws near, looking pretty in a pink checked dress. "I didn't know you were coming."

I pull my bottom lip from between my teeth and smile. "Neither did I. I'm...uh...trying to track down Dr. Alexander."

"He's here." She points to where I saw him moments earlier. "Oh! And here he comes."

Determined to make the best of it, I glance at him, but only long enough to note the absence of a smile.

"Luke Warren's going home today," Jessica says.

I return my regard to her. "That's wonderful."

"Of course, he'll have to come back like me."

"I understand he's been here for three months."

"Yeah. His arms and chest got all burned, and one of his legs, but he's better now."

"I'm glad to hear it."

"Kate," Clive says.

I meet his gaze, which is less than warm. Regardless, were I made of butter, I'd melt. "Cli—er, Dr. Alexander."

"I didn't expect to see you today."

"I dropped by to thank you for cleaning up my mess in the domed room." I shrug. "Sorry. I didn't mean to crash the party."

"I'm glad you did." He looks to his left. "It gives me the opportunity to introduce the man who recommended your work to me."

Cranking up my smile, I start to follow his gaze.

"Oh! What happened, Miss Kate?"

"Hmm?"

Jessica points at my chest, and I find I'm once more tugging at my blouse, the material of which has become increasingly irritating. Self-consciously, I lower my hand and pull the lapels of my sweater over the stain. "Nothing. I just—"

"Spilled your coffee, hmm?" drawls a familiar voice—*painfully* familiar.

Emotions slamming into one another, I come face-to-face with Christopher Stapleton the Second. The one who said he'd love me forever. Who put his ring on my finger. Who made me give it back.

Lord, You've got to be kidding!

"Are you all right, Ms. Meadows?"

I blink at Christopher. He's pretending he doesn't know me.

Which is for the best as his wife is probably lurking nearby.

I give a vigorous nod. "I'm fine."

He extends a hand. "Christopher Stapleton."

I briefly consider passing on the nicety; however, my behavior is suspect enough. Hoping I'm not trembling as bad as I
feel, I allow him to encase my hand in his, which is still big and
soft. Big is fine, I tell myself as memories of last night return,
but rough is better.

"Kate?" Clive says in a sharp voice.

What did I do? I pull free of Christopher. "Yes?"

"I asked if the coffee was hot."

Seriously off-kilter, I say, "They were out of…um…cream,
so I used one of those little packets of powder…you know…" I
grip an imaginary packet and give it a shake. "So, yeah, it was
pretty hot. But I'm okay."

Appearing unimpressed, he lowers his gaze to my neckline.

"You should check her, Dr. Alexander," Jessica says.

Huh?

Jessica gives a motherly nod. "Burns aren't anything to fool
with, Miss Kate. Believe me."

I do. Still, I shake my head. "I'm fine. Really."

Clive takes my arm. "Come with me."

"Really, this isn't necessary." However, a few moments later
he ushers me out of the playroom and into a small room down
the hall.

He closes the door, leads me to an examining table, and
releases my arm. "Hop up." He pats the table and turns toward
a sink.

"Hop? Look, Dr. Alexander, I'm not eight years old."

He slowly turns, revealing a grin. "Sorry—habit. Would you
mind getting up on the table?"

I clutch the lapels of my sweater. "Yes, I would."

Losing the grin, Clive takes a step toward me. "What's the problem, Kate?"

As if he doesn't know! "In case you've forgotten, last night you wanted to date me. And you…kissed me."

"Believe me, I haven't forgotten."

Really?

"Well, don't you think it's a bit uncomfortable that you want to, you know, look at me?" I wince. "I mean, examine me? Like a doctor."

Oh, Lord! My mouth runneth over!

He folds his arms over his chest. "I am a doctor."

I snort. "Of course you are, but last night—"

He steps nearer. "Have you changed your mind about last night?"

"No." Well, perhaps a tiny bit, but I'll get a grip. *Must* get a grip.

"Then you should have no objections to me, in the capacity of a doctor, examining your burn. Now let me—"

"No!" I clap a hand to my chest and gasp at the sting that zings across my skin.

Clive closes the distance between us, takes my arm, and steers me toward the table. "Up, Kate."

And I go like a lamb to slaughter.

Pushing aside the sweater, he peers at the skin above the neck of my blouse. "When did this happen?"

He's looking at me. But if he thinks he's going to get a closer look, if he thinks I'm going to take off my blouse and let him gawk at my unwieldy breasts, he can think again.

He touches me with those rough fingers and probes the skin above my neckline. And I can't be sure if my gasp is born purely of pain.

"When, Kate?"

I stare at the ceiling, which is the most uninteresting shade of white. "Maybe an hour ago. I was on my way into my Sunday school class when I sloshed coffee down my front." No need to tell him the reason.

"And you've done nothing for it?"

"I was going to put ice on it when I got home."

"No ice."

I look into his serious face. "What?"

"It's too harsh and can cause tissue damage."

"Then butter?"

"No." He returns his attention to the burn and, a moment later, pronounces, "It's superficial, or first degree if you prefer."

"That's good, right?"

"No, but it could be far worse."

"Oh."

"And it might be." He straightens. "I need to see the rest of your chest."

I yank my sweater closed. "I am *not* letting you—"

"Then you'll have to be my eyes."

"What?"

"I'll turn around and you open your blouse and tell me if there are any blisters."

"There aren't. I already looked."

"Look again."

I eye him. "How do I know I can trust you not to...you know."

"Peek?" His mouth tilts. "I give you my word."

"Is that all?"

"It's all you need, Kate."

It is, isn't it? Still, I hesitate before motioning for him to turn around.

As he gives me his back, I start on the buttons.

"How's the finger?"

I glance at the flesh-colored bandage binding my paper cut—a definite improvement over the tissue I first wrapped around it. Of course, the one Clive tied did the job pretty well. And that's when it hits me: If I'm not more careful, availing myself of his medical expertise could become a habit.

"It's better, thank you." I grimace. "Of course, I imagine you're getting tired of playing doctor with me."

I jerk my gaze to his unmoving back.

"Not at all," he says with a note of amusement.

Rolling my eyes, I pop the rest of the buttons free and lower my chin. "My chest and upper abdomen are just red, but it does hurt."

"Is the skin's appearance the same as that on your upper chest?"

"Not quite as red. I guess my blouse took the worst of it."

"You're fortunate." He steps to the sink and opens a drawer. "I'm going to give you an antibiotic cream. When you get home, apply a cool, not cold, compress. Are you decent?"

I pull my blouse closed. "Sort of."

He turns. "The burn should heal in five to seven days. Until then, wear loose tops. If you experience discomfort, a mild pain reliever will help." He uncaps the tube. "I suppose you'd like to do the honors."

"Yes!" I grab the proffered tube.

Mouth tucking at the corners, he turns around again. "If you're worried about the cream staining your blouse, I can give you gauze bandages to cover the burn."

"Not necessary." I squeeze a glob onto my palm. "I've already accepted that the blouse is a goner." Fortunately, it was clearanced at 75 percent off. Unfortunately, I really liked it.

Keeping an eye on Clive's back, I part my blouse and gingerly smooth the cream over the affected areas. And it feels somewhat better.

Clive widens his stance. "How far back do you and Christopher Stapleton go?"

That eye I've been keeping on his back nearly pops out. Hands frozen on the button I'm coaxing into its ridiculously small hole, the accomplishment of which is hindered by my bandaged finger, I search for…well…a lie. Which Operation: Perfect Faith has a lot to say about. But this time it's 1 Timothy that warns me about being honest—keeping my conscience clear to prevent my faith from being shipwrecked.

I sigh. Though I may not be able to bring myself to reveal my inability to bear children, I certainly can be honest about this. "How did you know?"

Continuing to face opposite, he crosses his arms over his chest. "The look on your face, the way your hand trembled when you shook hands. Then you began to babble, and I had to ask twice if the coffee was hot." He pauses. "But the real clincher was the way Stapleton stared at you."

I frown. What way was that?

"Decent?" Clive asks.

Realizing I'm still mostly unbuttoned, I say, "No!" and force the button into its hole. "Just a moment." A moment I badly need, and which I stretch to nearly a minute. "Okay, I'm decent."

He turns, and from his raised eyebrow I know he expects an answer. "How do you know Christopher?" I stall with a question of my own.

"The hospital leases equipment through his company, so we've had dealings, but most recently I got to know him through his son—"

Son...

"—who has visited his cousin several times a week since Luke was admitted."

"Luke?" I scrabble after the familiar name.

"Luke Warren, the little boy being discharged today."

That's right. Jessica told me about him.

"When he knocked a pot of boiling water off the stove, he was burned over 20 percent of his body."

My imagination does a number on me, conjuring images that cause a chill to travel across my shoulders.

Clive nods. "It was bad. Thought we might lose him those first few days, but he pulled through. He's what we call a *save*."

My heart jostles at how amazingly beautiful that unremarkable single-syllable word sounds in the context of life.

I smile. "That must make you feel good."

"It does." He studies my face, making me self-consciously aware of my emotions.

"So you—" I swallow—"don't regret leaving your cosmetic surgery practice?"

"I don't. Though helping burn victims reconstruct their lives is hardly glamorous, the hours are unpredictable, and the compensation is beneath what I previously earned, it's what I was called to do."

"Called to do? If I didn't know better, I'd say you're getting spiritual on me, Dr. Alexander."

He momentarily looks aside. "It does sound that way. Of course, it hardly qualifies me as a *practicing* Christian."

I flush at the reminder of my objection to dating him. Thus, I return to a relatively safe topic. "So Luke is Christopher Stapleton's nephew."

Clive settles back on his heels. "Yes—rather, soon-to-be *ex*-nephew."

"Ex?"

"According to Stapleton's son, his parents are divorcing."

Then Christopher and the woman who bore him a child are calling it quits, untying the knot.

Not that I'm gloating. Quite the opposite, as not until I put aside my anger and resentment over his rejection was I able to heal. True, from time to time I'm pained by his abandonment, but I no longer wish ill on him, which I did before giving my life to Christ. How sad for Christopher…his wife…especially their little boy.

Clive steps nearer. "I assume the two of you were involved at some time or other."

Uncomfortably aware that I'm still on the examining table—in more ways than one—I hop down and search out the cap for the cream. "Yeah…we were."

His open hand appears inches from my face, at the center of which is the cap.

I pinch it. "Thanks."

"How far back do you go?"

As much as I hate talking about my past, I don't want Clive to believe of me what I believed of Adelphia. "Years and years—eight, I believe."

"And?"

"It didn't work out." No need to go into our engagement or the reason for breaking it off.

"So he married someone else."

Then Clive knows we were engaged? Or is he just guessing? "So it appears."

"Which didn't work out either."

Where is he going with all this? Well, he's not going there with me. "Guess not." I start for the door. "Thanks again for cleaning up my mess." A moment later, I reach for the handle, only to jerk back when Clive's hand arrives ahead of mine.

"It was the least I could do after running you off."

"You didn't run me off."

"Yes, I did." He calls me on the lie.

Oops. Sorry, Lord.

"And I apologize. I didn't mean to make you feel cornered."

"I didn't—"

"Yes, you did."

Ashamed at how quick I am to resort to falsehood to protect myself, I sigh. "You're right. I *did* feel cornered." I force a smile. "You are, after all, persistent."

"When the situation warrants." He eases open the door. "But under the circumstances, I suppose it all worked out for the best."

"Yeah." I step ahead of him into the hallway, only to turn back. "What do you mean 'for the best'?"

He raises his eyebrows. "Stapleton and his pending divorce."

I feel my face tighten. "You think he and I…? Oh no. Absolutely *not*."

"You sound certain of that."

"I am!"

"As certain as you are about you and me?"

I scoff. "More so!"

He smiles. "I'll take that as encouragement."

"What?"

He steps forward, slides a finger up my throat, and lifts my chin. "Persistence has its advantages, Kate Meadows."

Set a-tingle by his touch, I lower my gaze. And a repeat of last night's kiss is there on his lips. The kiss I want. The kiss I should deny myself.

But surely one more won't hurt, I reason, as the space between our mouths narrows. Just one...

And just who do you think you're kidding!

"Don't," I whisper, the slight movement causing our lips to
graze.

"I'm not."

He's not? It's then I realize that I'm the one who moved—
that I've gone up on my toes and leaned in.

I drop to my heels and step back. "Sorry, I don't know—"

A commotion to my left pulls me around, and with a guilty
flush, I watch as the noisy occupants of the playroom spill out
into the hall.

Clive steps alongside me. "Good timing, Kate."

Thank You, Lord.

Not that I care if Christopher sees me with another man, as
any feelings I had for him are dead. It would just be awkward.
More, had I claimed a second kiss, it would have sent Clive the
wrong message. Not that the message I *did* send by taking the
initiative is anything to be proud of.

Lord, I'm in trouble, aren't I?

"Miss Kate!" Jessica runs toward me. "Are you giving us a
tour of the new burn unit?"

Is that where they're heading?

I glance at Clive, who inclines his head, and give him a
dirty look. "So you cleaned up the mess for *me*, hmm?"

"I did. Of course, two birds with one stone is always better
than one."

"It's still murder," I mutter.

Jessica halts before me. "Are you, Miss Kate?"

I look beyond to Christopher Stapleton, who is flanked by a
miniature version of himself, who is flanked by a woman of average height and plain countenance—doubtless the soon-to-be

ex–Mrs. Stapleton. And they're heading our way.

"Miss Kate?"

"I'd love to give you the tour, Jessica, but I have somewhere else I need to be." And it's true. I *really* need to get back to Operation: Perfect Faith.

"Did I hear you say you won't be taking us on the tour, Ms. Meadows?" Christopher says as he and his family approach.

Feeling Clive tense beside me, I smile apologetically. "I'm afraid it's not possible."

"Pity." He halts. "It would have been nice to have the artist's take on the project." He looks to his right. "This is my wife, Nora. Nora—Kate Meadows."

The woman gives me a warm smile that turns her plain countenance lovely. "A pleasure to meet you, Ms. Meadows."

I accept her handshake. "And you, Mrs. Stapleton."

Our hands fall away, and if not for the familiar way she settles her freed hand to her belly—seen it a hundred times with Belle—I wouldn't have noticed the slight bulge. Nora Stapleton is pregnant. Pregnant and soon-to-be divorced. Unless Clive is misinformed.

I look to her left hand. She *is* still wearing a ring. A very familiar ring. Ignoring the accompanying wedding band, I stare at the diamond engagement ring that once resided on my hand.

"And this—" Christopher ushers forward a little boy of perhaps six—"is our son, Chris."

Exactly.

Realizing I'm heading toward moroseness, I focus on Christopher Stapleton the Third, who until now has remained faceless.

Smiling his mother's smile, the little boy sticks out his hand. "Hi."

My heart gives a ferocious tug, but a moment later I'm

marveling at how small his hand feels in mine. "Nice to meet you, Chris."

"You, too." He pulls back.

I consider Christopher and his wife, then return to their son, who bridges the palpable distance between them.

"Can we go, Mom? I want to see the painted room."

Nora nods, extends her smile from me to Clive, then leads their son away.

Aching at the unexpected turns life can take, I watch mother and child join the others heading away. Though I knew it was possible I would one day run into Christopher—and perhaps the family he made without me—I never expected to. After all, the Bay Area is huge.

"Dr. Alexander." Jessica breaks the silence. "You're coming, aren't you?"

"Of course." He glances at me. "Take care of that burn." And just like that, he walks away.

Once he's out of earshot, Christopher steps nearer. "It's good to see you, Kate."

"And you."

He zooms in on the absent mole, then the missing gap. "You've made a few changes."

So glad he doesn't know how recent. "Some."

"For the better."

Ouch. But is it really an ouch? Telling myself I will not take offense, I smile tightly.

He smiles back, then runs his gaze down me. "Gained a little weight, but otherwise you look great."

Otherwise… Okay.

"Thank you." Mouth aching with the effort to hold up the corners, I skim his figure. "You look…"

Dare I say it? Oh, why not.

"…married."

Surprise causes his light-colored eyebrows to rise a moment before a boyish grin spreads across his face. "I suppose I do."

Determined I won't let on that I'm aware of his pending divorce, which might open doors best left closed, locked, and sealed, I say, "Wife…son…and another on the way. Congratulations."

His smile fades. "Thank you. Unfortunately, Nora and I are going through a difficult time right now."

Oh, no. No. No. No. He's not opening that door! "I'm sorry to hear that, but I'm sure you'll work things out."

Silence. But just as I'm about to announce that I need to go, he says, "I gather Clive didn't tell you I'm the one who recommended you for the burn unit."

"Clive" rather than "Dr. Alexander"? Of course, Clive referred to him as Stapleton, so it must be one-sided. At least, I hope. "No, he didn't."

Of course, he tried, but Adelphia's interruption the night we met left me in the dark, and I'm about to clarify that when Christopher says, "I'd seen your work in a magazine, and when I heard the burn unit was short a gifted artist, I brought the article to Clive's attention."

"Thank you. Though it's been a challenge, I believe this job is just the boost my business needs."

He cranks up his smile. "Glad I could be of assistance. So, outside of work, how's life?"

"It's good."

He gives my bare left hand a meaningful glance. "Are you with anyone?"

Clive rises to mind, and before I know it, I'm nodding a lie that I justify with the remembrance of his kiss. "Actually, I am."

Sorry, Lord, but unless I'm way off, the last thing Christopher and his family need is for an old flame to reignite.

Christopher's face tightens. "And you're happy?"

"Yes."

"Then wedding bells are in your future."

That hurts. Oh, how I'd like to confirm that a wedding is, indeed, on my calendar, but that would be another lie. Still, neither can I bring myself to deny it, so I merely smile.

After a long moment, Christopher forces a smile of his own. "I'm happy for you."

Guilt washes over me, but I can't bear to correct him. "Thank you."

"Well, I ought to catch up with Chris."

Just Chris. Not Nora.

"I'll let you go, then."

"It was nice running into you, Kate." He lingers a moment longer, then turns away.

As I watch him distance himself, I call out, "I'll pray for you and Nora."

He halts and looks over his shoulder.

I smile. "And Chris. And, of course, your new little one."

His lips thin. "I appreciate that." Then he's walking away from me—again. But this time it hardly registers on the hurt scale.

Sunday, June 3

Dear Lord,

You're testing me, aren't You? That's what this is all about—first Michael, then Clive, now Christopher. A smorgasbord of men! But are any of them the answer to my prayers? Well, of course Christopher isn't. He's married—and with kids, just like he wanted. As for

Michael, I think You'll agree he's not "The One." So that leaves Clive, who wants biological children. Could it be that You have someone else You haven't yet made appear? Or is there no one? What ARE your plans for me? I know. I know. WAIT.

Please, Lord, give me patience. Help Christopher and Nora work out their marriage—for their sakes and their children's. Please continue to watch over Belle and Beau's baby. Please help me figure out what to do about Clive and my attraction for him. And please heal my burn.

Thank You for cool compresses and antibiotic cream. Thank You for Maia making eye contact and smiling this afternoon. And humming. Wonder what she's so happy about...?

Kate

PS: Time for an Old Testament reading. Maybe Ruth. I like Ruth.

m I good or AM...I...GOOD?
I draw back to further survey my artistic genius. Yep,
I'm good.
Thank You, Lord.

Returning the smile of the little girl whose formerly life-
less eyes are smiling in concert with her mouth, I triumphantly
whip my paintbrush overhead. She's the last. Other than touch-
up and the addition of details likely to become apparent once I
move into the hallway, the dome is done!

Feeling my burden lighten, I singsong, "Uh-huh"—swing
hips left—"Uh-huh"—swing hips right—"Uh-huh, uh-huh,
uh-huh!" All punctuated by a snap of my brush. My celebration
is interrupted by a blur of red that falls from my paintbrush, and
I jump back. Too late.

"NO!" I stare at the paint that streaks the right thigh of
my hip-hugging jeans—my previously undefiled *seventy-dollar
version*, which due to mounting laundry found their way up my
legs this morning.

"Bad, Kate! You are the clumsiest, klutziest clod!" Of course, if I hit it with solvent—

I whip around, grab the frame of the scaffold, and lose my balance at the sight of the man crossing the room toward me.

Grip slipping, I scramble to right myself at the platform's edge—even have the forethought to release the paintbrush and make a grab for an overhead rung. And, for one relief-filled moment, it seems I might save my neck. But my hands slip…feet fall away…and the cement floor hurtles toward me with disastrous enthusiasm.

I hit—hard—but rather than the floor, it's Clive Alexander's chest I slam into…his arms that come around me…my weight that thrusts us back. No sooner do I register his gusting breath against my brow than we meet the floor.

Not daring to breathe, let alone move, I gape at the cement floor just inches from my face and marvel that, if not for Clive's save, I would likely have broken my nose, among other things.

But he caught me, just like in the movies.

Well, maybe not. Were this a movie, I would have landed in his arms and he would be standing like a rock. Of course, it might help if I weighed less…

"Are you all right, Kate?"

I jerk my face around and come nose-to-nose with him. And in that moment I become ultra-aware of where our bodies touch—which is just about everywhere.

Oh my…

"Yeah." I scramble onto my knees alongside him.

He sits up and winces as if pained. "Sure?"

"Thanks to you."

He smiles wryly. "You're forgetting that I'm the one who caused you to lose your balance."

He noticed, then. And knows his effect on me. Wonderful.

"Still, I'm grateful. You saved my neck."

"And missed the opportunity to play doctor again."

"Oh." I blush. "Yeah."

He flexes his shoulders. "Unfortunately, it didn't work out the way I envisioned. Hardly hero material."

"I don't know about that." I give a nervous smile. "It seemed pretty heroic to me."

He rubs his back.

"Are you all right, Clive?"

"Will be." He pushes up and offers a hand.

I reach out for it only to snatch my arm back and thrust to my feet under my own power.

Clive's knowing gaze awaits mine. "It was just a hand up, Kate."

Embarrassed by my avoidance of further contact, I shrug. "I…uh…didn't want you to strain anything else." I look away and pretend an interest in my watch. The digital numbers show that it's 6:57 p.m.

I draw a deep breath. "So—"

6:57…6:57…

I frown over the tap-tapping that arises from a corner of my mind with the persistence of an SOS.

"So?" Clive prompts.

I shove my hands into the pockets of my jeans. "So you're working late again, hmm?"

"I was. Thought I'd drop by and check on your progress before heading home."

"What do you think of it?"

He takes in the countries and children that have become a part of the landscape.

6:57…6:57… What?

"It's wonderful." He turns back around. "You're done here?"

"Pretty much." I sigh. "A really good feeling."

"Obviously."

I start to nod. "Obviously?"

"I caught your little victory dance. It was…enlightening."

I roll my eyes. "Okay, so you know the truth. Kate Meadows does *not* have rhythm."

"And talks to herself."

Well, at least he didn't catch me talking to my breasts again—

In the next instant, I remember the reason for my one-sided conversation on the scaffold.

Oh, no!

As feared, the paint on my jeans is smeared. And a glance at the left leg of Clive's charcoal gray pants reveals its inkblot match. "I am *so* sorry." I reach to him. "Let me—"

I snatch my hand back. "Um…I have some solvent. If you catch it soon enough, it's possible to get the paint out."

"Don't worry about it. They've been hanging in my closet for years."

"Still…"

"Really." He smiles.

And my heart goes tripping—while that corner of my mind keeps tap-tap-tapping.

6:57…?

I clear my throat. "Did Sunday's tour go well?"

"Everyone was impressed with your work, especially Stapleton."

Oh, how I hope—pray!—the two didn't discuss me beyond my artistic ability. "I'm glad he doesn't regret recommending me for the job."

"Far from it," Clive says, then lets me off the hook with, "How's the burn?"

Though it has only been three days since my mishap, the skin has lost most of its angry flush, and the discomfort is all but gone. "Better."

He eyes my modestly scooped neckline. "May I?"

I startle. "What?"

"Have a look—in the capacity of a doctor."

"Uh…"

He raises his eyebrows.

"It's…" I flutter a hand down my neck to my upper chest. "As I said, it's better."

Still, he steps forward, and his shadow that falls over me feels warm. And the head he bends toward me makes me catch my breath. And the hand that pushes aside mine causes my breath to release in a rush. And his light touch across my healing skin sends shivers hip-hopping along my spine.

I stare at his fingers beneath my collarbone, which, in the capacity of a doctor, are entirely innocuous. But in the capacity of an attractive man for whom I have feelings….

He nods. "It looks good."

I meet his eyes near mine, and my attraction for him strains its seams. "That's, uh, pretty much representative of the rest of it." Just in case he's curious about what's not revealed below the neckline.

He continues to gaze into me. "Good."

Oh, boy. Not good. "Er, thank you for the antibiotic cream."

"Sure."

Though I know I should grab my brush, climb the scaffold, and not come down until he's good and gone, it's not what I want. I want—

His hand moves up my neck and slides along my jaw.

—what he wants.

His head lowers.

"Kate!" Michael's voice hails from beyond the domed room. "You here?"

Not 6:57, but 6:30! *Tap-tap-tap!*

I throw open lids that were on their way down. "It's Michael."

Clive's eyebrows converge. "You said it was over between you."

"It was—is! I mean, I told him…"

So hard to think with him so near.

"But Michael wanted to talk it over, clear the air. So I agreed to meet him for dinner, but I guess I lost track of time."

Clive doesn't appear convinced. And neither am I. What if the dinner I agreed to over the phone last night isn't about clearing the air? What if Michael *is* still pursuing me? How do I prove to Clive that I'm not some wishy-washy—

"Kate! It's me, Michael."

His voice carries easily across the domed room, and I become aware of how close Clive and I are and how it may appear. I lurch back. But not soon enough, making me look ten times guiltier to the man whose hurried step slows as he approaches the threshold of the domed room.

Michael stops and glances between me and Clive. "Sorry to interrupt."

Hearing the hurt in his voice, I force my feet forward. "Michael, I…uh…forgot about our dinner."

He crosses his arms over his chest. "I wonder why."

I halt before him. "I'm really sorry."

"How long have you two been seeing each other?"

"We're not." The dinner on the roof doesn't count, does it? Of course, Clive did kiss me. And was about to kiss me again tonight. "Well, not exactly."

He glances past me. "Surely you're not telling me this is a first."

"No, but…"

Lord, this is uncomfortable!

Of course, I have nothing to feel guilty about. Or do I? After all, though I'd accepted it was over between Michael and me that first time Clive and I almost kissed, I had yet to break it off with him. If not for the honor Clive exhibited, we would have kissed. Guess I do have something to feel guilty about.

I draw a deep breath. "It's true I was attracted to Clive." How I hate that he's listening! "But nothing happened while you and I were together."

Michael considers me through narrowed lids. "All right, but he is the reason you broke it off with me, isn't he?"

Surprised he would think that after all I threw at him that night in the kitchen, I open my mouth to remind him of his push to perfect me, only to press my lips closed. We really don't need to rehash it. But then, what if he concludes that his magnification of my every flaw wasn't hurtful after all? And does it to someone else?

I open my mouth, then close it again.

And suddenly, his mouth turns up. "Okay, not the *only* reason, but some of it, huh?"

Good compromise. "Yeah."

He sighs and drops his arms from his chest. "I won't say that seeing the two of you like that didn't throw me, especially considering you used to be my girl, but it's not as if we're not broken up."

Did you hear that, Clive?

"So now we're back to my reason for asking you to dinner."

I nod. "To clear the air."

"That's right. But rather than waste your time or Dr. Alexander's—" he glances past me—"I'll just say what I had to say and let you two get back to…whatever."

I *so* feel like squirming. "Okay."

"Can we talk somewhere private?"

I peer over my shoulder at Clive, who watches from alongside the scaffolding. "Of course." I lead Michael into the winding hallway.

"This is good," he says when we hit the second curve.

I turn to him. "Okay?"

"You were right about Maia and me. I am attracted to her—just like you were attracted to Dr. Alexander."

"Go on."

"I fought it because I didn't want to care for a woman like her. After all, she's not exactly marriage material. She's…"

"Gorgeous? Sophisticated? Educated?"

He gives a relieved nod. "Yeah, not at all like you, Kate."

I gasp.

He startles. "What I mean is she's not grounded, you know, girl next door and all."

Unintentional or not, that was a slam, though not quite as hurtful as "potentially fat."

I tilt my head. "So?"

"I just can't imagine Maia in wedded bliss. As for toting a kid on her hip, that's pretty far-fetched."

Did he not notice my jerk of surprise? "A kid? So it's not just about finding someone to settle down with? Now you're talking kids? You told me you could take them or leave them."

"Sure, but what if I change my mind?"

I knew it!

I grit my teeth. "That could be a problem."

"Yeah, and yet it's almost worth taking a chance."

"Then you feel strongly about her." Hmm. I sound a bit like a shrink.

"I'd like to give it a try."

"Does she know how you feel?"

"We've…uh…been talking.

Mystery of Maia's smile solved. And the humming. "It sounds like you should talk some more."

"I think we will."

I place my hands on my hips. "Air cleared?"

"One more thing. I apologize for trying to perfect you, for dumping all those business cards on you and making you feel inadequate. It's just that in my line of work, every imperfection is so…glaring."

Grudgingly, I nod. "And Kate Meadows had a lot of glaring going on."

"Sorry. Of course, you have to admit that the recommendations you acted on improved your appearance considerably."

Other cheek, Kate.

"I'm pleased with the outcome. Now may I offer some advice, Michael?"

"Sure."

"Maia will appreciate your business cards less than I, so keep them to yourself."

He grins. "Good advice." Then he just has to add, "Of course, it's not as if she needs any work done. She's…you know…"

"Perfect." On the outside, that is. Absolutely *everyone* can stand ongoing inner improvement—specifically the perfection of one's faith in Christ, which is a far better pursuit than the perfection of one's physical body, which in the end will be left behind.

I'm working on it….

Michael nods and, with a far-off smile, says, "Yes, Maia's perfect."

Which brings us back to that inner stuff. "I hope you'll continue attending church."

"Yeah, I've really enjoyed it."

"Great! And bring Maia along, if you can convince her."

He hesitates. "I'll see what I can do."

"Well, I'd better get back to work."

"Kate?"

"Yeah?"

"I meant it when I said I like who you are on the inside." He shrugs. "I guess I just wanted to make the outside as beautiful."

I stare at him and swallow hard as unexpected emotion tightens my throat. "Thank you."

He starts to lean in, pulls slightly back, then lunges forward and kisses my cheek. "See you later, Kate."

"I hope so."

I smile. He smiles. Then he turns away.

I linger in the hallway to work through the emotion roused by Michael's statement that he likes who I am—grateful that, despite my difficulty in making time for God, He still shines through.

When I return to the domed room, Clive is where I left him. He captures my gaze as I cross toward him, making me uncomfortably aware of what Michael interrupted. With three feet separating us, I stop and clasp my hands before me. "All better."

He just stands there.

I glance down, then back up. "Turns out Michael is attracted to Maia, as I suspected."

Did his eyebrows just move?

"I think they're going to start dating."

He blinked. I think….

"He also wanted to apologize for trying to perfect me."

I believe that was a nod.

"So—" I throw my hands up—"where were we?"

Oh! That didn't come out right. Sounded forward. Brazen.

His lips curve—definitely a smile. Then he straightens from the scaffold and steps to within inches of me. "About…" He lays a hand to my jaw. "…here." He tilts my face up and lowers his mouth to within a breath of mine. "Right here."

Then he's kissing me, pulling me in, taking me to my toes… And there's that queasy little flutter.

"Kate?" He lifts his head.

I open my eyes. "Yes?"

"This changes everything."

It does, doesn't it? The acknowledgment of which causes panic from another room in my heart to spill out. Though I want this to change everything, it can't. Not *everything*.

I take a step back, and thankfully he releases me. "Clive, I like you—very much." I press my lips inward and momentarily revel in the kiss that lingers there. "But we're different. We want different—"

"I have news for you, Kate. There is no such thing as a completely compatible couple."

Couple. That is what he's suggesting, isn't it? That we become a couple—at least in terms of dating. Even so, "couple" doesn't usually stay "couple." Along come children and, in my case, *not*.

"I know, but—"

I'm bit by Deuteronomy, which I stopped by on the way to Ruth last night. Though the Scripture commanded that accurate scales be used for weighing, it was really all about honesty. Again.

"No, Kate."

I blink Clive back to focus. "What?"

"You can't talk your way out of this."

"Oh, yes, I can." I give a vigorous nod.

He shakes his head slowly. "Not after that kiss—or this one." And he does it again.

Okay, Lord, I know he's not a practicing Christian, but that doesn't mean he isn't part of Your plans for me, right? Or that I'm not part of Your plans for him. Maybe I can bring him back. It's possible. And I know You'd like that. So here goes. Lord, please guide me through this relationship. I trust You.

But only so much, I admit, when five minutes later Clive departs—smiling over my agreement to have dinner with him Friday night. Still ignorant of my inability to bear children.

Wednesday, June 6
Dear Lord,

It's just a date. Just two people getting together to eat, enjoy each other's company, maybe kiss a little. As it's too early in the relationship to think about marriage, let alone children, why complicate matters? Why bare myself when this might not go anywhere anyway? If we even get past square one and I start feeling that he really is "The One," there'll be plenty of time to come clean. By then, maybe he'll feel enough for me that it won't matter. Maybe I'll be enough. Just me. Just Kate.

Oh, Lord! I'm not fooling You, am I? I'm going about this all wrong. Which means it's time for the next phase of Operation: Perfect Faith. Time to hunt down what You have to say about dating. Of course, people in biblical times didn't date—arranged marriages and all. This could take a while.

Forgive me my toddler's faith,
Kate

There are circles under my eyes, the likes of which I've rarely seen. Of course, yesterday's night shift to graveyard shift to today's day shift is largely responsible. But it was the only way I could free up Friday night for my date with Clive.

Telling myself it's worth it, I apply another layer of concealer beneath my eyes and determine that nothing else can be done for my face. Or my outfit, which is beyond peachy thanks to Michael, who months past convinced me I could pull off a lacy black crocheted top over a raspberry knit top. Very feminine, especially matched with a mid-knee black skirt that masks the state of my thighs. Not that they're as bad as that liposuction business card keeps telling me—or so I keep assuring myself. And the promise to get serious about an exercise regimen once the burn unit is complete is second only to the promise to stick with Operation: Perfect Faith. Or should be…

Remembering my search for Scripture to guide me through my decision to date Clive, I grimace. Though, as expected, the Bible had nothing to say about dating, it had plenty to say about deep relationships with non-Christians—as in "don't," since being with an unbeliever can draw a believer away from God. But as I keep telling myself, Clive isn't an unbeliever. He's on hold. Sort of.

I turn from the mirror and consciously avoid looking at my prayer journal, which hasn't seen pen or pencil for two days. As for my Bible...

I'll get back to them. Really.

I grab my purse and head for the door. Per Maia's shouted announcement minutes earlier, Clive is waiting for me at the base of the stairs. And no Maia in sight, which I'd find odd were it not that she has a date with Michael.

I pause on the landing and smile. "Hi."

Clive's appreciative gaze sweeps me, and I glory in it until his eyes falter at the level of my knees. It's then that I realize how much my hemline reveals from his vantage point. Squelching the impulse to slap hands to my skirt, I hasten down.

"You look pretty," he says as I step from the last stair.

"Thanks."

Here comes that smile I like so much, not even remotely á la carte. "Ready?"

I lift my purse and give it a shake. "Ready."

He leads me outside into early evening. As is proper—unfortunately only early in a relationship—he opens the car door for me.

"So where are we going?" I ask when he settles in beside me.

He eases away from the curb. "That's up to you."

Huh? "You want *me* to pick the place?" *Not* how I envisioned the evening. I don't mind having a say, but the romantic in me— I think that's what it is—would prefer Clive to have it worked out. Of course, he didn't have candlelight or a linen-covered table that night on the roof—

"What I mean is that you have a choice."

So it's not completely up in the air. "Okay, so—"

I catch my breath, as I do when my mind strays from the steep streets for which San Francisco is known. Built on over forty hills, the sudden drops inherent in traversing the city by car, especially at speeds faster than posted, often tempts my tummy to pay a surprise visit to my throat.

Clive glances at me. "Sorry. Got going a little fast there."

I nod. "Okay, so what are my choices? Seafood versus steak house? Mexican versus Chinese?"

"Bistro versus in-laws."

Did he say *in-laws*? I can't have heard right. In…inlos? Some newfangled cuisine I haven't heard of? Or maybe he meant Indian food…

Braking for a light, he gives me an apologetic smile. "I'd planned to take you to a bistro across the bay, but the option is to take you to meet my in-laws."

Grateful for the green light that draws his attention from my expression of disbelief, I shake my head. "I've heard of taking a woman home to meet one's parents, but in-laws?"

"Obligation." He snaps his blinker to turn left. "My niece's birthday."

"Oh. You forgot about it, then?"

"Conveniently." He eases into the mob of cars heading toward the Golden Gate Bridge. "Her mother called to remind me, and I didn't check caller ID before answering. So I can come up with an excuse—tell her there was a hospital emergency—or you can accompany me."

I'm ashamed at how tempted I am to urge him to make the call so we can head for the promised bistro and the intimacy of the two of us.

"So what do you think?"

Realizing I've scrunched up the hem of my skirt, I release my grip. "You know, Clive, it would have been perfectly fine for you to cancel our date."

"I considered that, but it would have been short notice, and I know you worked through the night to free up the time."

Yep. Home at 4 a.m. and up again at 8 to get to my other job—late. So did someone inform him of my extended hours, or is this a case of under-eye concealer failure?

He noses into the traffic on the bridge. "More, though, it doesn't bode well for a relationship to begin with a cancellation."

Nor for a relationship to begin with a nonbeliever. Operation: Perfect Faith elbows me.

"On-hold" believer. Clive is merely on hold.

He switches lanes, accelerates past cars that aspire to the bridge's forty-five-mile-per-hour speed limit, finds another opening, and snags it. "So bistro or in-laws?"

Oh, the temptation of the bistro! I struggle as I stare out the windshield past the cars heading in the opposite direction along a bridge that, despite the name Golden Gate, is actually painted a deep red-orange.

"As I don't want you to lie and your niece expects you, in-laws it is." There! That ought to appease my conscience after the nonbeliever versus on-hold believer argument.

Were I not watching Clive closely, I would've missed his tightening jaw and thinning lips, both of which evidence that he was hoping I'd go the other way.

"Not what you wanted to hear?" I venture.

He glances at me. "It will be awkward. If they're expecting anyone to accompany me, it's Adelphia."

That casts a whole new light on the situation. As we pass the Vista Point exit and come off the bridge, I say, "Then they've met her?"

"A few times."

Awkward doesn't begin to describe what I'm about to walk into.

An instant later, I startle when Clive's hand covers mine in my lap.

"They like her, Kate, but only to a point."

I drag my gaze from his hand. "And that point is?"

"Date, don't mate."

My reaction earns me a halfhearted smile.

"Their words, not mine. You'll understand when you meet them. *If* you meet them." He nods at the signs in the distance. "Last chance. Mill Valley and the in-laws, or Tiburon and the bistro?"

I zoom in on the latter. Never has a sign been so appealing—nor more closely resembled a crisp, shiny apple. Of course, I know that this temptation in no way compares to Eve's, but at the moment I feel a deeper than usual kinship with the woman.

"Mill Valley," I croak.

Clive takes the exit and, for the duration of the drive, fills me in on his in-laws. His niece is celebrating her fifteenth birthday at her grandparents' home. There will be twenty or so people that will include relatives and friends, and the Murphys are good people.

He gives me a knowing glance. "They're *practicing* Christians, which should make you feel more comfortable."

It does—until he mentions that I might want to avoid his father-in-law, a boisterous, doesn't-read-body-language retired salesman whom Clive credits with the "date, don't mate" comment. Is it Adelphia Clive's father-in-law objects to, or just the idea of her replacing his daughter? If the latter, this could be a long night.

A while later, we draw up to the curb in front of an immaculate one-level home that hails from the sixties. The long driveway is lined with cars, and the curtains are drawn wide to reveal the partygoers.

With a little cough, I clear the nervousness from my throat. "So this is it."

"Sure you want to do it?"

Knowing I'm being given one last chance to chicken out, I look into Clive's shadowed—and hopeful?—face. "No, but I'm willing, especially as it's something you should do."

His lids narrow.

I smile and take a chance. "Remember the things you missed out on with Jillian and Sam? If you miss out on this, you'll regret it."

The air between us changes abruptly, the only sound and movement Clive's breath as he regards me across the dimming day. But then he nods, leans in, and touches his mouth to mine. "Thank you, Kate. I appreciate that."

So do I. So…do…I…

He pulls back and, a few moments later, comes around the car to open the door for me.

As he hands me out, I realize something's missing. "What about a gift?"

Clive closes the car door behind me. "At fifteen, cash is all they want."

"Okay, but you ought to at least present it in a card. I don't suppose you have one?"

He spreads his empty hands.

"So you're just going to open up your wallet and whip out a few bills?"

He grimaces. "I see what you mean, but we're late and—"

"Wait! Give me the money."

Wavering between a smile and a frown, he says, "Is this a holdup?"

I shove my hand forward. "Come on."

He pulls out his wallet.

Using the roof of his car, I fold and fold until the twenty dollar bills are fashioned into a graceful swan with outstretched wings.

"Ta-da!" I turn to where Clive leans against the car watching me. "Origami."

He picks the swan from my palm and turns it left and right. "You are a woman of many talents, Kate Meadows."

I curtsy. "Why, thank you."

He zeros in on my mouth. "Do you realize you bite your tongue when you're concentrating?"

Though I knew he was watching me, I thought he was focused on my hands. "Uh…I do?"

"Seen it a dozen times."

"When?"

"When you don't realize you're being watched."

"And you've been watching me?"

"More than you realize." He smiles. "I've seen you dance on top of scaffolding."

That I know about.

"A couple of times now."

Oh.

He takes my arm and turns me up the driveway. "I've heard you sing."

I grimace.

"Once you were talking to a somewhat misshapen little boy near Australia."

Caught conversing with a layer of paint! "And you still wanted to date me?"

"More so. You were comforting him, assuring him you'd get his face right." He frowns. "Sounded a bit like me, actually."

I roll my eyes. "Big difference between what I do and what you do." As we start up the porch steps, I ask, "What else?"

"You rub that bracelet of yours a lot."

I turn it on my wrist. "A gift from my friend Belle, the one who owns the children's shop where we met."

He halts before the door and lifts my hand to examine the bracelet. "*Believe?*"

I nod. "In God and His plans for me—at least, I try."

And fail, that conscience of mine kicks in again.

To my surprise, Clive doesn't drop my hand like a hot potato but rubs the little medallion—just as I do more often than I realize.

"Do you ever question God?" he asks quietly.

His question nearly robs me of breath. On top of that, we're standing so near that I can feel the heat coming off his body.

I give a jerky nod. "I do. But I still believe."

He looks into my eyes. "So do I, Kate."

My heart leaps…rolls over…plays dead…. And the sound that squeezes through my vocal chords sounds more like a toy squeaker than a human voice. "You do? You really do? Then you haven't—"

He releases my hand. "I even heard you curse once."

Hardly a smooth change of topic, but to be expected. Knowing that the opportunity to delve into his faith has passed, I wonder what foul word burst from my lips. And what must he think of me, a Christian, talking like that? "Sorry."

He presses the doorbell. "Don't worry; it was one of the lesser curses."

Still a curse, and one I would never have spoken were I aware of an audience. I cross my arms over my chest. "You do know, don't you, that it's bad manners not to announce one's presence?"

"Yes, but character is who we are when no one's watching."

"When we *think* no one's watching."

He smiles.

I narrow my lids. "So you were trying to determine my character, were you?"

"To some extent. More, though," he reaches up and runs a finger down my cheek, I enjoy watching you work."

"You—?"

The door explodes inward, and I startle at the appearance of a big man in the doorway.

"Clive!" he booms above the din. "You're late."

"Jack, this is Kate Meadows, my—"

"Date." Jack thrusts a shovel-like hand at me. "Jack Murphy."

We shake, and I'm somewhat surprised when I withdraw with all my bones intact. "Nice to meet you."

He lumbers back and waves us in.

"Uncle Clive!" A big-boned teenage girl breaks from a group of girls and hurries forward.

Clive pecks the cheek she offers, then draws back and thrusts the origami swan at her. "Happy birthday, Heather."

"Oh!" Holding it by its scrawny neck, she turns it side to side. "Clever. Thank you, Uncle Clive." Her eyes light on me. "And thank *you*."

Then it's too much of a stretch to think Clive fashioned the little creature. Duh.

"You're welcome."

"Heather, this is Kate Meadows. Kate, my niece, Heather."

Though the teen's hand isn't as large as her grandfather's, it engulfs mine. "Glad you could make it. And you, too, Unc.

Enjoy!" With a little wave that doesn't quite work for her, and a somewhat ungainly flounce, she swings away. The teenage years can be *so* awkward.

"And this is just the beginning," Clive murmurs, his breath in my ear sending a shiver down my center, "so buckle up."

I look around. "You *are* going to stay with me—"

"Clive!"

A woman not much taller than me, and somewhat wider, hastens toward us.

"My mother-in-law," Clive says. "You'll like her."

And I do. For the next hour, she and I make the rounds while Clive disappears and reappears among the guests. Gloria Murphy, though dwarfed by her husband, is nearly as boisterous as the big man, but not in any way offensive. Most times she reins in her laughter before it rises above the other voices. As for playing the good hostess, there's acceptance in her twinkling eyes, reassurance in her hand on my arm, and interest in my person and profession. Though her older daughter—Jillian's sister and Heather's mother—is distant when we're introduced, Gloria whispers, "She likes you," as she leads me away.

I meet everyone and am greeted warmly by most; then Gloria offers a tour of the house, at the end of which we pause in a hallway lined with pictures.

"I suppose you'd like to see pictures of Jillian and little Sam."

Her forthrightness nearly makes me jump. "I would. How did you know?"

"Clive brought you tonight, which must mean he's serious." She smiles. "Which hopefully means you're serious."

Hopefully?

She looks momentarily down, then back up. "Which means

you ought to know more than he's told you about my daughter and grandson."

Did she give this same speech to Adelphia? "I understand Clive also introduced you to Adelphia."

"Oh—" she waves a hand—"not the same."

"What do you mean?"

She steps past and motions for me to follow. "Clive didn't watch her as he watches you. You know, maintain situational awareness."

Is that what he was doing while I followed his mother-in-law around? Though I kept an eye on where he was in relation to me, I was certain he'd forgotten about me.

Midway down the hall, Gloria halts and looks to me. "He was the same with Jillian." Remembrance curves her mouth. "He loved our daughter very much." She sighs. "Adelphia is a nice enough woman, but she was little more than appease-ment."

"Appeasement?" I keep my eyes on her though I want badly to look at the pictures.

"Yes. About six months ago, Jack and I told Clive it was past time he came out of mourning and started dating."

As my eyes widen, she nods. "I know. Sounds strange com-ing from the parents of the woman he loved, but that's just it—he loved Jillian. And Sam."

"But, he—" No, it's not my place to mention the guilt he carries.

"Of course, he needs to release that, too." She reads my thoughts. "Yes, he got caught up in his career and should have spent more time with them, but had he been there the night of the fire—"

She breaks off. "You do know about the fire?"

"Some of it."

She draws a deep breath, and I can almost feel the pain in her chest. "It was an electrical fire—faulty wiring in their new home. If Clive had been there, he would have been lost as well. And yet, he's certain he could have brought out Jillian and Sam sooner."

"Sooner? Then he…"

"Yes. He came home from a function, ahead of the fire trucks, and went in after them." Her eyes mist. "He brought them out and not only suffered smoke inhalation, but was badly burned."

Clive is burned?

She nods. "His back and upper arms."

Which explains why I haven't seen the burns. Of course, he may have undergone reconstructive surgery.

"I understand your daughter—"

Dare I?

"Go ahead, Kate." She pats my arm. "I don't mind."

Amazed at how forthcoming she is—I could *never* open up with a stranger—I say, "I understand your daughter and grandson died within days of each other."

Her gaze wavers. "Sam succumbed to smoke inhalation in the ambulance and Jillian… Her burns were too extensive. Though she regained consciousness the following day and asked about Sam and Clive—and we assured her that *both* were doing well—it wasn't long before she slipped into a coma. She passed away two days later."

"I'm sorry."

Gloria Murphy draws a finger beneath her pooling eyes. "It was painful for all of us, but especially Clive. You see, he believed he'd saved them. And just as we lied to Jillian about Sam, we lied to him during his lucid moments—he was heavily sedated. By the time he recovered sufficiently to demand to see them, funeral arrangements had been made." She sighs. "A funeral he was unable to attend due to the extent of his injuries."

Heart feeling as if it could use a good wringing out, I sniff.

Gloria smiles bravely. "He won't forgive himself for not getting home sooner…for not being home in the first place…for putting work above his family…"

"And yet it sounds as if you do."

She tilts her head to the side. "We're not saints. We had our moments of wanting to blame him for our loss, but Jillian wouldn't allow it. Before she slipped into the coma, she told us that Jesus wanted us to hold Clive's hand." She leans nearer to me. "Just as he was holding hers and Sam's."

"Sam's? But you told her—?"

"She knew, as if her little boy were standing right there with Jesus. Waiting for her."

Chills run up my spine, down my arms, and across my chest.

"Um-hmm," Gloria murmurs as I rub my arms. "The story tends to do that to people, especially believers."

Then she knows I'm a Christian. "Has Clive talked to you about me?"

"Not by name, but I'm good at addition."

"Sorry?"

"Putting two and two together. When Clive came to dinner a couple months back, he was riled. When I pressed him, he said he'd had a run-in with the burn unit's artist over the inclusion of Christianity—meaning the artist had to be a Christian." She shrugs. "And so here you are, and now I better understand why he was so bothered."

I think I know what she's saying, but it never hurts to clarify. "Do you mind explaining that last bit?"

"He was attracted to you, Kate. Thus, he couldn't simply

dismiss your disagreement. Of course, in the end you got your way, didn't you?"

"Yeah," I say, sheepishly. "I was…sneaky."

She nods. "We do what we have to do. And I'm glad you did."

Whew! Though, as a fellow Christian, I can't see her objecting to the inclusion of Christianity in my painting, she might not have approved of the way in which I went about it.

"It told me that not only was Clive ready to pick up his life, but he may be receptive to returning to God. My guess is you're the one who convinced him to go to Guatemala."

I shrug. "He credits me with it, but all I did was make a pronouncement on a situation I knew nothing about."

She shakes her head wonderingly. "Amazing the way God uses people, hmm?"

I smile. "Amazing."

Gloria turns to the pictures. "This is my Jillian."

I step nearer the picture of a young woman who greatly resembles the one beside me—with somewhat softer features and deeply green eyes.

"She's lovely."

"Yes." One by one, Gloria goes through the pictures that tell the story of her daughter's life. Of course, those that hold my attention the longest are the ones in which Clive is present—their wedding and the progression of their son from infancy to his fifth birthday. His last birthday…

I respect the silence into which Gloria descends as she stares at the picture of her grandson, whose breath causes the flames at the tip of each candle to strain in that split second before the light is snuffed out.

She squares her shoulders and returns to the picture of the glowing bride and her captivated groom. "The wedding was a simple affair. They were happy. And I want Clive to be happy again."

"You really care about him."

"Though Jillian and Sam are gone, he's still our son." Eyes watering further, she dons a lopsided grin. "If you're what you seem, Kate Meadows, I'm counting on you to keep him heading in the right direction."

Sounds like a vote of confidence, but what if I fail her? What if her expectations are higher than what I'm capable of?

"Time for us to return to the party." She takes my arm and leads me down the hallway. "I'm surprised Clive hasn't come looking for you. My guess is Jack corralled him."

As we turn into the living room, she drops her hand from me. "I can't wait to see the work you've done on the burn unit."

"Then don't. Drop by anytime and I'll—"

She shakes her head. "Jack and I have decided to wait until the grand opening."

"Oh. Certainly." Knowing I've monopolized her long enough, I say, "Thank you, Mrs. Murphy—for everything."

"You're welcome. And call me Gloria." She smiles as if in parting, but then her brow furrows. "I understand that Clive commissioned a memorial plaque."

"Yes, and it's beautiful—especially the words."

She nods. "It was a big step for him. Do you know if there'll be a picture of Jillian and Sam?"

Does she know about his sterile office, the walls of which are conspicuously absent of family photos?

I shrug. "He hasn't said anything about it to me. But that doesn't mean he won't have one hung."

She looks down, then back up. "He needs to get past it, Kate," she says with an intensity that makes me feel the matter's entrusted to me. "Until he does, how can we?"

I lay a hand to her arm. "I'll do what I can."

Oh, Lord! Did I just accept a mission? I am not cut out for missionary work. You know it. I know it. What have I done?

"Kate."

I turn to Clive, whose questioning face makes me feel as if I've been caught doing something dishonest.

He halts alongside me. "Enjoying yourself?"

"Uh…yes. Gloria has introduced me around and we've visited a bit." *More* than a bit.

He turns his regard to his mother-in-law. "Thank you, Gloria."

She inclines her head. "Well, it's past time we lit the candles." She steps past me and raises her arms. "Everyone! Cake! The dining room! Now!"

"Welcome to the Murphys," Clive murmurs.

"They seem very nice."

He parts his lips as if to say something; however, a moment later he's covering my hands with one of his. At which point I become aware I'm rubbing the medallion.

"What is it you want to believe, Kate?"

So many things that have to do with him—that he'll get past his loss, that he's capable of loving another woman, that a biological child isn't more important than his love for a woman. But it's not the time or place.

I try to smile. "I'll tell you later."

An hour and a half later, filled up on finger foods, cake, and ice cream, we say our good-byes. On the porch, Gloria gives me a hug while her husband pulls Clive aside and rasps, "Date, maybe mate."

Gloria gasps. "Jack!"

Shrugging off his failure to be discreet, he claps his son-in-law on the back and follows his clucking wife back inside.

"Jack likes you," Clive says as we make our way through the darkness toward the car.

"Hmm. And we didn't exchange more than a dozen words."

"He trusts Gloria's judgment, and I believe you did more than exchange a dozen words with her."

Does he know?

I glance at his night profile. Hard to tell.

He opens the car door for me, and shortly we leave the neighborhood behind.

Clive looks at me. "It's early yet. Would you like to go somewhere?"

"Sure."

"Where?"

"Uh, I don't drink, so…"

"Bars are out."

What if he's an alcoholic? What if, all these years, he's been grieving at the bottom of a bottle? Of course, I've never seen him look anything but in control, and have yet to catch the scent of alcohol on him. Still, I have to ask.

"Do you drink?"

"An occasional glass of wine with dinner."

Okay. Falls within the guidelines of many Christians. Actually, if not for the fact that I don't particularly like the taste of alcohol, I might have an occasional glass myself.

"Does that bother you, Kate?"

"That you drink? Occasionally? No. Everything in moderation, right?"

He gives me a glancing smile. "Right."

I sink back in the seat, and it hits me—I am *so* buzzing.

Sleep deficit having caught up with me, I have a sudden longing for a plump pillow. And so I lower my lids against the glare of headlights. And sink deeper.

"So have you decided where you want me to take you?"

"Um-hmm." I sigh. "To bed."

ilence—until I sit bolt upright and start choking on saliva.

"I didn't—"

Hack! Hack!

"Didn't mean—"

Hack! Hack! Hack!

Clive thumps me on the back. "Do I need to pull over?"

"No! I'm all right." I clear my throat. "I didn't mean that the way it sounded. You know, about...the..."

Come on, Kate, it's not a four-letter word!

"Be-ed!" I spit out in a voice cracked straight down the middle.

Clive smiles. "Can't say I'm not disappointed."

Oh, boy.

Grateful for the dim interior, I say, "I'm just tired."

"Then I should take you home."

"No!"

Ack! What is my problem? And, yes, he should take me home, as I could really use some uninterrupted sleep. But it's not what I want.

I look to him. "Wherever you'd like to go is fine with me."

"You sure?"

I press my shoulders back lest the seat once more tempt me to muttering about B-E-D. "Absolutely."

"It's clear tonight, and unseasonably warm."

Funny things, San Francisco's summers—cool, foggy, and with temperatures averaging fifty to sixty-five degrees. "Yes. Very pleasant."

"Do you trust me, Kate?"

"What do you mean?"

"There's a place I'd like to take you, but I want you to feel comfortable, as it'll just be the two of us. Trust me?"

"Wouldn't have got in the car if I didn't." I grin. "Besides, I carry pepper spray."

"Wise." He takes a sharp right onto Highway 1.

"Stinson Beach?" I venture.

"Not quite."

When the ocean comes into view, the moon cuts through the darkness to spill stars among the waves.

I sigh. "It's beautiful."

"It is."

Ten minutes later, he pulls off the highway. "And now we walk."

"Walk? Where?"

"You'll see." He opens his door and comes around to hand me out.

As I straighten alongside him, the cool breeze coming off the water whispers at my hem, reminding me that I'm hardly dressed for a walk—especially a walk in the dark.

Clive closes the door. "I forgot about your skirt, but your shoes are sensible."

Yes, but is a night walk sensible?

I look to the hill that rises at his back. "Maybe this isn't such a good idea."

"It's an easy walk."

"But—"

"Trust me." He entwines his fingers with mine, causing prickles to take up residence on my limbs.

"All right, but you should know I'm not the adventurous, spontaneous type."

"I know." He draws me toward the hill.

"This should do." He releases my arm, leaps onto a rock, and reaches back to assist me. Shortly, he turns me to face the ocean and the salted breeze that has badgered my backside throughout the climb. I sigh into it and momentarily ponder the reason it's so much warmer up high.

Ah, exertion. That would be me.

"Worth the climb?" Clive asks at my back.

I have to admit that it's breathtaking, but worth the climb? That might be stretching it.

He pulls me back against him. "Worth it?"

Absolutely. Positively. Irrefutably. Indisputably.

I close my eyes and concentrate on his warm breath swirling in my ear. "Definitely worth it."

"Good." To my groaning disappointment, he drops his arms from me, takes my hand, and draws me toward the topmost rock. Somehow, I make it with minimal scrapes.

Sitting shoulder to shoulder with Clive, I stare out across the ink-spilled ocean to pick out lit boats and ships. And it's then that I realize how high up we are. "First rooftop dining, now this." I smile at him. "You're partial to heights."

"Actually, it's the night sky to which I'm partial, but height certainly improves the view."

Fighting the urge to touch his breeze-swept hair, I look

lower. "I do believe, Clive Alexander, that you're a romantic."

"And if I am?"

I watch his mouth shape the words and feel a rush of attraction that borders on woozy. Or maybe that's lack of sleep?

"In that case, I'd place a check mark in your pros column under *romantic*."

He regards me across the dark. "Pros column?"

"As opposed to cons." Speaking of which, maybe I *should* formulate a pros and cons list for Clive as I did for Michael.

"And what other qualities besides *romantic* would be on your list?"

I stop on that. Oh, dear. Did *not* mean to reveal my mental tallying. How juvenile!

Unfortunately, the hole I've dug is too deep to back out of, so I shrug. "*Considerate* is a good one."

"And you rank me...?"

I laugh. "Pro, of course."

"Go on."

"*Attractive*—another pro."

His teeth flash through the dark. "Thank you."

"And *intelligent*—pro."

He leans near. "I'm listening."

I dip my gaze to his mouth. Is he thinking what I think he's thinking? "*Good kisser*. Definitely a good kisser."

Yes, he *is* thinking what I think he's thinking, as evidenced by the touch of his mouth on mine. A nice, lingering kiss...

He draws slightly back. "Keep going."

"Er, *self-sacrificing*—you know when you caught me...the scaffolding. A pro."

"What about the cons?"

How I wish he'd either kiss me again or remove the temptation of his mouth! "I haven't really—"

"Yes, you have. Tell me."

I roll my eyes. "And ruin the moment?"

"*Would* it ruin it?"

Uncomfortable with the conversation's turn, I say, "Well, *ruin* is a bit extreme."

He waits but, when I continue to flounder, says, "Let me guess—the first con falls under the heading *religious*."

Rather, *spiritual*. But it's not as if he's never believed. He's just on hold. Though his relationship with God is of utmost importance, the biggest obstacle is his desire for biological children.

"Kate?"

"Uh…yes. I mean, your spiritual state is important to me."

Ack! Spiritual state! Where did that come from? It sounds so… superior.

Clive's moonlit eyes consider me; then he turns his attention to the great, dark expanse. "As I mentioned earlier, Kate, I still believe."

And as happened earlier, my heart leaps like a tadpole that suddenly discovers it has grown legs. However, rather than burst forth with questions as I did before, I bite my tongue.

Shortly, I have something to show for the discomfort when Clive says, "I know very well that God exists." He pushes a hand through his hair and shakes his head. "I've just stopped trusting Him."

"Do you think you'll ever trust Him again?" The question is out before I can think better of it.

Fortunately, he doesn't slam the door and hang the "closed" sign. "I want to. It's just not easy."

"I know."

His mouth tightens with a forced smile. "And yet you trust Him, hmm?"

I nod—an automatic response that my conscience grabs hold of and gives a good, hard shake.

Well, aren't you "holier than thou," Kate Meadows? Yes, you trust God, but not when it's easier to play it safe. Not when what you want doesn't match what you have to give...

"No." I draw a breath. "That's not exactly true. Though I know I should trust God completely—that He's the only One who doesn't need to earn my trust—I sometimes fail." I give a halfhearted laugh. "Actually, more than sometimes."

Clive stares at me, and I feel his pain between us. Pain I long for God to heal.

I touch his hand and spread my fingers across his. "God loves you."

His hand tenses.

"He's never stopped loving you."

His fingers curl.

"He wants to heal you of your losses."

His hand clenches.

"If you could just—"

He pulls his hand from beneath mine. "Let's talk about something else."

I blew it. Saw—rather, *felt*—the signs, but ignored them. And now I've gone and scared him back to the other side.

Pulling my hand from his knee, I finger my way around the bracelet.

Lord, I'm not cut out for evangelism, so why do You put it on my heart to talk to him? Of course, maybe it isn't You. Maybe it's me. Me wanting to fix his beliefs. To make him more datable. What if he never comes back to You? And even if he does come back, what if he never gets past his loss? What if that wedding band becomes permanently embedded in his finger? Three going on four years, Lord!

I startle when Clive covers my hand with one of his, halting my unconscious medallion-rubbing.

"You're doing it again, Kate. What is it you want to believe?"

"You." I don't mean to thrust the word at him, but that's how it comes out. "That you really are available."

Once more, his hand tenses. "Are we talking about religion again?"

"No! I mean, not exactly. Well, some, but…" And the dam breaks. "Gloria showed me the pictures in her hallway. She told me about Jillian. And Sam. And the fire. And—"

Cool air rushes in to replace the warmth of his hand upon mine. "I didn't expect that." He draws back. "From Jack, perhaps, but not Gloria." His silence stretches to keen discomfort. "How did you manage it, Kate?"

"What?"

"How did you get her to give you the lowdown?"

"I—"

Wait a minute! He thinks I was prying. That I forced my way into her confidence. That I could be that nosy…

Deep breath, Kate.

…that desperate…

Deep breath.

…that insensitive…

Deeeeep.

I narrow my gaze on his dark countenance. "You've got it wrong."

"Do I?"

"Yes."

With a rumble in his throat, he rises. "It's late. I should get you home."

That's it, then? He's not going to give me a chance to explain what happened in that hallway with Gloria? Not that I couldn't unload on him. And I would if not for the realization that it would be a waste of time. Clive Alexander *isn't* ready—in fact, he's surely searching for a way out of his attraction toward me. And I…

It's for the best, as it saves me the unnecessary awkwardness of revealing something intensely personal. In fact, I'm relieved—or will be once I move on.

With a lump in my throat, I look up.

Though Clive doesn't offer me a hand up, when I straighten, he takes my arm to lend me his sure-footedness.

I suppress the temptation to jerk free. In my present circumstance, it could prove dangerous—cutting off my nose to spite my face and all. Of course, it has been brought to my attention that that particular member of my face is violating my personal space by as much as a quarter inch—

Get your mind out of the bottom of your purse, Kate!

Yes, I have yet to toss all those business cards, but I'm going to. Just as soon as I get home. And half an hour later, following a ride so bereft of conversation that I repeatedly renew my "thou shalt embrace singledom and be unbelievably, inconceivably happy" creed, that's where I find myself.

As Clive pulls to the curb, I reach for the door handle.

"Kate." His voice closes over me as effectively as a hand on my arm.

I look around.

The porch light illuminating his features, his eyes meet mine. "I'm sorry."

As I frown at him, the angst that's been building throughout the drive teeters toward forgiveness.

He shifts his jaw. "It's difficult for me to talk about what happened. And you surprised me. I didn't expect Gloria to open herself—or me—so wide to someone she'd just met."

Does this mean we're not fighting anymore? That he wants to kiss and make up? A thrill skips up my spine a moment before the renewed creed singsongs through my head.

I sigh. "I understand your reluctance to speak about your past, and though I admit to being curious, I didn't pry. Gloria wanted me to know."

He continues to study my face.

Opting for lightheartedness, I flash a smile. "Can I help it if she likes me?"

He leans toward me and slides a hand up my cheek. "I like you, too, Kate."

The creed!

Struggling against attraction, I say, "It's late. I should—"

"I'm driving up to Fairfax tomorrow. Will you come with me?"

"Fairfax?"

"I've bought an old house that sits on twelve acres and has an incredible view of Mount Tam that I think you'd like."

"You live there?"

"No. I keep an apartment here in the city, but once the renovations to the house are complete, I'll move out there."

"A bit of a commute."

"Worth it." His thumb caresses my cheekbone. Tempts me. I shake my head. "I have to work tomorrow."

"Sunday, then?"

"Church." Of course, I could—

Not! Remember Operation: Perfect Faith? You know—your getting-back-to-God exercise that you've let slide for the past two days?

"What about after church?"

And what about the creed? Hmm, Kate?

"Uh…my friend, Belle, is having her baby shower right after church."

"So you should be done by…?"

Creed!

"Hard to say. You know, baby showers can go on for hours. But if I can swing it, I'll call you."

He looks momentarily down, then draws back, opens his car door, and comes around.

Clasping his hand, I step to the sidewalk. "Good night, Clive."

"Good night, Kate."

He doesn't walk me to the door, but as I fit my key in the lock, I glance around and find him right where I left him beside the car.

"'Night," I murmur across the darkness, then open the door and slip inside. As I climb the stairs, I hear his car pull away. And feel empty.

Upon entering my bedroom, I kick off my shoes and drop to my knees beside the bed.

"Lord, I want him to be 'The One.' I want him to be right with You. I want him to make it past his loss." I clasp my hands tighter before my mouth. "Of course, then there's still the matter of what I can't give him. I know I should tell him, but then he might not be The One. But if I don't tell him, and he really is The One, when I finally do tell him, it could be too late. But then, if it's too late, that would mean he isn't The One. Unless he would have been The One if—"

I drop my forehead to my clasped hands and shake my head. This is why I journal. Though I'm capable of verbal expression—to a point—when it comes to actually talking to God, I'm all over the place.

I blow a breath up my face. "Let me start again." And I do.

Several times. Until I decide to just…be…still. Which is hard, especially when silence is all I hear on the other end.

My head gives a warning throb. Knees creak. Back aches. Clenched fingers tingle. But, in the end, my bladder is my undoing.

When I emerge from the bathroom, I stop at the sight of my journal, which stares blankly at me—as in "plenty of room here to talk to God." And my Bible, which gives me a knowing look—as in "plenty of Scripture here to guide you."

I avert my eyes. "I know. Just…not tonight."

Telling myself that Operation: Perfect Faith will get back on track first thing tomorrow morning and that talking to God will suffice for now, I crawl into bed and stare at the ceiling. "Lord, if I don't get it right soon, my life is going to be in the toilet."

18

and me that roll of toilet paper!"

"When I'm jolly well done with it."

I eye the young woman unwinding another length of the ultrasoft fluffy stuff that is the means by which we guess the size of Belle's belly.

Andrea wiggles her eyebrows at me, rolls off another half dozen squares, then tosses the roll to me. "Kate's up!"

Eyeing her wad of toilet paper, I rise from the sofa. "Sheesh, Andrea, we're measuring her girth, not wrapping her for mummification."

Belle's younger sister guffaws amid the chuckles of the other women attending the baby shower.

I tear off twelve squares. "That ought to do it. What do you think, Belle?"

"That you're too kind." She shifts her bulk in the recliner. "I feel twice that size."

"Told you so." Andrea waves her toilet paper.

Belle's mother stands. "Everyone line up—and be quick about it. Belle doesn't need to be on her feet." As we scramble for position, the older woman turns to her beautifully pregnant daughter and helps her out of the chair.

We take our turns wrapping the toilet paper around her belly, and it's not long before I discover that I *was* too kind—by two squares. As for Andrea, she pulled off ten too many. Delia Speck, a boutique employee, is the winner at fourteen squares, for which she takes home a cute little tin of rose petal soap.

It's another hour before the shower winds down, and when I glance at my watch and discover it's only two-thirty, the first thing that pops to mind is that I *could* have gone to Fairfax with Clive. Not that I had any intention of doing so, but I definitely could have fit it in.

And still could.

Which brings me back to all the wrestling I've done since Friday night. Fortunately, I didn't awaken with a limp like Jacob after his all-night wrestling match with God. Unfortunately, I'm *this* close to a headache.

"What's up?" Belle asks.

I look up from the gift bags I've been folding and meet her gaze across the sofa table. "What?"

"You're agonizing. Please tell me it's about a man—preferably Dr. Alexander—and not your work."

Though I hadn't meant to say anything, when we talked by phone Friday afternoon, my pending date with Clive slipped out. She was thrilled and, undoubtedly, has been on pins and needles since I arrived with the other guests. Now we're finally alone.

I sigh. "Yes, it's Clive."

Her left eyebrow arches. "He didn't try anything funny, did he?"

"Other than take me to meet his in-laws, no."

"In-laws? In-laws! You've got to be kidding."

"I'm not."

Belle points to the ottoman upon which her feet are elevated. And I'm almost grateful for the summons. After all this "agonizing" over Clive, I need to talk to someone.

"Start to finish," she says as I lower alongside her feet, "and don't leave anything out."

I tell it all—from my initial attraction to Clive, to his advice against "instant" self-improvement, to his desire for biological children, to his wanting to trust God again, to the fallout from Clive's mother-in-law's disclosure.

"But at least it seems to be working out between Maia and Michael," I say. "I heard them come in after midnight. They sounded happy." Even past the pillow I'd dragged over my head.

Belle narrows her lids. "Tell me Michael didn't spend the night."

"Nope. He left ten minutes later."

"That's progress." She shifts her bulk around. "So you really like this Dr. Alexander, hmm?"

"Yeah."

"But?"

Here we go again. "Remember our disagreement over the inclusion of religious symbols in the burn unit?"

"Yes."

"Well, though I was finally able to convince him to allow the symbols, he's still turned away from God."

"Hmm. That is a problem. Of course, from what you've told me, it sounds as if he's receptive to turning back. What else?"

"There's the matter of him holding on to his loss—wedding ring and all."

"Better than him not holding on. Shows he's capable of real love, Kate."

True. "And then, when he learned that his mother-in-law told me about the fire, he closed down on me."

Belle raises an eyebrow. "Do you think you're the only one who's afraid to let someone in? The only one with secrets?"

I flush guiltily. "Of course not."

"I'd guess once he accepted that you knew more about his past than he was prepared to tell, he was actually relieved. Hence, the apology and invitation to accompany him to Fairfax—which you were right not to accept, of course."

I was?

She smiles. "He likes you, Kate. I'd say very much."

And I like him. Very much.

Belle sits forward to reach a hand to my knee, but her belly gets in the way.

I smile, scoot closer, and clasp her hand. "Yes, Belle?"

"Have you prayed about you and Clive?"

My smile crumples. "A lot—especially since Friday."

"What's God telling you?"

I shrug. "He's not speaking much to me these days."

"More than likely, *you're* not listening."

Or reading my Bible. Or journaling. Though I had every intention of doing so this morning, especially after missing Saturday on top of Thursday and Friday, time got away from me as I lay in bed rehashing my date with Clive.

Well, actually, I *let* time get away from me. Did *not* want to open my Bible and be confronted yet again with more truths that I'm not ready to act upon.

"*Are* you listening to God, Kate?"

I shake my head. "I know God wants me to tell Clive about my infertility, but he seems to thinks I'm stronger than I am."

Belle makes a sound in her throat. "And we know how often God is wrong."

I drop my forehead to our joined hands. "I argue with myself all the time—tell myself it's too early to reveal something so personal, but that Clive should know so neither of us wastes the other's time…that the more time he has to get to know me, the more likely he'll choose me over biological children, but knowing there'll be consequences for not telling him…that I won't have to suffer his pity if it doesn't work out, but that he's taken a chance by revealing his painful past to me."

"That's right, he did."

I lift my head. "Grudgingly. And with regard to the fire, that was all his mother-in-law."

She sighs. "I'm not going to side with you—not when it sounds like this is something more than a onesie-twosie date. Regardless of how you came by Clive's past, if you're going to continue seeing him, you have to let him in."

If I see him again.

"You have to be a friend first, Kate."

As she was to Beau. But how do you do that if you've already progressed to the kissing stage?

Belle moves her hand to her belly, taking mine with it. "I think you should call him."

I want to. I really do. And maybe I will. It is, after all, just a phone call. Nothing at all to tempt either of us. Yeah.

Cell phone—no answer.

Hospital work phone—not expected in today.

In-laws' phone—miracle of miracles, they were listed, and Jack whipped off the directions to the Fairfax property in no time flat.

I know this isn't what Belle meant for me to do when she said I should call Clive, but here I am giving my brains a good shake as I negotiate a crumbling old asphalt driveway stretching toward a Victorian-style home that appears charming until I draw near. *Definitely* in need of repair.

As for the vehicle parked out front, it's not Clive's car. Though I suspect the dark green truck I pull alongside belongs to him, I glance at the cute little canister of pepper spray that swings from my car keys.

Hmm. Relatively remote…may not be Clive's truck… "truck man" may not be alone…no one to hear me scream….

I pull the keys from the ignition, unsnap the flap on the pepper spray, and twist to disengage the safety tab. Finger on the button, I step from the car and approach the house.

"Clive?" I call, though I doubt he's outside as he would have heard the shudder and jolt of my car over that savage driveway.

I mount the porch and call again when I see that the front door is open, but no answer. And no doorbell despite the cracked yellow button I repeatedly jab.

Rubbing the button on the pepper spray, I step inside a shabby foyer and call again.

No answer.

Okay, doesn't hear me—or perhaps "truck man" does and is lurking.

Rub, rub, rub!

Forcing my trigger finger to relax, I turn into a living room that's not much better than the foyer. Nor is the dark-paneled office to the right. The kitchen, however, shows definite signs of renovation. In fact, with the exception of unfinished drywall, it appears to be near completion—a gorgeous open room with a central island and plate glass windows that offer an unobstructed view of rolling hills and Mount Tamalpais in the distance.

"Wow." I peer across the valley and pick out fewer than a

dozen residences that share the view. Not a single one within shouting distance. And suddenly I realize how much I miss this kind of privacy. Having become accustomed to the squeeze of a crowded city, I've almost forgotten what wide open spaces look—and feel—like. I could get used to it again.

As I turn away, I catch a faint *shloop shloop* sound. Leaving the kitchen by a second exit on the other side of the room, I step into a dim corridor and halt before a flight of stairs down which the *shloop shloop* travels.

Pepper spray or not, maybe this isn't such a good idea...

I cross to the bottom step and look up the stairs—creepy, shadow-shrouded stairs that turn halfway up. "Clive? Is that you?"

Shloop shloop. Shloop shloop.

I glance at the pepper spray from which my keys swing and rub the button.

"Clive?" Louder this time.

Shloop shloop.

Surely if *I* can hear him, *he* can hear me. "Clive?"

Shloop shloop. Shloop shloop. Shloop shloop.

An instant later, I place the sound—at least, I think I do. Sounds like sanding. However, it isn't a sound over which a person can't hear a shout. Unless he's deaf. Or pretending not to hear—

The shiver that's been building at the base of my spine shoots like an arrow straight up my vertebrae, and I whip around—pepper spray at the ready.

But no one's there. Regardless, I'm tempted to track down Clive from the safety of my sealed and bolted car. But I do have a weapon. And it probably *is* Clive up there. Maybe he's plugged in to music. Headphones would certainly account for his lack of response.

I almost laugh at my silly fear, but the shiver that coursed my spine has yet to dissipate.

Glancing up into the unknown, I grip the little canister tighter and set foot to the first step. "Dear Lord, protect me."

Twice more I call to Clive as I ascend the stairs, but the *shloop shloop* continues.

I turn at the first landing and keep my eye on the second floor above me, which opens into what appears to be a sitting room. And it is, I confirm as I step up to it.

Shloop shloop goes the sandpaper.

"Clive!" goes Kate.

Shloop shloop. Shloop shloop.

It's coming from behind the closed door at the far end of the hallway—the *really* dark end.

Surely it's Clive. Or maybe not. He's a surgeon, not a sandpaper guy.

I continue past two rooms and rub the button on the pepper spray. I will use this if necessary.

Halting before the door, I reach to the handle. "Clive!"

Shloop shloop. Then silence.

Okay, he heard me. I curl my fingers around the doorknob only to stumble forward when it's ripped out of my hand. And there, against an eerie mist, is a monster—a white, chalky monster with a round muzzle and piercing, flesh-ringed eyes. And are those wires connecting its head to its neck? Impossible, and yet my throat opens and lets out an eardrum-breaking scream. And my hand shoots upward, wielding the pepper spray.

The monster's eyes above its expressionless muzzle widen; then it barks or growls or something LOUD and lurches toward me.

At about the level of its chest, I jab the button.

There's a shout, and as I raise the canister to nail the thing between its ghastly eyes, it knocks my hand up and back. But I continue to press the button, determined that nothing will keep me from defending myself. Nothing—except the pepper spray that rains down. On me.

"Oh, my!" Heat pours into my eyes. "Ow!" As if from a distance, I hear my keys clatter to the floor. "Oh!" Then I'm lurching back…desperately rubbing at my flaming eyes…dropping to my knees…coughing….

"Kate—no!"

The pain intensifies. "It hurts!"

My hands are yanked from my eyes and a voice commands, "Don't rub! It'll only make it worse."

I flail, slip a wrist free, and reach to my eyes. I barely get in a good rub, which makes me cry out louder, when my wrist is recaptured.

"No, Kate!" A hoarse cough. "Don't rub!"

Is that Clive? With a moan that ends on a cough of my own, I shake my head and realize I'm flat on my back. I gasp. "I'm—"

"Stop it!"

"—being burned alive."

In spite of the excruciating pain, I sense hesitation from the one who has me down on the floor…who's refusing me the comfort of rubbing my eyes…who sounds a lot like Clive….

"Listen, Kate—" another cough—"I've got to get you to the—"

"It burns!" I splay my hands. "Lord, help me!"

"*I'll* help you," Clive growls. "If you'll let me!"

It's Clive. Clive. Clive.

"Okay." Deep breath. "Okay." Deep, deep breath. "Help me."

He drags me to my feet and releases my wrists to slide an arm around me.

I reach again to my eyes.

"Don't rub!"

I clench my hands at my sides and chant, "Don't rub, don't rub, don't rub," as he guides me through the hallway.

"We're going down the stairs now, Kate. Hang tight to me."

I cling, allowing him to bear much of my weight down the treacherous steps. In between my admonishments of "don't rub" and his throat clearing, I whimper and cough and become aware that it's not just my eyes that burn, but my entire face.

Off the stairs, we turn one way, then the other, walk a straight course, turn again, and halt. Then I hear the squeak of a faucet and feel a mist.

"We're getting into the shower now."

"Okay," I say, only to startle when I realize that he really does mean "we're"—that *he's* getting in with *me*.

"Your pepper spray got me, too." He reads me right. "Not to the extent it did you, as I was wearing a mask and safety glasses, but I need to rinse off."

Mask? Safety glasses? At the moment, my eyes hurt too much to figure that one out. However, propriety is an entirely different matter.

"Isn't there—oh, it burns!" I grit my teeth as he urges me forward. "Isn't there another shower you can use?"

"This is the only one that works. Besides, you're in no state to be left alone."

I groan—three-quarters pain, one-quarter humiliation. "And once again you're stuck doctoring me."

"Once again." He shifts me around, and the shower spray hits me in the chest—my clothed chest. I am showering in my clothes. My nice going-to-church clothes. My dry-clean only clothes. My soon-to-be-ruined clothes. Well, at least the loss will be a memorable one.

"Lift your face into the spray, Kate."

Oh sweet, blessed relief—at least until he orders me to open my eyes and irrigate them. "Ee-ow! Ow! Ow!" I jump back into him, lift my hands to rub at the burn, and am once more thwarted when he pins my arms to my sides.

"Give it a minute," he speaks into my ear, "then we'll try again."

Unsure which is stronger—the burn in my eyes or the tingling in my ears—I nod and he moves us forward. Considering the amount of water that rushes down my neck, I guess he's put his face into the spray. And the shake of his head a moment later provides further evidence.

Clive draws us back, and once more I'm the recipient of the downpour. It feels good, but what feels better is my back against his chest. Who would have thought that two people standing in a shower, fully clothed, could be so—

I catch my breath. Funny things are happening to my insides... Not good.

"Clive, I really think we should—"

"Try again, Kate."

"What?"

He grips my chin and lifts my face to the spray. "Open your eyes."

I force my lids up, and though the water increases the pain, it's not as bad as the first time. Or is it?

"I'm blind!" I squeeze my lids closed. "I can't see a—"

"A temporary condition."

I turn my head toward him. "Are you sure?"

"Positive."

I turn my face back into the spray. "Okay."

"Kate, you're wearing contacts, aren't you?"

"Uh-huh."

"We need to remove them." He turns me to face him. I was wet before, but this makes it complete as the spray douses my backside and causes my clothing to cling to every inch of my body. *So* glad I can't see the inevitable bump and bulge. Unfortunately, Clive can.

"I…uh…think I can take it from here."

"Tilt your head back."

"But—"

He eases my head back, pries open the right lid, and slides the contact off.

I hold my breath. Though our bodies are no longer touching, I feel him. In fact, impossible though it is in the darkness behind my lids, I know the beat of his heart. And, at his hesitation, I'm certain he knows mine.

Oh, my! Is he looking at me? At my pitifully wet, sopping figure with all its imperfections? Does he see my tummy roll? Not that it's *that* big, but it certainly runneth over. And my thighs! Which I never did have the fat sucked out of. Encased in the clinging black material of my slacks, they must appear positively bulbous.

I hear him draw a rough breath. "One more," he says, and removes the second contact.

I squeeze the lid closed and realize that though my eyes sting horribly, the pain is no longer excruciating. Thank God.

Oh, and Clive! Clive who—

Whose mouth brushes the tip of my nose, down which water trickles.

Surely he's not going to kiss me. That would be…

Dangerous!

I strain back. "My contacts! Where did you put them?"

His breath stirs across my face as if suddenly released; then he's turning me back around. "Down the drain."

"Down the drain!" I open my eyes wide only to find that I'm still on the blind side—and it hurts!

"You won't want to wear them again. In fact…" He lowers his voice and, with apology, says, "You need to get out of these clothes."

"What?"

"Not only will they have to be laundered to remove the oil residue, but you're soaked."

"But—"

"One more irrigation." He urges me forward. "Open your eyes."

Deciding that the matter of my clothing removal—and what, exactly, I'm supposed to wear!—will have to wait, I force my lids up.

Ooh! I see shapes, indistinct but shapes. I blink into the water for as long as I can stand it, then step back—back into Clive's arms again.

"I think my vision is clearing."

"Good." After a pause I feel straight through my back, Clive says, "Kate?"

Why the feeling he's going to ask something better left for when I'm dry and decently attired? I squeeze my eyes closed for the relief found behind my lids. "Yes?"

"I'm assuming it was Jack or Gloria who gave you directions."

"Jack."

So strange conversing with my back to him. *More* strange conversing in a *shower*!

"I gave up on you calling hours ago."

"But I did call—your cell phone—though I suppose *after* you gave up."

"Must have been. I left the phone downstairs when I decided to tackle the drywall."

I frown. "You do drywall?"

"It's how I put myself through college."

"Oh." Then no rich parents footing the bill.

"Why did you drive out here, Kate?"

Why be coy? "I wanted to see your property. And you."

After a breath-holding moment, he says, "So you came bearing pepper spray?"

I almost laugh. "I wasn't sure it was your truck outside. And when I heard the noise upstairs and called to you and you didn't respond…"

"I was listening to music, didn't hear you until you were at the door."

Remembering the "thing" that ripped the knob out of my hand, I say, "I thought you were a monster."

His chuckle warms the back of my head. "Never been called that."

"You were all white and chalky and had this muzzle, and your eyes were wild, and there were wires connecting your head to your neck…" *So* strange carrying on a conversation like this!

"I was sanding the joints of the drywall, which is why I was dusted. As for the mask, it keeps me from inhaling dust, and the safety goggles keep it out of my eyes."

"And the wires were earphones," I finish, determined to nip "stupid" in the bud.

"That's right."

The awkwardness of our conversation is almost enough to make me scream. "I'm sorry about the pepper spray. Good thing you didn't take off the mask and goggles before opening the door."

"Yeah."

"I did get you in the chest, though."

"You did."

I can stand it no longer! I swing around, lift my lids, and try to focus on him, where he stands back. The first thing that "crisps up"—at least, as far as it can without contacts—is his wet long-sleeved shirt, the chest of which I hit with pepper spray. And which is molded to his torso.

"You…uh…should get that shirt off."

I sense, more than see, him stiffen and only then realize how that sounded—about how it sounded when he told me I'd have to remove my own clothes. Oh, dear.

I jerk my gaze to his face, which around the hairline bears evidence of white dust. As does his hair. "I mean, not in here, but out there. It will have to be laundered as well."

He reaches to the tall glass door. "I think you can handle it from here. Take your time."

He closes the shower door behind him, and through the pane I watch him retrieve a towel, cross to the doorway, and pull the door closed as he steps into the room beyond.

I don't take my time. Though I have no idea how to solve my clothing dilemma, I rinse another minute, then reach to the faucet; however, remembering the dust Clive will want to wash away, I leave the water running so he can step in after me.

Dripping great puddles, I sink my toes into the thick rug on which Clive's mask, safety glasses, MP3 player, and head-phones lie. I don't remember him removing them. But then, I *was* a bit preoccupied.

I grab a towel, wrap it around my sopping clothes, and open the door into…a bedroom.

Averting my gaze from the full-size bed, I land on Clive, who appears unaware of my presence where he stands before a dresser with his bare back to me. Even so, I'm very aware of him—especially what he reveals that he wouldn't want to reveal. There's no mistaking the scars above the waistband of the clean jeans he's pulled on—scars that witness his attempt to rescue his wife and son.

What a painful reminder…

19

I know the instant Clive becomes aware he's no longer alone. It's in his tensing shoulders, the slight turn of his head, the breathless moment he listens to confirm what slipped past him while his thoughts were elsewhere.

"It's bad manners not to announce one's presence." He throws my words back at me.

Slowly, he turns to present a firm chest unmarred by fire. *Don't look! Don't look!*

"I..." I lower my gaze, squeeze my eyes closed to soothe the sting, then whip my lids up so fast that everything below his chin passes in a blur. "I would have announced myself, but I was surprised to—"

"You don't seem surprised. More like pitying."

Do I? Of course, maybe he means *pitiful*, which certainly fits the picture I present in sopping clothes and hair—nowhere near the beauty that was Bathsheba. I suffer a pang of regret, only to remind myself of what happened when King David saw the bathing beauty on her rooftop. In such a state as I now present, there's no way Clive would summon me to be his mistress.

So this is good—even if I feel like puppy doo.

"Don't, Kate."

"What?"

"Pity me. If I wanted that, you would have known long before now—or should I say before Friday?"

I really wish he would put that shirt on. Though I may be no Bathsheba, he too well fits the image I hold of King David.

"I assume she told you," Clive prompts.

He makes it sound like gossip Gloria and I indulged in, but it wasn't. Still, I flush. "Your mother-in-law mentioned you'd been burned but didn't elaborate. I thought you would have had reconstructive surgery."

"No."

A memory rises of my first day at the burn unit, when I'd rebuked him for preaching at me about my self-improvement by pointing out that he had nothing that needed improving upon. For a moment, it had appeared he might contradict me.

"I decided to leave it."

"Another reminder? Like the ring?" Only after the words are out do I realize how bold I sound. And how far I've trespassed. Times like these I wonder if I ought to have a lip zipper installed. Of course, were I staying on top of Operation: Perfect Faith, perhaps God would help me with the guard on my tongue that I keep laying off.

Fortunately, Clive doesn't appear to take offense. If anything, weariness settles about him. "For a while it served as a reminder. Now it's just part of me. In fact, most times I only give it enough thought to keep me in long-sleeved shirts."

I lower my gaze to the shirt he holds and, on the downward journey, travel across the breadth of his unscathed chest. *Perfect-ly* unscathed.

I really wish he'd put that shirt on!

Lifting my chin, I catch his grim smile a moment before he drags on the dark blue shirt.

Wish granted.

"People tend to ask awkward questions." He jerks the hem down over the waist of his pants and looks past me. "Did you mean to leave the shower running?"

Guessing the subject of the fire is closed—and wishing he trusted me enough to talk about it—I glance over my shoulder at the misted room. "I thought you might want to rinse off. You were kind of…shortchanged."

"I'll treat myself to a long shower tonight." He turns back to the dresser.

Right. Probably for the best.

"I don't keep many clothes here." He rifles through a drawer. "However, I'm sure I have something you can change into."

"Thank you. That would be nice."

Hold it! I'm about to crawl into Clive's clothes? Something *he's* worn? Something big, soft, and lightly infused with his scent? And, perhaps, button-down? I conjure an ad of a woman wearing her man's oversized shirt unbuttoned to the point of cleavage, a cup of tea poised before her lips, and bare legs curled beneath her—

"Sweatpants." Clive drops a black garment atop the dresser.

So much for bare legs. Not that I'd go bare-legged around him. I am *not* that kind of woman!

"Sweatshirt."

So much for button-down. And cleavage. Not that I'd be so brazen as to show off that much flesh.

"You're good to go." Clive drops a blur of color atop the sweatpants—one that makes me see red.

Feeling a twist at my center, I zoom in on the red sweat-shirt. I don't do R-E-D.

Though I know I should "stiff upper lip" it—that my refusal to wear Christopher's favorite color is childish—I say, "Do you have a different top?"

Clive turns. "That's my last clean one. Hardly stylish, but I promise not to hold it against you."

Feeling incredibly shallow, I give my stinging eyes relief with a prolonged blink. "Then red it is."

He arches an eyebrow. "It's the *color* you're opposed to?"

Beginning to chill beneath my waterlogged clothes, I give a shrug that ends on a shudder. "Not my favorite color."

"Because it's associated with the devil and his pitchfork?"

Well, if you wanted to call Christopher a de— "No!" I'm ashamed at where my thoughts nearly took me. True, my con-tinued aversion to red rests in what Christopher did when I most needed his strength and support—

I know! Get over it. Grow up. Get a life.

—but he's no horned dude.

"Kate?"

I shudder again. "It's just that—"

"Back in the shower." Clive scoops up the clothes, crosses the bedroom, and thrusts them at me. "After you've warmed up and irrigated your eyes again, get dressed and we'll talk."

Knowing that I must resemble a wet mutt, I snatch the clothes from him, step into the bathroom, and firmly shut the door.

Ridiculous as it seems—especially considering the lock on the door—I once more step beneath the spray fully clothed. Though nowhere in the Bible does it say "Thou shalt shower in one's Sunday best if one finds oneself sheltered by a man not one's husband," I'm in a man's bedroom for goodness' sake!

When I finally step out, I can't peel off the clinging clothes fast enough. When it's time to don the R-E-D sweatshirt, I do it behind closed lids.

And there you have it. I'm wearing Clive's sweatpants, drawstring pulled tight to keep them from slipping down my hips (nice to know they can) and his sweatshirt, which does, in fact, carry the faint scent of…a man.

I wipe the above-sink mirror and eye Katherine Mae Meadows done up in red. Difficult as it is to admit, the bright color does me good. Not that I like red any better, but it likes me.

I peer at my face, where not a trace of makeup remains. Nothing I can do about that. However, the brush I find in the top vanity drawer can do something about my hair. I will *not* obsess over the short sand-colored strands woven between the bristles. I draw the brush through my hair. And leave behind a few dark strands to mingle with the sandy ones.

Draping my wet clothes over the showerhead, I exit the bathroom. "Clive?"

"In the kitchen—down the hall and take a left."

I know where it is, but he doesn't know I know.

Self-consciously patting down the sweatpants, I traverse the hall and walk into the kitchen, which is no longer as bright as it was earlier. Caressed by the rays of the setting sun, the room frames the man at its center where he leans against the island.

Clive looks over his shoulder at me. "Like it or not, red's a good color on you, Kate."

Though he's in line with the consensus, I feel a strange absence of resentment. "Thank you." I give the elasticized hem a tug. "Guess I'll have to wear it more often."

"Not for me, I hope."

I raise my eyebrows. "But you like it on me, don't you?"

Did I say that? Sounds so codependent! So "Lead me around by the nose, and I'll follow you to the ends of the earth"! So "Wannabe Mrs. Christopher Stapleton the Second so bad!"

I could just puke.

"I do like it, Kate, but that doesn't mean you should wear red if *you* don't like it."

The self-loathing that rises like bile begins to ebb. I could kiss him—Clive Alexander, a man after my own heart.

"You seem surprised. Is this another Michael thing?" He taps his nonexistent mole and missing gap.

"Oh. No. It's…"

It's the moment of truth. And why not? Considering how much I know of Clive's past, it's only fair that he knows mine—well, some of it.

I cross the kitchen and lean back against the island alongside him. "Actually, it's a Christopher thing." I glance sidelong at him. "Red was his favorite color, and I aimed to please. After he broke off the engagement, I cleared out my closet." I huff derisively. "Childish, but it helped."

Wow! I said it. And without a flinch or quiver.

Clive angles his body toward me. "Are you telling me that in all these years, you haven't worn red?"

"Yep."

"Because it's *his* favorite color?"

Feeling my defenses rise, I mentally stomp on them. My continuing aversion to red really is ridiculous. "'Fraid so."

He considers me. "He hurt you badly."

My emotions tighten, but more for what caused Christopher to hurt me—which I have yet to tell Clive.

I will, Lord.

"It wasn't easy getting over it."

He lifts my right hand in his left. "I understand that." As evidenced by the wedding band that glints on his ring finger.

And I can't help but note that as I've clung to the *absence* of red, he's clung to the *presence* of gold. As I've lost a man I loved who was to be my husband, he's lost a woman he loved who *was* his wife. As I've lost the ability to bring forth a child from my body, he's lost a child who was fully brought forth. No, my tragedy isn't as great as his, but we've suffered similar losses.

"Did your faith help?" His thumb circles the back of my hand. Strains my senses. Draws me to him though neither of us moves closer.

"Did it, Kate?"

I meet his gaze, and in his eyes see that he really wants to know.

"Unlike you, at the time I didn't have faith. My grandmother dragged me to church every Sunday, but I secretly sided with my grandfather, who thought it was cute that his little wife believed in the existence of a higher being. I humored her, and it wasn't so bad, as church filled many of my social needs. Not only did several of my friends attend, but I gained a few boyfriends—the last being Christopher, who had moved to Redding to finish out his degree at the university."

"Then he was a Christian."

"No. He dabbled in Christianity, said he liked the idea of it, but was no more committed than I."

Clive nods for me to continue, and all the while his thumb keeps circling.

Knowing it's only a matter of time before I start babbling and tell more than I'm ready to tell, I gush, "So we fell in love, were engaged, moved to San Francisco, started planning the wedding, and never made it to the altar."

He wants to ask the reason—I see the question move from his eyes to his lips. And I panic.

"Whereas your loss made you step back from faith, mine made me step forward."

His hand on mine stills. "I'm sorry for the pain Stapleton caused you, but you really can't compare our losses."

I search his face, see the pain there…search my heart, feel the pain there. And I whisper, "I think you'd be surprised."

He steps nearer. "Surprise me."

Here's your opening, Kate.

As I stare at him, I realize he's taken a piece of my heart. And I may never get it back—which would be fine were it an even trade. If he cared as deeply for me and that were enough for him. Perhaps given more time…

"You're right." I nod. "They don't compare."

Suspicion crosses his face. However, when nervousness makes me moisten my lips, he looks to my mouth, cups my face in his hands, and lowers his head.

I know I should pull back as Belle would advise, but I hold my breath.

"Kate," he whispers against my lips, then kisses me. Deeply. Urgently. And is that his hand sliding around the back of my neck…trailing down my spine…urging me closer?

Not good! Though I ignored the voice that told me to be honest with Clive, the voice that warns me not to go where I vowed never to go again outside of marriage, this time it's too loud to shove aside.

I pull my head back. "I can't."

He opens his eyes. "What?"

"Do this. It might get out of hand, and I don't believe in premarital sex."

He frowns. "Then you and Michael—"

"Yes! I mean no! We didn't…uh…we didn't."

Keeping his hold on me, Clive takes a step back. "Are you telling me you've never been with a man?"

The question—and his disbelief—are to be expected, but I'm broadsided. As for the answer… Despite having repented and been forgiven for my promiscuity with Christopher, I'm tempted to shame.

You're forgiven. Once and for all, Kate!

But no matter how often I assure myself of God's grace, there's this voice that tells me my infertility is a punishment from God, and were I truly forgiven, He would restore the most precious part of my womanhood.

"It's a simple question, Kate."

I blink Clive back to focus. "What?"

"Are you a virgin?"

I shake my head. "But the mistake I made years ago is one I'm not willing to repeat."

"Was that mistake made with Christopher Stapleton?"

I catch my breath.

Clive's regard deepens a moment before he releases me. "None of my business." He thrusts his hands in his pockets and shifts his attention to the valley's lengthening shadows.

Though I know better, I lay a hand on his arm. "Clive—"

His head snaps around and his gaze drops to my touch.

I snatch my hand back.

When he looks up, a strained smile stretches his mouth. "I'm sorry you had to push me away, Kate." The smile strains further. "It's just that it's been a while since…"

I nearly reach to him again, but this time stop myself.

He draws a long breath. "You're wise not to allow it to go any further without a commitment."

Then he understands.

I nod. "Or without God's blessing."

His lids narrow. "That may be more difficult than the commitment."

In the next instant, I find myself repeating words Belle once spoke to me. "It's however difficult you make it. God's ready when you are."

Silence. Is it time to leave? It *is* getting dark. And I do have to be up early tomorrow if I'm to stay on sched—

"I failed them, Kate."

The emotion in the taut lines of Clive's face is all the confirmation needed that he's talking about his wife and son.

"I kept putting them off. There was always something that needed to be done. Money and connections that needed to be made. And Jillian did her best to understand. But I knew there were problems the night I suggested we have another child, and she said it was hard enough being a single mom with just the one. So I promised her I'd get my priorities straight."

He shakes his head. "For three weeks, I was home by six, let the answering machine take my calls, helped put Sam down, and refused all distractions when it was just Jillian and me. Three Sundays in a row we attended church as a family. Not once were we late, and not once did I pass out a single business card."

Clive breathes deeply. "Then there was a function my partner had to pull out of due to a family crisis. As I believed it imperative that one of us be present, I reasoned that after all the giving I'd been doing, I could be forgiven one late night. There was disappointment in Jillian's voice when I phoned, but she assured me that she and Sam would be fine."

He swallows. "I pulled in close to midnight, and by then the upper floor of the house was ablaze. Though I heard sirens in the distance and a neighbor tried to stop me, I entered the house."

Silence.

"I brought them out, Kate—was certain I'd saved them. And Gloria and Jack let me believe it. Not until after the funeral arrangements were made did I learn the truth. I wasn't even there to see them buried."

More silence.

"I was facedown in bed for weeks while my burns healed." His eyes close as if to replay the memory against the backs of his lids. "A long time to decide whether or not to live. A long time to curse God."

I clasp my hands tightly as it seems the only way to keep them to themselves.

He sighs. "A long time to torture oneself with 'if only.' A long time to hate—not only myself, but my profession. A long time to consider Adam MacPhail's offer of a position working with burn victims."

I blink. "The favor."

He smiles grimly. "It gave me a reason to get out of bed and pick up what was left of my life. To try to make restitution for failing Jillian and Sam."

Aching for his ache, I unthinkingly say, "Jillian didn't blame you."

He tenses. "What *didn't* Gloria tell you?" Though there's resentment in his voice, I don't sense anger.

"She wants to see you happy—for you to come back to God."

"And believes you're the woman to make it happen."

Where is a really good sinkhole when you need one? "That's not her decision. It's yours."

A long moment passes. "And yours, Kate."

He meant that the way it sounded; I'm sure of it. But then he has to go and give my hand a squeeze. And I feel the edge of his wedding band.

I catch a glint of gold. "Are you certain you're ready for a relationship, Clive?"

"It's been almost four years."

"Yes, but to the world, you still claim to be a married man."

His gaze shifts downward, then slowly rises to mine. But he doesn't say a word. He just stares at me. Then he releases my hand and slides off the wedding band.

Oh, Lord. He said he wouldn't remove it until the right woman came along. Am I the right woman?

Of course, this means *I* have to tell *him*. And I'm not ready. Too, what about Belle's advice to first be friends? This is *way* past that.

Clive slips the wedding band in his pocket. "I'm ready to get serious."

Nervousness flies all over me. In fact, had I any tics, they'd be rolling out one after the other.

"Kate?"

I regard him with wide eyes, and before I realize what's happening, my tongue develops a tic all its own. "That's great. Really great. Provided you don't think this…uh…changes any-thing—you know, with regard to us…um…sleeping together." I shake my head. "No can do."

Ugh. That didn't sound like English. Did he understand any of it?

He's still—as if listening hard to a translator. Then a half smile eases out. "I understand."

He does? Hmm…maybe there *are* wedding bells in my fu-ture.

If you can change his mind about biological children.

20

You *showered* with him?"

I jerk the phone away and, half-expecting Belle to emerge from the earpiece, hold it at arm's length.

"Please tell me I heard wrong," her miniaturized voice pleads.

I gingerly put the phone back to my ear. "Do you have any idea how effective pepper spray is? I couldn't see a thing. It felt like my eyes were being burned out of the back of my skull."

"Hmm…"

"He's a doctor, Belle."

"Yeah, a doctor who's getting way too accustomed to playing doctor."

How I wish I'd kept Clive's ministrations to myself! "Nothing funny happened."

"I'm not worried about *funny*, Kate."

I groan. "You know what I mean. We didn't do anything inappropriate."

"Did you kiss?"

"Yeees."

"Okay. Let's see—the two of you are alone in a house in some secluded valley—"

"*You* told me to call him!"

"*Call* him, Kate. Not drive out there."

True.

"And then you go and take a shower with him—"

"I was fully clothed!"

"Even so, you know where a kiss might have led."

"Well, it didn't. I told him no."

"Ah!"

I yank the phone away again.

"So you had to tell him no, did you?"

Thank goodness for her blessedly miniaturized voice.

She snorts. "Should have known. After all, a man who takes a date to see his *in-laws*—"

"Belle?" I gingerly return the phone to my ear.

"What?"

I draw a deep breath. "I think I'm in love with him."

Did I lose the connection? Or is she about to take another whack at my eardrum?

"Oh, dear." I hear her blow a breath. "Tell me all of it."

I back away from the wall I've been transforming into hills and lean against the opposite wall where I can survey my progress. Not bad—though maybe I went too far with that one hill. I zoom in on the three crosses that point heavenward. Hardly subtle—

"I'm waiting," Belle singsongs.

Phone wedged between ear and shoulder, I pick up the story where I left off: postshower.

At the end of my retelling, Belle says, "All right. Sounds like he's fallen for you, too. Now the question is: When are you going to let him in like he's let you in?"

"I'll tell him."

"When?"

"Soon."

"As in yesterday, Kate. If you wait much longer, this could become more complicated than it already is. Do you know what I'm saying?"

I know what I'm *feeling*—like a novice brought before a ruler-wielding Mother Superior. "I know that I'll end up more hurt than if I'd told him earlier."

"That's putting it mildly, but at least you're not tucking tail and running."

If I didn't feel so strongly about Clive, I would. "I'll tell him."

"You'd better."

Eager to turn the conversation, I say, "So how are you feeling? Only three and a half weeks to go."

Her silence is telling, but finally she says, "Or less."

"Less?"

"The doctor says that if he decides to come tomorrow, it won't be necessary to stop labor again."

I refuse to fall beneath the wheels of my inability to experience what she's going through, so I surrender to joy. "Really?"

"Uh-huh. He's well developed."

Praise the Lord!

"Kate, I can hear Beau on the stairs." She gives a sniff. "Smells like vegetable soup."

"Okay, I'll let you go. Have a nice dinner."

"Hey! I expect a good report."

"I'll do my best. Talk to you soon."

But when Clive shows up bearing gyros an hour later and, in the midst of sharing his meal, turns his attention to my work, the timing proves wrong.

For what seems just shy of forever, he stares at that hill with its none-too-subtle crosses.

Why didn't I do something about them before he came?

When he finally shifts his gaze, it's to the rendering of woodland. My momentary relief is shot full of holes when I see the scene through his eyes. Though I believed I'd deftly formed crosses among the tree limbs, there's nothing deft about it. Rather than a few, I placed a dozen. And that crown of thorns hidden amid a thorny bush—glaring.

"Kate, it—"

"I know. I messed up." I lower the remainder of my gyro to its wrapper, drop my head back against the wall, and close my eyes. "Sorry."

His hand covers mine. "If your faith is as strong as you say it is, why do you need to splash it everywhere?"

Maybe because it isn't that strong. After all, though I got home early enough last night, determined to jump-start Operation: Perfect Faith, instead I hunkered under the covers. I didn't even say a real prayer, opting for a quick "Now I lay me down to sleep…" Still, it was an hour or more before I did sleep. I just couldn't bring myself to talk to God. It's awkward—asking Him again to help me with Clive, being convicted again to do the right thing, then…

Awkward. But once I tell Clive—and I will!—everything will be better.

He leans nearer. "You know, Kate, Jesus doesn't come because there are paintings and symbols of Him. He comes because He's needed and called upon. Even if you hadn't painted a single cross or child at prayer, He'd still be here."

It takes me a moment to place myself, but when I do, his words come at me in waves—the first bearing the message he intends, the second and every one thereafter revealing something else. I smile.

"You have to—" He frowns. "What?"

"I'm surprised to hear you talk like this. I didn't know you could."

Apparently, neither did he, as evidenced by the momentary alarm that sounds in his eyes. Then he's pulling his hand from mine, settling back against the wall, and touching the emptiness left by the removal of his wedding band.

Is he missing it? Regretting taking it off?

He draws a breath. "As I told you, I still believe in God. Trust is the problem."

Gulp. "Would you consider attending church with me, Clive?"

Regret crosses his face. "If I did, it would only be to impress you, rather than a genuine attempt to heal the rift between me and God. If you're all right with that, I'll come. But I'd prefer not to—at least, not now."

I'm tempted to push him, as it's possible that something in the pastor's sermon might be the trigger he needs, but I know that until he's ready to seek God himself, Clive won't find Him. That's how it was for me.

"Okay." I smile. "Later, then."

He looks at his watch. "I should get going. I have an early morning surgery."

I'm disappointed, but I know it's for the best as I have tons to do, especially considering the alteration required to make the woodland, hills, and valleys appear more natural.

Clive gathers up the cast-off wrappers, rises, and helps me to my feet. "Same time tomorrow."

"Then you're going to make a habit of bringing me dinner?"

"With the exception of Saturday nights, when you're all mine."

All his...

He frowns. "Unless you object."

"No!"

"Good." He leans in and lightly kisses me. "Don't work too late."

"Only as late as I have to."

Then he's gone.

Saturday, I tell myself. Five days until Saturday. Five days to prepare for what I need to tell him. It can wait. Sure it can.

"Kate, it's Christopher. I'd really like to talk to you."

Talk? How stupid does he think I am? Or should I say how wanton?

"You know, maybe over lunch."

Well, at least he isn't proposing dinner. Might I be over-reacting?

"Or dinner, if you prefer. Call me. My cell phone number is 555-3048. Bye, Katie Mae."

Katie Mae! Along with red, Christopher's exclusive pet name was tossed out when I returned the engagement ring.

"Message received at 11:50 p.m." An automated voice time-stamps the message.

Just what is he doing calling me at midnight?

"To save this message, press—"

As if!

"—to delete this message, press seven."

I jab seven, snap my cell phone closed, and return it to my purse, which I dug the beeping little creep from as I pulled out of the parking garage.

Determined not to dwell on Christopher's call, I ease down the lightly trafficked street and glance at the digital clock. Going on 1 a.m., which gives me five and a half hours of sleep before I have to get to my day job.

Just where did he get my cell phone number?

Aha! My business answering machine! Well, I'm not calling him back. Hopefully my silence will say all that needs to be said. But what if he shows up at the burn unit?

I groan. How I wish there were a seven I could jab on the side of my head. Better yet, a way to snap my mind closed like a cell phone.

Not in this lifetime.

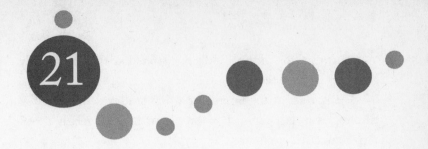

21

t's Christopher again."

Third call this week, and it's barely Saturday. I push seven, bypassing the remainder of the message to pick up another that came in while I labored over Pilates alongside Maia.

"Kate, it's Beau. Looks like the little guy isn't waiting any longer. Uh...hold on."

"Breathe, honey, breathe," he muffles.

"So we're heading to the hospital—"

"That's it, sweetie. You got it."

"Hope to see—"

"Ow! You're crushing my hand!"

"Uh...we hope to see you there, Kate. Bye."

Oh, my! The baby's coming! The baby's—!

"Kate!"

I find Maia's wide-eyed face above mine; then she gives me a jerk that nearly pulls my arm out of its socket, and I stumble to the sidewalk amid a blare of horns.

"What are you doing?" She rounds on me. "Are you nuts?

You can't just stop in the middle of a street like that. You nearly got yourself flattened."

I look back at the intersection that still evidences the fog that rolled in last night. For the life of me—or nearly so—I can't remember stopping.

Wide-eyed, I return my gaze to Maia. "Thanks."

She rolls her eyes, but as she starts to turn away, I wave the phone at her. "Belle and Beau are heading to the hospital—the baby's on its way!"

She scowls. "Not exactly news I'd care to be killed over, but good for them. Now let's have some coffee; Michael's waiting." She heads for the corner coffee shop where Michael said he'd meet her after Pilates.

Relieved to have an excuse to back out of the invite I accepted before she mentioned Michael would be present, I say, "I have to get to the hospital."

Maia looks over her shoulder. "Oh, really, Kate, what's twenty minutes?"

"Twenty minutes! She could have the baby in twenty minutes."

"More like twenty hours. Believe me, Belle has a long day ahead of her. Why should you waste your time pacing a hospital waiting room?"

Waste? I will not take offense. Will not take offense.

"You don't understand. I have to go." How's that for guarding one's tongue?

She scoffs. "It's not as if *you're* having the baby."

That cuts, though she has no idea how sharply. I curl my fingers into my palms. "You stay and enjoy your coffee with Michael. I'll—"

Michael sticks his head through the doorway. "What's up?"

Maia brightens, closes the distance between them, and plants a juicy kiss on his mouth.

Ew. Not that I'm jealous. It's just weird watching someone kiss someone you kissed, especially when it wasn't that long ago.

Maia pulls back. "Belle's having the baby, and Kate's determined to rush to her bedside to hold her hand." She snorts. "Like she needs Kate when she's got her husband."

The truth of Maia's words sink in like claws. Belle *does* have Beau. And her mother. And her sister. Have I been assuming something I shouldn't, that Belle needs me, too? But Beau called—said *they* hoped to see me at the hospital.

Michael steps from the shop. "That's wonderful. We should go, too."

Maia startles. "What?"

"My car's around the corner. We can head over right now." He gives me a smile. "Kate?"

Being arm in arm with Michael and Maia isn't how I envisioned this day. "That would be great."

Thankfully, Maia's pout fades when Michael puts an arm around her. And, as we walk to the car, she slips an arm around him.

When we arrive at the car, I don't question that I ought to take the backseat; however, I sense Michael's uncertainty when he straightens from pushing the passenger seat forward.

I step past Maia and catch Michael's eye. "I may be potentially fat, but I can still squeeze into tight spaces."

Discomfort draws lines across his brow, but I pat his shoulder and grin. "No hard feelings."

He raises an eyebrow.

"Well, maybe a few, but I'll get over it." I duck my head, stick a foot then a hip into the gap between front- and backseat, and find myself…stuck. As embarrassment rolls up my cheeks, I squelch the impulse to point out that it's my breasts, not my rear or thighs, that are responsible. Why bother?

Emptying the air from my lungs, I manage to shrink my bosom just enough to drop into the seat. So much for squeezing into tight places…

"It's a boy!"

We jump to our feet and step toward the door across from the waiting room—only to have Beau close it in our faces.

We exchange glances, then start to lower back to our seats.

He sticks his head out again. "At least, I think it's a boy."

"You think?" Maia shrills.

"Oh, Lord." Belle's mother moans where she leans against the wall, twisting her purse handle.

"Well, it's supposed to be a boy." Beau looks wildly disheveled despite only two hours having passed since Belle was admitted. "That end hasn't come out yet."

"Ugh!" Maia gives a full body shudder and drops back in her chair. "Go away, Beau."

He reappears thirty seconds later. "Lots of hair. And there's this white stuff all over him—kind of gross—but the doctor says it's normal."

"Let's sit down, Mom." Belle's sister encourages their mother back into her chair while Michael and I gauge Maia's reaction.

She pulls her long legs to her chest, wraps her arms around them, and glares at the ceiling. "And I gave up a latte for this!"

"Umbilical cord visible." Beau peers over his shoulder. "Oh! Wow!" He wiggles his eyebrows. "It *is* a him, no doubt about that."

Maia drops her forehead to her knees.

"And he's out! All the way! Whoosh!"

Belle's mother whimpers while her younger daughter fans her with a magazine.

"Beau!" Belle calls. "SHUT! THE! DOOR!"

"Gotta go."

And the door closes as a squeaky little cry turns into a wail.

Michael lowers to his chair beside Maia. "Isn't life amazing?"

I sigh and reclaim the seat on the opposite side of Maia. "Amazing."

Maia pops her head up. "Reality check. Their lives will *never* be the same."

I raise my eyebrows. "That's the idea, Maia."

"Not in my cards. I can tell you that right now."

"Really?" Michael leans toward her.

Uh-oh. Is Maia unaware that his take-'em-or-leave-'em attitude isn't screwed in real tight?

Maia jerks her chin. "Really."

"You wouldn't even *consider* children?"

She sneers, which transforms her face into something approaching a work of Salvador Dali. "And put myself through what Belle has for the past nine months *and* today? Ugh!"

Looking as if someone has stolen his collection of makeup brushes, Michael sits back. "Oh."

Oh, dear. Wishing Beau's florid, stubbled face would reappear, I start to avert my gaze only to catch the widening of Maia's eyes as she clues in to Michael's "Oh."

She struggles—doubtless warring with her desire for the man beside her and the desires of his heart. "Well, I suppose children *are* a possibility." She threads her fingers with his.

"I'm just a bit shaken by all that howling…and grunting…and screaming…and panting."

Mercifully, my cell phone rings. Snatching it from my purse, I step away. "Kate Meadows," I say, only to cringe at not having checked caller ID. What if it's Christopher?

"Kate." It's Clive.

"Hi!"

"I stopped by the burn unit to see you. Taking Saturday off for a change?"

"No. I mean, not intentionally. I'm here, but in the maternity ward." I draw a quick breath. "Belle just gave birth."

"That's wonderful."

"It's a boy. I'm hoping they'll let me in soon to meet him."

Another pause. "It could be a long wait. Want to join me for lunch in the cafeteria?"

I'm tempted—until I glance down my front. Though I sprung for a new exercise outfit, I'm still not certain I wasn't better off in shapeless sweats. This sporty, overpriced, form-fitting, logo-enhanced stuff leaves no room for error. Add to that the absence of makeup and hair that would have nothing to do with a brush this morning…

I shake my head. "I'd better wait." Then, for fear that he might offer to wait with me, I add, "But I'll see you tonight—picking me up at six, right?"

"Right. The symphony, then a late dinner."

Can take or leave the first, but *love* late dinners with Clive. "See you then."

It's an hour before any of us are allowed inside, but Beau pops his head in and out to recount the cord-cutting (Maia flaps her hands before her face), the pediatrician's exam (Maia sighs deeply and rolls her eyes), the difficulty in getting his son to latch on to Belle's breast (Maia protectively crosses her arms over her own), and the measurements.

Finally, Belle's mother and sister are allowed inside.

Maia lifts her head from Michael's shoulder. "I'm hungry."

He pushes the silken hair off her brow and plants a kiss on her forehead. "As soon as we've seen the baby, I'll take you to someplace nice for lunch."

A half hour later, Beau motions me inside, then says to Michael and Maia, "You're next."

"Mind keeping an eye on my purse and jacket?" I ask as I rise.

Michael nods. "We're not going anywhere."

Smiling encouragement over my shoulder, I step inside and accept the mask Beau shoves at me. As I fit it, I look to Belle's mother and sister, both of whom have slid their masks down now that they're no longer touching the baby.

Belle beams as I step forward. "Kate, meet our son, John Mark."

I cross to the bed where the bundled infant rests beside Belle and sigh as I take in his wide eyes staring out at this new world.

That's when it hits me—how well I'm handling Belle and Beau's blessing. Though I've avoided acknowledging my misgivings over this moment when my friends' prayers would be answered, I twinge. Well, maybe a little more than twinge, but I'm fine. My joy for Belle and Beau is much bigger than "if only I…"

"Would you like to hold him?"

Should have known that was coming. Shouldn't be surprised. It is, after all, to be expected. And yet I'm jolted.

"Kate?"

I look to Belle and, past her encouraging smile, glimpse her own uncertainty over my reaction to this blessing. Uncertainty I do not want her to feel—uncertainty she shouldn't feel. Though John Mark is not of my body, his blessing extends to me as well.

I smile from behind the mask and know that the expression reached my eyes when the tension between us falls away.

Beau pokes me in the back. "Pick him up, already."

"Okay." I slide hands beneath the little bundle and ease him into my arms. And all the while he stares at me without the slightest show of concern. As if he trusts me completely.

"Oh," I breathe, drawing him in and settling him against my oversized chest, beneath which beats a heart swelling with adoration.

He smells new…and pure…and sweet.

Opening his perfect little mouth, he gurgles.

And that swollen heart of mine threatens to burst. And my stinging eyes threaten to tear. And my voice comes out all choked. "Welcome, John Mark."

"He's alert, isn't he?" Belle says.

I nod. "And beautiful."

I touch one little fist above the blanket wrapped around him and hold my breath in anticipation of him grasping my finger. But he doesn't. With a little sigh, he lowers his lids to half-staff, remains thus for several moments, then lowers his lids the rest of the way.

He does trust me. Completely. And I can't help but wonder if this is how God feels when I trust Him. Completely. Of course, He's probably never experienced this with me. Always some part of me I hold back.

"Oh, look there," Beau croons over my shoulder. "Kate's bored him to sleep."

"Beau!" Belle protests.

I make a face at him, but it's lost behind the mask. Deciding to let him off easy—*this* time—I return my attention to the bundle in my arms as a knock sounds. Guessing I'm about to be shuttled out so Maia and Michael can have their turn, I hold John Mark closer, the better to savor God's gift one more moment.

"Dr. Alexander," Beau says.

I give a little jerk which, fortunately, doesn't rouse the baby.

"I understand congratulations are in order."

Slowly I turn to where he stands in the doorway, wearing his doctor's coat.

He meets my gaze above the oh-so-flattering mask, and a light enters his eyes that I suspect arises from the memory of when I attempted to subdue the powder-coated monster with pepper spray. As for the smile slung from his mouth, that would be the shower we shared…

"Babies look good on you, Kate."

Suddenly spitless…uncomfortable with my armful…grateful for the mask, I murmur, "Thank you." Aware of my trembling hands, I gently return Belle's son to her, all the while wishing she wouldn't seek my gaze. But she does.

I know, I tell her with my eyes, *I know. And I will.*

Her mouth purses. She is *not* happy with me. That makes two of us.

I focus on the little one's sleeping countenance and experience another melting moment; this one, however, is spiked with regret for what can never be.

I step back, remove the mask, and settle my hands to my thighs as I turn to Clive. "So—"

Oh, no. The smooth microfiber beneath my palms thrusts me into an awareness of my appearance, and I suck in my tummy lest it peek from the gap between bottoms and top.

Unfortunately, my hips and thighs don't respond with equal enthusiasm. Or my breasts.

I don't know them! I long to pull a Peter. However, unlike
Peter, who three times denied Christ and succeeded in sowing
doubt, it won't work for me no matter how many times I deny
the speed bumps that force one to slow as they travel the lines
of my body. They're *all* mine.

The silence of the room growing louder, I smile tightly at
Clive, who's beginning to frown. "I doubt you dropped by to
witness a mushy, gushy sentimental moment."

"Actually, I did."

"Oh."

He looks to Beau and Belle. "May I?"

Belle nods. "Of course."

He eases the door closed and crosses to where I stand
alongside the bed.

"Mask?" I thrust mine at him.

He shakes his head. "A look will suffice."

And I'm grateful, as the only thing worse than him seeing
an infant in my arms would be me seeing one in his.

As he peers into the little face, I ease my protesting stomach muscles.

"He's handsome," Clive pronounces.

Belle smiles her gratitude. "Thank you."

Clive turns to me. "You'll be here a while?"

I suck it in again. "Actually, I'm on my way out."

"To work on the burn unit?"

That *was* the plan, but now the day is half gone. "No, I think
I'll just enjoy a day off." Rare beasts that they are.

"Then spend it with me."

I startle. "But you're taking me out tonight."

Beau drapes an arm across my shoulders. "Kate doesn't get

out much. You'd be doing us all a favor if you'd sweep her off her boring little Birkenstock feet."

From the crown of my head to the top of my chest, I break out in red.

Fortunately for *Beau-zo*, Clive takes my elbow and draws me away. "I'll do that."

I look over my shoulder to give Beau warning of what to expect the next time I see him; however, he's turned to Belle. As she shakes her head at him, he cranks an arm up behind his back and gives me a wave.

When we step into the hall, Michael and Maia straighten in their chairs. Great. The ex-boyfriend and Wonder Woman in a workout outfit—not a bulge in sight. So why torture myself? Especially when my jacket is within reach.

Easing my tummy muscles, I grab the third piece of my exercise ensemble from the chair and meet Maia's gaze. "Your turn."

"About time." She rises and slides a hand through her silken hair to redirect it over the opposite shoulder, then steps past with Michael on her heels. "Dr. Alexander," she acknowledges Clive with a sweep of her lashes.

Ah! Despite the cover afforded by my jacket, I tighten those lazy, good-for-nothing tummy muscles. I may have handed over Michael, but I am *not* handing over Clive.

"Oh!" Maia turns back. "Your cell phone rang, Kate, and it's been beeping ever since—Christopher something or other came up on caller ID."

Oblivious to the slap she just landed across my face, she steps into Belle's room.

"Stapleton?"

Though I wouldn't say it's condemnation in Clive's voice, there's certainly wariness.

Nothing to feel guilty about.

"He's been calling." I turn to him.

"Then this isn't the first time."

"No."

He scans my face. "I understand he's still married."

"I wouldn't know, as I haven't spoken to him since the day I crashed your party."

"And yet he persists in calling you?"

I draw a deep breath. "And I persist in not returning his calls."

He considers me a long moment, then nods. "Good. Shall we go?"

Not until he guides me into an elevator do I ask, "Where are we going?"

The doors swish closed. "I need to stop at my office; then maybe we can grab some sandwiches and head to the park."

I imagine lounging on a blanket alongside Clive, the spongy grass our mattress, the cloud-laced sky stretching above us. "Sounds great." At least until I remember my state of dress. "*After* I stop by the house and change."

"Why?"

I snort. "Are you blind?"

"Are you, Kate?"

I throw my palms up. "I can't go out like this."

"You came in like that."

"Yeah, but Belle was in labor."

The doors open to reveal a janitor who's wiping down windows that pour light into the reception area.

Dropping the matter of my clothes, I follow Clive to his office.

Inside, he sheds his coat and crosses to his desk. "I just need to get a few things together, and then we can leave."

"No rush." I look around. As with the first time I visited his office, I'm struck by the absence of pictures depicting his life beyond these walls. Will he ever get over his loss enough to set Jillian and Sam's faces before him?

"It bothers you, doesn't it?"

I jump as Clive comes around the desk. "What?"

"You believe there should be photos."

"Uh…"

"There are, Kate, and I will put them up. Soon."

My heart gives a little leap. "That's great. It would really warm it up in here."

He nods, but before he can change the subject, I become the voice of his mother-in-law. "Have you considered a picture of Jillian and Sam for the domed room?"

From his sharp breath, I'm certain he'll concur that it's not my place, but he doesn't. "I've considered it, but haven't had time to do anything about it."

Though I open my mouth to offer assistance—to tell him I'll coordinate it with Gloria—he says, "Is it really necessary to stop at your house?"

It takes me a moment to place myself, but when I do, I wrinkle my nose. "I'm a mess."

"No, Kate, you're real." He steps close, tips my chin up, and slides a hand around my back to draw me nearer. Nice—until the sensation caused by skin on skin alerts me to his hand on the bulge between my pants and top.

I pull back. "Yes, we should definitely stop at my house."

With a smile so crooked it appears as if knocked askew by seismic activity, he says, "Definitely."

• • •

A perfect day. A perfect night.

Following a change of clothes, Clive and I picnicked in the park—on a blanket…side by side…fingers entwined…while I asked and Clive answered about his parents and a sister he rarely sees since her marriage and move to Australia two years ago. Then the second change of clothes, and the symphony, and a candlelit dinner overlooking the bay. Too perfect to end on a bad note.

Belle will just have to be mad at me. As for God—

I punch my pillow, toss and turn. Toss and turn.

22

ree. Unleashed. At large. On the loose. Done. And a week before deadline.

If not for the buzz of activity around which I've had to work these past three weeks while the unit is fit with equipment, I'd do a little dance. Guess I'll have to content myself with another sigh. And another. And one more.

"Hey, brushing up on your Lamaze breathing?"

Lamaze...

I swing around to where Dorian stands three feet back, a broad smile showing teeth. "Yes?"

"Cleanup complete." He nods at the double doors that have replaced the plastic sheet through which I've so often passed. "How does it feel to put the final brushstroke on your masterpiece?"

I sigh again. "Wonderful."

"Well, I'd take you out to celebrate, but I'm afraid the good doctor wouldn't approve."

He's right. Clive and I are definitely a couple, spending as much time together as possible. Which is how Dorian knows about us. As I hired him to assist with touch-up, he was here when Clive brought me dinner yesterday. Though Clive left shortly thereafter, there could be no doubt about our relationship.

"No, he wouldn't approve," I concur. "Besides, if I get out of here in the next hour, I can pick up that picture I told you about."

His eyebrows rise. "The surprise."

A good one, I pray.

Not my place, I kept telling myself. And yet I did it—coordinated with Gloria to ensure that not only will Jillian and Sam's names be present for the opening, but also their likenesses. Gloria chose a picture of mother and son taken a few months before the tragedy, and I'd had it enlarged and framed with an engraved plaque.

"I hope I've done the right thing."

Though I haven't revealed intimate details of Clive's loss, when Dorian commented on the memorial plaque and tied it to Clive, I'd told him about the picture. He asked if Clive knew, and I confessed he didn't. Dorian had looked doubtful, making me question if I was making a mistake. Gloria didn't think so.

"Just don't spring it on him, Kate."

That I've already decided—no ta-da! and whipping the cover off during the grand opening. By presenting it to Clive tonight, he'll have time to adjust if needed. "I won't spring it on him."

Dorian gives me a peck on the cheek. "Let me know when you have more work for us." Then, with a tug at his low-riding jeans, he hefts his tool bag. "Good luck, Kate."

Amazing how painful silence can be, especially from someone who a short while ago was smiling and making a careful examination of my hand in his. Now he's still as stone.

You should have prayed about this, Kate. But you didn't. Just as you haven't prayed about anything lately. Oh, you're still talking to God—rather, at God—but there's no conversation. You're too afraid of what He'll—

"You should have asked." Clive continues to stare at the framed picture on the drafting table in my office. "Why didn't you?"

My expectant smile having long since faltered, I open my clenched hands. "I wanted it to be a surprise."

"It is." He looks to where I stand alongside the drafting table.

"I'm sorry." And I am. *Lord, I'm sorry!* "I just thought—"

"Gloria."

I shake my head. "*I* approached her."

"Did you?"

"Yes."

"Without any prompting?"

I wet my dry lips. "The night of the birthday party, she showed me the pictures in the—"

"I thought so."

This is *not* going well. "Do you remember when I asked about a picture of Jillian and Sam for the domed room? You said you'd considered it, but didn't have time."

He blinks—a sure sign of life. "My mistake."

I stare at the air between my nose and chest as my emotions roll over and defenses rise. "I'm really sorry."

Shortly, his shoes come into view. "Kate, I understand your wanting me to get over what happened, but neither you nor Gloria has the right."

I jerk my chin up. "I wanted to help."

His eyebrows lower. "No, you wanted me to push through it. For me to get on with my life."

I thrust my shoulders back, which causes a sharp pain to slice down between my shoulder blades. "And don't you want that?"

"I do, but…for God's sake, Kate! I took off the ring."

I blink at him and dive in though this little voice urges, "Pull up! Pull up!"

"For God's sake?" I take a step toward him. "For *God's*? Really? But you've turned your back on Him."

As have you, Kate.

Skipping over the wounded look in Clive's eyes, I say, "Tell me, do you miss the ring?"

His wounded eyes harden. "I do today."

I nearly lurch back.

"You're right, Kate. I took off the ring for my sake, not God's. Because of what I thought I wanted. But perhaps I'm not ready after all. Of course, perhaps you're not either."

I feel as if the world has stopped spinning. "What do you mean?"

"You ask and I answer—as well as I can. But when I try to understand you better by asking about your relationship with Christopher and the years between then and now, you hold out." He draws a deep breath. "How do you think I feel knowing he's calling you?"

I knew it bothered him, especially last week when Christopher called while Clive and I were out. I'd grimaced at the name that came up, and he'd guessed correctly.

"I wonder if you still have feelings for him, and because of those feelings, don't want to talk about your past together."

At last, I pull out of the nosedive that crash-landed me in this very bad place. "You're wrong. My feelings for Christopher are gone."

He steps nearer. "Why didn't it work out between you?"

Another step, forcing me to tip my head back. "And why does he seem to think it will work out now?"

I look down and strangely enough find myself relating to a guitar string—this must be how it feels when one of those little knobs is turned too far…

"Kate?"

And further yet…

"You don't trust me, do you?"

Taut. Straining.

"Even though I've told you things I've told no one else."

Near snapping.

"You won't even look at me."

If it breaks, it can't be fixed, can it? Too short…too frayed…

He retreats a step. "I should be going."

Tell him, Kate! You've blown every other opportunity. This is the last one.

I toss my chin up. "Christopher wanted children, and I…"

Say it!

"I—"

"Didn't," Clive says with finality.

"No!" I catch his sleeve. "I did want children. He just… wouldn't consider adoption."

Clive's lids narrow. "Then you were afraid of ruining your body."

I shouldn't be surprised. After all, he suspected as much the first time I felt him out with regard to adoption.

"No." I release his arm, grope for the bracelet, and rub the *Believe* medallion. "After Christopher and I were engaged, I started having problems—female problems." I open my mouth to go into detail, but the realization growing in his eyes makes it moot. "The short of it is that, over the next year, I went through menopause—Premature Ovarian Failure. I can't have children. Unfortunately, you, like Christopher, believe that only biological children will complete you."

He stares, while across his face pass emotions too raw to name. "No, the problem is that Christopher knew adoption was the only option. I didn't."

Believe.

"I know I should have told you." I moisten my lips. "And I wanted to, but…"

"What?"

Believe. Believe.

"I like you too much."

Love you.

"I kept thinking that once you got to know me—"

"I wouldn't care. That my feelings for you would be strong enough for me to abandon the desire for a biological child. That I'd be hooked."

He makes it sound so manipulative. And I long to deny it, but he's right.

Believe.

He glances at my hand on my bracelet, and when he looks back, there's an emptiness in his eyes. "I suppose it could be worse. I could be dangling from your hook."

Ow.

Not until the silver and glass beads hit the wood floor do I realize what I've done. I stare in disbelief at the scattered pieces of the bracelet Belle gave me. Will I ever be able to pick them all up and put them back in order? I catch the sound of something small and metal hit the floor. And realize that *Believe* has also slipped through my fingers.

"Apparently," Clive says, "it's not enough to wear your belief around your wrist, Kate. You have to wear it here." He taps his chest.

"Guess I'm not the only one who needs to get back to God."

I catch sight of the picture that led to my downfall—

No, that's not right. I'm to blame. My *dis*belief.

"Wait!" I snatch the picture from the drafting table, tread beads underfoot, and halt before Clive as he turns at the door.

"I'm sorry." And that's all I can say.

He glances over my face, as if for the last time. Then, without so much as a brush of fingers, he takes the picture and leaves me to cry myself silly. Which I do for hours, in between sobs crying out to God, who is suddenly more important than my work, weight, makeup, clothes, thighs, and Clive.

After midnight, I hear Maia and Michael return. As their voices reach to me from the entryway, I squeeze my inflamed eyes closed. Which reminds me of the pepper spray incident. Which starts the tears flowing again. Which leads to the systematic destruction of my Bible.

Plop! goes another tear. Which sinks into the fibers of the thin page. Which I anxiously wipe at. Which causes the page to ripple. Which makes me wipe harder. Which tears the paper.

I whimper, sink back against the headboard and, through tears, stare at my poor Bible—rippled and warped pages from Psalm to Proverbs all the way to Galatians. Every one of them evidencing my pitiful attempt to get back to Operation: Perfect Faith. Too little, too late.

With a lumbering heart, I flip to highlighted, tear-stained Proverbs 30:15–16: "*There are three things that are never satisfied, four that never say, 'Enough!': the grave, the barren womb—*"

I draw a bumpy breath, then turn back to Galatians 4:27, which has sustained the most damage: "*Be glad, O barren woman, who bears no children; break forth and cry aloud, you who have no labor pains; because more are the children of the desolate woman than of her who has a husband.*"

Oh, Lord, I'm desolate.

I close my Bible and wince at the bent gilt-edged pages. Unfortunately, the damage will never pass as simply thumb-worn.

In addition to a new heart, I'm going to need a new Bible.

Sunday, July 8
Dear Lord,

The Holy Spirit sends its regards from the pitiful person of Katherine Mae Meadows. I miss You. It's been a while since my last entry. Forgive me. Though I know You've been chasing me, I didn't want to be caught. I was too afraid of listening and losing, and now look what I've done. Who I've hurt. What I've lost. It's beyond me how You continue to love such a sinner.

Lord, I've put my insecurities and appearance and heart and desire for success above You and Your Word. And if I were You, I'd have a hard time forgiving me, so if You need to think about it a while, I'll understand. But I'm grateful I'm not You, because I know Your forgiveness blankets me. Even though I don't deserve it.

I need You. Please pull me through. Help me fight this urge to pull a no-show at the grand opening benefit. I have to be there, especially as Clive will be present. Even if I've broken something beyond repair, I owe him more than that sorry apology. As You know, I've been less than a model Christian despite my attempts (yes, feeble) to convince Clive of Your love for him. Please don't let me have set him further back than he already was. Which may not be as far back as I am...

Thank You for forgiving me and allowing me back in

what must seem a revolving door. And thank You, thank You, for the blessing of John Mark. All things are possible.

Badly in need of a _spiritual_ makeover,
Your Kate

PS: With the exception of breast reduction, cosmetic surgery is out—I've purged my purse. Please help me remember that it's more important how I'm seen through Your eyes than the eyes of those who focus on the external and pick at my imperfections. Help me to embrace 1 Peter 3:3–4: "Your beauty should not come from outward adornment, such as braided hair and the wearing of gold jewelry and fine clothes. Instead, it should be that of your inner self, the unfading beauty of a gentle and quiet spirit, which is of great worth in God's sight." Tall order.

23

inderella is going to the ball. And she's wearing—

"Red is definitely your color." Maia shakes her head. "I can't believe it fits. Amazing."

No, what's amazing is, outside of a curling of toes and tightening of mouth, I don't react. She doesn't mean to offend, and besides, I can't believe it fits either. But then, the dress *isn't*—

"Of course it isn't fitted."

Picked up on that, too, did she?

I stare into the mirror that occupies a corner of Maia's bedroom and eye the scooped neckline that required me to move the patch—couldn't take the migraine threat any longer—from my chest to my thigh. My gaze skims the folds of the elegant, something-of-a-baby-doll dress that flatters my overly endowed figure. Now *that's* amazing. And suddenly I'm grateful that Maia let out a shriek at the sight of my evening attire—the black, fuchsia-edged outfit.

Reminding myself that inward appearance is what matters, I'd protested. But Maia pulled me after her and, following a frantic search through a family-sized closet, produced this. The color nearly made me recoil, but then a booming voice told me to unclench my fingers and let the past go. Told me that though God is more concerned with my inner self, that doesn't mean I should sink back into post-Christopher. Told me God made beauty, and provided I don't allow it to replace Him, He wants me to shine.

"Better, hmm?" Maia prods.

I turn sideways, thrill as the soft material whispers against the backs of my knees, and smile at the realization that I won't have to suck in my abs. Not a soul will know if I "let it all hang out."

"I like it, Maia. Of course, it was probably designed to be worn above-knee."

She glances down her long body. "Make that midthigh."

I roll my eyes. "Well, rub it in, why don't you?"

Her smile falters. Why? Did my quip prick her conscience? Or was she merely surprised by my response to her gibe?

She reanimates and pulls me toward a dressing table. "Let's do something about that hair."

"But I'm already late."

"Good." She presses me down onto a stool. "The better to make an entrance. Now let's get your hair up."

I sigh and give myself into her hands.

"How are you and Michael doing?" I ask as she sweeps up curls and wields bobby pins.

She smiles softly. "He's wonderful—cares about me in spite of everything."

"Everything?"

"My past. Who I am. What I've done. He's…well…a friend first."

Just like Belle was to Beau….

Another curl joins the others atop my head. "I've always had the 'boy,' but never the 'friend.'" She laughs. "He hasn't even tried to get me into bed." Then she frowns. "Not you either, hmm?"

That I wasn't expecting, and though I'd rather change the subject, I know she's looking for confirmation. "Me neither."

Her shoulders ease.

"Michael respected my convictions. I'm pleased he respects yours as well." Was that pushing it too far?

She meets my gaze in the mirror. "You're kidding, aren't you?"

I shrug.

Smiling broadly, she tugs tendrils down around my neck, then my brow, all of which lend an ethereal look to Katherine Mae Meadows.

"I like him, Kate." She picks up a bottle of hair spray. "I really like him."

I sense a "but" in there. "So?"

"I can see myself married to him, but this religion kick he's on…" She sighs. "He wants me to go back to your church with him. And kids. If he decides he wants them after all, well, I just don't see myself all round and roly-poly and bursting at the seams." She huffs. "And you should have seen him with Belle and Beau's baby! For a man who told me he could take 'em or leave 'em, he was way too interested."

"Obviously, that's something the two of you have to discuss before you get much more involved." Such easy advice to give, so much harder to take.

Maia spritzes my hair. "I know. And we're going to. Not that kids are completely out of the question, but he needs to know my feelings and I need to know exactly what his are."

My throat tightens. "I admire you for that."

"After all the mistakes I've made, I guess I'm finally learning from them."

She *has* had more relationships than I.

She tugs a tendril near my ear. "So what do you think?"

I stare at the woman in the mirror. "I think you really know your stuff."

"Thanks. Now one more thing." She pops into her bathroom and comes back with a familiar little bottle. "Visine!"

I know the stuff, went through a bottle just this week. Though it's true I'm crawling my way back to God, I still hurt, and that hurt most often finds its release in tears.

"I've heard you, you know." Maia hands me the bottle. "Crying at night."

So much for stuffing my face in a pillow. "I hope I didn't keep you awake."

"Not much. When I'm worn out, I can sleep through even the most obnoxious heavy metal music."

How sad to be equated with that. I drop my head back and, with a well-practiced hand, squeeze a drop in each eye.

"It's that doctor, isn't it?"

I startle and meet Maia's gaze through the excess moisture.

She nods. "I thought so." Then, to my surprise, she gives me a hug. "You look beautiful, Kate. Make the most of it."

Why does that sound easier said than done?

When I walk into the crowded room forty-five minutes late, I don't exactly stop the show, but I do turn some heads. Unfortunately, one of those heads belongs to Christopher Stapleton. Though I suppose I should have guessed he'd be here, I never considered it.

I grip my little purse tighter and look around the room that's festooned in blue and silver and hung with little white lights. Servers balance platters brimming with drinks and appetizers, and everyone who presses around me is dressed for the occasion—evening dresses that would have made my black outfit seem terribly plain, and tuxes, white shirts, and bow ties that turn every man into a gentleman. Deserved or not.

"Kate, dear!" Gloria Murphy appears before me wearing a sparkling green jacket and black slacks. "The artist herself." She kisses my cheek, then pulls back and sweeps her gaze around the room. "I'm amazed at what you've done."

"Thank you."

"And you…" She looks me over. "You're so pretty." She grips my arm and tugs me back the way she came. "Join us."

Us? I know the answer before we break through the circle of a gathering of guests, but I don't resist. I have to face him eventually.

"Don't worry about Clive, dear," Gloria whispers. "He's not happy with me either, but he'll get over it."

I survey the group. There's Jack, his older daughter, son-in-law, and granddaughter. Past them are a man and woman I don't recognize, the stout, bushy-browed Dr. Adam MacPhail, Adelphia, and Clive, wearing a tuxedo. Clive, who looks too good to be true, as does the bit of smile he gives me—not much, but it's something.

Over the next half hour, conversation shifts between the process of transforming the domed room to the subtle symbols of Christianity that have generated a buzz, then talk of how the new burn unit will serve the community. Throughout, I contribute when called upon, even though it's a struggle when what I really want is to slip away from the sight of Clive with Adelphia and the looks that pass between Gloria and Jack.

After a while, Adelphia asks Clive to dance. Strange, but only then do I become aware of the music pumping through the room and the beat of my heart, which doubles its efforts at the thought of Adelphia in Clive's arms. But maybe he won't—

He inclines his head and leads Adelphia away.

Beside me, Gloria frowns over her son-in-law's exit, then bends near her husband.

Taking the opportunity to slip away, I back out of the circle and weave among the other guests. Along the way, I acquire a long-stemmed glass of sparkling water but wave away the plat-ter of art the server assures me is all edible. Not where I come from…

As I head for the restroom, I pass the dance floor, where couples are moving in each other's arms. Lest I see Clive and Adelphia, I avert my gaze and glimpse something familiar on the wall to the right. I falter and peer closer at a picture partially obscured by guests who stand four or more deep.

He hung it.

Altering my course, I halt before the framed portrait and stare at it as I'm flooded with memories of when I presented it to Clive six nights ago. Six long nights.

Emotions trembling, I slide a finger across the brass plaque engraved with the names of Jillian and Sam Alexander.

"You were right," a voice says over my shoulder. "It was needed."

I turn. Though I fight the attraction roused not only by Clive's proximity, but by his tuxedo-clad figure that makes me long to savor him sip by sip, I'm dangerously close to abandon-ing my conviction to give us both time and space to get right with God. And when Clive shifts his gaze from the picture to me, I know my eyes reveal my struggle.

I moisten my lips. "The picture…I didn't think you would—"

"Neither did I, but it seemed the right thing to do. It be-longs here."

I don't know what to say, or if there is anything to say. But surely there must be or he wouldn't have left Adelphia to—

I frown. "I thought you and Adelphia were dancing."

"Dr. MacPhail cut in." He sweeps his eyes over me. "You look nice tonight."

Warmth melts into my cheeks. "Thank you."

"Of course, I am surprised by your choice of color. Did you wear it for Stapleton?"

Foreboding creeps in. "What?"

"He's here, you know. Or perhaps you don't know."

"I know—I mean, I saw him when I came in."

"Ah. Well, he's asked after you twice." His brow furrows. "Odd, especially as his wife accompanied him tonight."

Inappropriate is what he means, and the implication stings. Still, I feel compelled to explain. "Maia loaned me the dress. As for the red, I wore it for me, not Christopher."

"You might want to tell him that."

"I have no intention of speaking with him."

His eyes move to my mouth, as if to measure the truth of my words. And the silence stretches so taut that I long to take scissors to it.

Clive sighs. "We need to talk."

That's a positive sign, I think.

"There you are!" Adelphia's voice jostles our shoulders. "Thank goodness Ms. Meadows's dress makes her easy to spot."

Then she guessed Clive was with me? I look to where she and Dr. MacPhail appear alongside Clive, then the arm that Adelphia threads through Clive's to stake her territory. Territory that was mine not so long ago.

"Would you care to dance, Ms. Meadows?" Dr. MacPhail asks.

Not really, but better than watching another woman put her paws all over the man who still has his paws all over my heart. "I'd like that."

When I go into Dr. MacPhail's arms a few moments later, he says, "I'm sorry I couldn't convince Adelphia to partner with me one more dance."

I pull back. "What?"

He presses a hand to the small of my back and eases me into the music. "So you and Clive could have more time to-gether—to work things out."

I blink. "He told you?"

"No. Gloria and Jack are my pipeline. Not that Clive tells them much either, but Gloria did play a starring role in getting that picture to you."

Ah. "I hope he wasn't too angry with her."

He pushes up one of those scraggly eyebrows. "The picture's on the wall, isn't it?"

"That surprised me."

He maneuvers us past a couple who are more enthusiastic than the music calls for. "Take it as a sign, Ms. Meadows."

"Kate," I offer, "and what do you mean 'a sign'?"

He turns me around. "That it's all going to work out."

Though on the surface it may appear that way, he doesn't know what lies beneath. "Unfortunately, it's more than just my trespass over the picture."

"I know."

At my dismay, he shakes his head. "Deduction only. He hasn't said a thing."

I relax; however, in the next instant the music fades, and he guides me to a halt.

I smile. "Thank you—"

"Another dance?" His eyes sparkle, and I'm struck by how

much he resembles a smaller-than-life Santa Claus.

As another melody unfurls, he gathers me back to him. "I've known Clive since before the fire."

I stare into his face, which is on level with mine. "Then you knew his wife and son."

"Jillian—somewhat. She attended a few functions with Clive. Unfortunately, I never had the opportunity to meet their son."

We bump into another couple, but Dr. MacPhail is surprisingly quick on his feet and sweeps us toward a less-crowded corner of the dance floor.

"Why are you telling me this?"

"To establish credibility."

"I don't understand."

"So that when I advise you not to give up on Clive, you won't."

I'm touched. "You must care deeply about him."

Around we go again. "I do. Clive's a good man."

"I know. The problem is…" Dare I be so open? I hardly know this man. But then, what have I to lose? "The problem is that even if I don't give up on him, I'm afraid he's given up on me. I wasn't as honest with him as I should have been, and now my past has—"

"May I cut in?" Christopher's voice precedes his appearance.

Oh, Lord, can You help me out here?

Dr. MacPhail slows and looks to my past, which has just caught up with me again. "Actually, I'm holding Dr. Alexander's place."

He is? Does Clive know about this? Or is this matchmaking?

"Are you?" Christopher glances at me, and I know the glint

that enters his eyes and narrows his lids—a combination of suspicion and calculation. If he hadn't guessed there was something between Clive and me before, he's guessed now.

He steps nearer, indicating that he expects me to be relinquished. "I'm sure Dr. Alexander won't mind if a couple old friends play catch-up."

"Old friends?"

Grudgingly, I nod to Dr. MacPhail. "We go back quite a few years."

He eases his hold on me. "By all means, then."

And suddenly I'm back in the arms of the man around whom my world once revolved.

"Nice dress," Christopher says as Dr. MacPhail disappears among the dancing couples. "As you know—" he slides his gaze back to mine—"it's my favorite shade of red."

"I didn't wear it for you."

His mouth tightens. "For Dr. Alexander, then?"

"For me."

"But he is the one you're seeing."

"Yes." Though I'm not seeing him anymore, am I? Clive did say we need to talk, but it doesn't change anything. At least not at this time.

Christopher pulls me nearer. "Why haven't you returned my calls, Katie Mae?"

Piqued by the pet name, unnerved by the brush of his chest against mine, I draw back. "You have to ask?"

Thankfully, he doesn't attempt to pull me back, which is wise because I just had this not-very-nice vision of bringing a stiletto down on his instep. Of course, the flats I'm wearing wouldn't produce quite the same effect…

"As I told you, Nora and I are having marital problems."

I don't like where this conversation is heading, but it has to be had. "And as I said, I'm praying for you and your family."

He sighs. "It's only a matter of time. It can't be fixed."

"I wouldn't know. But what I do know is that I'm not the solution, and I'd appreciate it if you wouldn't attempt to cast me as such."

He draws us to a halt and searches my face with increasing intensity, as if to find the smallest glimpse of something. And when he doesn't, weariness settles over him that threatens to sag his shoulders. "I still have feelings for you, Katie Mae. Laugh if you like, but I've never stopped thinking about you."

I stare at him as closed doors within me fling themselves open to grasp at his words. Overwhelmed, I catch my breath.

Lord, forgive me for that lapse. Forgive me for glorying in the hold I've had over him all these years. Forgive me for that sweet feeling of vindication and the laughter of my wounded soul. Give me the right words that won't crush him, but send him back the way he should go.

"Say something, Kate."

"I've stopped thinking about you, Christopher. I'm sorry." I let apology run to the corners of my mouth. "Like it or not, you're dancing with the wrong woman."

His hand flexes on my back. "You're in love with Alexander." He gives a short, bitter laugh. "And to think I'm the one responsible for introducing you."

It *is* ironic. As gently as possible, I say, "What I feel for Clive has nothing to do with you. I've been over you for a long time." At least, the love part.

"Does he know that you can't give him a child?"

I didn't see that coming. And that it's made to sound like a threat causes anger to spurt through me and the guard on my tongue to look the other way.

Beginning to fantasize about stilettos and insteps again, I

jut my chin forward. "The real question is this: Is he different from you? Or how about: Is it more important that he pass on his DNA to a junior than that he love the woman with whom he promised to spend his life?"

Oh, I could go on and on, but the dismay on his face causes the tongue guard to return to its station.

Christopher heaves a sigh. "I'm sorry. Chalk it up to injured pride."

So maybe just a good stomp on the toes with my flats….

I draw my hand from his shoulder, and it's only then that I'm struck by how odd we must appear standing in the middle of the dance floor. I grip his forearm. "Go back and love your wife and son and that sweet baby who's on its way into your life. Make it work."

After a long, grudging moment, he nods. "No promises, though."

I drop my hand from him. "As it's no longer to me you should be making—or keeping—promises, I don't expect any. Good-bye, Christopher." I smooth my dress and turn opposite to weave among the couples.

At the outskirts of the dance floor, I walk straight into the tuxedo-clad chest that steps into my path. I know the hands that steady me before I look up into Clive's expressionless face.

"I would have cut in, but it seemed as if you had a lot to say to each other."

I have no reason to feel that I've been caught doing something wrong, but I know it looks bad—especially as I told Clive I had no intention of speaking with Christopher.

"He cut in when Dr. MacPhail and I were dancing." I take a step back that causes him to drop his hands from me. "As for us having a lot to say, I assure you I left no doubt as to whom I wore the dress for."

He inclines his head. "Can we talk?"

I glance around at the press of bodies. "Here?"

"No. My office."

"All right."

He leads the way among the other guests—a crooked course that presses in on me and requires sidesteps and a few squashed toes not to lose sight of him.

Midway, he reaches a hand to me. "I don't want to lose you."

In the right context, I'd puddle. Sliding my hand into his, I allow him to draw me from the room and down the corridor. However, once we're through the double doors, he releases me.

Shortly, he flips the switch in his office, sending light rushing into the dark corners. "We shouldn't have any interruptions here." He steps farther inside.

A sweep of the walls confirms that though he allowed the picture to be hung in the domed room, he isn't ready for Jillian and Sam to look out at him from close quarters.

He turns to where I stand inside the doorway. "I want to apologize for Saturday night. I behaved poorly…said things I shouldn't have. My only excuse is that there was too much coming at me. Of course, now I better understand your reluctance to get involved in the first place. And why I shouldn't have pushed."

I clasp my hands before me. "I should have told you sooner."

He draws a deep breath. "Kate, you have to realize that when I began to imagine a future with you, it went beyond just the two of us."

"I know."

He looks momentarily away. "I've read up on Premature Ovarian Failure, and though, in some cases, women do become pregnant, it's tenuous at best." He shakes his head. "I hate that I'm like Stapleton in wanting a biological child, but I can't reconcile myself otherwise."

As numbness settles deeper, I'm grateful I haven't allowed myself too much hope these past days—that I've turned back to God and His promise of endless love. "I understand."

Not surprisingly, silence steps in and expands to fill the space between us, then winds tightly around us until I feel like I might suffocate.

I toss my chin up. "Well, I guess that's it then. Time to get back—"

"I'm sorry for your loss, Kate."

He is. It's in his eyes—full-blown pity.

He steps nearer. "I can't imagine what it must have been like to go through what you did, and at such a young age."

Eyes moistening, I lower my chin. Does he have any idea how deep his words cut, especially now that he numbers among my losses?

"Kate?" He lightly touches my cheek.

Though I don't mean to overreact, I'm unable to suppress the survival instinct that makes me jump back. "You're right." I meet his gaze. "You can't imagine what it was like—what it *is* like."

Regret shifts through his eyes.

I shrug. "Of course, you're not exactly immune to loss yourself, are you?"

As he stares at me, I summon a smile that feels almost natural. "Well, back to the party, hmm?" I swing away.

"Are you all right, Kate?"

At the door, I turn. "Yeah. Good thing it wasn't love, right?" A lie—a big, fat, not-even-close-to-little-white lie. "Good night, Clive."

And he lets me walk away.

Refusing to give in to the longing for home and the comfort of tear-stained pillows, I return to the party. Throughout the remainder of the night, I catch glimpses of Clive, and more often than I can stand, his eyes are on me.

Friday, July 13
Dear Lord,

I'm broken. In more ways than one. When I chose to follow You all those years ago, I thought Your healing would be complete—or at least enough to help me accept for all time what I can never give a man. But here I am again aching for what is lost in not being able to provide it. I know it's not Your fault—that it's me who allowed my cracked places to be held together with paste rather than the heavy-duty glue of faith. Me who chose to ignore that not only was I not spiritually ready for a relationship with Clive, but he wasn't ready for one with me. I should have followed Belle's example of first laying a foundation of friendship upon which we could both learn to trust one another. I'm so sorry. Though this hurts really bad, all I'm asking is that You forgive me for not trusting YOU.

Repentant Kate

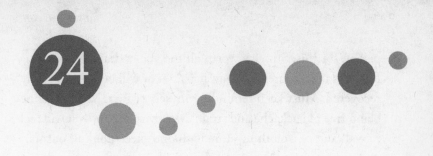

o, I never asked to be made over. But was I really content with Katherine Mae Meadows just the way she was—*thirty-three* years old (now thirty-four), five foot *three*, 134 pounds (now 127), and *way too manless* to fuss with hair and makeup?

No. I was apathetic. And self-deluded. As for Beau's comment on my shortcomings to Dr. Clive Alexander... He meant well. As for Clive... I told you the good doctor bore mentioning. And that's to say the least.

Sigh.

So here I am, laid out, packed in ice—

No, I haven't died, but I do have this vague memory of going on and on about death as I surfaced from the anesthesia and was seized with a coughing fit—something along the lines of: *Hack!* "I'm dying!" *Hack! Hack!* "Dying, do you hear me?" *Hack!* "Ohhh, dearrr Lorrrd."

Two days ago, I finally underwent surgery for breast reduction, and I thought I was prepared, but *nothing* prepares a person for this. Still, it's worth all the yucky drainage, discomfort, and take-your-breath-away pain—or will be once I've fully recovered. Must keep reminding myself of that. Must imagine being free of backache and strain. Must visualize how it will feel to walk out of a clothing store with one-piece nonknit outfits.

I am content. Not that I don't miss what might have been. And think of him sometimes—

Okay, more than *sometimes*, but every day it gets better. And it *has* only been three months.

I sigh and reach for the bottled water Belle set on the bedside table before she and her little dumpling, John Mark, left.

"Unh!" I gasp as the movement sends a sharp pain across my bandaged chest. Maybe I should take a pain pill…

I eye the vial, but before I can give it further consideration, the phone rings—line two, meaning it's business. Which I shouldn't take, but other than my prayer journal (two entries today) and my Bible (what made me undertake a study of Leviticus?), how else am I going to fill my bedridden time?

On the fourth ring, I lift the handset. "Kate Meadows."

"Ms. Meadows, this is Becky Standish. I'm calling from the hospital."

My heart lurches. "Yes?"

"We're planning a remodel of the waiting room in our children's cancer center and are considering a mural like the one you painted for the burn unit—on a smaller scale."

"Oh." Nothing to do with Clive, er, the burn unit.

"We'd love to have you take a look at the room and discuss cost and time frame."

And if I run into Clive? "Uh…where is the cancer center in relation to the burn unit?"

"Excuse me?"

Mouth feeling more desert-y than moments earlier, I rasp,

"Just a moment, please." I grab the bottled water, grimace at the pain caused by the sudden movement, and take a noisy gulp.

"Ms. Meadows?"

"Sorry. You…uh…would like me to take a look at the room."

"Yes. Can we set up an appointment?"

I should say no. After all, regardless of where the cancer center is in relation to the burn unit, they're both in the children's hospital, and if I accept the job, eventually I'll run into Clive. And if I run into Clive—

You'll be fine. Besides, after all those prayers for him, maybe you'll get a chance to see God's answer.

"Okay."

"Great! How about next Thursday?"

"No! I mean, I'm up to my eyeballs." Or should I say chest? It'll be two weeks until I'm allowed to resume social activities and another two before I can return to work. "How about mid-November?"

A prolonged pause. "That's farther out than we'd like, and really, it shouldn't take more than an hour. Could you, perhaps, squeeze us in…say…end of this month?"

It *is* just to take a look—hardly strenuous activity. "All right."

We agree on the day and time, and she hangs up.

As I lower the handset, I draw a breath that causes the elastic bandage around my chest to stretch past the point of tolerable discomfort.

I groan, take another drink of water, and settle into my stacked pillows. "Lord, please tell me I didn't make a mistake."

Hoping to sleep away a few hours of discomfort, I close my eyes, but it's no use. Clive is on my mind.

"Okay, Leviticus it is." I gingerly reach for my Bible on the bedside table—the warped one I have yet to replace. Lowering it to my lap, I finger the beads of the *Believe* bracelet that I restrung into a bookmark when several of the beads came up missing (down the heat register, I imagine). At the *Believe* medallion, I pause.

"I do," I say, then open to the page marked by the thin silken cord.

"Need anything?"

And there's Maia standing in the doorway. Still can't believe she took the week off to be here for me. "No, but thank you."

From behind her back, she pulls a glossy catalog. "How about the new Victoria's Secret catalog?"

I stare at the perfectly proportioned, bra-and-undie-clad, some-teen female on the front who gives me a sultry look from beneath long lashes. And who I will *never* resemble no matter how much I torture my credit card. And that's okay.

Maia waves the catalog. "There are some pretty scrumptious selections in this issue."

Though I'll definitely need some new bras, I say, "I think I'll start cheap and work my way up from there."

She makes a face. "Not even a peek to give you some ideas?"

"Not even a peek. Besides, that stuff is for women who have someone to share it with."

Maia snorts. "I still wear it, and believe me, the most Michael has seen is an errant strap."

I smile. Despite the downs and the ups, including Maia's continued refusal to join Michael in his pursuit of God, they're still seeing each other. Don't know how it will work out, but God does.

Maia gives a little shiver. "My 'secrets' make me feel so good underneath."

I smooth a hand down the sixth chapter of Leviticus. "Think I'll stick with my Bible. It makes *me* feel good underneath."

Predictably, she should roll her eyes, but she doesn't. "Well, once you're up and about, you and I are going shopping."

"We are?"

"Uh-huh." She tucks Victoria's Secret under her arm. "I'm not letting you go cheap. Frugal? Sure. But not cheap." She smiles, then disappears down the hall. As she thumps down the stairs, she calls out, "Look out, world! Here comes Kate Meadows—a B-cup at last."

25

I'm a walking, talking 36B who, thanks to Maia's shopping know-how, has inflicted very little damage on her credit card. And for it has an updated wardrobe to fit a figure altered not only by a sizable decrease up top, but also by a couple pounds that have disappeared from around her middle. Best of all, 36B has an updated spirit. Well…getting there.

As I follow Becky Standish around the waiting room, I smile as her expressive hands paint her vision on the air. Three times around we go; then she halts and turns to me. "As I said, it's on a smaller scale than the burn unit, but Dr. Alexander assured me—"

I startle.

"—that, schedule permitting, you'd consider it. And as we're not in a big hurry…" She frowns. "Are you all right, Ms. Meadows?"

"Yes! I was just thinking."

"Oh. So how about it? Is it something you can take on?"

Determinedly, I push Clive aside. "I'm booked for the next six months—" largely due to the publicity received from the burn unit—"but I could fit the job in sometime during the spring."

"Hmm. That's a bit far out."

Never again. I will not overextend myself as I did with the burn unit. Will *not* cheat on God again. "I'm sorry, but that's the best I can do."

She sweeps her gaze around the room. "Then six months it is."

Wow. That wasn't so hard. "Great. I assume Adelphia Jamison will be contacting me to draw up the contract?"

She seems taken aback. "Oh, no. Ms. Jamison is no longer with the hospital. I'm her replacement. Sorry I didn't make that clear."

None of my business. None of my bus—

"So she…quit?"

"Yes. She got married a couple of weeks ago."

Though I'd like to think it's the constricting support bra that's responsible for the sudden compression of my chest, it's Clive. Did he and Adelphia—?

"To one of our doctors, as a matter of fact."

If I don't get to a bathroom and adjust this bra soon, I'll suffocate.

"Are you sure you're all right, Ms. Meadows?"

"Absolutely!" I whip my purse up, pull out a business card, and thrust it at her. "Give me a call and we'll discuss the specifics."

With a bewildered frown, she accepts the card. "I'll do that."

"It was nice meeting you."

"And you, Ms. Meadows."

And with that I go in search of a restroom and find one just outside the children's cancer center.

"36B," I mutter as I fumble with my bra. "Feels more like a 40B trying to squeeze into a 36B." I free the hooks and eyes, but it does little to relieve my constriction. And I have no choice but to admit that Clive's marriage to Adelphia is responsible.

I lean back against the bathroom door and look up. "In all things God works for the good of those who love Him." I nod. "I know, Lord. I do."

Still, it's ten minutes before I emerge, bra hooked, chest somewhat less constricted. At the elevators, I push the Down button as a family of four push the Up button. A few moments later, twin *pings* announce the arrival of both. However, as I step toward the Down elevator, I feel a tug in the vicinity of my heart, and I look to the elevator into which the foursome clamor.

It *would* be nice to peek in on the burn unit. After all, I've yet to see it used as intended—for the children.

As the doors of both elevators start to close, I yield to impulse and join the family of four.

What am I *doing*? Of course, not much chance of running into Clive, as he and Adelphia are probably still honeymooning.

The moment I step into the winding corridor, my worries dissolve as I find myself caught up in the feel of something alive and breathing. All those weeks spent in relative solitude so this place could now be filled with children and their families, friends, nurses, doctors...

From some of the rooms I pass comes the silence of grief and healing, but others are lit by little voices, words of encouragement, and laughter. And it gets better as I near the domed room, from which excited voices and laughter flow. I halt at the threshold and watch the family of four join another family that is on the floor with a toddler who seems oblivious to the bandages covering his legs. All that matters are the blocks he stacks one upon the other.

Next, I pause on a girl about Jessica's age who leans against a wall with an arm flung out to finger the smile of a painted child. And with each child I look upon, my heart grows fuller.

I should have come sooner. It's one thing to create something, another to see the response of those for whom it was created. How God must have delighted in Adam and Eve's exploration of the Garden…

Speaking of whom—well, not exactly—Dr. *Adam* MacPhail catches my eye next to a teenage boy in a wheelchair.

I smile—until he says something to another white-coated man who's conversing with a woman alongside the boy in the wheelchair.

Over his shoulder, Clive meets my wide-eyed gaze.

Catching my breath, I swing away.

"Kate!"

Feeling childish at the thought that I can outrun him, I turn back.

Oh, Lord, Adelphia's husband is heading toward me.

Despite how tight the bra once more feels, I smile. "Hello, Clive."

He halts within reach. "I hoped you'd stop by."

Huh? "You did?"

"Yes, I asked Becky to let me know when you were coming to take a look at the cancer center."

"Well…" I shrug. "Here I am."

"Yes, you are." He runs his eyes down me and pauses on my chest. "So the procedure was a success."

"What? Oh!" I clap my hands to my breasts. "Yes!"

Lord, did I just do what I think I did?

Blushing ten degrees of red, I jerk my arms to my sides. "It went well."

"Good. I considered calling, but…the timing didn't seem right."

I imagine not. Let's see, that would be about the time he was getting married to a woman who can give him what I can't.

I put my chin up. "I appreciate the thought. Now I really must go—"

His hand falls on me. "Kate…"

I stare at his fingers curled around my forearm.

Dear God, forgive me for this thrill I have no business feeling for a married man.

"I was wrong. I shouldn't have pushed you away."

That was one short-lived honeymoon, and suddenly I feel sorry for Adelphia, who probably has no idea that her husband has buyer's remorse. Anger rising as much for her plight as for my disillusionment over a man I never would have believed capable of this kind of behavior, I yank my arm free.

"But you did push me away. And now it's too late."

"Is it?"

The world really *is* morally bankrupt. I take a step back. "If you think I'm going to allow you to pull a Christopher on me, think again. Cliché though it may be: You chose your bed; now sleep in it."

Refusing to linger on the hurt that rises on his face, I turn and, thanks to sensible shoes and an absence of frontal bounce, quickly step through the double doors and head for the elevators.

How could he do it? I was certain he was different from Christopher! Would have sworn—

"Kate!"

Before the elevators, I turn, and there's Dr. MacPhail.

Somewhat breathless, he halts before me. "Look, Kate, I know Clive hurt you, but—"

"You, too?" I jab the Down button. "I can't believe you're siding with him. The man is married, for goodness' sake."

"No, Kate. He really has let Jillian—and Sam—go."

I drop my jaw. "I'm not talking about Jillian! I'm talking about Adelphia."

This time it's his jaw that drops. "Adelphia?"

"Clive's *wife*."

"But…" He blinks. "Ah."

"What?"

His mouth tightens with what seems like an attempt to suppress a smile. "Will you come to my office? There's something I'd like to show you."

"I'm sorry, but—"

"It's important."

I long to refuse him, but in spite of his twitching lips, his pleading eyes get to me. "All right."

During the elevator ride, my gaze is drawn to him repeatedly, and I wonder at the smile that twitches its way into being, followed by the grin that elbows aside the smile. But the real curiosity is the spring in his step as we walk down the hall toward his office. What is he up to?

On the verge of demanding an explanation, I catch sight of Clive's office ahead, the door of which is open. Though I know he can't be inside, I look away as we pass.

A few moments later, Adam motions me into his office. "Have a seat."

I step into an office on par with Clive's—excepting the presence of pictures—and lower to a chair before Adam's desk. Behind me, he closes the door. As I wait for him to come around, I consider the pictures on the wall. Family…friends…children…dogs…a boa constrictor—

Ew!

I lower my gaze to the credenza and a picture of a newly wedded couple. Very nice.

Wait a minute! I peer at a tuxedoed Adam MacPhail posed alongside…Clive's wife.

"So are you going to congratulate me?" Adam comes around to face me.

I know I'm gaping, but there's nothing I can do about it. When I finally break free, all I can manage is, "I'm confused."

"Yes, you are."

I shake my head. "Are you telling me…?" No. Adam must be twenty years her senior. "I mean, are you…?"

He settles back against the desk. "Adelphia and I were married two weeks ago this past Saturday." He slaps his thigh. "Been chasing that woman for years. Only when she realized that Clive's heart wasn't into her did she finally accept."

My chest constricts, head swims, thoughts twist back on themselves. And like a punch between the eyes I relive my exchange with Clive.

"Oh no!" I drop my head between my knees. Not Clive, but Adam. Adelphia and *Adam*. Clive is *not* married—no more married than the night we met and I momentarily believed the woman who glided into the children's shop was attached to his wedding band. No more attached to Adelphia than when I wrongly concluded that she was his mistress.

It's almost funny. And to prove it, a snort of laughter exits my nose, only to be followed by a hiccupping sob, another snort, another sob. Though aware that the sounds coming from me could be mistaken as coming from a seriously disturbed donkey, it's not until Adam lays a hand to my back that I'm able to gain any control over them.

"Are you all right, Kate?"

I open my eyes and stare at the carpet between my feet. "No. Not all right." I swallow the snort-sob that attempts to sneak up my throat. "I thought…"

"I know." He rubs my back.

"I said…"

"I can guess what you said."

"He thinks…"

"Probably."

I raise my head. "When Becky Standish said Adelphia married one of the doctors…" I swallow hard again. "I thought it was Clive. And when Clive said he was wrong and shouldn't have let me go…" I drop my head back between my knees. "Oh, no."

Adam grips my shoulder. "Listen, Kate, it's a simple misunderstanding."

I jerk my head up. "It's not simple. It's complicated. Very complicated. This means maybe he and I…" My throat convulses. "But I can't give him kids. And he wants kids." Another convulsion. "And I've worked so hard to get over him. To get right with God. And he doesn't want anything to do with God."

"Kate." Adam drops to his haunches before me. "If you talk to him, I believe you'll find that you're not the only one who's been trying to get right with God."

I look at Adam. Did I hear right? Does he mean that the way it sounded? Is it possible that Clive—

"Gloria tells me he's started attending church again. And not long ago, he hung pictures of Jillian and Sam in his office."

"Really?"

He nods. "And yesterday I walked into his office and found

him praying. Of course, he said he was dozing, but I know what prayer looks like."

Lord, is Clive in Your plans for me after all? Or do I just want to believe he is?

Adam straightens and grabs a box of tissues from his desk. "Wipe your face."

I pull a tissue, wipe my eyes and cheeks, then pull two more and blow hard.

"Better?"

"Sort of. I'm still not sure—"

"Talk to him, Kate."

"Now?"

"Now."

"Okay." On wobbly legs, I stand and cross to the door. "Uh…" I look around. "Thank you, Adam."

He waves me away.

In the hall outside, I pause.

Lord, is this You? Your timing? Are what I long to do and what You want me to do in line with each other? I don't want to mess up again. As You know, I'm not the outdoorsy type—do not *like camping out in the wilderness.*

Though I'm not one of those who hear God's voice loud and clear and know exactly His will for them, I feel a nudge toward Clive.

"All right, I'm going." Smoothing my outfit, I set a course for the domed room. However, as I near Clive's office, I notice the door closed to within an inch, whereas a while ago it was wide open. Meaning he's inside? I push the door inward.

Clive doesn't notice me where he sits at his desk with his head in his hands, but when I step inside, he looks up.

"Kate." He drops his arms to his desk. "What are you doing here?"

And out of my mouth pops stupid. "You're not married."

"What?"

I cross the room and halt before his desk. "I thought you were married."

His brow furrows.

"To Adelphia."

His eyes widen.

"That's why I said what I did."

The transformation to disbelief complete, he shakes his head. "You thought I'd married Adelphia?"

"Yes, but now I know it was Adam. That you weren't pulling a Christopher on me. That what you said…" I look down and, as with each time I do it, am amazed to see beyond my chest to my shoes.

I hear his chair roll back, then the creak of wood and leather as he rises. "What I said…?"

I nod. "About being wrong, that you shouldn't have pushed me away. You meant it. Didn't you?"

After a painfully long moment, he nods. "I did."

Why does that sound so past tense? "Do you still?"

"Should I, Kate?"

Though fear of rejection urges me to retreat, I step around the desk. "I hope you do."

Clive turns to me, and I ache for how tautly he holds himself—for the defenses he's raised in the short time since he approached me in the domed room. Not that I should be surprised, as it can't have been easy to humble himself and then have his attempt at reconciliation thrown back in his face. Even if it was all a misunderstanding…

"It's been a long three months, Kate."

I clench my hands to keep from reaching to him. "It has, but I needed the time. And you did too, I understand."

He inclines his head only to narrow his gaze. "So you and Adam had a nice long talk, hmm?"

Hand in the cookie jar, but I will not feel guilty. "You have a good friend in him. Of course, I'm sure you already know that."

He looks momentarily away. "What did he tell you?"

"That you're attending church again. Seeking God." *Dare I?* "Praying."

Feeling a rise in Clive's discomfort, I'm struck by a vision of an overinflated balloon at the mercy of a small but very sharp pin. But then he sighs. "A month after I pushed you away, I came to the end of myself."

The *end* of himself? "What do you mean?"

He sidesteps and crosses to the right of the door, where two pictures hang—the first identical to the one of Jillian and Sam I had blown up for the domed room, the second an eight-by-ten candid shot of the three of them.

For a long moment, he just stands there with his back to me, but then he speaks. "I looked back and saw all the broken pieces I'd been dragging behind me—everything I'd lost." He draws a breath that broadens his shoulders, then turns back around. "But you weren't there. And neither was God. I tried to write off the two of you as losses, but you wouldn't get behind me. Do you know why?"

Beginning to tear up, I shake my head.

"Because I didn't want you behind me, didn't want to lose either of you."

Pain cramps my heart.

He takes a step toward me, only to halt as if thinking better of it. "Finally, I got down on my knees and from there gained a perspective I lost years ago. I can't say I liked the answers I demanded from God, but I accepted them. And forgiveness."

I think I'm going to cry. "Then you and God…?"

"Are reconciled? To a point."

My hopeful smile falters.

Clive takes another step toward me, then stops. "I won't lie to you, Kate. I don't have a hand around my faith yet, and I don't know how long before I get to where I need to be, but I am getting there." His grim mouth lightens. "Bit by bit. Prayer by prayer."

Which is the best way. The only way.

I smile. "I'm happy for you."

"I knew you would be." He starts to smile, and his body tenses as if to take another step toward me, but he doesn't. "Now the question is: What do we do about us?"

Us. And all this space between us.

I press my shoulders back, thrill at doing so without the ache that once accompanied the shift in weight, and cross to where he stands. "What do you want to do?"

He stares into my upturned face. "First, I want to apologize."

"You don't need to—"

"Yes. I do. I'm sorry for requiring you to be a perfect fit. Sorry for marking you off. Sorry for using your distrust of me to justify walking away."

"But I should have told you—"

"I wish you'd felt you could, but I understand why you didn't, why you were afraid to trust me. Had I known earlier, I probably would have walked away that much sooner. And we might not be here now."

But we are. *Thank You, God.*

"What else do you want, Clive?"

He steps nearer. "I want what I never should have pushed

away—to be with the woman who can give me far more than she can't."

Please, Lord, let this be Your will. I want it so bad. But Your will be done, not mine.

How I hope I truly mean that!

"Provided it really isn't too late."

"Oh, no! It's not!" I shake my head. "You didn't marry Adelphia."

"How could I when I don't love her?"

Please, God. But Your will…Your will…

"Your turn, Kate. What do you want to do about us?"

As much as I long to grab hold of the love he dangles in front of me, Belle and Beau come to mind. Belle and Beau who are so happy. "I want to be your friend, Clive."

His brow furrows. "More than that, I hope."

"Yes, but first your friend."

He considers me, then steps nearer and cups my face between his hands. "All right. Friends. *Kissing* friends."

I grin. "Nice compromise."

He lowers his head, and I feel his breath against my lips. "Do you remember when I told you it was a waste of time to expect God to act on prayer?"

"Yes?"

"I was wrong, Kate. You're here, and it isn't too late."

I draw a trembling breath. "No, it isn't." I start to lean in to claim his kiss, but there's still something that needs to be addressed. "I know we're not discussing marriage at this point, but we still need to talk about children."

He brushes his mouth across mine. "There's only one non-negotiable."

I hold my breath.

"You."

Never did I expect a man to say that to me. "You're certain? I couldn't stand it if—"

"I love you."

He loves me. Clive Alexander loves me.

He draws his thumbs across my cheeks. "You were right about there being plenty of children who need a home. All we have to do is believe that God will provide."

I am going to cry. "I believe." I nod. "I really do." And I don't need a medallion to convince me of it. "I love you, Clive."

His eyes close momentarily. Then he kisses me again.

Yes, I'm content. Thus, I shall embrace datingdom and be unbelievably, inconceivably happy! And why wouldn't I be, considering He loves me JUST THE WAY I AM—God, that is.

And Clive Alexander, too.

Thursday, July 12 (Five years later)

Dear Lord,

And baby makes three. Thank You for our recent addition, eight-month-old Teresa, who arrived back in the States with us two nights ago, following a looong flight from the Ukraine. Thank You for Joshua and Mariah, who welcomed their new baby sister with oohs and aahs and way too much argument over whose turn it was to hold her. Help!

Lord, You are amazing! Each time You add to our family, I turn to my warped and tear-stained Galatians 4:27. And I quote: "Be glad (am I ever!), O barren woman, who bears no children (but is now the mother of three!); break forth and cry aloud (late-night feedings, here we go again!), you who have no labor pains (surely loads of laundry, piles of dishes, and chauffeuring qualify!); because more are the children (three and counting!) of the desolate woman (not anymore!) than of her who has a husband (I certainly do!)." Thank You, Lord.

And thank You for the latest blessing You're sending Belle and Beau's way in January. You are so faithful. As for Maia and Michael, thank You for an amicable end to their relationship. I pray that whatever wounds they have will heal and that Maia will remain open to attending church services—this time for herself.

Forever Yours,

Kate

PS: Thank You for my incredible wife and three— THREE!—children. This is Clive, BTW, and yes, Kate fell asleep over her journal again. Think she'd scalp me if I suggested we hire a housekeeper to help out a few times a week?

PPS: I love you, Kate.

Clive

Discussion Questions

1. Kate's story begins with "I never asked to be made over," and yet her desire to please her makeup artist boyfriend causes her to become caught up in the pursuit of physical perfection. When have you allowed others to prioritize your life? What were the results?

2. In Kate's words, "there's something somewhere on every someone's body that could benefit from some type of beauty enhancement." What about your physical appearance bothers you? If you could have one procedure—surgical or nonsurgical—what would it be? Why?

3. Kate's growing concern with her looks interferes with her pursuit of God. What have you allowed to come between you and God?

4. Kate is uncomfortable with sharing her faith. How do you feel about sharing yours? How do you react when your efforts are met with resistance?

5. What is the importance of dating others with similar beliefs? What can happen when your beliefs are incompatible with those of the person you're dating? Marrying?

6. Have you personally experienced or know someone who has experienced infertility? How did it impact your/her faith?

7. Clive's relationship with God is shaken when he loses his wife and son in a tragic accident. Has your faith ever been so shaken that you turned your back on God? If so, how?

8. Have you experienced deep grief? Did your faith help?

9. Throughout the story, Kate keeps a prayer journal. How does this means of conversing with God differ from prayer? What are the benefits of journaling with God?

10. Though Clive was set on repeating the experience of a biological child, in the end he and Kate opt for adoption. How might this experience differ from having a biological child? What added blessings do you think Clive and Kate received?

"You're fired."

With those two words, my favorite TV program ends its season, and I'm left hanging as usual.

Wishing summer were already past so I could get back to *The Coroner*, the one program I follow, I push the remote's Off button, then close my eyes to savor the night breeze sifted by the screen door.

But it's no use. My middle and index fingers start to twitch, my lips purse, and a vague memory of nicotine wafts across my senses.

Jelly Belly time.

I reach into the container, scoop up a dozen pebbly beans, and pop them in my mouth. I'm usually more discerning about how I combine the flavors (there's an art to it, you know), but tonight I don't care. Tonight they're comfort food as opposed to pleasure food. Something to take my mind off the silence of the phone, which has yet to ring its death knell.

I look at where it perches on the side table. Though I know it will eventually ring, and I'm not going to like what the person on the other end has to say—as in "Good-bye, Harri," or "So long," or in the style of *The Coroner*, "You're fired"—I want to get it over with.

No, my mistake wasn't as serious as the one committed by my show's female lead, but there will be consequences. Have to be.

Once I returned home to First Grace Church's Senior Mobile Home Park—yeah, *Senior*—and prayed through the encounter with Pastor Paul (not to mention *that* man who, according to the pastor, I now answer to), I accepted I was wrong. Not that that makes Pastor Paul right, but legitimate though my complaints are, I shouldn't have confronted him as I did.

I heave a sigh. Though I believe a leopard *can* change its spots (or in my case, tattoos), it takes a miracle. Or expensive laser surgery. Unfortunately, God's making me take the long way around. No blinding light on the road to Damascus for Harriet Bisset, just a battered conscience and an impending sense of doom.

Stuffing my mouth full of another helping of Jelly Bellys, my anxiety eases as I taste sizzling cinnamon…green apple…cotton candy…margarita (virgin, of course)…coconut…strawberry cheesecake…buttered popcorn and…? Is that tutti-frutti? Too late, as they're all jelling into one sweet-sour-spicy mouthful. Regretting that I wasn't more discerning about how I combined the flavors, I swallow and chew some more.

Then comes the death knell.

I look to the phone as it takes a breath between the first and second rings. Though I refuse to waste money on caller ID, I know it's him. And that *I'm* about to be fired.

Get it over with.

Now the second death knell.

Pick it up!

I reach and, only when I attempt to bolster myself with a deep breath, remember my mouthful. I chew faster.

The third death knell.

I desperately look around, but the only thing at hand is…my hand. Spitting the remains of my Jelly Bellys into my palm—gross!—I grab the receiver.

"Hello!"

"Harri, it's Harriet."

Harri/Harriet always glitches me, and tonight is no exception. Actually, it's worse, as I was expecting *him*, not my namesake. The remains of Jelly Belly juice trickle down my throat, and I turn my head aside to cough.

"Are you all right, Harri?"

"Uh-huh. Just a tickle in my throat." Swallow, swallow. "What's up?"

"Brother Paul."

Then he asked Harriet to—?

No. As disillusioned as I am with the man, canning me is not something he'd send the church secretary to do. And certainly not over the phone. "What is it, Harriet?"

"He's been visiting some of us fogies this evening—"

He's here? In the park? Now?

"—and asked me to let you know he'll stop by to chat with you on his way out."

Foul words slip to the edge of my tongue. Just the edge.

Sorry about that, Lord. And that one. Oh, that was a really bad one. Sorry. Sorry.

"Harri?"

I startle, gape at the gooey mess in my hand, and finally shrill, "It's nine o'clock at night!"

"Is it?" A pause. "You're right. Well, just a quick chat, and I'll be a couple minutes behind. Thought I'd bring you a batch of my famous biscuits."

I jump out of my recliner. "But I'm wearing house slippers and lounge pants and a T-shirt." New, out-of-the-box house slippers with big pink roses (last year's birthday present from Mom). Pilled flannel lounge pants with a motorcycle insignia (a relic from my rebel days that I keep meaning to toss out). A "Got Jesus?" T-shirt that hasn't been white in ages (the short sleeves of which barely conceal my armband tattoo).

"Well," Harriet says, "throw a robe over it."

"I can't! I have to change!"

"But, Harri, he and—"

"Stall him. Gotta go!" I drop the handset in its receiver and, closing my fingers over the mess in my hand that's starting to ooze, with the other grab the Jelly Belly container. Four strides carry me past the screen door to the kitchen, and two more to the sink where I slam the container on the counter and turn on the taps. One good shake and the sticky mass slops to the drain.

Ew! Can't believe I did that to Jelly Belly, which is as close to a friend as something edible can come considering the beans and lots of prayer helped me kick the nicotine habit. Were there a Jelly Belly fan club, I'd ban me for life.

The stainless steel soup pot in the drain rack catching my eye, I grab it and peer at my distorted reflection. Not only is my "somewhere between red and blond" hair wisping all over the place, but beneath my blue eyes are dark shadows beget by mascara that should have been removed hours ago.

Hoping Harriet can stall Pastor Paul at least ten minutes, as the mobile home where she lives on the opposite side of the park is a mere two-minute walk, I quickly soap and rinse.

Jeans and a light sweater, I determine as I reach to the taps. But no sooner do I tighten the knobs than a tinny knock sounds behind me.

I swing around and, as I light on Pastor Paul's mesh-shadowed face on the other side of the screen door, feel my arm connect with something.

Oh, no. NO!

All the colors of the rainbow—and then some—sail past me. Little bean-shaped colors. Melt-in-your-mouth colors. Very expensive colors. With a sound akin to spring hail, they hit the linoleum floor.

Reflexively, I step forward. And glimpse surprise on Pastor Paul's face as the beans beneath my slippers sweep me off my feet.

With a screech, I go down. My rump hits first, followed by my shoulders, then the back of my head.

"Harri!" Pastor Paul shouts, and I hear the squeak of the screen door, followed by its slam.

As I lay on the kitchen floor, I can't say what hurts more: the places where my body hit, the embarrassment, or that I'm spread-eagled among fourteen—fourteen!—dollars worth of Jelly Bellys that were supposed to last me all month.

"Harri?" Pastor Paul gives my shoulder a shake. "Are you all right?"

"No." I squeeze my closed eyes tighter. "Not all right."

"Would you like me to call an ambulance?"

I shake my head. "No, I—"

Hold up! *That* wasn't Pastor Paul. *That* voice came from somewhere to my right and, instead of concern, reflected amusement.

Oh, no. Not *that* man! Not here. In my kitchen. With me flat on my back amid colorful little beans that surely confirm I'm the silliest woman he's ever seen.

As the heat in my face deepens, I decide embarrassment does hurt more than the loss of Jelly Bellys. Definitely embarrassment.

As much as I long to stay behind my closed lids and wave my uninvited guests away, that would make me appear sillier yet. Thus, with burning cheeks, I lift my lids to look into the familiar face above mine.

Pastor Paul smiles uncertainly. "All right, Harri?"

Avoiding looking to my right where, peripherally, I see khaki pants alongside the kitchen cabinets, I return a twisted smile. "Tell me, are there any Jelly Bellys left in the container?"

He frowns and looks around. "Maybe a handful."

Might get me through the night. Of course, that depends on whether or not he's about to string me up and kick out from under me the horse I've been riding.

I shrug. "Then I should be all right."

With a sigh, he straightens and reaches a hand to me.

Refusing to look toward the lurker from Pastor Paul's office, I ignore the juvenile temptation to reject the offer of a hand up and allow the hangman to pull me to sitting.

It's then I'm socked with a visual reminder of my state of dress—house slippers, lounge pants, and T-shirt. Lovely.

"You okay, Harri?"

Telling myself it can't get any worse, I mutter, "Yeah," pull my hand free, and look to the destruction around me: dirt, dust, Jelly Bellys. I wish I hadn't neglected to mop the floor. Of course, it's not easy holding down two jobs, even though both are "officially" part-time—mornings waitressing the breakfast crowd at Gloria's Morning Café and afternoons fulfilling the duties of the Women's Ministry at First Grace.

Still, it is a *very* small kitchen made even smaller with the addition of two men, one of whom I'm going to pretend doesn't exist. At least until my embarrassment-induced first degree burn fades.

Sweeping beans aside, I place my palms to the floor and lever up.

Oh, my rear! And lower back!

As I unfold to standing, I turn to Pastor Paul to keep the lurker behind me. Then to the tune of "snap, crackle, pop!" I press my shoulders back.

"You sure you don't want me to call an ambulance?" says the one who doesn't exist.

Can't take a hint, hmm? With a glance at Pastor Paul, I give the hem of my T-shirt a tug and turn. "I'm a lot tougher than I look." It's then that I get my first real faceful of the man where he leans back against the counter.

Not bad looking, but not great, and all because of a nose that's a little too narrow, a little off center, and a little too long. Speaking of long, that curly hair of his could use a haircut. Not that it's long long, but in my humble opinion, the cleaner cut, the better. I do *not* like men with long hair. At least, not anymore…

As for the eyes that engage mine before traveling down my T-shirt/lounge pant/house-slipper-clad body, they're unremarkable. But, oh, those lashes! Why would God waste them on a man?

"Actually—" he sweeps those lashes up—"you look pretty tough to me."

That was *not* a compliment, and I can't help but be miffed, especially considering all I've given up to project my feminine side. I *am* the director of Women's Ministry, and though I hardly reflect that position at the moment, he did see me in my "getup" at church.

Pastor Paul steps alongside. "Harri, this is Maddox McCray. Maddox, Harriet Bisset."

Maddox McCray pushes off the counter, and all slender six feet of him steps forward. "A pleasure to meet you, Harriet—or do you prefer 'Harri'?" He extends a hand.

Must I?

"Harri's best, as it avoids confusion with our church secretary, Harriet." I slide my hand into his and am relieved when no current of electricity passes from him to me. Good. Though his ringless left hand attests to him being single, I do not want to be attracted to this man whose eyes are laughing at me. Again.

"Confusion?" He gives my hand a squeeze. "I can't imagine anyone confusing you with that sweet little woman." Before I fully register that his comment wasn't a compliment, he lowers his gaze and draws out a smile. "Nice tattoo."

Somehow I manage to keep from clapping a hand over what was revealed when my short sleeve rode up.

"Leftovers," I mutter and pull my hand free. Dropping my arm to my side, I inwardly sigh as the sleeve slips down to hide the crown of thorns circling my upper arm.

"Leftovers?" McCray's smile widens. "As in PK?"

He knows I'm a Preacher's Kid? I jerk my chin up, though not too far, as he's only a few inches taller than my five foot nine.

"Or, more accurately…" he hikes an eyebrow into a gathering of curls on his brow, "…PKS?"

And he knows about Preacher's Kid Syndrome.

"Exactly who are you?" The abrasive question is out before I can think better of it, but I don't care.

"Maddox is a consultant." Pastor Paul steps forward with the air of someone about to referee a fight.

"Consultant?" I repeat, knowing I am *not* going to like the answer.

"Yes, First Grace has hired him—"

"*First Grace* hired him?"

Now Pastor Paul looks like *he's* the one about to go head-to-head with the preacher's kid. However, a glance in Maddox's direction causes his jaw to ease.

Wishing I'd caught the look that passed between them, I clench my hands.

"Yes, Harri." Such measured calm! "The board has approved and budgeted for a consultant."

The board, which didn't leak a word to me. Of course, it's no longer my father's board, as the faithful dozen have been weeded and replaced with younger members "handpicked" by Pastor Paul—and with the blessing of my father who convinced several of the older board members to step aside. Now only five of the faithful remain—a minority.

"And exactly what's this consultant supposed to do?" I ask as if said consultant isn't present.

Yes, I'm revving up to be difficult. And I know that I should back off. That—

"Maddox is here to observe the staff and workings of our church." Pastor Paul crosses his arms over his chest. "Once he understands where we're at, he'll help us map where we need to go and how to get there."

He will, will he?

I look to Maddox McCray, one of those new-fangled church growth consultants who thinks that without a fasten-your-seat belts Gospel delivery system, we're just a bunch of backward, puddle jumping, tobacco chewing—

Stop it, Harri! You are at stake here, and so is God. Above all, try not to disappoint Him any more than you've already done. Show a little R-E-S-P-E-C-T.

Unfortunately, the best I can do is dumb it down. I wish I could take a big pink eraser to McCray's self-assured mouth, not to mention those loose curls that give him a deceptively boyish look. "I suppose you had something to do with the decision to junk our organ."

"Actually, that was me," Pastor Paul says with…regret? "And according to Maddox, I went about it the wrong way."

He did? And he's admitting it? And it was this new-fangled consultant who made him see the error of his ways?

I narrow my gaze on Maddox, to which he raises his eyebrows. Something's not right here. But before I can question it, the screen door squeaks.

"Oh, my girl!" A tin of biscuits in one hand, Harriet halts inside the doorway. "What have you gone and done now?"